Trapped

Brooke Morgan is an American living in London. She is also the author of *Tainted*.

Also by Brooke Morgan

Tainted

Trapped

BROOKE MORGAN

arrow books

Published by Arrow Books 2010

1 3 5 7 9 10 8 6 4 2

Copyright © Brooke Morgan 2010

First published in Great Britain in 2010 by
Arrow Books
Random House, 20 Vauxhall Bridge Road
London SW1V 2SA

www.rbooks.co.uk

Addresses for companies within The Random House Group Limited can be found at:
www.randomhouse.co.uk/offices.htm

The Random House Group Limited Reg. No. 954009

A CIP catalogue record for this book
is available from the British Library

ISBN 9780099536284

The Random House Group Limited supports The Forest Stewardship Council (FSC), the leading international forest certification organisation. All our titles that are printed on Greenpeace approved FSC certified paper carry the FSC logo. Our paper procurement policy can be found at
www.rbooks.co.uk/environment

Mixed Sources
Product group from well-managed
forests and other controlled sources
www.fsc.org Cert no. TT-COC-2139
© 1996 Forest Stewardship Council

FSC

Typeset in ACaslon Regular by Palimpsest Book Production Ltd,
Falkirk, Stirlingshire
Printed and bound in Great Britain by
CPI Cox & Wyman, Reading RG1 8EX

1

The whole idea was crazy, especially for someone like her. Other women might not blink at the thought of an internet date. They could saunter into a restaurant and meet whomever it was they'd communicated with and sit there making small talk without even a hint of nerves. But Ellie had had a pit-of-the-stomach feeling of anxiety all day, heightened when she spent hours trying to decide what would be appropriate to wear, and finally paralysing her as she stood outside of the restaurant door.

She wasn't the type to do internet dating: she'd been pushed into it by Debby. 'Think of me as the eighth dwarf, babes,' Debby had said. 'My name is Dating. I'm going to whistle a happy tune and be at your side and make sure you do this, OK? There's no way out.'

There was no way out. Debby had signed her up, chosen her profile picture, overseen all the personal information she'd offered up. They'd laughed so much as they did it that Ellie had thought it was all a joke. And it had been funny for a while, in an agonising way. It was mean, she knew, but Debby and she had laughed about the various men who had contacted her, all of them truly weird. Until Daniel Litman had popped up and they'd both thought: 'Whoa! This one's different.'

He was a nice-looking, forty-two-year-old oncologist who'd never been married.

'It doesn't get much better than this, babes,' Debby had said. 'No ex-wives, no children. An income. If you don't reply to him, I'll steal your identity and do it myself.'

'No way – he's mine,' she'd responded instantly, surprising herself. Up until that moment she hadn't been sure whether she'd actually moved on from Charlie, or was still too wounded by his betrayal to allow herself to consider a new relationship.

After two weeks of trading emails with Daniel, he'd suggested this dinner and she'd accepted.

But now she wished they'd had a coffee date instead. If it were too awkward, one or the other of them could make an excuse after five minutes and bolt for the door. But this was a fairly expensive restaurant, she knew. They couldn't get up and leave in the middle of the main course.

Two middle-aged women stood side by side, their backs to the restaurant's front window, smoking; Ellie wished she could join them so her loitering would have a purpose, but taking up smoking just to feel a little more comfortable for a few minutes was way too extreme. She went towards the door, then stepped back away from it.

One more minute.

'Hi, Daniel, nice to meet you,' she tried out. Or how

about: 'Daniel, hey. It's great to see you'? Both sounded lame. Maybe: 'Listen, Daniel, I'm a nervous wreck. How are you?'

This meeting wasn't that important – she had to remember that. They'd exchanged a few emails and were getting together for a meal, that was all. It was only hugely meaningful to her because she hadn't been out with a man other than Charlie for seventeen years.

No big deal, Debby had emailed. *You're just putting a toe in the sea where plenty of other fish are swimming, if you see what I mean. I know I pushed you into signing on for this, but he seems like a nice guy. Just relax and talk to him, El. If you like each other maybe you can meet again. If not, well, adios.*

Which was fine for Debby to say, but she wasn't here. If she had been, she could have come with Ellie to the restaurant, given her a pep talk and sent her inside. Debby had set this whole thing in motion and then – boom – taken off. 'Sorry, kiddo, but I can't turn down Cal Tech. Think about it . . . California. No snow. Movie stars. As much as I love you, you can't compete with Rob Lowe.'

Emailing or talking on the phone with Debby wasn't the same as actually having her here – but that was the whole purpose of the evening she was about to have, Ellie knew. She couldn't keep trading emails with Daniel indefinitely.

He's just asked me to dinner. I want to say yes, but I'm nervous, she'd typed in a Facebook chat with Debby.

Say yes now. If you don't have dinner with him, you might get into some email romance that works great in cyberspace but

3

is a total bust in real life, was the message back. *Don't be nervous. Hell, you might fall desperately in love. And this time he won't be a sewer rat like your cheating, lying creep of an ex-husband.*

But what if he's nothing like what I expect or I'm nothing like he expects? I'm not sure this is the way to meet someone. It feels so staged.

Staged-schmaged. People do this all the time now, El. Stop making up excuses and say yes.

The two women simultaneously threw down their cigarettes on the sidewalk and stepped on them, then turned to go into the restaurant. Ellie looked at her watch: 8.05. He'd said he'd be at their table by eight and that he was never late – unless he had an emergency call, in which case he'd text to tell her.

She pulled out her cell phone. No messages.

He'd chosen Acquitaine because he lived in Chestnut Hill. She was glad he'd picked it rather than an even ritzier restaurant downtown. More casual was easier to dress for. After throwing clothes around her bedroom as if she were in a RomCom 'what will I wear for this date?' movie scene, she'd finally decided on what she'd tried on in the first place: black linen trousers, a white sleeveless shirt and a black jacket. And black, medium-heeled sandals. According to his profile, Daniel was 5'11" – and she was about 5'5" in these shoes.

Not that she had killer high heels in her closet anyway. One of Charlie's rules. No stilettos. And no red nail polish.

'Women who wear red nail polish are whores or call girls,'

he'd announced early on in their relationship. 'They may not think they are, but that's the signal they're sending. It's what they are underneath.'

When they were out at a party and a woman wearing red nail polish came up to them, Charlie would give Ellie a sidelong glance and meaningful nod, as if to say 'Clock the slut', and she'd be terrified those women could read the contempt in his eyes.

Stiletto heels were one step away from red nails in Charlie's mind. They weren't as absolutely hookerish, yet they signalled a louche attitude.

The almost laughable irony of these prejudices of his hit her with a knockout blow when she finally saw, in a photograph in the social pages of *Boston Magazine*, the woman he'd left her for. There she was, decked out in some designer dress, wearing impossibly high heels and bright red nail polish.

She's ten years older than I am, she does all the things you didn't want me to do, and you fell head over heels in love with her. What's the deal, Charlie?

Ellie had stared at it for way too long, her heart thumping, before throwing the magazine in the trash.

She hadn't worn high heels tonight, but she had painted her nails red in a small, but meaningful, gesture of independence.

Enough. Stay outside any longer and Daniel will think you're rude.

Taking a deep breath, Ellie pushed through the door and into the restaurant. Immediately on the left was the maître d's desk, and a young, dark-haired woman said 'Can I help you?'

before Ellie had time to process the notion of walking straight back out.

'I'm meeting someone . . . he should be here. Daniel Litman?'

The young woman looked down at a big book propped open on the lectern.

'Yes, he's here. Follow me, please.'

Ellie did, passing by the packed bar at the front, a few booths, and then into the main body of the restaurant, which looked like a classic French bistro with banquette tables lining mirrored walls. The place was buzzing; no surprise, given that it was a Thursday night in June. She could see students and their parents celebrating graduations; couples out on dates; and one table of six older women, two of whom were the smokers.

And then she spotted him at the table beside the smokers in the middle of the room. He was facing in towards the mirror. And he was looking at himself, combing back his hair with his hand – a gesture which instantly sent her back sixteen years.

She and Charlie had been playing a game of 'what do you like/what do you hate' a few weeks after they'd met.

'*I hate it when men stare at themselves in mirrors in public places,*' had been near the top of her Hate List. And one of his, almost matching, had been: '*I hate women who put on make up as they sit at a restaurant table.*'

Daniel Litman caught her eye in the mirror and immediately stood up, waving her over.

'Ellie,' he said as she reached him. 'Hi.'

He took a step forward to give her a kiss on the cheek just as she put her hand out to shake his. In a comic reversal, he then stepped back and put his hand out as she stepped forward and withdrew hers.

'Oops!' he said. 'Should we start again?'

He extended his hand and she shook it. She'd expected a bone-crunching handshake and was a little surprised when it wasn't. It wasn't limp, though, and she was grateful to him, too, for that 'Shall we start again?' which made an embarrassing beginning a little easier.

'I hope this restaurant is all right,' he said as she took her seat on the banquette opposite him. 'It was selfish of me to choose a place near where I live, I'm sorry. You probably would have preferred downtown.'

'No, no, this is great. I've been here before. I like it.'

'I wanted to get a table at the back but they were all taken.' He sat down and smiled at her.

'Why did you want one in the back?'

'To make a quick getaway out the back door if you weren't who I thought you were when you arrived. Wait a second.' He held up his hand. 'Don't look at me like that. You know how people put up doctored pictures of themselves online.'

Debby had told her people sometimes posted fake pictures, but the way he'd immediately introduced the topic sounded as if he'd done a lot of internet dating. Which wasn't what he'd said in his emails.

'Oh, God.' He sighed. 'Sorry again. That makes me sound like an old hand at this business. I'm not, I swear. This is only the third time I've met someone this way. All I meant by that was that you never know who's who in this internet world, you know? I guess it was a tasteless thing to say.'

Daniel looked exactly as he had in his photograph. Blondish, with a rugged physique as if he played a sport or climbed mountains. Which he didn't, she knew. And he had the same baby-face as in his photograph, one that was oddly out of synch with his physical heftiness and was surprising in a forty-two-year-old. She found herself wondering whether his patients would have preferred it if he'd had a craggy, creased face. When you were putting your life in a doctor's hands, you might want him to look older and wiser, be more reassured by an aura of experience.

'What I should have said was: you look as terrific as your photo,' Daniel continued. 'Would you like a glass of wine?'

'Yes, please.'

'Red or white?'

'Red, please.'

'Excellent. Let's decide what we're going to eat and drink and get that out of the way. Then we can get down to the talking business.'

'OK. Fine.'

He was good at getting the waitress's attention: they were given the menus, had time to look at them and then ordered without having to wait for ages in between each stage. Ellie's glass of wine arrived quickly too.

'Cheers to our first meeting,' said Daniel, picking up his glass of white.

'Cheers,' she replied.

She'd met Charlie at a party given by Rebecca, a friend

of hers who lived off campus at BU. She'd been in Rebecca's kitchen, looking for a glass of water after eating too many salty peanuts, when Charlie had walked in looking for a Coke in the fridge. They'd started talking, and ended up staying in the kitchen talking until 2 a.m. It had been so easy, so natural, and so completely unlike this contrived dinner.

'I really admire the work you do, Daniel,' she said, after taking her first sip of wine. 'Being an oncologist must be difficult.'

'It's not fun. But it's rewarding.'

'I was thinking on the way over here: everyone must be in such bad shape when they come to you. They must be so nervous and upset and terrified. It's the word cancer, isn't it? The way it's used in everyday language – you know, "terrorism is like a cancer spreading through the world". You'd never say "terrorism is like a heart attack spreading through the world".'

That sounds rehearsed. Because it was.

But he nodded, as if he were interested, and she relaxed a little.

'You're right. The word cancer carries so much weight because of the nature of the disease, how insidious it is. Heart attacks don't spread. Cancer does. Of course that doesn't mean heart attacks don't kill.'

'Of course not.'

'And you're right about my job, too. People *are* nervous and upset when they see me. In fact, no one wants to see me. But then again, no one wants to see any doctor, not

9

really. Or, for that matter, any dentist.' He smiled a smile that made her think he went to his own dentist often.

It was so odd to know a little bit about him, but then again, not really anything. She'd liked the way he'd answered the various personal questions on the dating site; he had a sense of humour and there was nothing weird, desperate or self-aggrandising about him. And the emails they'd traded had been short but fun. As nervous as she'd been about meeting him, Ellie had looked forward to seeing him in person. But that didn't change the fact that they were, effectively, strangers.

Still, she reminded herself, almost everyone on a first date barely knew the other person.

'I should be upfront right away.' Daniel leaned towards her, brushed away the lock of blond hair that had fallen over his forehead. 'I hate talking about cancer. I live with it all day. And if I go out there are always people asking me questions because they know someone who has it and they want me to fix it. The truth is, I can't stand to talk about it at night or when I'm not working.'

'I can understand that. Totally.'

Ellie began to search her mind for other topics of conversation, but within seconds realised that his job was one of the reasons she'd been drawn to Daniel: she didn't want to discuss cancer at length, but the fact that he helped sick people, actually *saved* people, amazed her.

In her imagination he'd been immensely kind and compassionate – which he could well be – but she had to admit that that first sight of him looking at himself in the mirror had immediately made her wary of him. It was an instinctive response of hers and it wasn't fair. She had to forget about that and try harder.

'So . . . you should tell me about your son,' he said, before she'd had time to think of another question to ask him. 'Tim. He's fifteen, right? Where is he tonight?'

'He's out with friends. It's his last night in the city except on weekends with his father because we're moving tomorrow. Which makes my coming out tonight pretty insane, but – oh, God – I already told you that in my emails, didn't I?'

'Yes. But I haven't told you that *I* may be moving too. Further than you are. I applied for a job in London a while ago and it looks like I've got it. I just found out this afternoon. So unless there's a hitch, I'm going to England for the next two years. I'll be leaving on Sunday.'

The waitress arrived with their first courses and set them down.

This announcement of his was disconcerting. It wasn't as if she'd been practising writing 'Ellie Litman', but she'd felt as if she'd taken a major step forward by allowing herself to get excited about a man. She'd signed up for the online dating mostly because of Debby's insistence, not really expecting to meet anyone she cared about when she did. So when Daniel had appeared in cyberspace, she'd been surprised and delighted. Even the whole drama of getting dressed for this date had been exciting, reminding her of what it felt like to have expectations. Now he was leaving the country before she had a chance to get to know him.

'I'm not absolutely sure whether I'm going yet,' Daniel

11

said. 'It's all about politics. People who aren't involved in the medical world don't know how political it can be. I can't begin to tell you . . .'

But he did begin to tell her, and he continued, in detail. She tried to keep up with all the different names of the many doctors and administrators he mentioned, and she tried even harder to hear everything he was saying and blot out the background noise. But the women at the table beside theirs were being so boisterous she found herself leaning forward and surreptitiously cupping her ears.

Almost all of what he was saying sailed straight over Ellie's head. He was clearly passionate about his subject and she admired that, yet she didn't know the people involved in his stories and the politics of the medical world were beyond her. At various points, her thoughts would stray – to Tim, to the move the next day – and then she'd mentally nudge herself and try to concentrate. His emails had been short. Now he was being so expansive she was having problems figuring out where one story stopped and another began.

They'd finished their main course, and he'd been as adept at managing to eat and talk at the same time as he had been at getting the waitress's attention.

Did she like him? she asked herself as he began an anecdote about a backstabbing, competitive colleague.

Yes.

Kind of.

He was intelligent, occasionally funny. And his bluey-green eyes were appealing.

12

But nothing was actually drawing her to him and her initial feeling of disappointment when he told her he might be moving was fading. She felt completely separate from him, almost as if she were watching him on television, not sitting a few feet away.

As inappropriate as her flashbacks were, she couldn't help but compare this meeting once more to her first with Charlie. That hadn't been love at first sight, but it hadn't been far from it. Love at first night was more like it. Because by the time they left that kitchen and he was walking her back to her dorm, she'd fallen for him. Completely, absolutely, stomach-churningly. For weeks afterwards, she'd feel her stomach roiling any time she was in his presence.

'What's happened to you, Ellie? You're so skittish all of a sudden,' her mother had commented when she'd gone back home to New York for the holidays a week after she and Charlie had met. She hadn't responded, but later on her mother had narrowed her eyes, stared over the kitchen table at her and said, 'You're skittish *and* you're not eating. What's his name?'

'*Happy birthday to you . . .*'

Jolted, Ellie looked around and saw their waitress and two waiters approaching the next table with a birthday cake. She switched her gaze back to Daniel who half-smiled and rolled his eyes, then joined in the singing of 'Happy Birthday' with the rest of the restaurant clientele. Ellie did as well, self-conscious about her awful singing voice. Five of the women stood up while one sat and received the cake. They all whooped and applauded as she blew out the candles.

'I *should* have gotten us a table at the back – but not so I could sneak out the door – to avoid all this noise. Oops again.'

'Oops' was so not what she'd imagine a successful forty-two-year-old oncologist saying, she couldn't help but wonder what Daniel's patients would think if he said it during a consultation.

'In any event, I've been droning on about hospital politics – we still haven't talked about you. I've enjoyed your emails.'

'Thanks. And I've enjoyed yours too. But it's so weird, this whole internet business.'

'I know. Absolutely. I don't know why I ever signed up for the whole thing: a friend convinced me to. And OK, I know everyone says that, but it's true. She said I'm too obsessed by work and it's criminal to be forty-two years old and unmarried and not dating. She said this was the easy way to do things.'

'Same here.' Ellie smiled. 'I mean, a friend of mine convinced me, and I'm telling the truth too.'

'But this really is such a strange way of meeting people, isn't it?' He leaned forward. They were bonding over their shared discomfort.

'Completely crazy.'

'I Googled you, you know. That sounds so intrusive, but it's gotten to be a reflex action these days.' His lock of blond hair fell forward again and he brushed it back. She found herself imagining him with a hair band, fixing it so it wouldn't fall, and smothered a smile. 'Anyway, I couldn't find you.

14

There were a lot of Ellie Walterses but none that seemed to be you. Did you Google me?'

'Yes.' She blushed. 'My friend Debby, the one who convinced me to do this – she told me to, just to make sure you were who you said you were.'

'Hey, don't apologise. Everyone does it. Sometimes I think that even though technology is supposed to bring us all closer together, it's actually making us more distant and suspicious of each other. We sit alone at our computers sending messages out into cyberspace and checking up on people instead of actually interacting in person. But, hey, I shouldn't be saying that. I'm pro-science. I shouldn't be dissing technology.'

'Sometimes *I* wonder how email has changed the way people write; whether when they used to write real letters they wrote differently. More intimately, or something.'

'Probably. So tell me, Ellie. Have you ever been to Europe? Do you like to travel?'

She felt immediately wrong-footed. He'd changed the course of the conversation unexpectedly and asked her a typical 'getting to know you' question just when she thought she actually was getting to know him better.

'I went to Paris once,' she replied, not adding 'on my honeymoon'. 'I've always wanted to go back to Europe. You must be excited about the the idea of moving to London.'

'Absolutely. I've been to London before, of course, but working there, seeing for myself what the National Health Service is like, that would be really fascinating.'

He was off again, discussing the pros and cons of universal

healthcare with the same intensity he'd talked about hospital politics. For an instant she'd thought they might have a conversation about writing emails, writing letters, how people communicated with each other, but that didn't happen. And she really didn't want him to fire questions like 'do you like to travel?' or 'what are your hobbies?' at her. They'd more or less covered all that in their online profiles.

It was all so much easier online. Sitting on the spot like this, being asked questions, is so awkward. And what do I have to say? My husband left me for another woman eighteen months ago. I've been married to him since I was twenty and I have no idea what life is like out in the single world.

So, why did he leave you, Ellie?

Even if he didn't ask it, he'd be wondering. Women sympathise with you when something like that happens. Scared that they might be next in the firing line. But men can't help but think of you as somebody some other man dumped.

The rest of the meal went by quickly as Daniel talked about living and working in London and then caught himself again, apologising once more for monopolising the conversation.

'I keep meaning to ask you . . . why Bourne? Of all the places to move to, why did you choose there?'

A few mintes before, he'd signalled for the bill and before she had a chance to reply, it arrived. She reached into her purse to pay her share, but he had already pulled out a wad of cash and was handing it to the waiter. 'This is on me, Ellie. You're in my neighbourhood, I pay.'

'That's incredibly nice of you.'

16

'No problem. You still haven't told me – why Bourne?'

'My aunt rented a house on Mashnee Island in Bourne when I was fourteen and I spent two weeks there in the summer. I had an amazing time, and when I thought about moving out of Boston, Bourne was the first place that came into my head.'

'It's at the very beginning of the Cape, right?'

'Yes, just over the bridge.'

There was a strained silence and she was struggling to think of a way to fill it when he said: 'Listen, you've probably figured out by now that I'm not very good at small talk – or medium talk. I either talk my head off like I'm in a presidential debate and I'm the only candidate or I try to be funny. You haven't heard me try to be funny yet. You're lucky. Anyway, that's why I've never married, I guess.' He winced. 'I'm very good at my job, I'm very comfortable in it, but I'm not good – or comfortable – with this dating business.'

This self-effacing confession touched her heart; it was more like the Daniel she'd met online and she wished he'd said it at the beginning of the evening. He was nervous too. For some reason she hadn't considered he'd be feeling the same way she was.

'I'm not comfortable with the dating business either, Daniel.'

'You seem fine to me.'

'I haven't dated anyone since I met my ex-husband when I was nineteen. Even the idea of dating makes me nervous.'

'Well, listen, could I see you again if something un-expected happens and I don't go to London?'

How could she say no after what he'd just said about himself and dating? And she wasn't sure that she wanted to say no. She'd had mixed reactions towards him: doutbless he'd had mixed reactions to her. A first date was a first date. It hadn't been straightforwardly fantastic, but it hadn't been a disaster either.

'Sure. We can keep in touch and you can let me know what's happening, whether you've moved or not.'

'Great. I won't hog the conversation next time, if there is a next time, I promise.'

'You didn't hog anything. What you were talking about was really interesting, honestly. I had a very nice evening.'

'OK then. Great. I guess it's time to go.' He didn't look at himself in the mirror before he stood up and he didn't try to take her arm or elbow to guide her out – both plus points.

She'd called a taxi on her cell phone as they were having their coffee. With any luck, it would be outside waiting for her.

'Take care of yourself, Ellie,' he said when they reached the sidewalk. 'You know, moving to Bourne might be a great thing for you. Think about it. You can be Bourne again!'

'Daniel . . .'

'I know, I know. Lousy joke. I told you, I can't help but try to be funny. So I bet you'll be glad to get rid of me. Look, there's your taxi. Perfect timing.'

A Red Cab pulled up and the passenger-side window zoomed down. Daniel leaned in and spoke to the driver, then turned back to her.

'Yup, it's yours. Goodnight, Ellie. Thanks for putting up with me.'

He went to kiss her as she put her hand out – an exact replay of their first meeting. This time they both laughed and he went ahead and kissed her on the cheek. She climbed into the taxi, gave the driver the address, then gave Daniel a wave as they drove off.

She collapsed against the back of the seat, realising when she did just how tense she'd been the whole time she'd been sitting on the restaurant banquette.

That's it. It was all right, but I'm not going on that dating site again. If he stays and asks to see me again, I might say yes. But I'm not trawling cyberspace any more. It's too strange a way to meet someone.

And what if Tim found out? Debby can say everyone does this now, but how embarrassed would I be if he knew I had done this?

The cab driver put his wipers on; Ellie watched the rain belting against the windshield as they travelled down Beacon Street. Outside one of the bars they passed, a young couple stood, clearly looking to wave down a taxi. The woman was pregnant, the man had his arm around her. Ellie turned in her seat, kept looking at them as they sped by.

That was Charlie and me fifteen years ago, she thought. *Young and happy and together, planning our future.*

You think you know someone and then they do something you never expected them to and your heart stumbles around, reeling, like a bad drunk at a horrendous party.

But she was making headway. She was getting there,

wherever there was. Away from Boston anyway. Tomorrow she and Tim would be out of this city, away from Charlie. They'd be living on the water with a view of their own.

She missed Debby, though. Hugely. Debby had a kind of magic to her, a way of bringing out the fun in any situation, seeing the absurdity and humour and going straight for it, whisking Ellie along with her.

'Jesus, you're almost as short as I am,' she'd said, the first time they'd gotten on the apartment building's elevator together. 'Please tell me you're the one who's just moved in on the fifth floor. I so need another short person in my life.'

Laughing, Ellie had said 'That's me', and their friendship began.

Every time she saw Debby, she pictured her playing Annie on Broadway, with her red hair and freckles, singing her heart out and dancing around. The idea of Debby teaching at MIT and being a maths prodigy was unimaginable. 'Are you telling me you can stand still in one place for more than five minutes? I don't believe you,' Ellie had said to her when she found out.

'Believe it, kiddo. I'm a fucking genius. Forget that at your peril,' was the reply.

Debby liked dissecting people's characters as if they were frogs in a laboratory. And when it came to Charlie, she did it with a vengeance.

'You know, your ex is a wannabee WASP with a chip on his shoulder,' she had stated one night when they were sharing a bottle of wine in her apartment.

'Deb, you've never met him.'

'As if I need to meet him! You told me he's from a working-class background, right? And he's pulled himself up by his Gucci bootstraps . . . not that Gucci shoes *have* straps or anything except those little gold bracelets on them. I mean, what's with that? Who thought of putting bracelets on men's shoes? And now you're telling me he joined the Country Club? That place teeming with all those dyed-in-J.Crew WASPS? It doesn't get any more social-ladder-climbing than that. His hands must be calloused as hell.

'Except . . . wait a second . . .' She took a swig of her wine, stood up, sat down again. 'Has he made it into the *Social Register*? That big black book with anyone who's anyone's name and address and telephone number? Like Facebook for snobs only without the internet part. Don't tell me he's in that thing?'

'No, not yet anyway. I know he'd like to be in it, though.'

'Oh my God! What's that bird that never lands? An albatross, right? His ego is like an albatross. Just keeps flying. And now he's swanned off with Sandra fucking Cabot, precisely because she *is* a fucking Cabot. What's that rhyme they say? Wait a second . . . right, I've got it: "Welcome to Massachusetts, the land of the bean and the cod, where the Lodges speak only to Cabots and the Cabots speak only to God." Charlie bagged a Cabot . . . It's so predictable, guys trading up. But he's put a spin on it, hasn't he? Because she's older than him. Where'd he meet her anyway?'

'I don't know. The Cougar Club?'

Debby laughed and Ellie did too, relieved that time and

21

a sense of humour could make a subject that had once been so painful almost palatable.

'I don't know how you lived with that idiot. Thank God you don't have to speak to him any more. I understand you have to be civil to him because of Tim, but at least you don't have to have any real contact with him. Let's toast to that.' Standing up again, Debby had clinked her glass against Ellie's.

Ellie stood too and took a sip, feeling uneasy. If Debby had actually met Charlie, she wouldn't dismiss him so breezily. Ellie could picture him, sitting in a chair, one leg slung over the other, eyes narrowed, asking Debby questions, concentrating on her with that considered way he had. Charlie didn't make you feel like the only person in the room when he talked to you, he made you feel like the only other person on a desert island – one you had no desire to leave because he was on it with you.

He wasn't classically attractive: he was short – only a half-inch taller than Ellie was, his eyes were disconcertingly close together, he had a mole on the side of his face which he'd often touch when he was concentrating. Charlie wasn't about his physical appearance; he was about his pull. People used that word 'pull' all the time now, instead of 'scored' when it came to dating, but Charlie's pull wasn't just about getting someone into bed; it was also to do with finding out exactly how they ticked, reaching into their psyche and gently lulling them as he lifted out information.

Debby could call him an idiot, but Ellie knew Debby would have been entranced by Charlie too, if he'd chosen to focus on her.

But she sipped her wine and kept quiet. Debby had labelled Charlie an egomaniac social climber. She liked making jokes at his expense and Ellie wasn't going to stop her. Defending him would be pointless and she didn't want to do it anyway. Charlie had left her. Charlie had gone.

The taxi pulled over to the side of the road in front of her apartment building. Ellie paid the driver then ran in, throwing her jacket over her head to shelter her from the rain.

I want Debby, she thought as she got in the elevator. I want to knock on her door now and tell her to come over and I'll debrief her on tonight. I want her to make me laugh.

Her apartment was as close to empty as it could get. For the past week she and Tim had been using sleeping bags on the floor, and she'd kept back only a few plates, pots and pieces of cutlery. Everything else was waiting for them at the cottage in Bourne.

Ellie had always thought of this place as temporary, so seeing it like this wasn't upsetting. When the divorce happened, Charlie had sold their three-bedroomed apartment in Back Bay, overlooking the Charles River, and they had split the proceeds. Instead of buying a new place, as he had done, she'd decided to rent. Because she knew she had to have some time to form a plan; she was too shaken to make any permanent decisions.

As the months went by, the plan gradually took shape. She wanted out of Boston. There were too many damaging memories here. If she were going to start a new life, she wanted to start it in a new place. Not too far from Boston, so Tim could visit his father easily, but away from the city. In the place she'd loved so much when she was fourteen years old: Cape Cod.

Finding a place she liked, buying it, moving into it, were part of the process of taking control of her own life; a new feeling for her. She'd always relied on Charlie before; even her part-time job in the Museum of Fine Arts had been one he had engineered through friends of his.

This move was symbolic on all sorts of levels. Tim was upset about it, but he was having big problems at his school and Ellie truly believed a new place, new school and new start would help him too.

One more night. Tomorrow at this time we'll be in the cottage.

Taking her jacket off, she went into her bedroom, sat on the floor and turned her laptop on.

Hey, Deb,

I so wish you were here so I could tell you about my night in person. Anyway, it was fine but I haven't fallen desperately in love and he hasn't either. Which is probably a really good thing because it looks like he's moving to London for two years.

We said we'd get together again if he didn't move. So – what else can I tell you? He was nice. But . . . he said 'oops' twice. Which was endearing, sort of. But it's a little too Hugh Grant, isn't it?

So, MY big move tomorrow! Tim is still not happy about this, but I think he will be when we get there and he sees how beautiful it is.

It's funny – you're on the Pacific and now I'll be on the Atlantic. I hope I find a friend like you in Bourne, but that's not going to be easy, I know. I really, really wish you hadn't moved.

OK I've had two glasses of wine and I'm going to get ready for bed.

Sorry Daniel and I haven't run off into the sunset. I know you would have LOVED that.

I miss you tons.

Love, Ellie.

She shut off the computer, went to her cupboard and pulled out a pair of pyjamas. Tim was staying the night with his friends, so she didn't have to worry about him coming home late. She'd get into bed now, read a little and fall asleep.

Just as she put on her pyjama top, she heard the sound of a siren.

Police car or ambulance?

It didn't matter which.

She sat down on the bed. The images were creeping in; she could sense them stealing in sideways, like some horrible slime oozing under a door.

Breathe in.

It didn't happen.

Breathe out.

It didn't happen.

Why? Why did she have to go to Starbucks that morning? Why did she have to overhear what the people at the next table were talking about?

All this time she'd managed to push the memories away but since that morning at Starbucks she'd felt them massing at the periphery of her mind; little things, tiny reminders, beckoning them back.

'Start with your toes, Ellie. Clench them, then unclench them. Now your ankles. Right. Move up your body, clenching and unclenching. Relax.' She heard an echo of Dr Emmanuel's voice. 'All right. Now do your breathing exercises. And let yourself forget.'

Breathe in.

It didn't happen.

Breathe out.

It didn't happen.

It never happened.

It never happened.

The memories began to recede. Her brain cleared.

Ellie opened her eyes. The sirens had gone.

2

This was not a great beginning. It was such a crucially important day, but everything seemed to be going wrong. The rain had been pelting down non-stop, with no sign of letting up, and they were stuck on the Bourne Bridge, wedged in a late Friday afternoon June traffic jam.

Tim kept fidgeting, taking his seatbelt off, pulling it as far as it could go, putting it back on, taking it off again. He was driving Ellie crazy and he knew he was. This was his way of saying: 'Mom, you're screwing up my life. There's no way I want to move to Bourne. Don't think I'm going to pretend to be happy about it.'

In the mood he was in, if she asked him to stop playing with his seatbelt he'd do it even more.

The car ahead of her moved two feet forward, and everyone behind followed; as if they'd won something precious, as if this were a war and they'd moved those cruicial feet further into enemy territory. Tim stretched his seatbelt again, pretended to be fascinated with it, while Ellie stared out the windshield, praying that the rain would stop and the traffic would clear.

27

This wasn't how she had pictured this trip. They should have been speeding over this bridge, windows down, catching a glimpse of the Cape Cod Canal beneath them. A week ago, when she'd made the same drive, the sun had been shining, the water had been glittering and sparkling, and she had imagined Tim, sitting beside her as he was now – except she'd envisioned him excited and impressed, maybe even saying 'Awesome' as he peered down at the sailboats.

A week ago she'd crossed this bridge in no time; she'd made it from Boston to the cottage in eighty-five minutes, and spent all afternoon unpacking and making the place look nice for Tim. She'd been so happy and so full of an unimaginable sense of freedom, she'd danced around the cottage by herself, like a teenager before a party.

You're driving me crazy – enough of the seatbelt-pulling.

No, don't say it.

He'll say something sarcastic back and you'll end up arguing and this day will become even more of a disaster.

'So, I put blue sheets on your bed.'

'Great.'

When Tim was a child, he'd loved blue sheets for some reason, and they became his special treat. Now she was hoping to get him to revert and be that little boy again, the one who cared about something silly like sheets and who adored his mother, instead of the truculent fifteen-year-old whose mother irritated the hell out of him.

Ellie didn't know whether he was being a typical teenage boy or whether he was suffering more from the divorce than he'd let on. When it happened he'd seemed to take it

28

reasonably well, but as hard as she tried to get him to talk, he'd never opened up to her about it. And then he'd done badly at school, flunking out of his year.

Now she was taking him away from his friends. Of course he'd be angry; she understood that. But what if he'd stayed in Boston and had to repeat his year there? She knew he'd hated that idea with a passion. And if he had moved to a new school in Boston, his friends wouldn't have been there either.

Meanwhile Charlie had been pressuring him to work like a demon and apply to a boarding school. The thought of sending Tim away like that made Ellie feel sick.

She leaned forward, hunched over the steering wheel. They were right in the middle of the bridge now, at the top of the hump.

'You know, the first time I came over this bridge, my aunt told me that the actor who played Superman in the original TV show, way back in the 1950s, got to the point where he'd played Superman so much he actually thought he could fly. He came here dressed up in his Superman costume and jumped, thinking he'd take off like a speeeding bullet, but of course he plummeted and died. It's a really sad story, isn't it?'

Tim craned his neck, looked out of his window, up at the top of the bridge. 'How'd he do that? I mean, those railings make it impossible to jump, the way they're curved at the top.'

'I guess they didn't have them back then. They must have made them later, to stop people jumping.'

'Yeah.' Tim squirmed, trying to get more comfortable.

Ellie remembered the first time she'd put him in his car seat. He was in a little white and blue polka-dot jumpsuit. Now he was wearing ripped jeans and a black T-shirt, and he was closing in on the 6' mark.

'Wow – how did a little person like you create a giant like Tim?' Debby had asked.

'I don't know. Charlie's short too, but he said his grandfather was tall, so maybe the tall gene skipped a generation,' she'd explained.

'But I saw that sign for the Samaritans at the beginning of the bridge,' Tim said now. 'Like a thousand years ago when we were at the beginning of it. So people must still try to jump off. Anyway, the Superman guy might have come here to kill himself in the first place. I mean, how would anyone know he thought he could fly? Did he go around telling people he could fly?'

'Good question. I don't know.'

Ellie didn't know, either, if the Superman story was true or an early not-so-urban myth, and she wasn't sure why she'd told it to Tim. But she'd gotten his attention: he'd stopped playing with his seatbelt. Instead he kept looking up at the curved railings protecting the bridge from the jumpers. Or, she corrected herself, the jumpers from the bridge.

'*Why did you and Dad get married in the first place?*' he'd asked when they'd first moved into the rented apartment. The question had come out of the blue. She'd answered: 'We loved each other, Tim. But sometimes things don't work out.' At that point, she'd expected him to grill her further but he'd simply nodded and continued unpacking. He knew about Sandra Cabot, but she didn't know how much he knew – whether he'd realised his father had had an affair with her.

When they'd told him about the divorce, she and Charlie had said that they had married when they were very young, had drifted apart, and that it was better for everyone if they split up now. Tim hadn't pressed them for more reasons and Charlie hadn't introduced him to Sandra until the divorce was finalised.

Although there had been times Ellie had wanted to tell Tim the whole truth and let rip about his father's infidelity, she didn't. She knew that wouldn't help his relationship with Charlie and using that type of weapon could only end up hurting Tim.

'This bridge – it looks kind of like a pregnant woman arched over backwards, so her stomach's pointing up.'

'You're right. That's exactly right. It does.'

Every once in a while Tim would come out with a description like this, and Ellie would be amazed and pleased. He was bothering to look at things, making comparisons, thinking in ways she wouldn't have expected him to. Not only that, he'd actually said it out loud. He still wanted to share with her; at least some things, some of the time.

'Look – we're moving – finally.'

As if some plumber at the far end of the Cape, in Provincetown, had unblocked the sink that was the Cape Cod Highway, the cars in front began to move, and not just to inch but actually pick up speed. They descended from

31

the top of the bridge down to the roundabout, in the centre of which the words 'Welcome to Cape Cod' were written out in bright, showy flowers.

'Look at that. How cheesy can you get?'

'Tim. Please. Give it a break.'

'Mom?'

'OK. It is cheesy. You're right.'

Elli headed right off the roundabout, past Tedeschi's the deli store cum bus stop, and on along winding roads. Tim wasn't speaking: he'd put on his iPod earphones, but when she glanced over at him, she could see he was taking in his surroundings and what he was seeing made him nervous.

This wasn't only a new house he was going to, but a new place. She could see his eyes scanning to right and left for signs of life: coffee shops, stores. Bourne didn't even have a main street. There was a small grocery store near their cottage and one coffee place not too far away; there was the High School he'd be going to, but if you wanted to shop, you had to go back over the Bourne Bridge and into Buzzards Bay.

The big A&P, a defunct movie theatre, stores and restaurants catering to summer tourists in Buzzards Bay, didn't qualify as Tim-friendly destinations, though.

He'd have to go to the Mall, a half an hour or more's drive away, to reach familiar territory. But he was fifteen years old, he didn't have a licence; he'd be dependent on her or his friends' parents for that kind of trip.

Long winding roads and cranberry bogs. That's what he was seeing now. What was he thinking? *I'm stuck in the sticks. With my mother.*

He'd steadfastly refused to come to the cottage before now, hoping, probably, that if he ignored the move it wouldn't happen. Now that D-Day had arrived and they were actually going to live here, Ellie could feel his panic setting in.

'Tim . . .' She motioned for him to take his earphones out and he did. 'It's going to be great, I promise. We're right on the water and there's a really nice beach just a few minutes away. And a lot of people who work in Boston live here year round. We're not in the middle of nowhere, even if it looks like it right now.'

'Yeah, right. Bourne, Massachusetts. What a Mecca. Everyone's lining up to come live here. There's practically a stampede.'

'Wow, look,' he continued, his voice flat. 'That sign for the Aptucxet Trading Post on the right there. What are they trading? Stamps?'

'It's actually a historical society. There's a museum there; I think it tells you the history of Bourne.'

'Oh, boy. Brilliant. Can't wait to go.'

'Tim, I know this is hard for you. But staying in Boston would have been hard, too. You told me that. If you could just be a little more positive, maybe look at things with an open mind, you might feel better.'

'Mom, I'm here with you, OK? I didn't run away.' He slouched in his seat. 'Let's just get there.'

Tim couldn't be excited yet because they hadn't reached the water. Once he saw the view and realised he'd be waking up to it every morning, he'd feel better.

The road they were on bottomed out at a small cemetery

where Ellie turned right, and then, about twenty yards further, she took a left, following the signpost to Mashnee Village. Which was where her aunt had taken her the summer when she'd been fourteen years old.

It had been a golden two weeks of her life, and maybe she was trying to recreate that special time in some way by buying a place so near to Mashnee, but so what? The cottage coming up for sale at the exact time she was looking to buy had to be fate.

During those weeks on Mashnee with her aunt, she'd spent hours daydreaming as she looked across the bay at this amazing house on a point – a huge grey clapboard house perched on a little hill. It was shaped like a witch's hat, with a wraparound porch on the ground floor and a beautiful balcony looking out over the Canal on the second floor.

A stone wall surrounded it, keeping the sea at bay. It stood there, on its own, both graceful and quirky, under its conical roof. When tour boats went down the Canal they'd always stop outside it, and she knew whoever was guiding the tour was saying something about it – maybe who owned it, who lived there. A few times, Ellie had asked her aunt if they could take one of those tours, but they never got around to it.

She often saw people on the lawn outside, though she couldn't tell from that distance what age they were or what they were wearing. But she'd imagined them leading a charmed existence in this Witch's House – a *good* witch's house – all of them playing games and gathering around a dining-room table telling stories and laughing. A house so different from the small apartment she and her mother lived in in Manhattan on their own, after her father had left.

Her aunt never rented the house on Mashnee again, but Ellie often thought of that summer, and when she did, the image of that house on the point was always part of her memory.

It was fate – it had to be – that her first thought about where to move was to Cape Cod, and that on her third visit to a real estate agent there, she discovered that the cottage which belonged to the Witch's House, the cottage which was only two hundred yards from that house, was up for sale. She made an offer for it on the spot, without even asking to see it first.

The view suddenly opened up a little; if it hadn't been so grey and rainy, Tim could have seen the Canal, the beaches, the water and maybe cheered up a little, but it was so dismal, Ellie could barely make out the cluster of summer rental houses that formed Mashnee Village straight ahead of them at the end of a causeway – on both sides of which were beaches. Good for swimming, perfect for teenagers hanging out on sunny summer days.

'See, ahead? That's Mashnee. They're mostly summer houses there, but there's a nice restaurant too and it's open all year, I checked. It's maybe a ten-minute walk to Mashnee from our place. We're on the point just before it. Here's our road – right here.' She turned into Agawam Point Road.

'It used to be a sand road but they've surfaced it. These condos at the beginning here? There weren't any when I first came to Mashnee. My aunt drove me down this road

35

once, exploring. We wanted to check out the big house at the end on the point, but then we started to worry they'd think we were trespassing so we turned back. There . . . can you see it? It's huge, isn't it?'

'That's ours? I thought you said it was a cottage. Wow!'

'No, no – that's not ours – ours *is* a cottage. A cottage that used to belong to the big house.'

Although the road had been paved, it was still narrow and the bushes on either side scraped the side of the car as she drove. Tim had had one moment of excitement when he'd thought the big house was theirs. How was he going to feel when he saw the tiny-in-comparison cottage?

A mini version of the Mashnee causeway lay ahead, leading to the circular driveway of the Witch's House on its own peninsula at the end. Their cottage was down a grass side road before that mini causeway began.

'This is it?' Tim asked when she pulled up in front of the door.

When Ellie had first seen it, she'd thought: 'This is it?' too, but that thought had been followed immediately by: 'This is all I've ever wanted.' Painted white, with rose bushes on either side of the old wooden front door, it looked like it could have been on the cover of any magazine heralding the virtues of small-town life. But it was even more perfect than a generic cosy cottage because it was on the shore-line. The living-room window had a view on to the Cape Cod Canal and the two back bedrooms looked out over a small cove.

'Yes, this is it. Come on. Grab your backpack. You can

get your luggage out later. I want you to see your room.' Ellie got out of the car, took the keys from her bag and opened the front door, feeling nervous and proud, ushering Tim out of the rain and into the living room.

'Jesus, Mom. This room's like a pumpkin,' he said as soon as he stepped inside, putting his hand up and mockingly shielding his eyes. 'It's like Hallowe'en orange. What's the deal? You own this now, right? You can paint it whatever colour you want, can't you?'

'I *did* paint it. I *wanted* this colour. I wanted it to be bright. Different.'

'It's different all right. And what's with all the seagulls?'

Since she bought the cottage Ellie had been collecting all types of little wooden seagulls which she'd arranged on table tops and bookshelves. Maybe she'd gone overboard and indulged herself in them because she knew Charlie would have thought they were the tackiest things possible, but she loved these little knick-knacks.

'They're fun. Anyway, come here . . . to the back of the house.' She led him to his bedroom. 'This is it, your room. See the cove right outside your window? Isn't it beautiful, even in the rain? You have a view of the water. You used to say you wanted a view of the water.'

'Maybe when I was four years old or something.' Tim turned away from the window. 'This room is tiny. It's not even half the size of my room at Dad's. It's smaller than mine in our apartment. And it smells.'

'I know, sweetheart. But after it stops raining, I'll open the doors and windows and let the air in, and it will smell fine.'

'If it ever stops raining.' He sat down on the bed, put his head in his hands. 'Face it, Mom. It's small, it smells. This place is a dump.'

Last week she'd imagined him saying, 'Cool, Mom. The view is great. I've always wanted a view of the water.'

'It's big enough for us, it's on the water, it's nice – it will be even nicer when it's sunny. It's just bad luck it's raining today. Everything's going to be good, Tim, I promise. You'll get used to it.'

'It sucks.'

'Come on. Just give it some time.'

Reaching down, he grabbed his backpack from the floor, pulled it up on his lap, opened it and fished out his laptop.

'Do I have a choice? Besides being homeless and living on the street by myself or whatever? Or dealing with Sandra, which would be worse than living on the street. This is so wrong, Mom.' He pushed the button that made his Apple MacBook whir into life. 'You said there's WiFi here, right? I'm going to get it going, log on.'

'Wait a second. We should talk more. You can tell me what's going on in your head. We can—'

'I've told you already, moving here sucks. There's nothing else to say. Right, OK, I've got it. Is there a password?'

'My usual one – you know it. But listen, I really want you to give this place a chance.'

'I get it, Mom. OK? I'm busy now.'

'Tim, I need to know you're all right.'

'I'm fine.' He sighed, stared at the computer screen.

Ellie wanted to hug him but he was so stiff and distant

she knew he'd back off if she tried. Instead she stood up, walked out of the room, leaving him concentrating on entering cyberspace and disappearing into it.

So what did you think, El? Did you really believe he was going to like it in this place? You were so excited about branching off on your own, you didn't think through the ramifications, did you? I thought you were smarter than that.

Ellie sank down into one of the living-room armchairs.

'No one will ever cry in this room.'

That's what the painter had said when he'd applied the first brushful of orange to the living-room wall. It was a crazy colour, she knew, but it was symbolic. A bright, crazy colour, full of life.

All right. I'm not going to cry. But . . .

But Charlie was back in her head, like a parasite that had wormed its way into her brain and taken up residence, or like the clinking chains the ghost of Jacob Marley carried around with him.

He'll be out of my head soon. I got him out of my heart, I'll get him out of my head.

Damn you, Charlie. This is all going to work out. I'll make it work out.

A knock at the door made her jump.

'Hello?' a voice called out – a female voice. Leaping up, Ellie went over to the front door. When she opened it, she saw a woman dressed in a neon yellow rainslicker with a voluminous hood. She looked like someone who'd just walked off a tunafish trawler.

'Hello, I'm Louisa Amory . . . Louisa. I saw your light on

and wanted to say welcome to this cottage. We've only communicated via the real estate agent before and I wanted to say hello in person. But I can leave right away if you're busy.'

'No, no. How nice of you. And you know already, I'm Ellie.' She put out her hand and shook Louisa's. 'Please, come inside. Get out of the rain.'

Louisa came in, rubbed her shoes on the mat and lowered the hood of her rain slicker.

'Wow.' She glanced around the room. 'I love this colour.'

'Really?'

'Really.' Louisa smiled.

She looked to be in her late fifties or early sixties. Tall and thin with shoulder-length dark wavy hair, dark brown eyes and a long, interesting face. *Striking,* Ellie thought. *She makes you want to keep looking at her.*

'Let me help you with your coat.' She went to help her and saw, as Louisa pulled her arms out of the sleeves, the plethora of silver bracelets stretching from wrist to elbow of her right arm. In one instant she was transformed from a tunafish trawler woman into a gypsy.

'Amazing bracelets,' Ellie commented.

'Thank you. The way I see it, there are a lot of things you can't wear when you get older, but I think you can always get away with lots of bracelets. At least, I hope so.'

'They look terrific.'

'That's nice of you to say.' Louisa's eyes studied the room again. 'I really like what you've done with this. It needed cheering up.' She stopped, shook her head. 'Anyway, as I said, welcome to Bourne. I know you've been in and out of

40

this place, but I always seemed to miss you. What's that phrase? Phone tag? This is like "new neighbour tag".'

'Would you like some coffee or tea or anything?'

'Coffee would be great, if you have any. But you've just moved in, so if you don't, I can—'

'No, it's fine, I do. I came down here last week to get the place ready. And I brought some groceries. Including coffee.'

'Coffee's crucial,' Louisa stated. She was wearing a bunch of silver necklaces too, of varying lengths; the longest, which came halfway down her chest, had a small turquoise heart dangling from the end.

'Absolutely,' Ellie said as she hung up the slicker. 'Sit down. Please. I'll go get you a cup.'

'This is great. I come to say hello and see if there's anything I can do, and I end up with you waiting on me. I think I'll come visit all the time.'

Ellie smiled and headed for the kitchen at the back, off the right-hand side of the living room.

'What would you like in your coffee?' she called over her shoulder.

'Black's fine.'

Louisa wasn't someone who played golf or went to cocktail parties in a little black dress, Ellie could tell. Which was a huge relief.

Some of Charlie's group of preppie friends were nice; but she'd never felt entirely at ease with them. 'Ellie, a little heads up,' Sukie Hancock had told her, pulling her aside after a dinner party one night. 'Don't say the word "carpet". I know it's stupid, but people care about things like that. It's "rug". Because "carpet" signals that you don't have nice floors, so have to go that hideous wall-to-wall route to hide your ugly boards.'

Ellie had blushed; but as Sukie walked off, had come dangerously close to screaming, 'Carpet! Carpet! Carpet!'

'I can't tell you how happy I am to have bought this place,' she said as she came in with their mugs of coffee and handed Louisa hers.

'And I'm happy someone's living here again.' Louisa took a sip from her mug. 'Thanks for this. I needed a hit of caffeine. Anyway, it's been a while since anyone was here. My son used to live here. He and his wife.'

'And now they've moved?'

'His wife Pam died.' Louisa put down the mug. 'And Joe . . . my son . . . moved to Washington, DC.'

'I'm sorry about your daughter-in-law.'

'So am I. My husband Jamie died ten years ago. I know how hard it is to lose your partner. Joe's lost his father *and* his wife. It's unfair. Anyway, when I put this cottage up for sale, I was hoping someone young would buy it.'

'I'm not exactly young.'

'Oh, please.'

'Mom? Is someone . . . ?' Emerging from his room, Tim stood still, stared at Louisa.

'Tim, this is Mrs Amory.'

'Louisa.'

'Louisa. She lives in the house at the end of the point. This cottage used to be hers. She came by to welcome us. Louisa, this is my son Tim.'

'Hello, Tim.' Louisa stood up and shook his hand.

'It's funny. I was hoping someone young *and* with a child would buy it. And now here you are. Not a child, but still . . . not a boring old adult. It's nice to meet you.'

'Nice to meet you, too.' He brushed back his hair self-consciously. 'Your house is great. It looks like a big witch's hat.'

'That's exactly what I always thought,' Ellie said.

'A lot of people say that.' Louisa sat back down. 'A big grey witch's hat. You know, the top of the hat, the attic, is really scary. When I was little, I was terrified of going up there. I still am. So, how old are you, Tim?'

'Fifteen.'

'Which means you had him when you were what, Ellie, ten years old?'

'Twenty-one.'

'You look disgustingly younger than thirty-six. It's really unfair for anyone to look as young as you do. So, Tim, what do you think about your new house?'

Louisa had narrowed her eyes, was looking searchingly at him, but in a kindly inquisitive way.

'I don't know what there is to do here,' he answered.

Given all the answers he might have made, Ellie was relieved he'd come up with this one.

'Well, it's summer so you can swim. That's one thing.'

'And he starts summer school in Bourne on Monday,' Ellie put in.

'You do?' Louisa raised her eyebrows. 'Is that going to be fun or is it going to be a bummer?'

'It's going to be a bummer.'

Tim actually laughed.

A 'bummer'. Louisa must have been a hippie in her youth. She was wearing khaki-coloured jeans and a long-sleeved white cotton shirt. Very simple, but also somehow very stylish. She'd done what most older women Ellie knew hadn't been able to manage – dressed in way that wasn't trying to be too young but wasn't fuddy-duddy either. Ellie couldn't stop staring at her; she seemed very sure of herself without being arrogant. And she'd made Tim laugh. Which was nothing short of miraculous. Not even Debby had managed that.

'You know, the older I get, the more I think we have everything the wrong way around.' Louisa sat forward, directing her words at Tim. 'What I mean is, little kids are the ones with all the energy, right? You know how you can never get them to stop running around? How they never want to take naps or a rest? So they should be the ones who go to offices every day and work their asses off. Then, later on, when they're thirty or whatever, they can go to school. At which point they'll actually appreciate it.'

'So there'd be, like, four-year-olds with briefcases going to banks and stuff?'

'Exactly.'

'Awesome.' Tim laughed again. 'I like it.'

'I know someone who teaches at the Bourne summer school. She's good, I think you'll like her. And there *are* things to do here, Tim.'

'Yeah, like what? Visiting the Aptucxet Trading Post Museum?'

'Tim—'

'Yes, absolutely. You *should* go to Aptucxet. There's some interesting local history there.'

'Bor-ing.'

'Tim—'

'It's OK, Ellie,' Louisa laughed. 'Tim's absolutely right. I lied. The museum *is* boring for the most part, but there is one good story they chronicle there – it's about the Billington Boy. In fact, the Billington Boy is my personal hero so I'll save you from going there and tell you about him myself now. Sit down. I can't concentrate when you're standing.'

Tim sat on the chair which flanked the other side of the sofa.

What did Louisa have that made him do what she said without even raising his eyebrows in protest? Ellie wondered.

'Right, here's the deal.' Louisa leaned forward, locked her eyes on Tim. 'My family are descendants of the Billingtons, on my father's side. And the Billingtons came over on the *Mayflower*. We're talking serious history here, right?'

'Right.' Tim nodded. 'Got it.'

'So the pilgrims on the *Mayflower* brought their children with them, of course. Some had unusual names – like Wrestling Brewster and Resolved White – but the two Billington kids, both boys, were more prosaically christened Francis and John. Howsoever, they were both little trouble-makers. And on the trip over Francis somehow gets hold of some gunpowder, makes little pellet bullets, and fires one into a barrel of explosive powder. That blows up, starts a fire and if some of the older pilgrims hadn't been able to put it out, the *Mayflower* would have been – well, history.

45

'In any event, Francis and John are not your average Pilgrim kids to begin with. Still, the *Mayflower* survives, lands on Plymouth Rock, and they all pile out and set up their community in Plymouth. But one day in 1586, six-year-old John Billington disappears. Vanishes. He's lost.

'Everyone goes nuts. Turns out he wandered off and was found by the Indian tribe who lived around here, the Massasoits. They took care of him, fed him, looked after him for a few weeks and then gave him back. Miraculous rescue of little lost boy, right?

'But the way my brother and I always saw it was that little John didn't get lost – he deliberately ran away from the tight-assed Pilgrims in their boring black clothes. I mean, it's a hell of a long distance from here to Plymouth when you can't drive. John hightailed it out of there and was probably desperate to stay with the Indians. A sad day for the Billington Boy when he was hauled back to Plymouth was the way we saw it.'

Louisa belonged in the Witch's House; she'd woven a magic spell with this story. Ellie was not the only one entranced: she could see Tim was too. Louisa had said she'd been scared of the attic when she was a child, so she must have grown up there; Ellie found herself wondering if the house you were raised in had as much effect on your personality as your parents or your genes.

'I went to Plymouth Plantation on a school trip. I bet you're right. I bet the Billington Boy did run away on purpose. I would have.' Tim grinned, looking positively happy.

'So, end of history lesson.' Louisa stood up. 'I have to get home.'

'Do you have to?'

Stay, Ellie silently pleaded. *You're making everything so much better.*

'Afraid so. In weather like this I get a lot of leaks. The pots I've put under them to catch the water are probably overflowing by now. I better go rescue the situation.'

'Thank you for coming over,' Ellie said as Louisa went to the coat rack and grabbed her slicker.

'You know, I really do like this bright colour, Ellie. Especially on a dismal day like this,' she said, nodding at the wall.

'Seriously? You like it?' Tim asked.

'I do.'

Tim, Ellie could see, was suddenly reconsidering. Maybe it wasn't such a bad colour after all.

His cell phone rang then and he reached into his pocket for it.

'It's Dad,' he said.

Ellie grimaced.

'Hi, Dad. Wait a sec.' He covered the mouthpiece. 'I'm going to my room. Goodbye, Louisa, nice to meet you.'

'Nice to meet you too, Tim.'

He headed off back to his bedroom.

'Come and visit me any time, Ellie,' Louisa said. 'My door's always open and it would be lovely to see you. And Tim, of course.'

'Thanks so much. It was really kind of you to come.'

'Right, it's time for me to brave the elements. One hundred per cent liquid sunshine. See you later.' She waved and set off.

Maybe it would be a good night now, Ellie thought as she

closed the door. *I'm lucky with neighbours. First Debby and now Louisa.* When she turned back, Tim had reappeared.

'Are you hungry, sweetheart? I thought I'd make some spaghetti for our first night. What do you think?'

'OK.' He scratched his forehead.

'Louisa's terrific, isn't she?'

'She's cool for an old person.'

'I can't wait to see inside her house. And I can't believe this cottage came up for sale when it did. We were really lucky, weren't we?'

He didn't respond. Ellie knew she was sounding like Pollyanna, but she couldn't stop herself.

'You will like it here, Tim. I know you will.'

'Mom.'

'What?'

'You're trying way too hard. And whatever you say, being here still sucks.'

He strode off back to his room and slammed the door. Ellie sat down, feeling deflated. She'd assumed he'd fall in love with this place the way she had, so had gone ahead and bought it in a rush of enthusiasm. She should have consulted him, made him an equal partner in their new life, brought him down here before the deal was done. Springing it on him as a fait accompli had been wrong. At what point did a mother begin to understand her son was not a boy any more? Tim was fifteen, not five, but Ellie knew that there was a part of her heart which would always think of him as a child.

She should go into the kitchen and start dinner, but she wanted to check her email, in case she had a message from

48

Debby that might cheer her up. Her own laptop lay in its sleeve beside the TV in the corner of the room. She went and picked it up, returned to the sofa and switched it on.

She had two new messages: one from Debby and one from Daniel – which took her aback. She hadn't expected him to contact her so quickly. She opened his first.

> *Hi there, Ellie,*
>
> *I hope the move went well and you're settling in. As it turns out, I am going to London. I fly Sunday night. Found out when I got back from our date. So I can email you about the National Health Service there, if you'd like. Because it was very nice to meet you. Maybe I could be like a foreign correspondent, and bore you with all the details of my life in London! Ha-ha. Let me know if you'd like to keep in touch, but in any event I hope you have a great time in Bourne and a great life.*
>
> *All best, D.*

How was she going to reply to that? Did she want to keep emailing him? He'd left the choice up to her. Her instinct was not to. Going on another date would have been a possibility, but what was the point of corresponding? He'd tell her all about his job and she'd say what in return? *The weather is nice here, Tim's settling in finally.* What? It would be a strain for both of them to continue. She sat for a few seconds, doing nothing. And then she clicked on Reply.

Hi, Daniel,

It was really nice to meet you too. Thank you so much for a

49

lovely dinner. You know you wouldn't bore me with your news, but . . . she stopped, frowned . . . *we're both starting new lives and . . .* and what? . . . *we should concentrate on our futures. You're going to be really busy, I know. If you ever come back to Boston, please get in touch and we can catch up with each other's progress. I'm sure you'll have a fantastic time there. Thanks for everything, and I hope you have a great life too.*

All my best, Ellie.

She hesitated, but then pressed 'Send' and quickly clicked on Debby's email.

Babes – too bad the date wasn't a major success. I wish I were there too, to discuss every detail. Maybe he'll be perfect second time around, if there is a second time. If not, I promise you, you will find someone perfect, and soon, I bet. You'll find friends, too. Better than me and then I'll be jealous, you unfaithful bitch! Am in a rush now but will email again soon. Love to Tim xxxoooo.

Debby had a new life too. Ellie was going to have to get used to not having her around.

As she rose and went to the kitchen, she thought of Louisa and then the Billington Boy. Had he really wished he could stay with the Indians, in Bourne? Was he lost or had he run away – like her? No, not run away, Ellie corrected herself. Run to. But run to what?

A place where there were fewer sirens.

3

Ellie dropped Tim off for his first day at summer school, hoping that the minute he walked through the door he'd find a whole new group of friends and come back home raving about them. The odds were heavily against that, she knew, but at least the sun was shining after the close to torrential rain over the weekend, and he'd woken up to good weather and the beautiful view she'd kept telling him about.

Heading back to the cottage, she saw Atwoods Café on the side of the road and decided to check it out. The times she'd come here before she'd been so busy moving and setting everything up, she hadn't stopped for a coffee break. She liked how unprepossessing it looked from the outside – clearly a hangout for locals, not summer tourists.

There were two cars outside and she pulled up alongside them, parked, got out and opened the screen door.

It was a cute place, with aluminium chairs, red and white checked tablecloths, little vases of flowers at every table.

'Ellie!'

Turning, she saw Louisa at a table on her left.

'Louisa, hi.'

51

'Come join me.'

'Thanks.' Ellie smiled, thinking: I'm becoming a local now.

'What would you like? Coffee?' Louisa asked as Ellie took her seat. 'And a muffin? They have countless varieties of muffins here now.'

'Coffee would be great. A cappuccino if they have it.'

'Of course they do. One cappuccino, please,' Louisa called out to the waitress behind the counter. 'You know, they never used to. Have cappuccino, I mean. This place has been here forever. Fishermen used to come here in the mornings, sit on stools at the counter, drink black coffee, smoke cigarettes and talk about how the fish were running. My brother John and I would come and listen to them. And we always wondered how that expression started . . . fish running.'

'Don't they come here any more?'

'No. It's too fancy now. I know it may not look fancy to you, but believe me, those guys wouldn't drink cappuccinos if you paid them. And forget the muffins. Dunkin Donuts, sure. But muffins? That's heresy.'

Louisa, dressed in jeans and a dark blue T-shirt so large the sleeves came down to her elbows, was still bedecked in the bracelets and necklaces. Her eyes, Ellie noticed, were lively, as if she were amused or intrigued by everything she saw.

'It sounds as if this place used to be hard-core Alpha Male.'

'Absolutely. You know, I miss that sometimes. I know it's un-PC and fatally unhealthy, but I miss that cigarette smoke and the way they hunkered down at the counter. Now it's all cheery and feminine – witness the flowers.'

'And the muffins.'

'And the muffins,' Louisa laughed. 'But Atwoods does nod to ancient history. Look . . .' She turned and pointed to the wall above her. 'Old photographs of men showing off the fish they've caught.'

There were about fifteen black-and-white photos of fishermen proudly holding their catch in front of them. All the men wore caps; not one of them was smiling.

'See that one at the top? That's my son Joe. I can't tell you how excited he was to join the ranks on this wall. That's a fifteen-pound striped bass he caught when he was eighteen. He said he almost broke his wrist reeling it in.'

Looking up, Ellie saw a tall, scrawny young man with eyes like Louisa's. His hand was hooked through the fish's mouth, presenting it to the photographer. His mouth was set in a straight, ultra-serious line.

'He looks so determined,' she said, quickly adding, 'and handsome,' partly because it was true and partly because she knew any mother would like to hear that. 'You said he lives in DC. What does he do?'

'He's the right-hand man of Senator Brad Harvey.'

'Wow. That's impressive.'

It was hard for her to envision this thin young man walking the corridors of power. When Louisa had mentioned him before, Ellie had immediately assumed he'd be an artist of some kind, working in a creative field. Was he a smooth operator instead, having dinners with lobbyists?

Not all politicians were sleazy, she reminded herself. And Brad Harvey had a good reputation. Besides, it was impossible to believe that any offspring of Louisa's would be sitting down to dinner or even coffee with gun lobbyists.

'Joe cares about politics. And he decided it was better to work from within the system. You'll meet him soon, I hope. He comes to visit pretty often in the summer. I like to think he comes to see me, but I know the heat in DC then is unbearable.'

The young waitress brought her coffee. Ellie said 'Thank you', wondering if all mothers were the same: intensely proud, hoping their children loved them as much as they loved their children, struggling with the inevitable truth – children grow up.

Except some children didn't get the chance.

'Ellie?'

'Sorry.'

She pushed it back down, buried it. It was so much easier to bury it when she wasn't alone.

'You disappeared on me there.'

'I know. I was just thinking about the summer I spent in Mashnee, how often I used to look over at your house and fantasise about it.'

'Well, I'll give you a tour soon. Anytime you want.'

'That would be lovely.'

'And bring Tim. I'm already really fond of him. In fact, he reminds me a little of Joe when he was that age. You know, I wish for Tim's sake that this place hadn't changed so much. When I was a teenager, we used to come here in the afternoons. The fishermen came in the mornings and the teenagers in the afternoons. There were booths then, and all of them had jukeboxes. We'd order black and white frappés and play songs. All those great ones, like "My Boyfriend's Back" and "He's A Rebel". But you're too young to know those, aren't you? God, one day I'll get used to being my age. Maybe.'

'You're not old, Louisa.'

'Yes, I am. But don't start me on the subject of age. Self-pity alert! Listen, I'm going to treat myself and buy lobster. There's a great little place to buy fish on the way to Pocasset. You could come with me and I'll drop you back here after-wards – unless you know it already? It's called the Lobster Trap.'

'I don't. I'd love to go with you.'

'Excellent.'

Louisa drove an old black Saab, one that had a gearbox. She drove slowly, occasionally pointing to a house and telling Ellie the name of the people who lived in it. When they were about to reach the graveyard, she stopped and said: 'That house on the right? It used to be an old Mom and Pop candy store. My brother John and I would walk here and stuff our pockets with chocolate bars. And there really were an old Mom and Pop running it.'

'Where's your brother now?'

'You're not going to believe this, but it's true. He's in Alaska. He's a dog musher, he races in the Iditarod and the Yukon Quest. He can do that even at his age. You know, I can never figure out how our parents, who were pretty straitlaced, produced the two of us. I run off to Haight-Ashbury and John runs off to Alaska with his huskies.'

Instead of turning right at the graveyard, they made a left, on the road to Pocasset, a town ten minutes away. They passed a boatyard, then pulled over to the right, parking in front of the Lobster Trap.

'One time when Joe was about ten,' Louisa said as they got out of the car, 'we came here and there was this giant lobster. It was huge. Mammoth. Joe got so excited and was desperate for me to buy it. I kept telling him big lobsters like that don't have the same taste, they're old and chewy, but he finally said: "Please. It can be my Christmas *and* birthday present. Please?" So I gave in.'

'What was it like?'

'First of all, it was a son-of-a-bitch to cook. Finding a pot to fit it in was murder. And it tasted disgusting. I knew Joe thought it was disgusting too. But he pretended to love it, poor boy. Worse, there was so much of the damn thing left over, he had to eat gross lobster salads and lobster soup for days.

'My husband Jamie and I tried not to laugh, watching him manfully struggle through it, but sometimes we couldn't help ourselves and Joe would get angry and say: "Stop laughing. There's nothing funny. This is delicious. This is the best lobster I've ever had."'

Smiling, Ellie thought of Tim. He would have done exactly the same.

They entered the store: one room with a big tank full of lobsters and a counter with clams, mussels, all kinds of fish.

'Hey, Mrs A. What would you like today?' a white-haired man in a white apron who was standing behind the counter asked Louisa.

'A nice lobster, Kyle. Not too big,' she answered, and then introduced Ellie to him. 'No, actually, make that three lobsters, please. You and Tim can come to dinner, can't you, Ellie? And we can have that tour tonight.'

'I don't want to ruin your plans. You probably want some time alone.'

'Are you kidding? I have too much alone time. Please come.'

'Great. We'd love to. Thanks so much.'

When Louisa dropped her back at her car and said 'See you later', Ellie felt as if she'd crossed a line and really had gone over to the side of the locals. Louisa, she could tell, by the way Kyle had chatted to her, was an institution in Bourne. She'd taken Ellie under her wing and Ellie was happy to let her. She'd been planning to explore more on her own, but having a guide was much more fun, like having the key that unlocked all the right doors.

And Louisa's happy-go-lucky attitude was contagious. Ellie found herself driving back over those roads, brightening each time she saw a house Louisa had mentioned, even picturing the old candy store and Louisa as a young girl with her brother, filling their pockets and walking back along these same roads to the point.

Ellie's own childhood had been more restricted, spent in a dark, cheerless apartment on the West Side of Manhattan, living with a mother who did her best, but who had never really shaken off the trauma of being abandoned by her husband after six years of marriage. Ellie could barely remember her father; she couldn't begin to picture herself in a family scene like the one Louisa had described with Joe and the lobster.

Self-pity alert. She smiled again as the phrase echoed in her mind and thought of how often she smiled when she was with Louisa.

She wanted Tim to smile more. He was alone with her as she had been alone with her mother, but his life was going to be so different: colourful and fun and interesting. He'd have memories of swimming and sailing and fishing. Maybe he'd even get a photograph of himself with a monster fish on the Atwoods wall. What he wouldn't be was stuck in a city apartment, glued to his computer.

Tim loved lobster.

Debby had always made her laugh.

But Louisa made her – and, more importantly, Tim – laugh *and* smile.

If I told that to Debby, Ellie thought, she'd say: 'See? I told you you'd find a new best friend, you unfaithful bitch.'

The tour started at the back of the house, in the kitchen. Louisa had greeted them at the door at 6.30 and asked Tim how much of a bummer his first day at summer school had been, to which he'd replied, 'On a scale of bummers one to ten, ten being the biggest bummer, I'd go for a seven.'

'OK.' She'd nodded. 'Seven's good. I was expecting a twelve.' Ushering them inside, she'd said: 'Tour first, then lobster. I'm going to try to make this interesting, Tim, but if you get bored, tell me. I won't stop the tour, but I'll invent a few ghost stories, maybe even a little vampire action, to spice it up. Come on, we're going to the kitchen first.'

She led them through the living room and dining room into a huge kitchen at the back: one that housed not only a fridge, an oven, a nice big wooden table and some crazy hand-painted chairs, two of which had the words 'Vino' and 'Splurge' writtten on the back, but also two enormous stone sinks.

'They used to wash all the laundry by hand in these sinks,' Lousa explained when she saw Ellie staring at them. 'And when I was a child, we had no fresh water pipes. The care-taker of the place, Allan Bourne, used to have to bring fresh water over. Gallons of it. Can you imagine?

'What I remember most is coming here in the summer, trying to run a bath and watching all this rusty red water pour out of the taps. We couldn't use the sink water either – that was just as bad. But what's really strange is every single summer I'd turn on the taps and be shocked. As if I didn't know.'

By the time they'd finished on the ground floor, they'd seen the formal dining room, which Louisa said they rarely used, plus a small sitting room, a massive living room, two bedrooms, a bathroom, a television room, a study – all of them interlocked by a maze of passageways, so you could go through from one of the bedrooms straight to the kitchen, or you could get to the kitchen through the formal dining room: there were so many doors, so many entryways, so much space. And, more than anything, so much light.

'It's amazing,' Ellie said. 'You can see the water from every single room, even the bathrooms.'

'You'll see it's the same upstairs, too. You have a view of the water from every room in the house.'

'I love all this light.' Again, Ellie couldn't help but compare it to her mother's sunless apartment.

'But the walls are dark,' Tim commented. He was studying the old wood panelling in the living room. 'So it feels deep in here. What I mean is, there's light, but there are shadows everywhere too. Outside in the sun it's so clear . . . maybe because there are no big buildings or mountains or whatever. But there are no shadows outside. In here there's more – I don't know – texture or something.'

'Tim Walters.' Louisa walked up to him, put her hand on his shoulder. 'You should have told me you're an artist, you little sneak.'

Tim shrugged. And blushed. Ellie's heart lit up.

'You should have a big steering wheel and compass set in the middle of this room,' he continued; emboldened, Ellie could sense, by Louisa's praise. 'Because basically this house is a big ship.'

'Come here.' Louisa took him by the arm, walked towards the staircase. Ellie followed. 'Look at that photograph.'

On the wall facing the staircase there were a bunch of photographs, mostly of what Ellie guessed were old relatives. Louisa took one off its peg, handed it to Tim.

'Shit!'

'Tim—'

'Sorry, Mom, but look at this. It's unbelievable.'

Ellie went to his side. The photo was of the house, but it was completely surrounded by water. The causeway had flooded, leaving the house marooned, cut off from any land.

'We took that the year of Hurricane Bob,' Louisa stated. 'This place really does look like a ship in that picture, doesn't it?'

'You're not kidding.' Tim kept staring at it.

'There have been worse hurricanes, but that's the only photo we have showing exactly what the house looks like in a big one.'

'Awesome. I want to see it like this. How cool would that be?'

'I'll get it copied and give one to you,' Louisa said. 'Just in case you have to wait a few years to see it in person. Now . . . time for the next floor.' She took the photo from Tim, laid it on the bookshelf underneath the other pictures, and walked up the large staircase. Tim was shaking his head in wonder and Ellie was too.

The Witch's House had lived up to her childhood fantasy, and that pleased Ellie immensely. She'd been right to imagine all the things she'd imagined. It was special, with special people living in it. Even better, Tim was sharing this discovery with her, as caught up in its magic as she was.

When they reached the landing, Louisa stopped.

'All right – here is the next floor: a subject of some strife. Because the bedrooms on one side all have a balcony and the bedrooms on the other don't. Hard not to play favourites when you have a full house.'

A full house? Christ, Ellie thought, peering down the

hallway. How many bedrooms were there? As it turned out, there were seven on this floor, which meant nine altogether. What happened in the old days, when there was no fresh water? How many trips had Allan Bourne had to make?

All the rooms were big enough for a large double bed, although three of them, the ones which weren't on the balcony side, had two singles. The furnishings in them felt nostalgic, although Ellie couldn't place exactly which decade they sprang from. Possibly the forties or fifties, but the bathrooms were definitely older. Somehow Louisa had managed to do with the house what she'd done with her own appearance: nothing was modern or trendy but it didn't come across as old and fusty either. There were lovely bright crocheted blankets on the beds, watercolour paintings on the walls, big cushions, big pillows, and one sweet rocking chair in Louisa's bedroom.

The house felt content with itself, Ellie decided. Nothing jarred, everything was peaceful, and it felt as if it had always been that way and would stay that way forever.

'So now we're in what we used to call the sewing room.'

They'd reached the last room which was tucked away at the back of the house, above the kitchen. It was the only room that didn't have a bed – only one small chair, a standard lamp and an upright piano.

'Does either of you play?'

'No,' Tim said.

'That's good. Because it's so out of tune, you wouldn't want to. My family was a lot of things, but not musical. God knows why we have this.'

'Can we go to the attic now?' asked Tim.

'You can, Tim. I'm not going near it.'

Ellie climbed the winding staircase opposite the sewing room with him. When they reached the top floor, he said: 'It's not so scary.'

But Ellie could see Louisa's point. Not only was the attic empty, dusty and dank, it had all these crawl spaces in the eaves, and the eaves themselves sloped so much they looked as if they were about to fall in and bring the whole house down with them.

They were at the peak of the witch's hat, the only part of the house that was dark. Ellie wouldn't have wanted to spend much time here either.

When they went back down, Louisa finished the tour by taking them back to the ground floor and then outside, to a small room at the right of the porch which housed rakes and tools. Louisa pointed to the wall at one side and Ellie saw a mass of lines with names and dates pencilled on top: a chart that reflected the growth of children through the decades. The earliest entry, she saw, was from 1918.

'There's Joe – look.' Louisa crouched down and pointed to a line. 'And there he is the next summer.' She pointed higher. 'Whoever first thought of doing this was brilliant. I still remember every single time we measured him.'

Studying the various names and dates, Ellie couldn't help but wish she had this kind of history in her life: one house that would have represented so many memories and lives. She could barely remember her father, much less his parents. And her grandparents on her mother's side had died before she was born.

I envy Joe Amory, she said to herself, as she looked at the line with his name pencilled on top. *I hope he appreciates how fortunate he is to have had all this.*

The train of thought halted abruptly as she remembered that Joe's wife had died. How could she have forgotten that? Because she'd been so caught up in what it would have been like to be Louisa's child, living in this house? That was no excuse. He must have been through hell, and here she was envying him. Chiding herself, Ellie followed Louisa and Tim as they made their way back to the kitchen.

'Right,' Louisa stated when they trooped in. 'Tim, you can set the table. I'll show you where everything is. And, Ellie, could you husk the corn? It's over there on the counter. I'm going to boil the lobsters now. If you're squeamish, look away and sing a song or something. And think butter. Butter with the lobster, butter with the corn. Think feast.'

She has such a generous heart, Ellie thought. That's all you need in life: people with generous hearts.

4

Pulling over to the side of the road to pick up the mail from the mailboxes, Louisa saw Ellie reaching into hers.

'There you are,' she said as she got out. 'Great minds think alike.' She walked up to Ellie's car. 'I just knocked on your door but you weren't there. I had a good idea this morning. There's a store in Buzzards Bay that sells aerial photographs of the area. I thought Tim might like one for his room. And that you could come with me to look for a good one.'

'That's brilliant,' Ellie smiled. 'He hasn't done anything with his room except put up the photo you gave him of your house in the hurricane. I'm beginning to think he's as obsessed with it as I was at his age.'

'Well, that makes me very happy. Look, let me check if I have any mail and then we'll go. If you're not busy now?'

'Fantastic.'

Ellie was dressed in white shorts and a green T-shirt; Louisa was pleased to see that she was beginning to get a tan and was looking much healthier than the first night they'd met. When she'd sold the cottage, Louisa had hoped someone nice would buy it, but she'd never imagined she'd like anyone as much as she liked Ellie and Tim. She and Ellie had had a few more coffees together at Atwoods and Louisa had gone over to the cottage for dinner with them once: they were developing a close friendship, all three of them, and Louisa couldn't believe her luck.

I couldn't have asked for anyone better, she thought, as she opened what turned out to be her empty mailbox. *I only hope Joe will feel the same when he meets them.*

Ellie hopped into the Saab and Louisa started it up, glancing at the few envelopes in Ellie's hand. 'Anything interesting?'

'No, just a few bills.'

'Jamie used to say: "Is this good news?" whenever he answered the phone. He never opened any mail; he left that to me. He said, "There's almost never any good news in the mail, is there? Only bills."'

'That's even more true now, because we don't get letters any more – everyone emails.'

'True.'

Stuffing the envelopes in her bag, Ellie sighed.

'I have this plan, you know. I need to get a job. I hate being financially dependent on Charlie. Taking half of the money from the apartment sale seemed fair to me, and child support for Tim seems fair, too. But I don't like taking alimony because it feels as if he still has a hold over me. I want to be independent, but I don't have any skills. So I signed up for a secretarial and IT course at Cape Cod Community College. It starts in September.'

66

'Secretarial? Ellie, no offence to you – or to secretaries – but I don't see you touch-typing all day.'

'No offence taken,' Ellie laughed. 'That's why I didn't tell you about it before. I knew it probably wasn't your idea of a good career move. But I couldn't think of any other options. I got married and had Tim when I was so young, and Charlie thought I should stay at home, not try to start a career when I was already a mother. He said paying someone to take care of Tim would cancel out anything I earned if I worked. Then he helped get me that part-time job at the museum when Tim was older, but all I did was work in the shop there. I'm not qualified. And I'm thirty-six years old.'

'Right.' Louisa nodded. 'I see your point.'

Sometimes she forgot how young Ellie had been when she got married. Why had she leaped into marriage before she'd finished college? She was an intelligent woman and a seriously attractive one: petite, with shoulder-length dark brown hair, dark eyes, and facial features that were reminiscent of Loretta Young's. Of course, when she'd said that to Ellie, Ellie had asked 'Who?' and Louisa had told her she'd find a DVD of an old Loretta Young film to show her.

Hadn't she wanted to explore a little before she settled down and had children? But who cared about exploring when you fell passionately in love? And when there was no fortune teller around to inform you your husband would run off with another woman fifteen years later?

'I understand the not-qualified business, but let me think about it. There must be some other way.'

'Please. Tell me if you come up with one.'

During the rest of the drive they talked about Tim and how he was doing at summer school. He was progressing, Ellie thought, but he still wasn't pleased about the move. 'He misses his friends in Boston,' she stated.

'Just wait until he finds a girl here,' Louisa said. 'He's fifteeen. He'll fall in love soon.'

'Tim? In love? God, that makes me feel ancient.'

'Welcome to my world,' Louisa laughed.

At the aerial photograph store they thumbed through dozens of large pictures of the area, until Ellie pulled out one she thought Tim would love.

'Look – your house is right there, almost in the centre. And it has the Railroad Bridge in it too. It's perfect.'

'Good. I'll buy it. This is my late moving-in present to you and don't even try to stop me from gettting it.'

As they were standing at the counter, paying, a thought occurred to Louisa.

'Listen, Ellie. It must be hard for Tim. He doesn't have a licence so he can't drive himself. He has to rely on people to give him rides. Why don't you get him a bike? There's a bike shop down the road here. We could look for one now.'

Ellie put her hand on the counter as if to steady herself.

'Ellie?'

She'd closed her eyes and her face was blank, expressionless.

'Ellie? Are you OK?'

Louisa reached out, put her hand on Ellie's forearm. As soon as she made contact, Ellie opened her eyes.

'Yes. Sorry. I'm fine. It's the heat, that's all.'

The heat? The weather was warm, but not hot. And the store was actually cool.

'Are you too hot to go to the bike shop?' Louisa asked as she paid the bill and took the photo from the man behind the counter. 'Because I really think Tim needs one.'

'No . . . I mean, he's never had a bike. We lived in the city. He didn't need one. And he doesn't know how to ride one. Let's skip the bike shop, all right? Besides, I like driving him places.'

'OK. Fine. It's a shame, though.'

'It's just the way it is.'

On the drive back, Ellie peppered her with questions about Jamie: what was he like, how had they met, where did they get married? Louisa was happy to answer them all, yet as she did so, she also found herself thinking that the way Ellie's face had gone blank in the store was very close to the way she'd zoned out that first morning they'd had coffee at Atwoods. And her 'It's just the way it is' comment had been an uncharacteristic remark. Also, this constant questioning felt more like an interview than a conversation. Any time she'd try to switch the topic back to Ellie, ask her something about her past – how she'd met Charlie, for example – Ellie would answer incredibly quickly and shift the focus back to Jamie.

'You must miss him like crazy,' she said as Louisa turned into the cottage driveway.

'I do. But we had twenty-five years together. Joe and Pam only had four. That breaks my heart. Pam's death would

69

have broken Jamie's heart, too, if he'd been alive. In a way, I guess I'm glad he was spared that.'

They sat in silence for a few seconds before Ellie turned to her.

'Why don't you come over for dinner tonight? I went to the Lobster Trap earlier and got some mussels. I got excited and overbought – there are tons of them. Please come. I know Tim would love it if you did.'

'I'd love to.'

'Great, see you later. And thank you so much for the photograph. It's brilliant.' Ellie got out of the Saab, retrieved the photograph from the back seat, shut the car door and gave her a wave.

Everyone had little idiosyncrasies, Louisa thought as she put the car into reverse. Jamie used to rub his knees when he was nervous. Joe used to be so superstitious he wore a T-shirt he thought was lucky all day and night every day and night for a month. If Ellie zoned out briefly occasionally, so what? Louisa's entire generation had zoned-out on pot in the 1960s. And they weren't zoning out briefly, either.

When she reached her driveway, she parked, got out, walked up to the porch, kicked off her sandals and sat down in her favourite chair, resting her feet on a stool.

Ellie had said she'd used to look over at this house from Mashnee; well, Louisa had a house she stared at sometimes too. It was across the bay, another old Cape Cod house, but this one had a widow's walk at the top of it. Wives of whalers used to go up there and stare out to sea, hoping to see their husbands' boats returning from their whaling trips. Because so many of those boats didn't make it back, these look-outs were christened widow's walks.

I'm the widow now, she thought. *All my friends still have their husbands. They invite me over, but I'm always the woman on her own. I wouldn't mind if I didn't see how sorry they feel for me.*

Now Ellie and Tim are here. They've brought life back to this point.

I'm inordinately fond of them.

And Joe will like them, too.

I hope.

5

27 June

'I don't want to talk about it.'

'Joe , this is ridiculous. I've apologised, but there's nothing I can do about it now. It's sold. Time to move on.'

'Do you have any idea how much I hate that phrase?' He threw the towel he'd brought from the beach on to the bench in front of the window. '"It's time to move on." Move on where exactly? To a place where the past doesn't exist?'

'Joe—'

'No, Mum, really. You sell the cottage without telling me. You don't even give me the chance to buy it. Now complete strangers are living in it, and I'm supposed to "move on"? Enough.' His heavy sigh sank with him into the armchair. Louisa wasn't going to tell him not to sit down in a wet bathing suit. It was too late and he was too old for that.

'It wasn't a happy place in the end, Joe. You know that. I thought you didn't need to be reminded of those times.'

'So you do an end run and sell it? And don't even consult me about whether I *want* to be reminded or not?' He shook his head. 'There were good times there too, Mum. Amazing times. We were happy there. You can't justify selling it,

72

however hard you try to. It was Pam's place. She loved it. I can't believe you don't understand.'

Louisa hated hearing the bitterness in his voice, but he'd been bitter since Pam had died and she understood. You don't lose someone you love so much and bounce right back; or at least, no one she knew and loved did. But she'd honestly believed she was doing the right thing by putting the cottage on the market.

Joe wouldn't want to live there with anyone else, if he ever found anyone else. And it was standing there, empty, an ever-present reminder of a lost love. Louisa hadn't been prepared for his rage when she'd told him. But then again, she'd prob-ably had a subconscious suspicion he'd react like this because she didn't tell him until the deal was done. He'd been angry when she'd finally informed him, but seeing a car in the cottage driveway when he'd arrived this morning had clearly made the sale real to him, ratcheting up his anger.

'I'm sorry, Joe.'

He didn't reply. He was staring out the window at the water, lost, she suspected, in memories. He did that so often it worried her: disappeared into his own world, leaving her wondering how far away exactly he'd gone.

'Maybe this won't help, but I want you to know that the woman who bought it is lovely. Her name is Ellie, and she has a son named Tim. I've seen them a lot since they moved in. I'm incredibly fond of them both.'

'I'm getting old, Joe,' she wanted to say. *'Having them here is like having a family again. I feel useful. And younger. I can't tell you they've brought life back to this place because that will*

make you think of Pam and all you've lost. But they have. They're *good company. And they've made me feel less lonely without you* *and Jamie.'*

That was verging on self-pity, though, and she would never want Joe to feel sorry for her. If he knew she got lonely, he'd feel guilty and she'd be a burden on him – the last thing she wanted.

'It's strange,' she said instead, although he didn't appear to be listening. 'Ellie reminds me of someone, and I can't figure out who it is. Anyway, she reminds me of someone, and her son reminds me of you when you were his age.'

'What – a sulking hulk?'

Louisa was relieved he had turned away from the window and was speaking again.

'A typical teenager. But with a really thoughtful streak.'

'And with an attitude, I bet, if he reminds you of me. Where's the father?'

'They're divorced – he's out of the picture. He's a lawyer in Boston.'

'I don't know why I even asked because I don't want to talk about them. Maybe at some point I'll get used to them being there, but not now.' He paused. 'You really screwed up, Mum.'

'I guess so.'

'So let's talk about something else.'

'OK.

She wished she could reach out and touch him and heal all his pain and sorrow. That's what mothers were supposed to do, and to some extent could do – when their children were small. But Joe was thirty-five years old; a tall, thin, dark, to her mind impossibly handsome man. What he really needed was for his wife to be alive; and Louisa couldn't fix that.

Perhaps I shouldn't have sold the cottage. But I couldn't bear looking at it and thinking of Pam. And seeing you look at it, watching you go over there and sit in it for hours on end. It had to stop.

'How's Washington?' she asked.

'Same old. It's crazy. But I like it. Harvey is one of the good guys, you know? A senator who will actually do something. So working for him does seem worthwhile. Sometimes.' He turned and stared out the window again.

When you're a parent, you can only be as happy as your unhappiest child,' someone had said to her once.

Joe was her only child, and for the past two and a half years he'd been deeply unhappy. Longer than that, in fact; he'd been unhappy since the moment Pam's illness was diagnosed.

Louisa missed her too, enormously. But she also missed the carefree Joe, the one who laughed and made jokes and messed around.

The boy – no, the man – with an attitude.

All these small breakthroughs added up, Ellie decided as she watched Tim making his way from the car park to the Bourne High baseball field. She could tell from the way he walked that he was feeling self-conscious, but he was going there, that was the point. He'd been asked to try out for the team, which made him both happy and nervous. It was another step on his way to fitting in here, and that made her probably even happier and more nervous than he was.

Starting her car, she drove out of the lot. The last thing she wanted to do was watch him. How parents could go to Wimbledon, or any major sporting event, and watch their sons or daughters compete, she'd never understood. Every lost point or dropped catch would tear you to pieces. Not because you wanted him or her to win, but because you knew how hurt your child would be if they failed.

He'll be OK, she said to herself. *He's not great at bat, but he's a really good fielder. They'll have to see that.*

The roads were completely familiar to her now; she was beginning to have a history here. People like Kyle recognised her when she went to shop; the waitress at Atwoods said 'The usual?' when she and Louisa called in; and she'd met some of the parents of other kids at the summer school. All these little breakthroughs.

Before she and Tim had left for the baseball field, Ellie had sat down in her living room and surveyed it. Because it was finally completely finished. Books were on their shelves, the sofa looked and was comfortable, the coffee table was a simple one made of driftwood, and the two chairs she'd bought the week before, covered in pretty orange-and-white striped material with white cushions to match, worked. OK, the seagulls were kitschy – but as far as she was concerned they were cute.

It was a far cry from Louisa's. But it was special too.

She'd done it all herself. As far as she knew, she hadn't been ripped off by anyone and she hadn't spent too much either.

Sitting on her sofa, looking around at the orange walls, she'd laughed out loud. Louisa hadn't thought of any alternative to secretarial school yet, but at one point when she

76

was over for dinner she'd said: 'How about interior decorating, Ellie?' and Tim had practically choked.

Louisa had told her Joe was coming this weekend. She'd also told her Joe wasn't happy about her selling the cottage.

'He'll get used to the idea,' she'd said. 'But it meant so much to him and Pam, it might take him a while.'

Joe Amory was a mystery man. In an odd way he was like Daniel Litman had been that night at Acquitaine: Ellie knew a fair amount about him but then again nothing at all. The prospect of meeting him in person was intriguing. Would he live up to Louisa's descriptions of him? If so, he'd be a super-hero, just as Tim would be to anyone listening to Ellie describe him.

Was any mother unbiased when it came to her children? No mother she knew. There'd been times, when Tim was younger and Ellie hung out with other mothers with kids the same age, when she'd wanted to say: 'Wow. Isn't it incredible? We all have genius, over-achieving kids. Not one of us has a child who's not a total star.' But it wasn't as if she didn't believe Tim was a total star. No – she *knew* he was.

When she reached the part of Agawam Point Road that straightened and led to Louisa's causeway, she noticed an unfamiliar car parked in front of the Witch's House. So Joe had arrived.

Louisa will be thrilled.

Turning into the cottage drive, she saw that her own front door stood wide open. Had Louisa come in for some reason and forgotten to close it? Or maybe she was in the cottage now, waiting for Ellie? But why leave the door open?

Puzzled, Ellie shut off the engine, grabbed her bag, got out, went over to the cottage.

What the fuck?

She stood on the threshold staring into her living room.

All the furniture had been upended. Books were lying all over the floor. Lamps had been knocked over. Clothes were scattered everywhere.

She took a step forward, stopped.

Wait. Someone could be in here.

In the kitchen? In her bedroom? In Tim's? Holding her breath, she listened for any sound.

Nothing.

She took another step forward. Both her bedroom door and Tim's were open.

'Whoever's here, I'm calling the police now,' she called out.

No answer.

Taking her cell phone out of her bag, she flipped it open.

'I mean it. Get out now. I'm calling the police.'

As if the police could get here quickly enough.

A police car . . .

Don't go there. You can't go there. Not now.

What do I do?

Pretend.

'Yes, Officer. There's been a break-in. Someone's in my house now. It's 101 Agawam Point Road. My husband will be here any second but come right away.'

There was no movement, no sound.

No one's here. Calm down. The front door was wide open. It's broad daylight.

Whoever did this has left.

Keeping hold of the phone, she skirted around the debris on the living-room floor and went to the kitchen. It was empty. So were her bedroom and Tim's when she checked them.

No one was there. The cottage was empty.

What had they stolen? She turned back to the living room. The TV in the corner was there.

Laptops . . . Shit! Tim will go crazy if they stole his laptop.

Back in Tim's room, she saw his laptop was sitting on his desk. Both the pictures on his wall were still there. In fact, nothing seemed to have been disturbed. Whoever did this hadn't come into this room.

My laptop?

But her laptop was on the floor beside the chair in her room where she'd left it. They'd been in here – the closet door was open, most of her clothes had been taken out and were now lying strewn around the living-room floor.

Jewellery?

Ellie didn't have anything worth much: the only expensive piece of jewellery she'd ever worn was her engagement ring, and she'd given that back to Charlie when they'd divorced. She kept her various earrings and bracelets in a small case on the top of her closet shelf. Reaching up, she grabbed it and looked inside. It was all there.

Nothing had been stolen.

Back in the living room, she stood and looked at the mess.

So someone wanted to trash the cottage. But why? For fun?

Stupidly she hadn't locked her front door when she'd left.

Was this technically a break-in if she'd left the door unlocked? But Louisa always left her door unlocked. This was Bourne, not Boston.

Maybe kids got bored in Bourne and one of them had dared another to do this. They'd tried the handle of the front door, found it open, walked in and made mayhem.

Maybe this had happened before, to other people. Ones living in the condos at the beginning of the road or cottages in Mashnee.

Louisa would know. This might have happened before and Louisa hadn't mentioned it because it was a pain in the ass, but no big deal.

Ellic could go ask her.

But Joe was there. She didn't want to bother her.

She could do it quickly. Go ask her and come right back. If this had happened before, maybe she should report it. If it hadn't, it must have been the one-off result of a dare or something.

Louisa wouldn't mind if she went over and asked. She would want to know if it was part of a spate of these things, and now it had reached this road.

Ellie took another look around the room, walked out and locked the door behind her.

Louisa heard a knock on her door and stood up.

'Maybe that's Ellie,' she said. 'Or Tim. He comes to visit sometimes by himself.'

'Shit.' Joe stood too. 'I'm out of here.'

'Joe—'

But he was off, heading for the kitchen at the back of the house.

'Ellie, hi. I was hoping it was you or Tim. Come in.'

She was in a pair of cut-off jeans and a Red Sox T-shirt, with her bag slung over her shoulder.

'I don't want to bother you, Louisa. I know Joe's here. I just need to ask you something.'

'Shoot. But you should come in.'

'No, really. I just needed to know if there have been any break-ins around here lately.'

'Break-ins? No. Not that I've heard of. Why?'

'Someone got into the cottage. I left the door unlocked when I took Tim to the baseball field. Anyway, whoever it was trashed the living room, but nothing's been stolen. I wondered if anything like this has happened before?'

'No.' Louisa shook her head. 'Not that I know of. Christ. That's awful. They trashed the living room?'

'It's a mess. But, like I said, they didn't take anything.'

'God, that's bizarre. And scary for you. Come in and have a cup of coffee. Or, hell, a drink. Have you called the police?'

'No. The door wasn't locked and nothing was stolen. What could the police do? And I won't come in, thanks. I should get back. I need to clean everything up before Tim gets back.'

'Joe and I will come help you.'

'No.' Ellie shook her head. 'Really. It's a beautiful day and he's just arrived. It's only one room. I can do it, honestly. But thanks for offering.' She leaned in, gave Louisa a kiss on the cheek. 'I'll see you soon, OK?'

'Ellie, please. Let us help.'

'No way. It's my mess. See you later.' She started back to the cottage.

Louisa rushed into the kitchen where Joe was sitting at the table with a mug of coffee and a bagel.

'That was Ellie. Someone broke into the cottage and trashed it. Nothing was stolen but we should go help her clean up.'

'Don't think so.' He picked up the bagel. 'Her problem.'

'Joe.'

'Mum.' He looked up, his eyes defiant.

'Well, I'm going to go help her now. You and I will talk about this later.'

It had been decades since she'd used that tone of voice with him.

Halfway down the road to the cottage, she caught up with Ellie.

'Louisa – I told you, I can do this. Go back. Really.'

'No. I'm here. I'm not going back.'

'OK.' Ellie nodded. 'But I'm not letting you stay long.'

When they reached the door, Ellie took out her keys and opened it.

'Christ!' Louisa exclaimed, surveying the wreckage. 'It's a mess all right.'

'I know. But Tim's room is fine. So is the kitchen. And my room's not trashed either, but they took all my clothes out of the closet and dumped them on the floor in here.'

'I don't understand. What do people get out of doing things like this? You're sure nothing's been stolen?'

'Nothing valuable anyway. No, I don't think they took anything.'

'I guess that's some consolation.' Louisa frowned. 'What can I do to help? Where should I start?'

'You shouldn't be doing this.'

'I'm *going* to help, Ellie. Don't even try to stop me. But tell me what I can do.'

'OK. Maybe you could put the books back in the bookcase?'

'Absolutely.' Louisa went to the wall at the back where the bookcases were. 'At least they couldn't pull these off the wall. And they dumped the books right in front of them.'

'It's funny how we keep saying "they".' Ellie had begun to gather some of the strewn clothes. 'It could have been just one person.'

Louisa leaned down, picked up a handful of books, then stood up and faced Ellie.

'You know, you're right. The fact that nothing's been stolen is strange. Almost as if it's personal. It couldn't be Charlie, could it?'

'Charlie? Why would he do this?'

'I don't know. He cheated on you, so he's a creep by definition.'

'He's not a creep. If I've made him sound like one, I shouldn't have. No, he'd never do something like this. Besides, he'd have no reason to.'

She carried the clothes she'd picked up into her bedroom while Louisa replaced books. When Ellie returned, Louisa asked: 'So Charlie has good points? I guess he must have. You fell in love with him.'

'He's really smart.' Ellie shrugged. 'OK, I'll try to be as fair as I can. He's not only really smart – he's charming.

He's the kind of person . . . if you were at a party with tons of people and Charlie were standing in a corner, you'd end up wanting to go talk to him even if you weren't sure why.

'And he's driven. Even he'd say he was driven. He expects a lot from people and I worry about that where Tim's concerned. But Charlie expects even more from himself. He's a perfectionist. I don't know if anything is ever enough for him.' She took another bundle of clothes into her room.

As Louisa bent to pick up more books, she saw one of Ellie's seagulls lying on the floor – crushed.

'Look at this.' She picked it up as Ellie came back in. 'It's been stamped on.'

'Shit!' Ellie surveyed the floor. 'There's another one over there beside the lamp. That's ruined too. Shit.' Her eyes went to the bookshelves and table tops. 'All of them.' She picked up more clothes. 'They're under here too. All wrecked.'

'I'm so sorry, Ellie. I know you loved them.'

'I can buy more.' She stood up straighter. 'I will buy more. What idiots! I could kill them. I'm going to get a garbage bag from the kitchen.'

When she came back she resolutely hunted through the wreckage, picking up the model seagulls and putting them in the bag.

'This one was my favourite,' she said, studying one of the smallest ones which lay in the palm of her hand. 'This really pisses me off.'

'I bet.' Wanting to distract her, Louisa asked: 'So do you think Sandra Cabot will be enough for Charlie or will he cheat on her too?'

'I don't know. I think he decided for whatever reason that he wanted her, so he set out to get her and he did. Nothing was going to interfere with that. Not me, not Tim. But he's not an overt womaniser, if you see what I mean. I don't believe he had other affairs.' Ellie grimaced, put the broken seagull in the garbage bag. 'Anyway, as far as I'm concerned now, Sandra's welcome to him. She can deal with all his rules.'

'Rules? What rules?'

'He didn't think anyone ever had to sneeze. That was one of them. He said any person can stop sneezing if they want to, and that if you sneezed you were rude – and you were spreading germs.'

'You're kidding?' Louisa laughed. 'So you had to stifle every sneeze?'

'Yes, and we could never drink out of containers. He hated containers.'

'You mean, like coffee cups with lids?'

'Exactly. None of those. And no bottles of water. He couldn't stand it if people sipped from bottles of water on the subway or on buses or planes. Basically he didn't believe in drinking or eating in public.'

'What about restaurants?'

'Restaurants are fine.'

'As long as you don't sneeze?'

'Right.' Ellie laughed. 'Seriously weird, I know. But most of them – well, they sort of made sense. Because they were about being polite. Another rule was that you should never tell your dreams to anyone else. His point was that you always think your own dreams are fascinating, but they bore the hell out of everyone else. He's right about that.'

What had it been like for Ellie, living with a man who had such rules? Louisa wouldn't have been able to stand it, she knew. Jamie would never have had rules; if anything, he was an anarchist.

She smiled to herself, remembering him trying out Joe's skateboard one afternoon, swerving crazily along the sidewalk, singing 'Born To Run'.

'OK, I sort of agree about the dream-telling. But making a rule about it? It sounds serious control freak.'

'Like I said, he's driven. But a lot of people are these days. And if you met him, you'd like him. The thing is, when he left me I blamed him completely. But as much as I'd like to keep blaming him completely, it's too easy to do that. I must have played some part in the failure of our marriage too. Looking back, I realise I relied on him too much. Because he took care of everything. And he made me feel safe.'

Louisa doubted very much that she'd like Charlie Walters. And it struck her as odd, again, that Ellie had married so young and that she'd want someone who took care of everything for her. Charlie had made her feel safe? Safe from what?

Stop trying to analyse the mysteries of love. You already know it will remain forever mysterious.

When all the clothes were back in the cupboard and Louisa had put all the books on the bookshelves, Ellie rapped her head with her knuckles and said: 'God, I'm a lamebrain.

I should have offered you some coffee before we started. I'll get you some now.'

'I'll come with you.'

They went into the kitchen and Louisa leaned against the counter as Ellie made the coffee.

'It must be nice for you to have Joe here.' She poured water in the jug, put a filter on top and went to get the coffee out of a cupboard.

'Wait a second.' She stared into the cupboard. 'I had a small bottle of vodka in there, next to the coffee. Debby gave it to me before she left for California and I haven't touched it. It's gone.'

'So they trash the living room and steal some booze? Has to be kids.'

'Definitely. I wonder if they took the bottle of wine from the fridge?'

Going over to the fridge, Ellie opened the door.

'What the . . . ?'

'Ellie?'

'Shit.'

'What? What is it?'

When Ellie didn't answer, Louisa went and stood beside her, saw the small white piece of paper Scotch-taped on to the front of the milk carton.

There were two typewritten words on it: 'Got you'.

Elie stepped back, sank into one of the chairs at the little kitchen table, put her head in her hands. Louisa could hear her taking deep breaths.

'Ellie?' She closed the fridge door, put her hand on Ellie's shoulder. 'Are you all right?'

'I don't understand . . .' She raised her head, shook it. 'Why . . . ?'

'These kids, whoever they are, are playing tricks. This is like some Hallowe'en prank. It's a terrible thing to do,' Louisa said, but Ellie didn't seem to be listening.

'Louisa?' Her eyes were suddenly full of fear. 'What day is it? What's the exact date today?'

'June the twenty-seventh.' Louisa stared at her. 'Why?'

Ellie shook her head again, kept shaking it.

'It's not July yet. Of course it's not July . . . could you leave me alone here for a few minutes? Please?'

'Are you sure?'

'Yes, please. I'll come outside. Just give me a few minutes.'

'All right.'

Confused, Louisa walked out, went and sat down on the lawn in front of the cottage. Joe and Pam had often talked about building a porch, but they'd never done it.

What the hell's going on?

A few minutes later, Ellie appeared and sat down beside her. All she said was 'Thanks', but her voice sounded composed, and the fear Louisa had seen in her before had vanished.

'Maybe you *should* call the police, Ellie. There might be fingerprints on that note. Or in the living room. They can—'

'It's kids. I checked again and the wine was gone. The note is a Hallowe'en type of prank, like you said. The last thing I want is for Tim to see a police car when he gets back. I don't want him to know anything about this, OK?

Please. He's trying out for the baseball team, beginning to settle in. This would upset him. Please, Louisa?'

It was a heartfelt plea, but still she hesitated.

'Louisa, I'm begging you. It would make things so much harder for me. Please.'

'All right. But promise me you'll lock your door from now on? And promise to call me if you're frightened for any reason?'

'I promise.'

She heard Ellie take those deep breaths again, inhaling and exhaling and then suddenly she jumped up.

'I'm going to finish cleaning up. You should go back home. I'm fine now.' She brushed off her jeans although there was nothing on them to brush off. 'I'm fine.'

'But the furniture. You'll need some help . . .' Louisa rose as well.

'No problem. I can do it. It will be good exercise. I told you I didn't want you to stay long. I meant it.'

Ellie's tone of voice was insistent.

'OK, but if you need anything, call me.'

'I'll be fine. Thanks for everything, Louisa.'

'Don't thank me. It didn't feel like work. We make a good clean-up team.'

'Maybe that could be my new career? Cleaning.' Ellie laughed feebly.

'See you later, OK?' Louisa gave her a hug, and set off back to her own house.

Yes, it could be kids, she thought. That 'Got you' could be a warped joke. Teenagers bored in the summer with nothing better to do. Still, it was upsetting and unsettling. Why, had Ellie kicked her out of the kitchen? And why, for God's sake, had she asked what day it was?

None of your business, Louisa, she could hear Jamie scolding her. *The last thing you want is to be the neighbour from hell, poking your nose in when it's not wanted.*

Fair enough, Jamie. But we're friends now, not just neighbours. Still, you're right. If she wants to tell me something — if there's anything to tell — she will. When she wants to.

Would she have to start locking her own house too? No, Jamie would have hated that.

But he would have hated the way Joe had behaved today even more.

Picking up her pace, Louisa strode down the road, through the stone gates piers at the end, and up the porch stairs.

Joe was sitting in the living room in his running shorts and T-shirt, BlackBerry in hand, typing. She sat down on the chair opposite and waited. When he finally looked up, she said: 'Have you finished?'

'Yes.'

'Then put it away, please.'

He placed it on the table beside him.

'I'm disappointed in you.'

He raised his eyebrows, cocked his head to the side.

'Ellie needed our help and you bailed. That was unbecoming of you, Joe. And uncharacteristic. How could you be so rude?'

'When was the last time you lectured me, Mum? I'm not sure, but I know you used the word "unbecoming" then too.'

'If I did, I had a reason to. And I have a reason now.'

90

'Look, it's her cottage, as you keep pointing out. It's her business.'

'That's pathetic.'

'It's true.'

'You would have helped anyone else. I know that.'

He shrugged.

'You have to get over this, Joe.'

'Whatever.'

'What? You've reverted to being a teenager now? That's the way you're sounding.'

'You've made your point, OK?' He stood up. 'I'm going to take a run now.'

'The place was trashed. And someone left a note on the carton of milk in the fridge. It said: "Got you". It might have been kids messing around, but it's worrying.'

'Or she might have made enemies. Maybe she's not as nice as you think she is.'

'If you'd deign to meet her, you'd realise she *is* as nice as I think she is.'

'I'm going now. I'll be back in about an hour.'

He headed for the door and she called out: 'Joe. Your father would have been disappointed.'

'You said that the last time you lectured me too, Mum.'

The screen door slammed shut.

Ellie had finished cleaning up. All the furniture was back in place: everything, except for the seagulls, was as it had been before. And she'd ripped up the note and thrown it in the trash.

Silly kids had had their stupid fun. They could have been hanging out in the cottage when it was empty and were pissed off now that it was inhabited. They'd made their point – they wouldn't do it again.

She had had that moment of real panic when she'd first seen the note, but she'd controlled herself with her breathing exercises. This incident had come at a bad time, just when she was feeling Tim and she were both finding their feet here, and on a day too close to the one she couldn't let herself think about.

But that was a coincidence. Coincidences happened.

I'll call Debby and tell her about it, and she'll tell me whoever it was decided my seagulls were an affront to good taste and wanted to teach me an artistic lesson.

Picking up the phone on the desk by the television, she dialled Debby's number, got her answer message and hung up. She wasn't in, but maybe she'd emailed the night before.

Ellie got her laptop from her bedroom, came back into the living room and sat down on the sofa. When she logged on, she was startled to see a message in her inbox from Daniel Litman, but using a different email address.

Hi, Ellie, it's me again. I know we weren't going to continue emailing, but I was out at a restaurant here in London on my own last night, and it was the birthday of someone at the next table and they all sang – just like at Acquitaine that night. I thought of you, of course.

The sad truth is, even though I've been here for a while now, I'm kind of lonely at the moment. I'm busy at work, finding out all the differences between medicine here and medicine in the

States, but the problem is that when you move countries you lose your past. I can't go out for a drink with someone and say: 'Remember when . . . ?' Starting fresh is good in some ways, but there's a core part of me missing. Do you feel that in Bourne at all? I know it's not far from Boston, but do you miss anyone? I know you have Tim with you, but are there moments when you feel alone? A little – what's the word? – stranded. I hope there aren't, but I'd like to hear how you're doing anyway.

I've switched to a British internet provider – which is why I'm at a different address.

I bet the sea at Bourne is beautiful. Where I'm living is not far away from the Thames, but I was thinking of going to the ocean, maybe Cornwall, next time I have a few days to myself. People say it's a good place for soul-searching. I hope I'm not too old to do a little of that, and I hope you don't mind me getting in touch. Don't worry, there's no need for you to reply. I felt like writing, that's all.

All my best, D.

Ellie re-read it twice. The way he'd admitted to his loneliness without being maudlin was touching. He was reaching out to her, but not putting any pressure on her to reply. When she'd met him, she hadn't thought of him as a soul-searcher. Clearly he was, and she liked that his first instinct, when he wanted to find peace, was to go to the sea.

Perhaps he'd remembered her point about letters being more intimate than emails and was trying to change her mind on that. Whatever the case, she wanted to reply, and to make her email as open and friendly as his had been.

Dear Daniel,

I'm really pleased you wrote. I think I might have felt lonely and stranded here too at first, but it turns out there's an incredibly nice woman who lives in the house next door and we've become close friends. In fact, she came and helped me clean up today. Some kids came in and threw things around and made a huge mess. It was my fault – I left the door unlocked when I went out.

Anyway, the ocean here really is beautiful. The cottage looks out on to the Cape Cod Canal and there are boats going back and forth through it all day – big tankers and small motor boats and lovely yachts. At night they look like ghost ships, especially in the fog.

If Tim or I walk around the back of the cottage and through a little marshy area, there's a small beach where we can swim. To the right of that is a little sheltered cove. I'm thinking of getting a rowboat so I can go out and sit in it in the cove: it looks so peaceful. I might even take sailing lessons. But I'll probably stick to the rowboat. Maybe I can do some soul-searching in it. I don't think anyone is ever too old to do that.

Let me know how it's going there. Cornwall sounds like a good idea, although I'm not sure why I say that. I don't know anything about Cornwall. But if it's on the ocean, it must be nice.

I haven't been to a restaurant since Acquitaine. Maybe whenever either of us goes to a restaurant now, someone will be singing 'Happy Birthday' at the next table. That's all right, as long as I don't have to sing it – you've heard my terrible voice!

Take care and all my best, Ellie.

She sent it, thinking how much easier it was to have this

94

kind of conversation than the one they'd had when they were sitting opposite each other at Acquitaine. Nothing was at stake: they didn't have to decide whether they were going to see each other again, or if they were physically attracted to each other.

This could be a male-female relationship with none of the usual tensions – Debby's point about having a cyberspace romance that didn't work in real life was a moot one. Daniel was thousands of miles away and would be for years. This was more like two people trading diary entries. It probably wouldn't last long – she suspected these type of correspondences never did – but it was fun and interesting, and a nice bonus on a not so nice day.

Ellie shut her computer off and looked at her watch. Tim was going to call her when he finished his baseball game.

Got you.

What did that mean?

Nothing.

A bad joke.

Going to her bedroom, she changed into her bathing suit, grabbed a towel and her cell phone and headed outside, to the little patch of sand at the back of the cottage. Not a beach: she'd exaggerated in her email to Daniel. But a big enough area of sand to put down a towel or two.

Halfway there, she turned back. She'd forgotten to lock the door.

6

7 July

They were all sitting around a table at the Windsurfer, drinking Cokes. It wasn't a bad restaurant – for a rinkydink place like Mashnee – but Tim was feeling out of it. Playing baseball with these guys was great: he'd made the team even though he'd batted badly that day of the try-out. Luckily he'd been responsible for a killer double-play, though, which had made up for it.

Now, though, they were talking about people he'd never heard of, the kids who hadn't had to go to summer school but would be back at Bourne High in September. He thought of his dad saying: 'People who show you holiday photographs should be shot. As if anyone cares. All they're doing is saying they've been some place you haven't been. Boring. Never show your holiday photographs to anyone who wasn't on the holiday with you. Another Walters rule, Tim.'

All of them talking about a gang of people he'd never met was the same, really, but it wasn't like he could tell them they were breaking a rule. Besides, they'd invited him along with them and he hadn't expected them to.

His mother would kill him for taking a lift to the

Windsurfer with Sam, who was a year older and had just gotten his driver's licence, because his mother was paranoid about safety shit. But he figured he could walk back from Mashnee to home and he'd tell her he got a ride from one of the guys' parents and she'd never have to know.

He was about to say something, maybe ask a question so he wouldn't be such an outsider, when Jared, the firstbaseman, started a riff about private schools and how crap they were and how all the people who went to them were stuck-up snobs. Tim kept his mouth shut, thankful that he hadn't told them he'd been at Boston Prep before.

The point was, he didn't want to talk about screwing up there so badly they'd wanted him to stay back a grade, so he'd said 'We've just moved here from Boston' when anyone asked where he'd come from. No one had been interested enough to follow that up, so he'd escaped the 'prep school jerk' tag, along with the 'dumb prep-school jerk' one.

'Hey,' he spoke up, making a show of looking at his watch. 'I have to get back home. See you guys later, and thanks for the ride.'

'Yeah, dude, later,' Sam said, echoed by the three others.

So he escaped before they started quizzing him about his old school.

I'll think up a good story. Make sure they don't find out.

Walking across the porch of the Windsurfer and down the steps to the road, Tim put his baseball glove on his right hand and began to pound it with his other fist. He'd broken it in already, but he liked the feel of hitting the leather hard. Besides, he felt like hitting something. Anything.

OK, he was on the team now. That was ace. And the sun was shining. And the beaches that flanked both sides of the road he was walking down were cool. But . . .

But he'd been cornered into this move. He'd had no choice about it. How come parents, who had screwed up their own lives and gotten divorced, had a right to make such big decisions for him? It didn't make sense. And it had been his Mom's decision. Not his dad's. No way did his dad want him to live here.

But his dad had wanted him to try to get into Groton so he could go to the same school as Sandra's kid, and that would have been even worse than coming here. He'd only met Fred once, but that had been enough. No way did Tim want to go to the same school as him, much less a boarding school which was in the middle of the sticks too. Not that he had a prayer of getting in anyway.

On the beach to his right he clocked a group of girls in bikinis, playing Frisbee in the water. Definitely a good idea to swim here more often.

His mother treated him like a two-year-old, his father had hooked up with a nightmare woman, and he was a total fuck-up because he'd flunked out of his year at school.

Life just kept getting better.

The only other bonus of moving was not having to face his friends at Boston Prep in September. No one survived staying back. They could pretend it was no big deal and act like they'd made great friends in the year below, but the truth was: you stay back, you're a doofus. So you either stay and be the doofus or you move, like he had, and go some-where different and start all over again.

He'd choose the second option, for sure, but not here. There were plenty of other day schools in Boston. Boston – a city. With movie theatres and stores and subways. Right now, because he hadn't made any real friends yet, the biggest entertainment he got was going over to visit Louisa. Yes, she was funny and cool and was even going to teach him how to play poker, but she was like sixty-something years old.

This move was all because his mom had this thing about living on the water. She'd had this stupid two weeks of one summer vacation in Mashnee that she talked about as if they were the best two weeks of her life. Shit – maybe they were.

But why didn't she rent a summer house on Mashnee if that was such a big deal to her? Why'd she have to buy a place to live in the whole year?

He kicked a stone, thumped his glove, turned into Grey Gables Road.

'Hey, nice glove.'

A man was suddenly beside him; a guy pouring sweat who was obviously on a run.

'Thanks,' he said.

'What position?' The man had slowed down, was now walking at the same pace. He didn't look sketchy so Tim decided to keep talking.

'Shortstop.'

'Ah. The best. How's your batting average?'

Tim hesitated.

'It sucks.'

'Yeah, mine did too, in the old days. But I went to the batting cages a lot, worked on it.'

'I guess I should do that.'

'Do you live around here?'

'Yeah. In the cottage near the end of the road.'

'Oh.' The man stopped. Tim stopped too. 'I see. Right.' The man bent down, retied one of his shoelaces, then straightened up. 'I used to live there. The house at the end is my mother's.'

'Louisa?'

'Yes.' The man semi-smiled. 'Louisa. I'm Joe.' He put out his hand and Tim shook it. He came close to wiping the sweat from it off his own hand but knew that would look rude so didn't.

'I'm Tim. We moved in at the beginning of June.'

'I heard.'

The man Joe wasn't moving and Tim didn't see how he could start walking away from him. The rude thing again.

'There are some batting cages on the Cranberry Highway, past Buzzards Bay not that far from here. You can practise there.'

'That sounds good.' Tim nodded.

'Where did you live before?'

'In Boston.'

'So you're switching schools? That must be tough.'

He shrugged.

'You must miss your friends.'

'Yeah. But I, like, blew off school last year. I mean, I

100

didn't do any work. So I had to repeat a grade. That's why I'm going to summer school. To catch up. If I do well enough, I can be in the right grade in Bourne High.'

Why was Tim telling him about it? He didn't have any idea.

'Right.' Joe smiled. And then he actually laughed, which pissed Tim off so much he forgot about not being rude.

'What's so fucking funny about that?'

'I'm sorry.' Joe wiped the sweat from his forehead. 'I didn't mean to laugh, Tim. I wasn't laughing at you. It's just that I was kicked out of school when I was about your age. I was remembering that, that's all.'

'You were kicked out?'

'Yup.' Joe started walking again and Tim went with him.

'What did you do?'

'I called the teacher a . . . well, I called him a seriously bad name. I got kicked out that day.'

'You must have been in deep shit.' Tim, guessing the missing word, was impressed. 'Your parents must have killed you.'

'Not exactly. We were living in California, in Haight-Ashbury, which was a real hippy place in the old days. My father was a rebel. He came from Boston, from an old-time WASP background, and so did my mother, but they were major left-wingers and they moved to San Francisco.

'Anyway, a few days after I got kicked out, my parents sent me off for the afternoon and, when I came back, they'd arranged this big party for me. They'd invited a ton of friends of theirs, artists and film people, all of them successful, who had been kicked out of school too. They were all patting me on the back. It was like I'd joined a great club.'

'I don't believe it!'

'It's true. Not that my parents didn't want me to go back to school and graduate, because they did. And I did too. But my father – he was pretty wild. My mother wasn't as wild but she loved him so much she'd go along with anything he wanted. He died ten years ago. Had a heart attack.'

'Louisa – I mean, your mom – told me. I'm sorry.' Tim couldn't think what else to say.

'So am I. Anyway, I don't think I'd do the same for my child if he or she got kicked out of school like that. I'd be a much stricter parent. But then I don't have any children.' He stopped walking again. It took a second for Tim to realise they'd reached the turn-off to the cottage.

'Listen, if you feel like it, I'll take you to the batting cages tomorrow morning.'

'Excellent. That would be great.'

'OK, come over around ten.'

'Cool.' Tim nodded. 'See you then.'

He watched as Joe began to run again, heading for Louisa's house. And then he turned away, but he didn't want to go into the cottage yet and be grilled by his mom so he skulked around the back and headed towards the cove. There was a small patch of sand there; a measly little beach, and – shit – his mother was sitting on it. He was about to turn around again when she called out 'Tim'. So he trudged on, sitting down as far away as he could get and still be on the sand.

'How did you get back?' she asked.

'I got a ride from the father of one of the guys.'

'And how was the game, sweetheart? Did you win.'

'Yeah. By one run.'

'That's fantastic!'

'Yeah.'

She gave him a look like 'please talk to me' . He turned away and stared across the Canal at a ship anchored on the other side. His mother had told him it was the Maritime Academy's training ship; he hadn't bothered to ask what it trained people for and he wasn't going to now.

At least she wasn't asking him any more questions. She'd stood up and was heading to the water for a swim.

A father who gave a party for his son when he got kicked out of school? How awesome was that? His dad was furious at Tim for having to stay back, totally pissed off. 'The only advantage to you in going to Bourne is that you won't have anything to do there so maybe you'll get your ass in gear and study! If you study hard enough, you can get back into your year and then you can apply to Groton. Because the alternative, Tim, is Cape Cod Community College. And there is no way I can countenance a child of mine going to Cape Cod Community College. Do you know what the word "countenance" means?' Tim had nodded, not knowing but figuring it out anyway.

He loved his dad and he hated him. Same with his mom. Neither of them bothered to consult him about anything. They just did whatever they wanted to do and assumed he'd be cool with it.

Picking up some sand, he flung it in the water.

Was he supposed to take sides between them? Choose his mother or his father?

At least his mom didn't have the whole weird rules business.

But his dad – his dad was successful and powerful and strong.

Still, when he got out of high school – if he ever graduated and got out – he wasn't going to be like either of them. He was going to be like Joe's father. He was going to rebel and live somewhere crazy and be wild.

Until then, though, he was trapped.

7

8 July

Ellie woke up to sheets so tangled it looked like she'd had a fight with the bed. As she sat up, trying to shake off the remnants of a nightmare, it hit her with a thud: the sickening knowledge of what day it was today. Lying back down, she curled herself up into the foetal position.

Twenty-four hours and it would be over. That's all she had to do. Make it through the day. But the memories were massing again, gathering strength. *You can't do it any more,* they were telling her, *we're coming. Look, pieces of the nightmare are here in your head still. We're coming. You can't escape us.*

Squeezing her eyes as tightly shut as she could, she clenched her fists.

'*It's July the eight, Ellie . . .*'

Breathe in.

It didn't happen.

Breathe out.

It didn't happen.

'*You can't get rid of us any more. You can't bury us. Stop trying.*'

Breathe in.

It didn't happen.

Breathe out.

It never happened.

Why wasn't it working?

Because she'd been doing it too much lately.

Because of that day in Starbucks.

'Mom, are you awake?'

Tim.

She sprang up. Leaped out of bed.

'Just a second, Tim. I'll be right there.'

Keep on the move. Keep busy. Keep so far ahead of them they can't catch up.

She went to her bathroom, brushed her teeth, washed her face, came back and got dressed.

'What would you like for breakfast?' she asked him when she went into the living room. 'I'll fix you anything you want.'

'You slept late.'

'Did I?' She looked at her watch: 9.30. Normally she woke up at eight.

'Yeah, remember I'm going over to Louisa's soon. Joe's taking me to the batting cages.'

'Right. Of course.' Joe was here again. Maybe this time she'd get to meet him.

Tim had on jeans and a Red Sox T-shirt. Walking over to him, Ellie hugged him.

'Mom – enough.' He stepped back, away from her. 'I hope I hit a few balls OK. I'm not totally hopeless. I don't want him to think that.'

'I'm sure he won't. I love you, Tim.'

'Yeah, I know. Are you OK? Is there something wrong?'

'I'm fine. Come on, I'll make you some fried eggs and bacon.'

The day was another sunny warm one. Tim was in a good mood and ate his breakfast quickly. Everything was going to be all right, Ellie knew. When he went to batting practice with Joe, she'd clean up. Maybe make some brownies for him after that. He was settling in, that was what she should concentrate on. And he'd even started talking to her, at least a little.

She'd been so careful the night before not to force him into speaking: she'd been quiet at dinner, and afterwards had sat down in the living room with her laptop. Holding back, not doing her usual desperate encouraging routine, had paid off. Tim had come into the room, sat down, and after about ten minutes of silence, ten minutes during which she knew he expected her to start quizzing him on his day so she held back and kept her mouth shut, he began to talk.

He told her about some of the boys on the team and then his meeting with Joe. When he recounted the story of Joe getting kicked out of school and having a party thrown for him, she'd laughed.

'That's brilliant,' she said. 'I wish I could do something like that, but I don't think I'd be able to.'

'Joe said the same. But he doesn't have any kids.'

When Louisa had told her she used to live in Haight-Ashbury, Ellie had pictured her with flowers in her hair, wearing mini-skirts and giving everyone the peace sign.

'Did you wear lots of bracelets then too?' she'd asked.

'Yes, and those Indian peasant blouses. And tie-dyed T-shirts. I went the whole nine hippy yards, believe me.'

The idea of Joe, now working for a US senator, calling his teacher a name – one Tim hadn't said but which she guessed was outlandish – amused Ellie. He had to have a streak of subversion in him too. Taking Tim to the batting cages showed he shared Louisa's generosity of spirit as well.

When Tim had gone off to meet Joe, and Ellie had finished cleaning everything there was to clean, she sat down, but stood up again immediately.

What next?

Keep busy.

Brownies. Bake those brownies for Tim.

Going into the kitchen, she prepared the brownies, put them in the oven.

What next?

Email.

Her laptop was on the kitchen table. Debby had sent her a long email about some man she'd fallen for, and Ellie responded, giving her encouragement. *He sounds fantastic*, she said. *And don't say it's your usual crush syndrome. It's obviously his crush too.'*

After she'd finished that one, she started one to Daniel. They emailed each other twice daily now, at the start and the end of their respective days, and Ellie was enjoying the correspondence more and more. Now she looked forward to seeing his name in the in-box, and during the day she'd think of things she was going to tell him in her evening email. She made an effort to write well, too. Something she hadn't done since college.

Just as she'd written *Dear Daniel*, she heard a car drive up. Going to the front door, she opened it and saw Tim climbing out of the front seat of Joe's car.

'Hi,' she called out, wanting to thank Joe, but the car was already reversing out the drive. 'Is he in a hurry or something?' she asked Tim.

'I don't know. He's really good at batting, though. He taught me a lot. And he said he's coming back next weekend. The summers in DC are too hot. He said he'll take me to a game next Saturday night. There's a Cape Cod league and they play minor league games. Joe's cool.'

'That's great.'

But why hadn't he said hello? She would have liked to meet him, compare the Joe she'd heard about to Joe in person. Ellie watched the car as it drove up to Louisa's house.

'I'm hot. I'm going to take a swim.'

Tim went to his room, changed into his bathing suit and headed outside. Ellie went back to her laptop. She'd write the email to Daniel and then make lunch. But after she'd written only two sentences, Tim burst back in through the door.

'Someone's dumped a load of garbage on the beach. It's disgusting. Dirty diapers. All this sh— all this crap. No way can I swim there.'

'What?'

Ellie got up and sprinted out and down to the beach. It was filthy, as if someone had emptied three big garbage bags full of junk on it: broken bottles, uneaten food, Coke cans, and, as Tim had said, dirty diapers. Putting her hand over her mouth, she backed away.

'See?' Tim was behind her. 'What asshole did that?'

'I don't know.' She shook her head.

'Why our little beach? Did some pleasure boat come over here and dump it? I've seen people throwing trash off their boats into the water. What assholes!'

Why our little beach?

Why?

'How are we supposed to clean this mess up?' Tim asked.

'I don't know.'

'It stinks.'

'We have to clean it up somehow,' said Ellie, but she didn't move.

The same kids who had trashed the living room? Had they done this too?

Or was Tim right, was it a pleasure boat dumping its garbage?

This feels personal.

'I can't deal with this right now.'

'You think we should leave it here like this?'

'I don't know, Tim. OK?'

'OK.' He held up his hands. 'Sam called me on my cell when I was with Joe. He invited me over to the beach at Mashnee. I wasn't going to go, but maybe I will now. If that's all right?'

'It's fine.' She nodded. 'Go ahead.'

He turned to leave.

'Mom?' He looked back. 'Are you all right?'

110

'I'm fine. Go on. Have some fun.'

As he picked up his pace, Ellie watched him.

Children grew up and got their own lives and left home. That's what was supposed to happen. Tim would be off to college in a few years and she would be a proud mother, watching, feeling the empty nest syndrome kick in.

That was the way it was supposed to be. Anything else was unthinkable.

Stop it, Ellie. Right now. Present tense. Keep in the present. Deal with this mess.

She swung her gaze back to the trash. She couldn't deal with it.

It feels personal.

But it's not. It can't be.

Looking out, over the Canal, she watched boats plying their way back and forth. Stupid people did dump their trash into the water. She'd seen them do it too, and when she'd seen it, had wished she could arrest the unthinking idiots who used the ocean as their garbage can.

A huge tanker passed by and she watched as its wake spread out through the Canal, finally landing on her patch of beach, lapping up over the smelly debris.

Later . . . I'll clean this up later.

Back in the cottage, she hit the bar to bring the computer out of its sleep, trying to distract herself by finishing that email to Daniel. But she couldn't concentrate and clicked on her in-box instead.

One new email. From Charlie.

'Shit, what does he want?' she muttered as she opened it.

Ellie,

I should tell you this before you hear it from anyone else. Sandra and I are going to get married. In December.

Charlie.

Ellie sat back, closed her eyes, put her fist up to her mouth and bit her knuckles.

She should have expected this, she *did* expect this, but not now. Not today.

Unwanted images rampaged through her brain: Charlie sitting at that table in the kitchen the first time they'd met, suddenly reaching out and taking her hand in his. Charlie in the church, standing waiting for her as she walked down the aisle. Looking so serious and yet so calm. Charlie staring down at Tim's face when he was born, grinning in a way she'd never seen him grin before. Proud and excited. Thrilled it was a boy. Charlie sitting in the chair in their living room, listening while she stressed about something silly like finding a plumber, and saying: 'I'll handle it, El. Leave it to me. If I can't fix it myself, I'll find someone who will.'

All these memories she'd dredged up. Why couldn't she remember something bad, something that wouldn't hurt so much?

Fuck it.

Snapping the lid shut, she stood up and headed for the door. She didn't want to be alone any more; she wanted to see Louisa. But as soon as she got outside, she felt them, those other memories, lurking at the edge of her mind.

Go away! Get the fuck out of my head!

The noise of a car engine startled her. It was the rental car

112

and Joe Amory was at its wheel, driving towards the main road. As she stared at him passing by, she saw him glance at her and then turn his eyes back to the road immediately, with no acknowledgement of her.

A fragment of her nightmare slammed into her consciousness: Tim was running down a road as fast as he could; she could see a car following right behind him, speeding up, and she was screaming, 'Stop!' She saw him trip, and she knew, as he fell, that he would die.

She couldn't be alone for one more second. She didn't care that she was going to leave the door unlocked. She had to get to Louisa's.

8

'It's so beautiful here. And so peaceful. You must love sitting here, watching the boats gliding and the seagulls flying. You said you used to play games. What kind of games?'

They were sitting on the wraparound porch together. Ellie had her feet curled up underneath her and was cradling a mug of coffee. Louisa's legs were stretched out, resting on a little wooden footstool.

Ellie had arrived at her door, a little breathless, and as they went into the kitchen together to make the coffee, had told Louisa about the beach, and then about Charlie's email.

'But I don't want to talk about it, Louisa. I needed to tell you what's happened, but I want to talk about something normal and forget it all.'

What the hell was going on? Louisa wondered as she turned the kettle on. First the cottage trashed and now this? Yes, boats dumped their garbage sometimes, and it was heinous when they did. But the idiots normally only threw a few items overboard. A couple of bottles or cans. Old cigarette packs. Not bagsful of crap. But Ellie was so insistent, Louisa could only do as she asked, take her out to the porch and have a 'normal' conversation.

'We played all kinds of games. Relievo, Sardines in a Can, Whiffleball. And games we invented. You know, if I ever went to a shrink, I'd say I had *too* happy a childhood. That would stump him or her. I think the phrase "happy childhood" is an oxymoron for a shrink.'

'Shrinks don't really help.'

'Don't they?'

'I don't think so. I think they all have their theories and try to make people fit in to those theories.'

'Maybe. I wanted Joe to go see a grief counsellor but he refused. I'm sorry you haven't had a chance to meet him yet.' Louisa uncrossed her bare feet. 'He had to catch a flight back to DC. Sundays . . . I hate them. Everyone leaves.'

'It was really kind of him to take Tim to the batting practice place.'

'He enjoyed doing it. All men are boys at heart.'

'I guess so.'

Louisa studied Ellie, who was staring out over the water, oblivious to her scrutiny. Although they'd been having this supposedly normal conversation, Ellie's tone of voice had been completely flat and disengaged. The news of Charlie's remarriage, coupled with the garbage on the beach, had clearly hit her hard.

'Hey!' Louisa clapped her hands, stood up. 'I almost forgot. I have a surprise for you.'

'Really?' Ellie swung around, her face becoming more animated.

'Yes, come on. Come with me. Bring your coffee. I'll show it to you.'

Louisa led her down the front steps and to the side of the house, where the garage was.

'You stay here. I'll bring it to you.'

Lifting the garage door by its handle on the bottom, Louisa went in and found Joe's old bike at the back. She grabbed the handlebars, wheeled it backwards out of the garage and into the sunlight.

'Here!' She smiled. 'This is for Tim. I know he doesn't know how to ride but we can teach him – it will be fun.'

Ellie stood staring. The coffee mug fell from her hand.

'Ellie?'

Turning, she raced away, running like a demon, but as she reached the end of Louisa's driveway, she tripped and fell.

'Ellie!' Louisa ran up to her. She was sitting hunched on the sandy gravel, her head down. 'Ellie, are you all right?'

'I have to breathe. Let me breathe.'

She closed her eyes, began to take deep breaths, but after a few seconds she stopped and opened her eyes again.

'It's not working. Oh, God. What am I going to do?'

'Ellie . . . sweetheart.' Louisa sat down beside her, pulled her to her. 'What's going on? I don't understand.'

'I can't . . .' Tears began to roll down her face. 'I don't want to. I can't! Don't make me!'

The tears had turned into sobs. Her hands started flailing in the air, as if she were chasing away a swarm of bees. Louisa grabbed her wrists and held them.

'Make them go away! Get them out of my head!'

'Make what go away? What are you talking about?'

'I can't bury them. They won't let me. I hate it, I hate it, I hate it . . .'

She's like a baby – like Joe when he was two years old having a meltdown.

'Stop it, Ellie. Now!'

'Make it go away,' Ellie said through her sobs. 'The bicycle. Make it go away.'

'I'll put it back in the garage. When you calm down, I'll put it back.'

'The sirens. All those sirens . . . it didn't happen. Tell me it didn't happen?' Her whole body was shaking.

'Shhh . . .' Louisa began to stroke her hair rhythmically. 'It's all right. It's going to be all right.'

'It's not. *She's* there. I see her. There's blood everywhere and . . . and then this woman is running and screaming, and my mother is screaming too . . .'

'Oh my God, sweetheart. What are you talking about?'

'And the sirens . . . the sirens are screaming and I'm screaming and it's today.'

'What's today?'

'Why did it have to be today? It happened today. But it didn't happen. So why . . . ? I can't make it not happen. The bicycle . . . it's in my brain. Get it out. Please. Make it go away.'

'Ellie. Calm down. Talk to me.'

'She's lying there. Oh, God. I killed her.'

What the . . . ?

'Ellie.' Louisa drew back, took Ellie's face in her hands, forced her to look at her. 'What are you talking about? Talk to me. Tell me.'

'No.' She shut her eyes. 'It didn't happen.'

Letting go of Ellie's face, Louisa hugged her again. Her heart was beating so hard against her chest, it felt like it was going to break through and explode. No one's heart should beat like this, Louisa thought. She'd have a heart attack if she didn't calm down.

'Ellie, breathe with me. Listen to my breathing and breathe with me.'

'I can't. Breathing doesn't work. She's lying there. She's dead. I killed her.'

'You're breathing with me, all right? Breathe with me.'

Louisa took long, even breaths, waiting for Ellie to match them. After a minute, she did. Her breathing slowed down but her heart was still pounding and the sobs didn't abate.

'Ellie, keep breathing with me, OK? Good. Good girl. Nice steady breaths.'

The sun was beating down on them. Louisa heard seagulls cawing and the sound of bouys ringing as they rocked in the Canal. She was afraid to move, to disturb Ellie in any way. They breathed in synch for about ten minutes until Ellie's heartbeat slowed a little. But Louisa didn't dare stop what she was doing or say something, ask the thousands of questions she wanted to ask. Anything might set her off again.

'It's gone now.' Ellie finally broke the silence. 'It's gone.'

'What's gone?'

'All of it.'

'Good.'

'But what if it comes back? What do I do if it comes back again?'

'Ellie, listen to me. I can't help you or answer any of your questions until I know exactly what you're talking about.'

'I need Dr Emmanuel.'

'Who's Dr Emmanuel?'

'A hypnotherapist in the ward.'

Hypnotherapist? Ward? A psychiatric ward? Had something actually happened or had Ellie imagined it had? Was the blood, killing someone . . . was everything she'd said so far real or a product of hypnosis or what exactly?

Louisa waited, sitting still in the same position for what felt like forever until Ellie's sobbing stopped and her breathing felt close to normal.

'I'm all right.' Ellie drew back from Lousia's hug, but gently. 'I'm so sorry, Louisa. I don't know why . . . it's all right. I'll be fine. It was the bicycle. It made me . . . I'm sorry. I'll go back now. You can let me go.'

'Ellie? You've just been through some kind of trauma. You're not all right. You're not going anywhere. What was going on? What was all that about? I'm not letting you go anywhere until you tell me.'

'Nothing.' Ellie turned her face away. 'Nothing.'

'But you said—'

'Nothing happened. There's nothing to tell.' Her voice was dead.

'That's bullshit and you know it is. Look at me, Ellie. Now.' Ellie did. Louisa put her hands on her shoulders, stared straight at her.

'Did someone die?'

Ellie closed her eyes. Louisa held her breath.

'Yes.' She shook her head. 'No. Dr Emmanuel said I could make it so it didn't happen. If it didn't happen, she didn't die.'

'Open your eyes, Ellie. Look at me. Right, I have no idea what's going on. But I *do* know that if something did happen, you cannot go on saying it didn't. If someone died, you can't bury that truth inside you.'

'I can. I have to. You don't understand . . .'

'No, I don't understand. But I want you to listen to me. Joe went wild with grief when Pam died. Not in the usual way. He didn't cry one tear. Because he couldn't accept it. Instead what he did was to deny it. He would do everything he normally did and pretend Pam was still there. He'd go to a movie and buy two tickets. He'd talk to her about it afterwards. Are you listening to me? Do you understand what I'm saying?'

Ellie nodded.

'I'm sure this denial actually did help him. For a while. But it was wrong and I didn't know what to do. He wouldn't see a grief counsellor or talk to anyone about it. I couldn't help. But then one day he came to me and sat down and said: "Mum, I know Pam's dead. I drove by the hospital today and I thought of her in there and how brave she was; I let myself remember that. She was amazing, the way she dealt with it all. I realised then – and it hurt like hell, but I did – that if I kept telling myself she was alive, I would be robbing her of all that courage, a whole part of her life. If I kept shutting out her death, I'd be disrespecting her."'

'Disrespecting her?' Something registered in Ellie's eyes, but Louisa wasn't sure what.

'Yes. Joe was right. Pam deserved to have her death acknowledged as much as she deserved to have her life acknowledged. I don't know what happened to you, Ellie, but if you did . . . if someone did die and you are refusing to accept that, you're refusing to accept that person lived and died. That's disrespectful.'

Ellie was silent, but Louisa could almost hear her brain whirring away. And yet nothing happened. Ellie didn't speak, but she wasn't trying to leave either.

'Stay here. I'll be right back.' Louisa struggled to get to her feet, feeling as if she'd been in a ten-round heavyweight fight.

She walked over to the bike, lying on its side in the dust, picked it up, wheeled it back in to the garage. When she returned to Ellie, she reached out her hand. 'Come on. You need something to drink. And you need to get out of this sun.'

Like a small child, Ellie obeyed, allowing Louisa to lead her back to the house. 'Sit down in the shade here,' she said when they reached the porch. 'I'll get you some water.'

It's too entrenched, she thought as she turned on the cold tap, then went to the freezer and got some ice. *She won't allow herself to get it out – whatever it actually is.*

'Here.' She handed the glass of water to Ellie, took hers and sat down in the same chair she'd been in when all this started. Now they were both staring out over the Canal.

'Louisa?'

Ellie was looking at her with mournful eyes.

'Yes?'

'I don't want to disrespect her. That's the last thing I want to do.'

'I believe that.'

'I can't . . . it's not working any more. I can say it didn't happen but it doesn't feel the way it used to. It used to feel real. But now . . . now *she's* real and I don't want to disrespect her. You believe me, don't you?'

'Yes. Who was she, Ellie? Can you tell me?'

'I want to, but . . .' She paused. 'Can you leave me alone for a few minutes? I need some time on my own.'

'Of course. I'll go sit on the wall, OK?'

'Yes. Thank you.'

Louisa went over to the wall that surrounded the house, a line of defence against hurricane tides. Ellie's breakdown had felt like a psychological hurricane, stranding her in a place and amid feelings Louisa had no concept of. She took a quick look over her shoulder, saw Ellie sitting in the chair, her arms wrapped around herself.

Did I do the right thing? Have I forced her into something she can't handle?

Jesus, I wish Joe were here.

If she killed someone . . . ?

Louisa tried to calm herself down by remembering sitting here like this when she was a child. Waiting to play a game or go swimming or out in the boat. But images of Ellie's distraught face, those sobs, hearing that weak 'I killed her', kept intruding, pushing away all other thoughts.

Why me? I'm too old to handle this. It's too intense.

Louisa saw Pam then, sitting in her hospital bed, tilting

122

her head to one side, the morphine-pumping device on her stomach. She was bald and she looked ten years old, angelic. 'You know what?' she said. 'A lot of people on this floor, they say: why me? Why did this have to happen to me? And I think, well, why *not* you? And why not me? Why would you . . . why would I . . . why would anyone think they're so special nothing bad could happen to them? I don't get it.'

Pam handled a lot worse, Louisa. Get a grip.

She gazed at a big pile of rocks about a hundred yards away in the water. Her brother and she had imaginatively christened it the Rock Pile, and would take their little rowboat out there on afternoons and bottom fish. Louisa remembered that feeling of baiting the hook with a piece of slimy minnow, unwinding the rope from the hand-held H-shaped block of wood, waiting for the tiny bump it made when it hit bottom. And then sitting there for ages, in the sun, hoping for a nibble, that moment when the rope twitched slightly in her hand. How many times had she thought she felt a nibble, pulled up the line excitedly, only to find the same piece of minnow dangling untouched from the hook?

'Louisa?' Ellie was by her side.

'Sit down. Join me.'

'I want to tell you.'

'Are you sure?'

'Yes. But can we go inside? To the living room?'

'Of course.' She rose and they walked together to the house.

'I love these panelled walls,' Ellie said as they sat down beside each other on the sofa. 'It's always so cool in here.'

They were silent for a minute, both looking out at the Canal.

'I want you to know who she was. I've never told anyone before.'

'Ellie sweetheart, take your time.' Louisa reached out and took her hand, squeezed it.

'Her name was Hope. July the eighth . . . today . . . was her birthday – her sixth birthday. Her parents had bought her a new bicycle. It was pink, with blue streamers on the handle-bars. She had strawberry-blonde hair and she was wearing it in pigtails. I think she was perfect.' Ellie stopped, took a deep breath.

'She lived in a suburb outside of New York City. New Rochelle. I don't know how many bedrooms there were in the house, but I know she was an only child. I don't know what school she went to.' She bit her lip. 'I killed her, Louisa. I killed her.' She closed her eyes, and Louisa could see the struggle she was having before she opened them again.

'I was seventeen and had just gotten my licence. My mother decided to go to her old hairdresser in New Rochelle. She used to work in the city but she moved there and my mother couldn't find anyone in the city as good as she was. My mother said we could drive there together. She'd drive on the highways and then, when we got out of the city, I could drive. I was really excited, you know?'

Louisa nodded.

'When we switched places and I started to drive, I was nervous, so I drove really slowly. We were on this street and I think Marie, the hairdresser, lived a couple of streets away. My mother had the directions, she was reading them to me. I was driving slowly, staring straight ahead, concentrating on the road in front of me.

'Hope's house had a sloping driveway. I guess she was really excited about her new bicycle, as excited as I was about driving the car, and she couldn't wait to try it out. She went down the slope and she lost control, kept going into the road. I didn't see her. I wasn't looking to the side. But I was going so slowly . . . I should have seen. I should have been able to stop.'

'Ellie, you couldn't—'

'No, wait. Let me finish.'

'There was a kind of thud. I didn't understand what it was. I thought something was wrong with the car. I stepped on the brake – and then this woman was screaming "Hope" and – my window was open, I could hear this scream and then my mother was screaming and I remember putting the car in park. I don't know what made me do that or what made me get out.

'I saw the bicycle on the ground in front of the car and there was all this blood. And I saw this little body lying splayed out and I began to scream and I – then I fainted. When I came to there were sirens and flashing lights all around. I couldn't look. I covered my eyes. Hope died before she got to the hospital.'

'I'm so sorry. I'm so, so sorry,' Louisa said, squeezing Ellie's limp hand as hard as she could.

'I ended up in a hospital too. But it wasn't the same – I mean, I was alive. Everyone kept telling me it wasn't my fault. I was going under the speed limit, she'd ridden her bicycle straight into the path of the car. None of them understood that none of that was the point. I should have been aware. I should have been looking to the left and right, not just straight ahead. I should have braked in time.'

'Ellie, everyone was right. It was an accident. It wasn't your fault.'

'I was alive, Louisa. Don't you understand that? I was alive and she wasn't. She was only six years old. I should never have driven that day. I shouldn't . . . I shouldn't . . .' She turned her head away, shook it, turned back.

'After it happened, I hid in my room. I didn't come out. I'd stay there, rewinding the tape, thinking: if we'd left three minutes earlier. If there'd been more traffic lights we had to stop at. If my mother had decided to find a different hairdresser . . . all these diffferent versions of that day so it wouldn't have happened. I'd do that, and when I wasn't doing that, I slept. I slept and slept and replayed that day with different outcomes and slept some more. My mother couldn't deal with it – how could she? I ended up in a psychiatric ward for six months. No one knew what to do with me. I mean the shrinks couldn't help me. I couldn't eat, all I could do was sleep. I wanted to curl up and die.' She pulled her legs up and hugged her knees, still keeping hold of Louisa's hand.

'But then this other doctor came to see me: Dr Emmanuel, a hypnotherapist. He didn't ask any of the usual questions or say any of the usual things about it not being my fault. He'd been a doctor in Serbo-Croatia and had switched from medicine to hypnotherapy. He said the mind could do anything, you know? That he'd seen people undergo operations without any anaesthetic, but with hypnosis.

'He told me if I couldn't bear to live with the truth, I should change the truth. I could tell myself it hadn't happened. I know it sounds strange, but the thing is, it worked. At first he hypnotised me. And I felt better when he did – for a while anyway. But still a while was a big deal for me . . . and then he taught me how to hypnotise myself. So that anytime I felt I was sinking back into it, I could do these breathing exercises and tell myself it hadn't happened.

'I felt so guilty because I realised I wanted to live. The thing is, the only way I could live and be normal again was to do what Dr Emmanuel said. It worked. And it kept working. I got better. I went home. I went back to school. It's weird. I don't know how to explain it, but I developed a kind of system, these self-defence mechanisms. If anything reminded me of what had happened, the first thing I'd do would be to try to push those memories down, bury them. And if that didn't work, I'd do Dr Emmanuel's exercises, the self-hypnosis. And as time went by, I had to do it less and less, until I didn't have to do it at all – or at least hardly ever. I guess I'd trained myself. But . . .' She shifted her gaze from Louisa, stared up at the ceiling.

'But what?'

'But then, a few months ago, I was sitting in Starbucks one afternoon, having coffee. And there were these two

127

young girls at a table beside mine, talking. And one of them – she was blonde, really cute, maybe twenty years old – she said to the other one: "I'm still shaking, you know? I mean, it was last week, but I'm still shaking. I could have killed him. He ran out in the street, straight in front of me, chasing a ball, and I hit the brakes so hard you wouldn't believe it and I came within inches. Inches." The other girl said: "You have to forget it, Janice. Move on. Nothing bad happened." And the blonde girl, Janice, said: "But what if I hadn't been able to stop? He was just a little kid. How could I live with myself? I'd never be able to get over it."

'I ran out of there. But the memories started chasing me then and they haven't stopped. They've gotten worse and worse. And last night I had this nightmare about Tim being killed. And it's the day it happened today. And then I saw that bicycle. And I couldn't bury it and the self-hypnosis didn't work and . . . I'm sorry, Louisa. I'm sorry to lay this all on you. But I couldn't keep it in any more. And what you said – I realise it's not right to keep it in. It's disrespectful to Hope.'

'It's not good for you either, Ellie. Living with this by yourself must have been hell. You said you didn't tell anyone? Not even Charlie?'

'No, not even Charlie. It's strange because he's so good at getting people to tell him things. And the first night I met him, I almost did. But I didn't want him to see me as someone who'd killed a little girl. And the hospital – I didn't want to tell him I'd been there. He hates losing control, you know. He doesn't drink, he's never even had a sip of wine. He would have hated the idea that I'd lost myself like that.

'That ward I was in, Louisa, it was so scary. Some of the other people . . . when I was sitting by myself outside before, I thought about that place and how scared I was and how young I was and how Dr Emmanuel seemed like a god to me then. What he did gave me a way out. It was the only way I could cope with what happened. I relied on him. Like I relied on Charlie during our marriage. I don't want to have to do that any more. I'm not a young girl. I'm a mother.'

'And you're a terrific mother.' Louisa let go of Ellie's hand and put her arm around her shoulders.

'But . . .' Ellie wiped her eyes with the backs of her fists '. . . Hope had a mother too. Mrs Davis. I never went to see her. I should have gone to see her parents. Hope would be twenty-five today.' She looked at Louisa with pleading eyes. 'She was an innocent child.' She put her head in her hands. 'Please tell me she's in heaven, Louisa? Please tell me she forgives me?'

'She is,' Louisa said, drawing Ellie against her, her own heart pounding. 'And she does.'

9

Tim tried not to stare at her. He'd look quickly, then look away. She was sitting cross-legged on the sand in cut-off jeans and a white cotton T-shirt, totally comfortable. Like she knew she didn't have to push how sexy she was; all she had to do was sit there and be herself. The two other girls were in bikini bottoms and tops, making moves that showed off their bodies, but Lauren didn't need to. She didn't giggle, either. Not like the other two – Kerry and Leslie – who giggled the whole time.

Sam and Jake were flirting with Kerry and Leslie, which was fine by Tim. Especially fine when Sam stood up, grabbed Kerry by the hand and dragged her into the water, Jake following with Leslie.

'Don't even think about doing that to me,' Lauren said.

'I wasn't thinking of it,' he answered her, keeping his voice low.

'You know they're trying to set us up, don't you?'

'Yeah. How more obvious could they get?' He shook his head, began to smooth out the sand in front of him.

'I told Kerry: "What's with this? Double dating's not

enough for you guys? You want to go for triple dating? Think about it. You'd need a bigger car."'

Tim smiled, began to draw a picture in the sand with his index finger. That way he wouldn't stare at her. That way maybe she wouldn't see he was beginning to blush.

'So.' She was picking up handfuls of sand, filtering it through her fists. 'You're the new guy. And you're from Boston. How do you like idyllic little Bourne?'

'I get the "little" part.'

When she laughed he felt like he'd hit a home run.

Jesus. He had to get a grip.

'What's that you're drawing?'

'A house. That one.' Looking up, he pointed across the water to Louisa's.

'I love that place.' She stood up, came over and sat a foot away from him, cross-legged again, her elbows resting on her knees, her chin in her hand, and watched him as he drew.

'Don't forget the porch. That's the best part.'

'The roof's the best part.'

'You think?'

He nodded.

'How do you do that? I mean, I try to draw and it's a mess.'

'So you're a modern artist.'

She laughed again. He could tell she was studying him now, checking him out.

'I *can* draw two things. A dog. Specifically a dachshund. And Fred Flinstone's profile.'

131

'The house could use a dog. If you draw it over there . . .'
He pointed . . . 'it could be about to go in and eat.'

'OK.' Leaning over, she began to trace a tiny dog in the sand.

'That's a dog?'

'Give me a break, Michelangelo.'

He allowed himself to look at her then. Her short blonde hair was hanging over her face a little. She had a slightly sharp nose – an intelligent nose, he decided. And her blue eyes were bouncing with light.

'What are you two doing there?' Kerry was suddenly standing in front of them, dripping wet. Flinging her long hair around like it was a lasso. 'What's that? Shit, Tim – that's amazing. That's amazing, isn't it, Lauren?'

Lauren shifted away from him while he swept the sand, obliterating the picture.

'Why'd you do that?' Kerry asked.

He didn't answer. The others had arrived too and they were back in their group, sitting where they'd been sitting before, the others being noisy and flirting and Tim sneaking looks at Lauren. Except this time, when he did, he'd catch her looking back at him.

10

For a week Ellie had felt as if she were recovering from a fever. Weak and listless, with no appetite, she struggled to do simple things like cook for Tim. Sometimes she'd spend hours on the beach – which she and Louisa had cleaned up together – sitting gazing out over the Canal. For some reason, she always ended up fixated on the Railroad Bridge, the imposing edifice with towers on either side of the Canal and a middle section which dropped slowly when a train was coming, allowing it to pass over the water.

The way the silvery top spikes of each tower glinted in the sun reminded her of the Chrysler Building in New York, and she found herself speculating about who had designed it, who had built it. Sometimes she wondered what it would feel like to sit on top of the moving middle section as it dropped downwards. It was operated by a hydraulic lift system, she decided. But what if it went haywire, suddenly started rising up again while a train was on it? What if whoever was operating it made a mistake?

And how would that person who made the mistake feel?

She'd tell Louisa about these thoughts because she told

her everything. Louisa would never say 'Don't be ridiculous' or 'Stop being so brooding and dark'. Instead she'd listen and nod and then she'd say 'What about taking a walk with me?' or 'How about we go out in the boat? Not far – just a little putter around'. And on those walks or in the boat, Louisa would tell *her* things too.

'President Cleveland used to have a house here, on the point over there, just before the Railroad Bridge. It looked exactly like my house and they called it the Summer White House, but it burned down ages ago. Sometimes I think my house might be sad, you know. Missing its twin.'

Ellie would listen, and if they were in the boat, she'd trail her hand in the water, feeling soothed. On any boat trip, Louisa would end up by motoring over to the cove behind the cottage, the place where Ellie had told Daniel she'd like to do some soul-searching. It was hidden away, distanced enough from the Canal that it didn't get any wake or waves: a placid, calm haven. Louisa would drop anchor, then pull out two Reese's Peanut Butter candy bars and hand one to Ellie.

'I often think about the Indians when I'm here,' she said, towards the end of the week. 'The original name for Bourne, the Indian name, was Mahamet, which means "Trail of the Burden Carriers". I ask myself: what trail? I mean, trail to where? Where were they going? Towards Hyannis? Provincetown? Or back the other way towards Boston? And what burdens were they carrying?'

'You're doing all this for me, Louisa. And I can never repay you for it. I feel as if I'm the burden you have to carry.'

'A burden? Don't be absurd. You know what I spent hours

134

doing before you moved in here? Playing solitaire games on the computer. I love having you here, Ellie – you know that. And *I* know you're feeling better. What's going on with you now, it's like a calm *after* a storm. You're learning to live with something you've spent decades struggling to repress. But you're doing it and you're coping and you're a strong woman and I admire you.

'Besides, who the hell else would sit with me in this cove eating Reese's Peanut Butter Cups?'

Laughing, Ellie wondered if Louisa was right. Was she learning to live with the truth? She'd had two nightmares since the day she'd told Louisa what had happened, but they hadn't been as frightening as the ones before. There was relief, too, in not having to attempt to bury the memories or hypnotise herself. Nothing could wipe out her sadness or guilt, but at least now she wasn't fighting them.

By the start of the second week she went to the beach on her own less often, began to cook again, was feeling stronger physically. Now, when she and Louisa took a walk, they wouldn't just go to the end of Agawam Point Road and back, they'd push on to Mashnee, end up at the Windsurfer and have a cup of coffee there. Or they'd drive to Atwoods. And with each successive boat trip, Ellie would ask Louisa to go further from home, until now they'd gone almost to the end of the Canal.

'Pretty soon, if it's a calm day, we can go to Cleveland's Ledge,' Louisa had suggested. 'There's a huge lighthouse there and it's in the open sea. You'll like it. I promise.'

Ellie believed her.

This weekend, though, Louisa had gone to Boston to visit a friend and Tim was in Boston with Charlie. Ellie had dreaded being alone in the cottage, fearful the memories would swamp her when she was by herself. When that didn't happen, she felt as if she'd made a breakthrough she'd never imagined she could.

Friday night she watched television, Saturday morning she took a walk to Mashnee and back, then wrote emails to Debby and Daniel, all without any sense of impending doom. She and Deb had joked about Charlie's upcoming marriage, she and Daniel had traded stories about their time in college. It was normal life.

I thought I had a normal life before. But I was always carrying my secret around with me. It was always there, and it was a secret I couldn't even tell to parts of myself. When I told Louisa, I was telling my whole self, too. The truth may not always set you free, but it's made me realise how much lies imprison you.

She was sitting on the lawn outside the cottage, catching the last of the afternoon sun, when she saw Joe Amory walking up the road from his house. She expected him to keep going; he hadn't spoken to her at any point, even though he'd taken Tim to a baseball game the weekend before – when once again Tim had gone over to Louisa's, Joe had taken him out and then dropped him back off without stopping. So Ellie was surprised when Joe diverted from the road and turned into her driveway.

'Hello,' he said, stopping five feet in front of her.

Tall, so thin he was almost scrawny, he had an angular

face which would have been really attractive if it weren't showing such a displeased expression.

'Hi,' she said back, standing up but not moving towards him. He was radiating unapproachability.

'I was waiting for Tim to come over, but he hasn't showed up. We're going to be late for the game.'

'Oh, no. I'm sorry. He must have forgotten. He's not here this weekend, he's with his father. He didn't know he was going until Thursday, but he should have told me he'd arranged to go to a game with you.'

'Oh. Right.'

He was going to turn around and walk back to the house without another word, she could sense that.

Ellie wanted to find out more about the son of the woman who had become, in such a short time, the most important person, after Tim, in her life. Louisa felt like family now: not having a conversation with her son seemed unnatural.

'Joe, don't go,' she said, searching for traces of Louisa in his face, but seeing only his stony expression. 'I want to thank you for being so nice to Tim. Taking him to the batting cages and to the game. You didn't have to do that. I'm really grateful.'

'I like Tim a lot. He's got a good sense of humour.'

'He told me the story about you being kicked out of school, and the party.'

'I probably shouldn't have told him. The message in that one's a little mixed.' He almost smiled.

'That's true.' Ellie did smile. 'But it's a great story.'

'My father was a great man.'

'I know. Your mother's told me about him.'

'Right, well . . .'

Ellie hesitated, then took a step forward. 'I hope you don't mind me saying this, but I'd really like to go to a baseball game. Tim refuses to believe I know anything about sports, but I used to be a tomboy. I love baseball. So I won't bother you with stupid questions, I'll just sit and watch. Is that possible? Can I substitute for Tim tonight?'

'I . . .' Joe shifted from foot to foot, searching for a way out, she could tell. 'Yeah. OK. I'll go back and get the car and come by and pick you up.'

'Thanks. That will be great. I'm Ellie, by the way. But you know that, don't you?'

He nodded. His acceptance had been grudging, given only because he hadn't been able to come up quickly enough with an excuse that worked, she guessed, but she didn't care. Because she was ready to take a risk. And for her that meant having a normal night out: going to a baseball game, eating a hotdog – all those things people did without worrying about hearing sirens or seeing police cars.

She'd walked through that door at Acquitaine and it had turned out to be a good decision. This wasn't a date; this was two people going out to a ballgame on a sunny Saturday afternoon in July. It didn't get more normal than that.

'I'll be back in a few minutes,' he said.

'I'll be ready.'

He turned and headed back to Louisa's; Ellie went into the cottage and to her bedroom, grabbing a sweater to keep her warm when the sun went down.

When she walked through the front door and locked it, Joe was waiting for her in his rental car, the engine running. She hopped in the front seat, did up her seatbelt and sat back.

'Thanks for this,' she said.

'No problem,' was his reply.

Terse, laconic, uncommunicative: absolutely unlike his mother.

Joe was steering with his left hand, his right elbow resting on the bottom of his open window.

'So who's playing?' she asked.

'Bourne against Wareham. It should be a good game.'

They spent the rest of the fifteen-minute drive in silence, Ellie thinking about Daniel and how their email correspondence just kept getting better. He was easy in print: sometimes informative, sometimes philosophical, sometimes funny.

Having a male friend at this point in her life was almost as much of a surprise to her as having Louisa, and made her realise how much of an emotional desert she'd been living in with Charlie. The people they had hung out with had been his friends, not hers, and whether or not it was necessary, she'd felt as if she always had to watch herself with them.

What would Joe be like in email? She imagined any communication with him would involve fewer than two sentences.

'Here we are.' He finally spoke as they entered the high school lot and he pulled into a parking space. 'Just in time.'

They got out of the car, walked to the stands a few hundred

139

feet behind the main school building, and found themselves seats behind first base, about ten rows up.

Ellie loved the feeling of the fading light of the sun combined with the big spotlights aimed at the green grass and baseball diamond. There was a friendly, excited buzz around the grounds as the fielders took their places and the first pitch was thrown. She settled back into the rhythm of the game, comfortable in the crowd, happy to be a spectator. Joe was relaxing too, occasionally talking to an old man with a huge pot belly who was sitting on his other side.

So he could carry on a conversation. Just not with her. He even let out a small cheer when the Bourne second baseman hit a single.

The game was close – 2–2 – until, in the bottom of the eighth inning, the Bourne shortstop hit a homerun with two players on, at which point Joe and Ellie both jumped up and shouted, and he turned to her, giving her a spontaneous high five. As he realised what he'd done, he looked embarrassed, and sat back down in his seat.

The ninth inning started and ended with no change in the score. Bourne had won. Joe said goodbye to the pot-bellied man, and they made their way back to the car. Ellie could hear the people around them talking about the chances of Bourne winning the Cape Cod League.

'So what do you think?' Ellie asked as they started the drive back. 'Is Bourne going to win the league?'

'Absolutely,' he answered. It was the first time she'd seen Joe really smile, and when he did, she could see a slice of Louisa in him, which gave her the impetus to keep talking.

'I'm curious. What did your teacher do that made you call him – or her – that name?'

'He accused me of stealing money from the charity box. He hated me anyway, probably because I was a pain in the ass, but still, I would never have done that, and I was so angry I couldn't stop myself from mouthing off.'

'And then you went to another school?'

'Yeah, and I had problems keeping my mouth shut there, too.'

'That's hard to believe. I mean, you talking a lot.'

He glanced over at her.

'I guess I haven't been exactly loquacious.'

'Not exactly.' Ellie laughed and was surprised when he did too.

'I'm not very good at small talk.'

Exactly what Daniel had said at the restaurant that night.

She tried to imagine Joe when he was young, running around that huge house, an only child. 'This place was built for big families and I always wanted a big family to fill it,' Louisa had told her. 'Jamie and I both did. But we couldn't have any more children after Joe. We tried to make up for it by inviting tons of people to stay in the summer. It's not the same. But it helped.'

'You know, Louisa's been telling me about her summers here when she was young. Were yours as fun as hers sound?'

'Yeah, they were, actually. We'd come back from California for two weeks every August, and I loved every minute of it. Mum and Dad would invite friends from Boston down, with their kids too, and we had a great time. We'd go out

141

in the boat or go fishing or play games outside when it was sunny, and when it rained we'd play Sardines in a Can in the house.' He drummed his fingers against the steering wheel. Ellie was about to ask another question when he said: 'One time when I was eleven one of the kids my age, a boy named Bert, managed to squeeze himself into the medicine cabinet above the sink in an upstairs bathroom when we were playing Sardines.

'We couldn't find him because no one thought to look there, it was too small. He stayed there for hours before he finally came out and told us where he'd been, and demonstrated how he did it. Whenever I think of that, I wonder whether Bert turned out to be a professional contortionist.'

'I hope so.'

'Why?' He glanced at her again.

'It would be a fun profession. And it would make use of his talents.'

'You're—'

'I'm what?'

He shook his head.

'You can't start a sentence like that and not finish it.'

'You're different. That's all. I guess I'm used to talking to women who inhabit the political world.'

'And what are they like?'

'Different from you.'

Feeling more comfortable with him, Ellie began to talk about Tim and what had happened at Boston Prep, and her worries about how he'd fit in at Bourne High in September.

'Kids are resilient. He'll work it out. If he's being a little

142

tricky now, that's natural. If I were you, I'd worry about him if he weren't. No one wants a goody-goody son.'

'Want to bet?'

'OK.' He shrugged. 'Mothers do.'

'Did Louisa want you to be a goody-goody?'

'Good question. I'm not sure. But I'd say she knew from the start that wasn't going to be the case. So if she did, she adjusted. Besides, I wasn't *that* bad.'

'Just bad enough?'

'Exactly.'

When they reached the cottage driveway, Ellie was disappointed that their time together was ending just as he appeared to be really relaxing.

The car was in park, the engine was still running: she knew she should be getting out, but she hesitated, debating the idea of asking him in for coffee. Just as she decided that would be way too pushy after she'd invited herself to the game, he said: 'Why don't you come over and have a cup of coffee or tea? I don't mean . . .' He paused. 'I mean, it would be nice to talk a little more.'

'Will you show me the medicine chest Bert hid in?'

'Absolutely.' He reversed and drove to the house.

Somewhere between the time Joe asked her to come over and when they went through the front door, he changed his mind and, instead of coffee, suggested they have a glass of wine.

Glasses in hand, they went upstairs and he opened the medicine cupboard above the bathroom sink. Ellie marvelled at any boy, much less an eleven-year-old, fitting in there, and they speculated some more about what Bert had ended up doing.

'He might be a lawyer . . . you know. "You're in a tight spot. I know all about those, I'm your man,"' she suggested.

'Or maybe he manufactures medicine cabinets.'

'Really, really small medicine cabinets.'

Joe laughed.

'If I had to pick a place to hide here,' she said, 'I'd choose that little cupboard in the sewing room, the one built into the wall near the piano.'

'Good choice. I remember someone did hide there once. Not medicine-cabinet level of difficulty, but pretty close.'

They went back downstairs to the living room. Ellie sat on the sofa, Joe on the chair beside the window, at an angle to her.

This was where she'd been sitting when she'd told Louisa about Hope. Yet Joe's presence in the room changed its whole atmosphere. Before, Ellie had thought of it as hers and Louisa's room, which was presumptuous, she knew, but she couldn't help it. In her mind it was a female room and she'd imagined old times in the house when men might have sat at the formal dining-room table next door, smoking cigars after dinner, while the women came into this room to talk.

When she'd asked Louisa if that were the case, she'd answered: 'Formal? *And* sexist? Well, maybe. But not in my lifetime.'

Sitting with his leg up, so that his right ankle rested on his left knee, Joe brought an air of masculinity into the living room. Ellie could now picture him in DC, having political discussions with senators.

'Do you smoke cigars?' she found herself asking.

'No. I hate the smell.'

He didn't continue talking or ask her a question. Feeling awkward again, she looked up at the ceiling. The chandelier above them was made of metal and looked like a hanging plant with small lightbulbs as the flowers, surrounded by bizarrely painted leaves.

'I keep meaning to ask Louisa. That chandelier – the way it's painted all these different colours – it's so unusual. Where did she get it?'

'She and my father and some friends bought it at some big hardware store and decided to paint it one rainy day. Even though my father sold modern art for a living, he had zero artistic talent of his own. That's why it looks like an art project kids did at school. And on that same day, they painted two of the kitchen chairs. You've seen those, right? The one with "Vino" painted in red on the back, and the other one with "Splurge". I haven't asked, but I'd guess they were stoned when they did it.'

'Did you take drugs?'

'I smoked a little weed, that's it. How about you?'

'No. Never. I was afraid of drugs.'

'See that lit-up yacht there going through the Canal?' He pointed out the window and she nodded.

'When I was eighteen, I'd smoked a joint and I went out fishing – right there, where the yacht is. And I suddenly saw this thing moving in the water – a huge grey head, surfacing, disappearing, surfacing again, slowly, in a rhythmic motion, making its way through the Canal. It came within a few feet of my boat – this astoundingly beautiful whale. I thought that the dope must have been much stronger than usual and I was hallucinating, but it turned out it actually was a whale. One that had gotten lost and was trying to find its way out of the Canal and to the ocean. I saw it on the local news later that night.'

'Did it make it? Did it get to the ocean?'

'Yes. I can't tell you how relieved I was. That beautiful fucker escaped.'

'Like the Billington Boy.'

'Jesus!' Joe laughed. His eyes, when he relaxed, widened, taking away the nervy tautness from his face. 'I should have known Mum would tell you that. She adores that story.'

'But she thinks he wasn't lost, that he ran away.'

'I think so too.'

They'd both finished their wine, both of them were still looking out the window at the night traffic of boats cruising through the Canal.

'Come on.' Joe stood up. 'You're making me reminisce about my childhood . . . I want to show you something.' He headed for the door, picking up a flashlight from a side table as he went.

Ellie followed him as he led the way, straight across the driveway and through the stone gate piers to the big garden flanking the beach.

'Are we going to the beach?'

'No. I had my own version of Bert's medicine cabinet. I want to show you.'

Shining the flashlight, he walked to the right, to the flower beds in front of the shrubbery at the edge of the garden.

'Nasturtiums . . . that's what we're looking for. OK.' He pointed the flashlight down. 'There they are. Dinky little orange flowers. I'm hopeless at the whole flower business, but I always remembered that name. Nasty nasturtiums. Here . . .' He swept aside some branches behind the row of nasturtiums, pointed the light inwards, at a hollowed-out space hidden in the bushes.

'This is where I hid when we played Relievo, a game which is a combination of Tag, Sardines, and Hide-and-go-seek. No one ever found me here.' He got down on the ground, crawled inside. 'Come on – there's room enough. Don't worry about the flowers. They'll bounce back. Check it out.'

She did exactly as he had done, and found herself sitting beside him in this strange cave, the flashlight illuminating it like a huge candle.

'Pretty amazing, isn't it? I kicked a soccer ball into the bushes once and stumbled across it and had my eureka moment. I knew it was the perfect place to hide.'

'I feel about ten years old in here.'

'I know. I'm thirty-five, but whenever I come in here, I feel like I'm five again and that's what's real. The rest of the time I'm just playing grown up.'

'I play grown up all the time. I hear myself telling Tim what to do and what not to do, and it's hard not to think: as if *I* know.'

'I can understand that.'

They were both sitting cross-legged and, as Joe adjusted

147

his position to get more comfortable, his knee touched hers. The contact travelled through her entire body, jolting her back to a time when she had felt such desire for Charlie it had made every nerve-ending spark. One second and then his knee was gone, but that feeling of yearning shocked her.

'My wife – Pam – she would have been an amazing mother.'

Ellie almost reached out to touch him then, but stopped herself. She couldn't speak either. It was too big a statement; it carried a weight of such loss, she couldn't bring herself to say something supposedly comforting but actually platitudinous in return.

Louisa, since that day she'd heard Ellie's story, had never said anything like all the stock, useless phrases the shrinks in the hospital had spouted.

What she had said once, as they sat on the deck of the Windsurfer, was: 'Terrible things happen in our lives, Ellie. Jamie shouldn't have had a fatal heart attack when he was fifty-two. Pam shouldn't have had cancer at thirty-one. Hope shouldn't have died when she was six. These terrible things happen and there's no way to get around that fact. But then there are those moments of joy . . . maybe just tiny moments, but those moments stack up. Whoever said "*carpe diem*" was wrong. You don't seize the day, you seize those moments. And hang on to them with all your strength.'

As Joe and Ellie sat in silence, the flashlight began to flicker.

'Uh-oh, looks like the battery's dying,' he said. 'Time to get out of here.'

'Right.'

They crawled back out, brushed themselves off.

'Let's go up and sit on the wall for a while,' he suggested. 'Unless you want to go back now?'

'No, I'd like that.'

Climbing the hill back towards the house, they went over to the wall where Louisa had been when Ellie asked her if they could go inside that day. Joe sat down and Ellie joined him. Half a moon was alight above them, while the noise of a freight boat chugging its way across the Canal slid across the water. Ellie could see the lights of houses on the other side of the Canal.

The further east you travelled down the Cape Cod Highway, the more wild the scenery became. Most people preferred the long beaches and sand dunes of places like Wellfleet, she knew, but she preferred this interplay of nature and civilisation. Seeing the lights reflecting on the water, watching the boats, she felt connected to other people and to the elements, all at the same time.

'It's high tide now,' Joe said. 'So you can't see it, but just beneath us here is a big stone slab. I don't know why it's there, but it used to be another special place for me. It's funny how kids find their own little sanctuaries. I'd come here at low tide and sit on it and think. God knows what was running through my head back then, but I could spend hours on that slab.'

'I grew up in New York City. There weren't any little sanctuaries there. At least, not that I could find.'

'That's a shame.'

'I never thought about it, but you're right. I hope Tim has some special places.'

149

'I hope so to.' Leaning back, Joe plucked some grass, put a blade of it in his mouth. 'I love chewing grass. Maybe I was a cow in a former life.'

'Have you noticed that most people who talk about their former lives say they were princesses in Arabia or Viking chiefs? I've never met anyone who thought he or she was a cow.'

'Hey – don't diss cows.'

'Sorry.' She put her hands in the air. 'Never again.'

They lapsed into silence as Ellie glanced over at the Railroad Bridge on the right. Whoever operated it must be off duty now. In a bar, having fun. Asleep in bed.

'When it's so calm and placid like this at night,' Joe said, drawing one knee up against his chest, 'it's mournful. If the wind is howling or the rain is pelting down or it's fogged-in, it feels to me as if nature is actually busy, doing something. But on a night like this it's empty. Sad.'

'But on a night like this you can hear everything so clearly. The crickets, the sound of boat motors, the buoys . . . everything. It's not empty. If whoever is piloting that boat that just passed through had been singing, we would have heard every word. So nature is still busy – amplifying.'

'Amplifying?' Joe laughed.

'You know what I mean.'

'I wish that boat pilot had been singing.'

'Can you sing?'

'Not a note.'

'Neither can I.'

Again, she wanted to reach out and touch him. So she stood up.

'I should get back.'

'Right.' Throwing the blade of grass away, Joe stood too. 'I'll walk you there.'

'Thanks.'

As they wandered down the road, Ellie was searching the stars for the Big Dipper, trying to concentrate so she wouldn't keep thinking of that need for physical contact.

'Look at them – the stars are so bright they're like the floodlights at the baseball park, lighting up the game we're all playing down here.' She breathed in deeply, loving the smell of the salt in the air. 'I wonder what the teams are. I wonder who's winning.'

Joe stopped.

'You know, you're really . . .'

'I'm really what? You've done it again. You have to finish that sentence.'

'Nothing.' He shook his head, resumed walking.

'Joe?'

'Nothing.'

They'd reached her door.

'That's great. Nothing.'

What was she doing? Fishing for a compliment? No. Because she had absolutely no idea what he was thinking. He could have easily finished that sentence with: 'you're really idiotic'. The force of her need to know what was going on in his head scared her.

'Ellie.' His back was resting against the cottage door. His hands were in his pockets. 'You know how sometimes people do the right thing? What I mean is, most people try to do the right thing, but they can get it really wrong. Back when we were sitting in that hiding place, when I said Pam would have been a great mother – most people would have said something or asked me about her, but you didn't. Thank you.'

She nodded, looking up at his face, thinking how much its expression had changed.

'What is it? What makes you so different?' He pulled his hand from his pocket, put it on her elbow.

'I'm not different.'

Her elbow now felt like the centre of her body.

'Ellie. What's going on here?'

'I don't know.'

'Neither do I.'

His hand left her elbow. It was on her shoulder.

'Do we have to know?'

'No.' She whispered it.

His hand moved to the back of her neck. He drew her face forward, kissed her, lightly, pulled back, but only for a second before pulling her close and kissing her again, this time with a strength and passion which she matched, until they were kissing with a kind of fury, Ellie feeling every pent-up part of her body letting go.

That release, the unconsciousness of desire, the way it swept away all thoughts, was like a drug to her. For so long now she'd been attempting to deny so much and then attempting to make sense of what she couldn't deny. But this was like a wind, clearing her brain, driving everything before it. Nothing else mattered. Only her body. And his.

Somehow she managed to be the contortionist, digging

into her pocket, getting her keys out, opening the door, all as the kiss continued, and they were backing into the living room, entwined, still kissing, making their way to her room, falling on the bed. Both of them refusing to end the kiss, as if knowing that if it ended, so would everything else; staying locked together as he unzipped his jeans and she unzipped hers and they both wriggled out of them, making love with the same intensity as this crazy endless kiss.

Until she felt him come, felt his body stiffen, but most of all felt the absence of his mouth on hers.

'Joe?'

He'd rolled off her, was lying with his elbow covering his eyes.

What was the 'right thing' to do now? She couldn't see his eyes, but his mouth was hard, set in a straight line.

'Joe?' she asked again, suddenly afraid to touch him.

'This is so wrong.'

He sat up, then got off the bed and started rummaging for his jeans and boxer shorts while she sat up as well, watching him as he dressed.

'Joe . . .'

'I shouldn't be here. You shouldn't be here. It's wrong.'

He walked out of the room. Without looking back.

23 July

A glass of orange juice and a cup of coffee sat on the table in front of Ellie. She knew she should eat something but she wasn't hungry. The word 'wrong' was revolving around her brain on a ticker tape. What had seemed so natural was wrong. The first time in seventeen years she'd had sex with a man other than Charlie had been wrong. Joe had walked out without even saying goodbye. Wrong.

She'd wanted a normal night out. Instead she'd ended up in bed with a virtual stranger. Wrong, wrong, wrong.

Reaching out for her coffee, she cradled the mug in her hands.

How had it happened?

Going over the night again, she tried to think how it could have been different, at what point it had become almost inevitable, how they might have stopped before it reached that point.

It took us both by surprise. Neither of us was thinking straight.

But I wanted him so badly.

And at the end, all he wanted was out.

She'd been dreading it, and when it happened, when she heard the knock on her door, she rose slowly, the mug in her hand, walking hesitantly, knowing this would be Joe, coming to tell her again how wrong they'd been. It would be awkward and awful, but this scene was inevitable too, she knew. Two people apologising to each other for becoming intimate. With the embarrassing kicker that one of those people wished the intimacy had been real and not just a moment of physical lust triumphing over sense.

'Ellie,' he said when she opened the door. She wasn't surprised that his face was set in that same rigid expression as it had been when he'd rolled off her.

'Joe, come in.'

'No, I can't. I have to catch a plane back to DC. I just wanted to say I'm sorry for walking out like that.'

'It's all right. I understand.'

This had been his and Pam's cottage. God only knew what emotions he was dealing with right now.

'Listen.' He rubbed his forehead. 'We should forget last night. What I mean is, we should try to treat it as if it never happened.'

'As if it never happened. Right.'

'It will be better that way.'

'Right.'

'OK.'

'OK.'

'I'll go now.'

'OK.'

He turned, walked away to his car. She shut the door, stood staring at it.

The awkward, awful scene was over.

So why had this feeling of misery enveloped her?

Because she'd retained that tiny little bit of hope that he would come in, sit down, talk to her. Tell her what he was feeling. And listen while she told him what she was feeling too.

Because 'it never happened' were the worst possible words he could have come up with to dismiss her.

11

Lauren's house was one of those newly built ones. All open-plan and full of shiny gadgets. It was all right in its own way. Not like Louisa's, for sure – but then Tim had never seen a house like Louisa's. Lauren's place was on the side of the road going to Pocasset and it didn't have any view of the water, but it had Lauren. Sitting in a big armchair, her legs slung over the side, while he sat on a stool at the kitchen counter.

She'd texted him, saying she'd got his number from Sam, and asking if he wanted to come to her place after school – Sam could drop him off. He'd been trying to think of a way to see her again for weeks. Of course he wanted to go – was she joking? But he had texted back only one word: 'Sure'.

They had been talking about divorce, which was kind of weird because it was interesting. He never would have thought that was possible before, but Lauren had a take on things that made him think differently.

'Tell me you're not one of those lamebrains who want their parents to get back together?' she'd said after she'd opened the door to him, ushered him inside and explained that this was her mother's house – her parents had been divorced for

156

three years; and he'd told her his had been divorced for almost two.

'As if,' he'd replied, thinking: That's exactly what I want. Or at least, I *thought* it was what I wanted.

'Whew! I don't get those idiots. I mean, do they live in Disneyworld? It's not as if people didn't get divorced for a reason, right? So these kids think that reason is suddenly going to disappear? They want to live with two people who don't love each other and listen to them rip each other up? I'll take step-monsters any day over that. Listen, I could do a stand-up comic act on the subject of my parents' fights. But, believe me, it wasn't funny actually listening to them.'

'My parents didn't fight. My dad had an affair and left. My mom and dad spun this whole story about how they'd grown apart, but it was because my dad went off with this woman Sandra.'

'Yeah, well, think about it. If he came back, he'd just have another affair and then you'd have to go through that whole crap all over again. Coke?'

He nodded.

She'd walked over to the fridge, taken two Cokes out and tossed him one. She was wearing her cut-off jeans again, and a black T-shirt with the words 'No, I Can't' on it. Her legs were tan, she was wearing bright pink lipstick and little star-shaped earrings.

He wanted to go over, take the Coke can out of her hand and kiss her. He wanted to figure her out.

'And you're an only child too, right?' she asked, strolling over to the chair, flinging herself back into it, draping her

157

legs over the side. Looking around for a place to sit, he'd chosen a seat the counter. A safe distance away. Possibly, in her head, a cool choice.

'Right.' Tim popped his Coke.

'Sucks, doesn't it? No one to talk to about how crazy your parents are. I mean, no one who really gets it.'

'I never thought about it that way.'

'And no one to tease, either.'

'But you can only tease a brother or sister if you're older than they are. Think about being the youngest child in a big family. You'd be teased more than the biggest geek in school.'

'True.' Lauren laughed. 'So what made you move here anyway? Why did Michelangelo leave Boston?'

'My mother has a thing about Bourne.' He swung round on his stool, took a sip of the Coke. 'And I flunked out of school last year. They wanted me to repeat a grade.'

'Hence summer school.'

'Hence?'

'I like the word.' She shrugged.

Tim told her Joe's story about being kicked out of school and the party his parents gave him, basking in the way she was reacting: the same way he had when he'd first heard it.

'That is so, so wicked! I want to meet these people.'

'I'll take you over there. They live in that house . . . you know, the one I drew in the sand, the one you love.'

'No shit!'

'Yes shit.'

'Oh, no.' She leaped off the chair. 'That's my mother's car driving in. She's back early. Look, just be polite, OK?

158

Stand up when she comes in, shake her hand firmly and look her in the eye – all that crap – and then you can get out. If you stay she'll question you as if you were a suspected terrorist. But I'll call you later, OK?'

'OK.'

When Lauren's mother walked in, Tim did exactly what he'd been told to do – stood up, shook her hand firmly, looked her in the eye – and then said he had to go.

'It was very nice to meet you, Tim,' she said. 'You're a polite young man. I hope I see you again soon.'

Lauren and he exchanged a look and Tim left, thinking it was probably a twenty-minute or so walk back. Twenty minutes when he could replay that whole time with her in his head. Maybe he'd walk slowly, give himself more time to go over it all.

Lauren's mother looked a little like her, except with brown hair and without that sharp, intelligent nose. She was pretty old, but he should be used to that by now. Almost all his friends' mothers were older than his mom; some of them were even almost fifty.

He could never decide whether having a young mother was a good or a bad thing. Sometimes people thought his mother was his sister, which really sucked, but it was nice on Mother's Day at school, when his mom always looked the best of any of them.

She had been acting a little weirdly for the past weeks. First she'd been all quiet and tired and not cooking or anything, and he was worried she might be sick. But now she was better, doing her normal stuff. Only spending much more time than usual on her computer. When he'd asked her what that was all about, she'd told him she had a kind of pen pal who lived in London and that she was writing him emails.

'His name's Daniel,' she'd told him. 'And he's a cancer doctor, an oncologist.'

'How'd you meet him?' Tim asked

'He used to live in Boston. He's a friend of Debby's,' she'd said. And then she'd blushed.

So she liked this guy.

But that was all right. He lived in London. He wasn't going to be showing up and moving in like that shit-for-brains Sandra. Although Tim hadn't seen her lately, which was a major bonus.

What was he doing thinking about all this when what he really wanted to think about was the way Lauren had been sitting, how she laughed at what he'd said, that look they'd exchanged at the end?

And, better than everything, the fact she'd invited him over in the first place. That had to mean she liked him.

Didn't it?

It wasn't raining but the air was wet, hot and cloying. Ellie had decided not to have an air conditioner in the cottage, but on a day like this she found herself reconsidering. She'd already sent him an email, but that was one of the boring details she would have been able to share with Daniel. For a second she wondered whether she could write another one, a one-liner saying: 'Air conditioner/no air conditioner – what's your stance?' then decided that was ridiculous. Sometimes she forgot he was a doctor, had a hectic life, wouldn't appreciate one-line unnecessary communications. Although, strictly speaking, all their emails were unneccessary.

Daniel Litman had morphed from an online date sitting across the table from her at Acquitaine to an online correspondent with whom she shared huge chunks of her life. He was beginning to know as much about her as Louisa did, although she hadn't told him about the accident. She couldn't bring herself to. Not yet. But she was close.

And, yes, this was the modern way to communicate, but increasingly she found herself thinking it was actually an old-fashioned way to get to know someone well.

She'd done modern and failed: how well had she really known Charlie before she married him? And how much did sex interfere with that getting-to-know you process?

A lot, she decided. Sex was a shortcut, negating the slow road to intimacy – that build-up of mutual knowledge you could gain when you weren't obsessing about figuring out the next time you could get each other into bed.

Or sex was a shortcut to a cul-de-sac, as it had been with Joe: a one-night stand leading straight into a brick wall.

Maybe modern dating worked for other women, but it didn't for Ellie. These emails worked for her. This was what real intimacy was about. She could talk to him without worrying what she looked like or what she was wearing. They could trade little details about their past and present lives, and feelings from the heart, too. They had even gotten to the stage where she had felt all right telling him a brief version of her night with Joe a few days after it happened.

Not too much information, but enough to say she'd felt a connection with him, they'd become close, but then he'd shut down. She couldn't tell whether he'd read between the lines and realise she'd slept with Joe.

I know I should feel strange talking to you about another man, but our relationship is different, isn't it? I can tell you I feel hurt and disappointed and sad because you and I aren't involved in that way. I want you to tell me about the women in your life, too. I don't mean I want you to say anything you don't think is appropriate, you know that. But I want you to be able to confide in me the way I've confided in you. I've told you before, I can be totally open with Louisa – but not about Joe, obviously. I hope you don't mind me telling you about him.

I'm sorry it didn't work out with Joe, Ellie, was part of his reply. *I'm sorry you feel hurt. And of course I want you to tell me about it. I have nothing to tell you on that front, I'm afraid. But I'll let you know if I do.*

She was relieved he didn't have a girlfriend, and she was disappointed in herself about that because she wanted Daniel to have a new, happy life too. Yet she knew if he became seriously involved with anyone – if either of them did – the correspondence would inevitably dwindle and die down.

These emails had become precious to her. She didn't want them to stop.

'Hey,' Tim said as he walked through the door. 'At the computer again, Mom? What's your pen pal saying now?'

'He just told me all about a soccer game he'd been to.'

'Yeah, they take it seriously over there.' Tim put some

envelopes down on the table, flopped in front of the sofa and picked up the remote. 'Hence all those hooligans and stuff.'

'Hence?'

'I like the word.' He shrugged and she smiled, turning off her laptop.

'Thanks for picking up the mail. Did Sam's father drop you at the end of the road?'

'He dropped me off at a friend's and I walked from there.'

'That was nice of him.' Ellie went over to the table, picked up the envelopes, thumbed through them, thinking about Jamie Amory's refusal to open mail. These were all bills, too. Except for the last one. Her name and address were typewritten on the front but she could see it was some form of letter. Opening it, she pulled out a sheet of paper. A few typewrittien paragraphs and then 'Joe' scrawled in black ink at the bottom.

Leaving Tim to watch his TV show, she went into the kitchen, sat down and read.

Ellie,

I need to make a few things clear. I'm worried that you have read too much into what happened between us. You should know there's someone else in my life here. We've been together for only a month or so but I think we have a real future. I'm sorry if I led you on, and I understand how difficult it must be for you on your own, not to mention your friendship with my mother and all the stumbling blocks that sets up in terms of a clean break between us.

*I think it would be for the best if we steered clear of
each other from now on. It would be a hell of a lot easier
than awkward meetings.*

*Again, I apologise for any way in which I may have
misled you. And I hope you have a very happy and
productive future.*

Joe

She read it again.

*I'm worried that you have read too much into what happened
between us?*

I'm sorry if I led you on?

I understand how difficult it must be for you on your own?

A very happy and productive future?

How much more patronising could he have been?

She'd accepted that gruesome meeting, the 'let's pretend
this never happened', because she'd thought he must have
been reeling with guilt and grief about Pam. But this? The
tone of it was galling.

She hadn't tried to contact him since the morning he'd
left. And yet he assumed she was pining away for him, that
she'd 'read too much into it'. And he was involved with
someone else yet had never mentioned it to her, hadn't taken
any responsibility or shown any guilt in this letter for cheating
on this other woman, whoever she was? Talk about an ego
like an albatross.

Fine. If that's the way you want it, Joe, fine.

Louisa would be appalled by this. But you figured I wouldn't tell her, and you're right. No way would I want to hurt her. She worships you, she's your mother. I won't rat you out. And, believe me, I will absolutely steer clear of you whenever you come here again.

Jesus! I never would have thought you could be such an asshole.

Nice work, Ellie. The first man you have sex with after Charlie thinks the world revolves around him. Way to go.

'Mom, come look at this.'

Picking up the sheets of paper, Ellie ripped them in half, ripped both those halves in half, threw them in the trash can under the sink and went into the living room.

'What?'

'Look – it's the news. And it's all about Senator Harvey – Joe's guy. He's been messing around with little boys. Can you believe it? Joe must be going mental.'

Ellie sat down and watched.

Senator Brad Harvey was a paedophile. Joe *must* be going mental. Ten minutes ago she would have called Louisa and gone over there to commiserate. Now, if she were to do that, Ellie knew she wouldn't sound as sympathetic as she should. She didn't believe Joe knew about his boss – he was an asshole, not a monster. But she was too angry to be sincere about any sympathising she did.

Not only had Joe treated her like some lovesick puppy, the single woman on her own who couldn't control her own emotions, he'd effectively driven a wedge between her and Louisa. And made her keep yet another secret.

Rewind the tape and don't ask yourself to that baseball game. You can never rewind the tape.

12

When Lauren and Tim walked into the kitchen, Louisa felt her heart light up. They were so young and so aware of each other. Everything was in front of them. Tim, she knew, wished he could have the guts to hold the girl's hand. And Lauren, she knew, wished he had the guts to too, but they were keeping their distance, sitting down across the table from each other, while she sat at the end, trying not to smile too much.

'Did you like the tour?' she asked Lauren – whom she'd liked from the second she'd met her at the door. The girl had a little edge to her, Louisa could sense. And something about her eyes made Louisa think she was shrewd, too.

'I loved it.' Lauren was sitting in the 'Splurge' chair, Tim in the 'Vino'. 'This house is like a person. One of those people it takes you forever to get to know.'

'Lauren plays the piano really well. She played a little on the one upstairs,' Tim put in.

'Fantastic. I'll have to get it tuned. I should have done that a long time ago.'

'I don't know, sometimes it's fun to play on out-of-tune

166

pianos. You get all these crazy notes. Wow – blueberry muffins! Can I have one?'

'That's what they're here for.' Louisa passed Lauren the plate. 'Betty Crocker blueberry muffin mix. It never fails.'

'That must be driving you crazy.' Lauren took a muffin, nodded towards the copy of the *New York Times* Louisa had beside her. 'All that stuff about Senator Harvey. Tim told me your son works for him.'

'Used to work for him,' Louisa sighed. 'Joe's so angry. He can't believe he didn't know.'

'How would he know? A secret's a secret, right? Harvey was obviously good at keeping it. His wife didn't even know.'

'That's exactly what I said to Joe. You know, at times like this, I miss the old days. When I was your age, we all believed in peace and love and flower power. And for a while there, we thought we could pull it off, change the world. But it didn't happen and we're still living in a world with despicable politicians and wars we can't win. Wars we shouldn't be in. Nothing's changed.'

'At least you tried,' Tim stated. 'Now all anyone cares about is their grade point average and what college they're going to go to and what job they're going to get.'

'Yes, we tried. But we ended up selling out en masse too. Anyway, this is too depressing a subject. What I want to know is how you two met.'

'On the beach at Mashnee.' Lauren raised her eyebrows. 'It was a set up. Friends from school.' She shrugged. 'Boring, I know.'

'No, it's not boring. That's how I met Jamie, my husband.

We were all going to a party and some friends of mine arranged for him to pick me up and drive me there.'

'And . . .?' Lauren leaned forward. 'Come on, spill the details.'

'OK.' Louisa laughed. 'He arrived and picked me up and he had a VW Beetle and he was probably the worst driver I've ever encountered. He stripped the gears almost every time he shifted them. But then there was this moment . . . We were driving along, listening to the radio; he turned up the volume, and it was a song I liked, too – and then he said: "Hold on to the wheel and drive for me, will you? I'm boiling." And I took hold of the steering wheel and drove while he pulled his sweater over his head. And that was it. At that precise moment I knew I was along for the ride, then. The whole ride.'

'I love that. That's so romantic. That moment when you, like, *know*.' Lauren glanced at Tim, who smiled the kind of smile that made Louisa want to hug him.

Young love, she thought. *Unbeatable*.

They finished the muffins on the plate as they talked about school. Louisa noticed how they were mirroring each other's way of talking, supporting each other's point of view, laughing at each other's jokes. And yet not in a mushy way. They were well matched, she could tell.

At least something was going right for someone.

When they left, they said they were going to walk over to Mashnee the short way, skirting the shoreline instead of taking the road. Standing on her porch watching them, she saw Tim take Lauren's hand and help her over some rocks. When he didn't let it go, Louisa allowed herself a quiet 'Yes!' and pumped her fist.

Being on each other's team – that was her definition of love and friendship. You can squabble, you can fight, get annoyed, get angry, but if you know you're on each other's team in life, you'll be all right.

She wished Joe had more people on his team. His world had collapsed with the revelations about Harvey and he'd been furious and at a loss. The first few days after the news had broken, he'd been hounded by the media. When Louisa had suggested he come back to Bourne to get a break, he'd wavered, but she'd pushed hard and finally he'd given in.

The first couple of days after he'd arrived, he'd stayed in his bedroom, reading.

'I feel like I need to detox,' he'd told her. 'So I'm reading Jane Austen. Interestingly enough, there are no paedophiles in *Sense and Sensibility*.'

During the day he'd read; at night they'd have dinner together and talk. But as much as she loved having him here for more than a weekend, Louisa hated the circumstances which had made that happen.

'Politics is all I know, Mum,' he'd told her on Wednesday evening as they ate a seafood chowder she'd made. 'At this precise moment I hate it, but it's what I do. I'm going to go to Boston for a couple of nights tomorrow, look up some contacts, see what's going on. Whether anyone will still speak to me.'

'Of course they will, Joe. They know you weren't involved in this.'

'Yes, but I was close to Brad Harvey. Shit – I still can't believe it. How did I not know?'

'Because he was good at keeping secrets.'

Now, hearing the sound of a car, Louisa turned, saw him drive up to the house, went down the steps to greet him.

'How was Boston?' she asked when Joe got out.

'Not as bad as I thought.' He collected his bag. 'I have a few interviews next week.'

'That's fantastic. Come on in. I have some blueberry muffins left over. Tim and his new girlfriend were just here. Come in and we'll talk.'

'Later, Mum, OK? I want to take a swim, clear my brain.'

'OK. I think I'll go over to Ellie's then. Why don't you come by after your swim?'

'No, thanks. I need to get working on my resumé.'

'Joe, it will be all right. I know it will.'

'Not for those young boys, Mum. It will never be all right for them.'

He trudged up the steps and Louisa set off towards the cottage.

How many people had known about Senator Harvey and kept their mouths shut?

How easy had it been for him to live a secret life?

It hadn't been easy for Ellie, she knew. The truth had been like that sci-fi creature, the Alien, burrowing inside her, waiting to leap out of her chest.

Wrapped up in Joe's problems, Louisa hadn't seen Ellie lately as much as she usually did. On Tuesday she'd thought it might be a good idea to invite her and Tim over for dinner, but as soon as she'd mentioned it to Joe, he'd nixed it.

'You should meet her, Joe. And you could use some distraction.'

'I met her when you were at Joanna's in Boston that weekend and I was here by myself,' he replied. 'You're right – she's nice. But I don't feel like seeing anyone now. I'm all talked out and Brad Harvey would be the elephant in the corner no one dares mention. Leave it, all right?'

'Fine.'

Ellie hadn't mentioned meeting Joe, which was strange, but it had probably just been a perfunctory 'hello'.

Ellie needs people on her team, too, Louisa thought. *Joe and she could use each other's friendship right now. But I can't push them together. That's a bad mother move. It never works.*

About fifteen feet away from the cottage, Louisa stopped. Took a few steps forward, stopped again.

What the hell?

It couldn't be.

But it was.

She started to run, knowing she had to get to it and get rid of it before Ellie saw it.

Just as she reached it and picked it up off the lawn, she heard the sound of the cottage door opening.

Panicked, Louisa dropped it.

A little pink bicycle with blue streamers on the handle-bars.

She could hear Louisa saying: 'Ellie, go back in the cottage,' but she couldn't move. It was lying on the ground, the handle-bars turned to one side, the blue streamers splayed out on the grass. In exactly the same position it had been in on that street in New Rochelle.

Louisa picked it up.

'I'll get it out of here. Get back in the cottage.'

Ellie couldn't take her eyes off it.

Hope's bicycle.

Louisa dropped it again, came towards her.

'Are you all right? Ellie?'

'It's Hope's . . .'

'No, it's not. It can't be.'

'But it is. Look at it.' She couldn't move. The bicycle was ten feet in front of her, and she couldn't move towards it and she couldn't move away from it.

'I know it looks like hers but . . .'

'Wait! There's no basket on the front. There was a little wicker basket on the front. What happened to it?'

'Listen to me.' Louisa put her hand on Ellie's arm. 'This isn't the same bicycle.'

'Was there a basket? I remember a basket. But maybe I don't . . .'

'You're in shock. Come inside with me. You need to sit down.'

'No.' Ellie shook her head. 'Wait . . . I can't remember. I can't remember if there was a basket. Was there a basket?'

'I don't know, sweetheart. Come inside.' She tried to move Ellie back towards the cottage, but Ellie still wouldn't budge.

'It was all smashed up . . . the front wheel. Who fixed it?'

'It's new, Ellie. This isn't the same bike.'

'Wait! I don't know . . .' She closed her eyes. 'There was this . . . the sun flashed off something silvery. Before I fainted, I saw the sun bounce off this silvery . . . bell. It had a bell.' Opening her eyes she took a step closer. 'There's no bell.'

'You need to come with me.' Louisa had her arm around her now, was shepherding her back into the cottage. 'Sit down.'

She sat. Her eyes were squinting, her brain was trying to put thoughts together, but the thoughts kept colliding against each other.

'I don't understand.'

'Neither do I,' Louisa said. 'This is horrible. Just horrible.'

'If it's not her bike . . . whose is it?' Ellie turned, stared at her. 'Whose bicycle is it?'

'I don't know. Someone must have put it there.'

'But why?'

'I have no idea. Let me get you something to drink.'

'No, don't go. Who would . . . It couldn't be somebody . . . I mean, could some little girl have ridden here and then . . . But where is she? Where is she, Louisa? What if she's hurt? We have to find her.'

'I don't think anyone rode it here. I think someone put it here on purpose to upset you.'

'But why?'

'I wish I knew.'

'I didn't mean to hurt her.' She reached out, grabbed Louisa's wrist. 'I swear to God, I never meant to hurt her.'

'I know. It was an accident, sweetheart. I know that.'

'I don't understand.' Ellie pressed her hands against her face.

'I'm going to get you some water. I'll be right back, I promise.'

She didn't protest. She couldn't think. Her brain felt empty, as if someone had shovelled every thought out.

'Here. Have a sip.' Louisa was back, holding out a glass of water to her. Ellie took a sip, handed it back.

'I think we should call the police. That bicycle . . . and this place broken into . . . and the beach. It may all be connected, Ellie.'

'Connected to what?'

'That's what we have to find out. And the police could help.'

'How?'

'Maybe there are fingerprints on the bike. Damn – I shouldn't have picked it up.'

'Fingerprints? Some criminal put it there?'

'No, maybe not a criminal, but . . . the same person who trashed this place and the beach. The one who left the note on the milk carton.'

'The note?'

Think. Make your brain work.

She made herself sit up straighter.

Think. Focus.

'The note. Wait . . . Whoever wrote that note put the bicycle there? But then . . . it doesn't make sense, Louisa. If it's connected . . . how could it be? No one knows about Hope. Only you and my mother. So no one would know about the bicycle. It doesn't make sense.'

'Could you possibly have told anyone else and forgotten?'

'No.'

'OK, I need to think. Let me get a quick cup of coffee. I'll be right back.'

Ellie tried to think too but she kept seeing the bicycle lying there. The little pink bicycle with blue streamers.

'All right, I have my caffeine now.' Louisa sat back down beside her. 'And it occurred to me in the kitchen . . . was the accident reported in the newspaper?'

'What?'

'The accident. Was it reported in the newspaper?'

'I'm sure now, it had a wicker basket on the front . . .'

'Ellie!' Louisa snapped her fingers in front of her and Ellie's head jerked back. 'Tell me. Was the accident reported in a newspaper?'

'I don't know . . . I think . . . wait. Yes. My mother told me it was in the local newspaper – one in New Rochelle. Her hairdresser told her that. But it was only one paragraph. "Don't worry," she told me. "No one we know will read it and it's only one paragraph." As if it mattered whether anyone we knew . . .' The image of the bicycle had receded. Ellie could think more clearly now. 'That was before I went to the hospital.'

'The hospital. Your doctors there knew, obviously.'

'My doctors? They asked stupid questions and said stupid things. Why would a shrink do this? I'm sure they forgot all about me the second I left.'

'But there was also Dr Emmanuel.'

'He's a hypnotherapist, Louisa. He worked helping war victims in Serbo-Croatia. He's not going to leave some "Got

175

you" note and throw clothes around a living room and stomp on seagulls.'

'I know, I know. I'm sorry. I'm trying out all the possibilities, that's all. Anyone who knew what happened.'

'I'm sorry too. I didn't mean to snap at you. It's just this is . . . it doesn't make sense. None of it.'

Ellie reached out, took the glass of water again and had another sip.

'Someone must really hate me,' she said finally.

'Someone wants to scare the hell out of you.'

'Do they want to scare me or do they want something else?'

'What do you mean?'

'Maybe they want me to pay. I've never paid for what I did, not really.'

'Ellie, it was an accident. And you were in a psychiatric ward for six months. You paid.'

'I'm alive. I went to college. I got married, had Tim. Hope never got to do any of that. She didn't get to fall in love. She didn't even get out of first grade.'

They were both silent for a while.

'Can you imagine,' Ellie finally said, 'if that happened to your child? When I think about Tim . . .'

'Don't, Ellie. It doesn't help.'

'I can't *not* think about it. Hope's parents must think about it every single day. And I never went to see them. I was so full of guilt and shame, I couldn't do it.'

'I'm not sure seeing you would have helped them.'

'It was so cowardly of me. I was afraid of what they'd say,

what they looked like even. I couldn't face them. I couldn't face myself.'

'Her parents . . .' Louisa started to slide the bracelets up and down her arm. 'They live in New Rochelle?'

'They did, but they moved. My mother's hairdresser told her that too. She was the local gossip and, you know, my mother kept going to her. I don't understand that. I never will. I don't know how she could go near that place again.'

'Where did they move?'

'To Newton. I remember because my mother said, "Newton . . . new town. That's good. They can start a new family too." As if Hope were a dog and all they had to do was go out and get a new puppy. I guess my mother was in denial too. In a different way. But still.'

'Newton, Massachusetts?'

'Yes.' Ellie looked at Louisa, saw what had just hit her reflected in her eyes. 'Oh my God.'

Did it make any sense? Nineteeen years later, had Hope's parents decided to do these things? Why now? And what was their purpose? To scare her? To make her suffer?

She and Louisa had discussed it all for a half an hour, but their conversation kept going around in circles, always ending up in the same place: why would someone do this? Could it be the Davises?

'I need some air,' Ellie had said finally. 'I want to go to the beach.'

'I'll come with you.'

'No – thanks, but you've done enough. I can't believe

you've had to go through all this again with me. I'm really sorry, Louisa.'

'This isn't your fault.'

'Could you take the bicycle away? Put it somewhere?'

'Yes, of course. Are you sure you want to be alone?'

'Yes.'

'I'll come over later and check on you.'

'Thanks. For everything.'

They left the cottage; Ellie locked the door, headed for the beach, keeping her eyes averted from the bicycle. When she got there, she took off her sandals, rolled up her jeans, walked down to the water. There was a jagged line of seaweed skirting the shoreline. She picked up strands of it, carried them up the beach, put them in a pile, went back, picked up more.

She didn't know what Hope's mother looked like: she'd heard her screaming, but she hadn't seen her, or if she had, she'd erased it from her memory. Someone had picked her up when she'd fainted, carried her to the other side of the road. When had the ambulance come? She couldn't remember. There was so much she couldn't remember. The police questioning her later: she remembered that. How she'd answered the questions, feeling as if she were in another world, some foreign place where her voice was robotic, where she felt as if she were looking down on herself, in a surreal dream.

Her mother must have driven her back to Manhattan but that trip was a blank too. 'Lie down, darling,' her mother had said when they'd arrived home. 'You need to rest.'

When she'd said that, she hadn't expected Ellie to lie

down and not get up. Or that Ellie would refuse to eat, refuse to have her sheets changed, sleep and sleep and sleep.

How long had it been, how much weight had she lost, before her mother called in doctors? She didn't know, had never asked.

'*You were in a psychiatric ward for six months. You paid.*'

'No,' she should have told Louisa. 'I hid. That's all I did. I spent my time trying to replay that day and have it turn out differently. I spent my time asleep, I talked to psychiatrists, and I finally found another way to hide – by trying to deny it had ever happened.'

Another girl could have gone to Mr and Mrs Davis, apologised. Faced them, acknowledged her part in their tragedy. Had the courage to do all that.

Bending down, she picked up the final bit of seaweed, took it to the pile she'd made, placed it on top. She walked back to the shoreline, sat down at the edge. The tide was coming in, lapping at her toes.

'Ellie?'

She turned her head, saw Louisa walking up behind her.

'Ellie – you're soaking. How long have you been sitting here?'

'I don't know.'

'Come on.' Louisa was at her side, holding out her hand. 'Get up. Get out of the water.'

She took Louisa's hand, stood. Her jeans were wet up to her thighs.

'I've decided I'm going to try to find Mr and Mrs Davis,'

179

she said. 'Maybe they've done these things and maybe they haven't, but I have to see them.'

'I'm not sure they'll want to see you, Ellie.'

'Tell me something. If it had been Joe, if he'd been involved in an accident like I was, wouldn't you think he should face the parents?'

Louisa inhaled deeply, blew the breath out.

'Yes. I would have gone with him, of course, but . . . yes.'

'So you see what I'm saying?'

'But nineteen years later? Wouldn't that be—?'

'It's better than never facing them at all – it has to be. They deserve an apology from me, Louisa. For Christ's sakes, talk about disrespect.'

Louisa put her arm around Ellie's shoulder, began to walk with her back to the cottage.

'If you do find them, I'll come with you.'

'No. Thank you, but I need to do this on my own. It's important.'

'It's going to be brutal, sweetheart, you know that.'

They kept walking, reached the door of the cottage.

'I still think you should call the police.'

'Louisa.' Ellie stopped, looked straight into her eyes. 'Clothes and things thrown around a living room, trash on a beach, a bicycle on the lawn – the police wouldn't take this seriously. They'd think I was crazy. It's not as if I haven't been crazy before.' She let out a shaky laugh. 'What's important to me now is doing what I should have done all those years ago. I can't deal with anything else until I deal with that.'

13

She'd parked the car across the street from the house. She knew she had to get out, cross the street and knock on the door, but she stayed in the driver's seat.

She'd gone to the Bourne Library, found their entry listed in the telephone directory that covered the Newton area. Davis, Sanders. Sanders was the kind of first name you didn't forget. It jumped out at Ellie from the page and she'd sat back, thinking: what am I doing? Do I call them now? If I do and they hang up on me . . .

Copying the adress and number down, she then drove back to the cottage. And sat still.

Was it crazy to go see them?

How would they feel if she showed up at their door?

But what if they thought she didn't care about what had happened? A teenage girl who'd swanned off after the accident, never apologised, never even thought about what they were going through. Was that the way they saw her?

Did it matter how they felt about her? Was she being selfish if she went? Hoping they'd hate her less?

What would you want, Ellie? If you were them?

It was a horrible question to ask herself, but she had to.

I'd want the girl who'd been driving that car to come to me and apologise. And I'd hate that girl and I would want to kill that girl, but I would want to see her.

And if that girl didn't come to see me, I might just put a bicycle on her lawn. Nineteen days later, nineteen years later – I might do it to make sure she remembered.

Ellie was shivering, even though it was boiling hot outside and she didn't have the car's air conditioner on. As soon as she'd turned down their street, she'd felt sick. Their area of Newton wasn't unlike the New Rochelle neighbourhood had been. A suburb with tree-lined streets, yards in front of the houses, a lot of basketball nets on garage doors.

Including the Davises' garage door, she could see when she pulled up. Did that mean they'd had another child?

Their house was painted white; it was two-storey, the windows flanked by green shutters.

The driveway was perfectly level. No slope.

Her cell phone was on the passenger seat beside her. She could call Louisa. For what? Moral support? This was her obligation, and she'd insisted on coming alone.

With no warning to the Davises.

How could she introduce herself on the phone? The impersonality of that would be worse than showing up at their door. At least that's what Ellie had decided, but now she wasn't sure.

She picked up her cell, looked in her bag for their number. Pulled out the piece of paper she'd written it down on and dialled.

After two rings, a woman's voice answered, saying, 'Hello?' Ellie hung up. Put the phone down. Gripped the steering wheel.

Shit.

What do I do now?

Get out of the car and go over there and do what you should have done nineteen years ago.

Stop hiding.

Forcing herself to move, she opened the door, walked slowly across the street.

There was a well-polished brass knocker on the door to the house, a bell to one side. She reached out to use the knocker, changed her mind and pressed the bell. When a chime rang out, Ellie stepped back.

'Hello?'

A tall slim blonde woman in a white skirt and white cotton top stood in front of her. Her hair was shiny, thick, cut in layers. And she was so much younger than Ellie had imagined. In her early forties, maybe. Was this the right woman?

'Mrs Davis?'

'Yes.'

Of course. Hope had been just six years old. Why had she imagined Mrs Davis to be Louisa's age? Because Ellie had been only seventeen when it happened. And she'd always thought of her as *Mrs* Davis.

'I'm sorry to bother you. I need to talk to you. I . . .' Ellie faltered.

'I'm not buying anything. You shouldn't waste your time here,' the woman stated. 'Try next door.'

'I'm not selling anything,' she said quickly. 'My name is Ellie Walters. Ellie Peters was my maiden name.'

'Ellie . . .' She stepped back. 'Ellie Peters?'

'I'd like to talk to you, Mrs Davis. Please.'

'What?' Her whole face sagged. 'What are you doing here?'

'I came to talk to you. To say how sorry I am.'

'Ellie Peters?' Ellie could see her struggling to regain her composure. 'I can't . . . I don't . . .' Turning her back on Ellie, she walked into the living room, sat down in a chair, put her head in her hands. Ellie stood at the threshold, not knowing whether to turn around and go back to the car or follow her in.

'Mrs Davis?' She took a step forward. 'Are you all right?'

She didn't raise her head.

Ellie took another step.

The living room was pristine. Everything in it gleamed: the glass coffee table looked as if it had just been cleaned, the bright blue cushions on the dark blue sofa were puffed up perfectly, the white rug underneath was immaculate.

'I'm so sorry, Mrs Davis. That's all I wanted to say. I know it doesn't help, but I—'

'But you what?' Mrs Davis looked up.

'I should have come to see you before, when it happened.'

'Why? To make yourself feel better?'

184

'To apologise.'

'Oh, for Christ's sakes! I'm sure you're sorry.' Mrs Davis's eyes locked on hers. The anguish Ellie saw in them made her want to curl up and disappear.

'But have you lived every day of your life being sorry? Do you wake up every morning thinking: why did I buy her that damn bike? Why, when Sanders yelled something out to me, did I go inside and ask: "What?" Why wasn't I outside with her where I should have been? Why didn't I see she was riding off down the driveway before it was too late?' Her voice was rising in volume with each question. 'Why couldn't I stop her? Why was I so goddamn *slow*? I was her *mother*. It was my job to protect her. Great, you're sorry. That helps a lot. God, if only you'd come here then and told me that, it would have changed everything.'

'I'm sorry, I'm sorry . . . I'll go,' Ellie said weakly.

'You know, there have been times I wish you'd been drunk. Or speeding. Or not wearing glasses you needed to wear.'

'Mrs Davis, I—'

'Why the hell did you come *now*?'

'I shouldn't have.'

'You want me to forgive you, right? You wish I'd say it was an accident, it's not your fault, say three Hail Marys or whatever and go on, lead your life. But I'm not Catholic. Sanders is. Sanders is the most forgiving person in the world. If he weren't out playing golf now with our son, he'd probably ask you if you wanted a cup of coffee. But not me. I *know* it was an accident, all right? But that doesn't mean I forgive you for existing, for being in that car, for driving down our street at that precise time. I wish you'd never been born. So I can't give you what you want.'

'I didn't mean to—'

'Listen to me.' Mrs Davis stood up. 'We've worked so hard to try to put that day behind us. We *have* to put it behind us, for the sake of our son. You know, I used to wonder what I'd do if you ever showed up. That's probably why I didn't slam the door in your face. I'd pictured all the things I'd tell you. About Hope. How beautiful, how precious, Hope was. So you'd suffer. But what's the point? There is no point.' She sat back down.

'There is no point,' she repeated, closing her eyes.

Looking at her, slumped in her chair, Ellie said: 'I'm so sorry,' turned and left the room, closing the front door softly behind her.

Before she'd gone into the Davises' house, Ellie had been freezing. Now she was sitting in the car, dripping with sweat. She had to start the engine and leave, she knew. If Mrs Davis got up, went to the window, looked out and saw her sitting there . . .

Go, go, go, she told herself; finally she put the key in the ignition, turned the car on, cranked the air conditioning up as high as it would go and put it in drive. Pulling out, she went straight ahead, then turned right, turned right again, parked on the parallel street, turned off the engine and sat there shaking.

On a Sunday morning in the winter, she and Debby had been sitting in her apartment, having brunch, reading

186

the *New York Times*. Debby had looked up from the book review section and said: 'OK, I'm boasting here, but I'm not only a mathematical genius, I was a hotshot in English and languages too. There's a new biography of Proust out – they're reviewing it here. Shit – I read Proust in French, every single word of *Remembrance of Things Past*. And after all that fucking time spent on it, I came away with one thing. The narrator goes on and on about how he wishes this girl were dead, right? But then she does die – and that's where the brilliant part comes in – he describes the difference between wishing something would happen and the reality of it actually happening. The reality of it was nothing like he'd imagined. He does that unbelievably well.'

What had Ellie expected to happen when she saw Mrs Davis? Had some part of her hoped she'd be forgiven? Was she really looking for a form of absolution?

Seeing Hope's mother slumped in that chair – her lost, bewildered, defeated tone of voice when she'd said 'There is no point' – that was the reality.

Her mother had been right, Ellie thought. They'd moved to a new town, started a new life. Had a child. How could she think, just because she'd been trying to come to terms with her past since she'd moved to Bourne, that they might have come to terms with theirs. How could they ever come to terms with it? They wanted to move on. And she'd dragged Mrs Davis right back into the painful heart of it.

Retrieving her cell phone from her bag, she turned it back on, dialled Louisa's number. When the answering machine kicked in, she said: 'Louisa, it's me. I fucked up. I should never have come. I can't tell you how much I fucked up. I made everything worse. I can't believe I thought it might be the right thing to do. I'm going to pick up Tim. I'll call you when I'm back.' She hung up.

Wrong. That word came back, hitting her in the gut. *Wrong, wrong, wrong.*

Her emotional instincts were egregiously out of whack, and had been for a long time. Going to the Davises' house. Thinking for one second even that they might have been responsible for leaving the bike.

Marrying Charlie . . . no, *trusting* Charlie. Having sex with Joe. Even semi-dismissing Daniel at first, not seeing him for the wonderful man he was.

'I don't trust people who haven't made major mistakes,' Louisa had said once. Ellie remembered smiling at that comment, but now she wondered: if you made major mistake after major mistake, how could you trust yourself?

Yes, she should have gone to see the Davises after it happened. She still believed that would have been the right thing to do. But, as Louisa had pointed out, not nineteen years later.

Had she gotten that wrong because she wanted to find out if they were the ones who'd put the bicycle there? Had that been what had really driven her to visit them? Ellie didn't think that was the case, but maybe she was wrong about that too. If so, it was shameful. However much fear she felt when she saw that bicycle, it didn't justify putting Mrs Davis through that scene.

Leaning forward, Ellie rested her head against the steering wheel.

I can't take it back.

It happened.

The noise boomed through the sky. Louisa, looking up, saw six Otis Air Force Base jets flying in formation, so close together their wings were almost touching. That precision and skill always amazed her.

'How do you think they train to do that?' she asked Joe, who was sitting in the stern of the boat, holding a fishing line in his right hand. 'I mean, how do they begin? Do they start off flying miles apart and then gradually get closer?'

'Probably.' He began to pull the line in, winding it around the block of wood as he did. 'I think I have something.'

But when it reached the surface, the hook was empty.

'Damn. Stole the bait and swam away. Another smart fish.' He leaned down, retrieved a minnow from the pail, baited the hook again. 'I think they've taken a training course. We're never going to catch one.'

They were anchored beside the Rock Pile, where she'd used to fish as a child. In those days they'd thought of it as the Magic Hole, a place where fish lurked just waiting to be caught.

The older Louisa got, the more pleased she was when she didn't catch anything. Even though they always ate whatever they caught, killing fish seemed more brutal to her now. What she enjoyed was sitting in the boat, idling away the time, talking. But Joe, she knew, wanted some success.

At least a few flounders he could clean and cook. So far the bottom of their boat was conspicuously empty.

She looked at her watch, wondering if Ellie had reached the Davises' house yet and whether they'd be in when she did. Whatever transpired there, it wouldn't be good.

'Are you late for something?' Joe asked.

'Just checking the time.'

She wanted to talk to him about it, but the subject of Ellie was now a closed one.

The night before he'd gone to Boston, Louisa had told him about Ellie's accident. She couldn't remember exactly what had led up to it – she knew they'd been talking about Tim – and she'd been thinking that if Jamie had been there she would have told him, and then she'd had another glass of wine, and suddenly she was telling Joe and he was listening intently.

'That's terrible,' he'd stated when she'd finished. 'For everyone.'

'I think she's beginning to understand it really was an accident.'

'Right.' He'd tipped back in his chair. 'But, Mum,' he rocked forward, sat up straight, 'it's not my business. It's your business, I know, but it's not mine. OK?'

'OK.'

Yet yesterday evening, after the bicycle incident, she hadn't been able to stop herself again.

'I know you don't think it's your business, but it's really worrying me, Joe. Someone's out there, doing these things to Ellie. And she's decided to go see the parents of the girl

190

– by herself. She wouldn't let me go with her. I care about her, Joe. A lot. I hate the idea of her doing that by herself. I know I shouldn't have told you about the accident in the first place, I should have respected her privacy, but I did and now I'm frightened by all this.'

They had been sitting in the living room. Joe was silent, staring out of the bay window. His expression was the one he always wore when his brain was churning away.

'I'd like to help,' he finally said. 'But I don't know how to. Someone clearly has something against Ellie, and it clearly has something to do with her past. Listen, Mum, I should respect her privacy too, but I need to tell you something. She and I – when you were away – Ellie and I . . . Well, we both forgot ourselves. I don't know how else to put it. It was a mistake. And I know for certain it's better if we stay away from each other. I can't get involved in her life. I don't want to and she doesn't want me to.'

'I see.' It was Louisa's turn to stare out the window.

'I'm sure she didn't want you to know what happened between us and neither did I. But you need to understand why I'm not going to get involved in this. Ellie needs help, but I'm not the one to help her. I think she should get a private detective.'

'You can't be friends even?'

'No.' He rubbed his forehead. 'But you know that doesn't mean you can't be. Look, I should be out of here soon. I'm going to have to pack up my things in DC, try to find a place in Boston. Find a *job* in Boston first, obviously. The point is, I won't be hanging around here much longer.'

'I like you hanging around here.'

'You know what I mean. Anyway, if something else happens, if she's threatened again, you have to tell me. You're up to your neck in this. And I worry about *you*. Really, I think you should tell her to hire someone to look into this.'

Joe and Ellie? Louisa had been surprised that her usually highly tuned mother's intuition hadn't kicked in on that. There she'd been, thinking she couldn't even get them together as friends. Meanwhile they'd raced beyond her, and ended up, evidently, crashing.

Now there wasn't even the possibility of friendship between them. Joe's 'No' had been adamant.

As much as she would have liked to discuss the situation with him as they sat in the boat, she felt awkward about bringing Ellie's name up. As she would from now on bringing Joe's name into conversation with Ellie.

Her son and the young woman she had begun to think of as a surrogate daughter at daggers drawn – well, not speaking to each other anyway.

Why did life have to be so complicated?

Another boom sounded. Another formation of jets raced against the sky. Louisa began to pull her line in.

'Let's get back,' she said. 'I really don't want to catch a fish.'

Lifting her head from the steering wheel, Ellie picked up her cell phone to check her messages. Tim had driven to Boston with her where she'd dropped him off at Charlie's, saying she was going to visit some old friends. He hadn't wanted to spend the night with his father because he was going to see Lauren in the evening, so they'd arranged that he'd call and tell her where he was and what time she could pick him up.

Mom, Dad's dropping me off at The Country Club for a quick swim. Can you pick me up here?

He'd sent it while she was in the Davises' house, half an hour ago.

After texting *I'll be there in fifteen minutes* Ellie started the car and set off. As she made her way to Route 9, she heard cars honking behind her. After a few minutes, she realised she was driving so slowly they were honking at her.

Go ahead and honk, she thought. I'm not going to go any faster.

This time, after she'd picked Tim up and they'd reached the Bourne Bridge, he'd be the one who wanted to get to the cottage in a hurry. And she'd be the one dreading their arrival.

Was the move to Bourne yet another mistake?

Someone wanted to torment her, and they'd only started to do it when she'd moved to Bourne. Louisa had talked about all the incidents being connected, but she hadn't made the original connection: the fact that this had all started shortly after Ellie and Tim had moved there. Why? What was it about them being in Bourne?

Mr and Mrs Davis weren't responsible, Ellie knew that now. What she didn't know was who was, or what they'd do next.

Was it safe to stay there? What about Tim? What if whoever it was did something to her son? Hurt him?

They should get away. Go to California and visit Debby. Yes, Tim was beginning to like Bourne. Because of Lauren. But they were fifteen years old – it couldn't be serious. He'd love a trip to California.

For how long?

Forever?

What about the cottage? Their *home*?

But how could it ever be a home if Ellie were sitting there waiting for something awful to happen again?

Louisa and she had discussed going to the police, but they'd always come back to the same problem. No one had made any real threat.

She could hire a private investigator but how much money would that cost and what would he or she actually do? Trawl through Ellie's life. She knew her life better than anyone else and she had no idea who could be doing this. Besides – she'd told Louisa about the accident, but she didn't like the idea of other people finding out, especially Charlie.

'You mean, you kept that a secret from me?' she could hear him saying. 'We were married and you never told me? And you say I lied to you about my affair. Come on, El. Who lied to whom? From the start?'

He wouldn't care about the difference between hiding something about the past and lying about the present.

California. Debby. Beaches. A different ocean, but an ocean.

Another new start.

It could be the answer.

It was a plan anyway. She needed a plan.

194

Because she could feel it – the fear creeping up on her.

Who?

Why?

What do you want from me?

Seeing the Heath Street sign in front of her, she realised she'd been driving for ten minutes in a trance. She must have stopped at all the red lights and made all the right turns, but she couldn't remember doing it. She had never lost her concentration at the wheel, never once since the accident.

She had to call Debby tonight. Make a plan.

The entrance to Pine Manor College was on her right. Ellie remembered Charlie calling it 'Pine Manure'. Had she laughed when he'd done that? She couldn't remember. Suddenly their marriage felt so long ago. Where did love go when it left your heart? she wondered. Probably straight into someone else's. Like an infectious disease.

She'd been to The Country Club twice, with Charlie, and teased him about its name. *The* Country Club. As if it were the only country club in the world. Charlie hadn't appreciated her joking about it: he'd been as pleased when he'd gotten into that place as he'd been when he made partner in the law firm.

The Country Club was in Brookline – like Newton a suburb of Boston. It spread over acres like an old country estate, complete with swimming pool, outdoor and indoor tennis courts, eighteen-hole golf course, even a curling rink. Before the 1960s it had been a haven for old money. No Afro-Americans, no Jews; even Catholics had a hard time getting in. But the old money began to dwindle at the same time as political correctness arrived on the scene, and now you no longer had to be a descendant of the signers of the Constitution or the families who came over on the *Mayflower* to be admitted into that magic circle.

What would the Billingtons and all their Pilgrim Brothers have thought of their descendants idling by the pool, living the life of luxury? Ellie wondered as she turned right on to Warren Street. The Country Club was definitely a different spin on Plymouth Plantation.

Debby lived in Long Beach. Was there a WASPy social hierarchy there too? Somehow she didn't think so.

A green sign with 'The Country Club' written on it in yellow letters appeared on Ellie's left and she turned into the drive. For a second she forgot that the small guard house by the entrance, a little yellow hut, was manned by a stuffed scarecrow-like figure, not a real person, and was about to zap down her window to explain what she was doing entering these hallowed grounds. As soon as she caught sight of its ridiculous stuffed face, she remembered this bizarre effort to ward off unwelcome types, and kept driving, down the long road that led to the Clubhouse.

'Give way to golfers' a little posted sign warned, because the road cut through one of the holes. After checking to see her car wasn't about to be hit by a stray chip shot, Ellie continued until she reached the large yellow clubhouse and another green sign, this one pointing the way to the pool.

When she reached the pool parking lot, she saw most of the cars had low licence-plate numbers: another sign of class.

Vanity plates with names or words on them were as bad, she'd been told, as wearing polyester. When automobiles first arrived on the scene in Massachusetts, the registry had issued licence plates starting from the number one and continuing up. The only families who could afford to have cars at that point in time were the families with all the clout, the old time WASPs, and they'd kept the original plates, passing them down from generation to generation like family heirlooms.

Charlie would have loved one of those.

Turning off the engine, Ellie sat for a few seconds, mapping out her plan.

She'd tell Tim about going to California when they got back to the cottage. Before he went to see Lauren, she'd sit down with him and explain what was happening.

I'll have to tell him about the accident.

How will he react?

If only she could go back to those first few weeks in Bourne when she was getting to know Louisa and exploring and taking such pleasure in being there. Before that day she'd walked in and found the living room a wreck. Before the garbage on the beach.

Before the bicycle.

Before the letter from Joe. Steering clear of him when he'd been in DC was simple. But now he was back in Bourne, and who knew for how long? Avoiding him while still keeping her friendship with Louisa would be tricky.

Everything had changed. The new life she'd created for herself and Tim had turned into a scary, confusing mess.

197

She'd been so proud of herself. Finally she was becoming independent; finally she was taking control of her life. Late in the game, but still. She was thirty-six. It wasn't hopelessly late. Now all those little breakthroughs she'd been so happy about had broken down.

At least she hadn't completely collapsed when she'd seen the bicycle. She could have felt that old overwhelming exhaustion; she could have gone straight to her bedroom and stayed there, sleeping. At least she was doing something, making a plan. She had that to hold on to.

Getting out of the car, Ellie locked it and made her way to the pool, passing an office where you were supposed to sign in by writing your name and your membership number. But there was no one there so she kept going. The Olympic-sized pool with two diving boards was surrounded by green deckchairs.

Everything here was yellow or green – except the water. She was surprised they didn't dye that. She put up her hand to shield her eyes from the sun and searched for Tim.

There were groups of families with small children, a few teenage girls, and over in the corner, at the edge of the grass behind, she spotted Tim. He was sitting on the side of a deckchair, talking to someone on the neighbouring chair.

The man he was talking to had on sunglasses and brightly coloured bathing trunks that came over his knees.

Oh, shit.

Charlie.

14

His dad suddenly stopped talking, sat up and waved. At his mom, it turned out, who was walking over, looking not so happy. His dad leaped up, grabbed an empty deckchair, pulled it over so it was beside theirs.

'El. It's good to see you. Come sit down and join us.'

'I'm just here to pick up Tim.'

'I know.' He patted the empty deckchair. 'But sit down. It's a beautiful day. You don't want to get straight back into the car. Relax.'

She started to look around the poolside. Tim knew she was checking the place for Sandra, but Sandra wasn't here. In fact, Sandra hadn't been around for a while now. He'd asked his dad where she was, and knew he'd looked disappointed when the answer was, 'Europe, on a little trip,' instead of, 'Hawaii. She's moved there forever.'

'El, sit down.' His dad was looking her up and down. 'You're not looking very well. Are you all right?'

'I'm fine. But I'm in a hurry. We should go now, Tim.' She stayed standing.

'You might be fine but you're obviously very very hot. Here.' Charlie reached inside the bag he'd put down beside his chair. 'I grabbed this bathing suit just in case. You can't be in that much of a hurry. You could use a swim.'

'Whose is that?' Ellie stared at the black one-piece bathing suit as if it were contaminated.

'It's Sandra's. You two are about the same size. It will fit, don't worry.'

'We're not remotely the same size. And I don't want it. We're going.'

'You're so pale, El. I thought you'd get more sun living by the water.'

'Sit down, Mom. Please.'

Tim could see she was shaking. Why had his dad insisted on staying here with him, not just dropped him off? He'd known Mom was going to pick him up. At some point he'd even gone and packed a bathing suit for her – Sandra's. He must have known that was a shitty thing to do.

But he'd been in his own world all day, pacing around the apartment with his hands behind his back like he was trying to figure out some massively hard physics problem, occasionally stopping and nodding his head as if he *had* figured it out. That's what he always did when he was thinking about work, so at one point Tim said: 'Do you have a really hard case or something?' and his dad had said, 'Yes. You can't shut off just because it's a Saturday, Tim,' and Tim had tried to let that dig bounce off him, but it hurt. He should have brought some homework with him, he knew. Even if he wasn't going to do it, he could have pretended to.

Now he was feeling protective of his mom: was that because he was still pissed about Dad's dig? But shit – had his father really expected her to put on Sandra Cabot's bathing suit?

She did sit down, though. Which was a good thing because she'd looked as if she might faint.

'So are you enjoying your independence, El?' He'd pushed his sunglasses up so that they rested on top of his head. 'Your own house?'

'Yes . . . yes, I am.'

'That's good. Tim told me you painted the living room a crazy colour. I'd like to see that.'

'Charlie, we have to go.' She stood up again. 'Get your things together, Tim. We're leaving.'

'That's a shame. It's so civilised, the three of us sitting here together like this.'

Tim caught his mother's eyes. He and she both signalled '*What*?' while he swiftly grabbed all his things, put them in his backpack. 'Goodbye, Dad,' he said.

'Goodbye, Charlie,' his mom said.

'Call me, El. Let's talk. I want to know how you're doing.'

His mother took off and Tim followed her.

Lauren was so right. Who were these kids who wanted their parents to get back together again? he thought as they walked past the other deckchairs and headed out. That really had to be some kind of warped Disney fantasy. Five minutes of his mom and dad in the same air space was five stressy minutes too many. He should have figured that one out before.

When they got in the car, his mother put her head on the steering wheel.

'Mom?'

'Just give me a second, Tim.'

'I'm sorry I didn't tell you Dad was going to be there. He inisisted on coming in with me and then my cell died so I couldn't text. And I had no idea he'd brought that bathing suit with him, I promise.'

'I know you didn't.' She lifted her head, put her hand on his knee. 'It's been a difficult day, that's all.'

'I thought you were meeting up with your friends.'

'I was. I did.'

'Wasn't that fun?'

'Not exactly,' she sighed, starting the engine.

'Umm . . . I've got a CD you might like.' He reached into the bag in front of his feet. 'Want to play it?'

'Sure.'

Fishing the Bonnie Raitt CD out of his pack, he slipped it into the player. Lauren had given it to him on Thursday, saying: 'Check this out. She's got a monster voice. It's old stuff, but she's really cool.' He'd already listened to it a couple of times. A little retro, but Lauren was right: she did have a monster voice. And his mother liked these kinds of songs, he knew. After the first song ended, he asked: 'Do you like it?' and she answered: 'Yes. A lot. Thanks, Tim. It's great.'

She was driving, she was listening to the music, but he could tell something was bugging her: probably that conversation with his dad, though Tim sensed it was more than that.

He'd given her a lot of shit about the move, but summer school in Bourne was turning out to be ace: he liked some of the guys and, well – Lauren. She was unreal. She had this way of teasing him, making him laugh at himself.

Sometimes they'd be sitting together and she'd do wicked imitations of him; not in a mean way but in this perfect flirty/unflirty way. He'd never met any girl like her. So instead of dreading going to Bourne High in the fall, he was actually really psyched about it.

But he'd been punishing his mom still anyway. He'd introduced her to Lauren on the day he'd taken Lauren over to Louisa's, but he only let her stay about five seconds before he dragged her away to the big house. Maybe he didn't want to admit his mom had been right about moving, so he'd barely told her anything about how great he was feeling. Which was mean, he knew.

Plus his mom was alone. His dad had Sandra, even though she was away in Europe probably on some clothes-buying spree because that's the way Sandra was, that's what she did – buy things. But still, his dad had gone off with Sandra and his mom had nobody. Except that pen pal guy in England and Louisa, but they didn't count. Not in the same way.

He used to tell her everything. When he was thirteen, he'd gone into her bedroom when his dad was working late, sat down on the bed and confessed that he'd smoked a cigarette. He'd actually cried like a little kid. And she'd hugged him and said, 'Don't do it again, Tim, all right? But I'm so glad you could tell me. Thank you so much for that.' And then they'd sat together on the bed, talking about other stuff. They used to talk a lot.

Bonnie Raitt started in on this song called 'Guilty' and Tim slumped a little. The right lyrics at the right moment could hit you hard.

So he put his iPod away, made himself sit up straight and started talking.

'Mom? I'm sorry.'

'Sorry for what?'

'I know I gave you a really hard time about moving to Bourne.'

'That's all right, Tim. I can understand why you didn't like it.'

'But I do like it now. A lot. I like it way better than Boston.'

'You do?'

'Yeah. And I know I haven't talked to you about Lauren and you only met her for like two seconds, but the thing is, I think I'm falling in love with her.' He half-laughed. 'I know, I know. I'm only fifteen. But it's the way I feel.'

She didn't say anything. She sat there, her eyes on the road.

'OK, too much information, but I wanted to tell you this is the happiest I can ever remember being. Except when I'm away from Lauren because all I can think then is how much I want to see her and how long it will be before I do. Lame, I know. But, anyway, all this good stuff happening is because of you and I didn't tell you because I was kind of punishing you.

'The thing is, when we first went to Bourne, I was still screwed up about the whole divorce, way more screwed up than either you or Dad knew, totally unhappy. I almost . . . anyway, I hated you and Dad because of the divorce and I hated you for making me move. Not really hate, but you know what I mean. And if this makes sense, I hated feeling that way about you. It made me even unhappier. Because I really love you, Mom. You're cool, you know? Oh, God, I'm being, like, eight years old. But I'll say it again anyway. I love you. And thank you for bringing me to Bourne. It's ace.'

He saw the tears begin to run down her face. She was so happy she was crying.

Sometimes being a good son felt really great.

The landline was ringing as they walked in. Ellie went to answer it while Tim went to his room – probably to charge up his cell and call Lauren.

'Ellie? How are you? I was on the porch and I saw your car driving down the road. Your message – I'm so sorry it was so difficult for you.'

'It was more difficult for Mrs Davis.' Ellie sighed. 'Your first instinct was right, Louisa. I shouldn't have gone.'

'And you're sure they're not responsible for the bike?'

'I'm sure.'

'I'll come over now.'

'No. Thanks, but I'm shattered. I don't think I could bear talking about it all right now.'

'All right. But I'll come over tomorrow morning, early, if that's OK?'

'That would be great. See you then.'

They said goodbye and Ellie hung up.

'Mom, I'm going to walk over to Lauren's now,' Tim said as he came out of his bedroom. 'You know, she told me I should get a bike and I couldn't admit I don't know how to ride one.'

'Walking's good for you,' was all Ellie could think of to say.

'Whatever. See you later.' He kissed her on the cheek. 'I bet it's pen pal time now, right?'

'Right,' she nodded, looking at him in wonder. He was so grown up. And so happy. 'Bring Lauren over again soon, will you? I really liked her that first time, but I'd like to get to know her better.'

'Sure.' He smiled. 'But not *too* many questions, OK? Don't go overboard.'

'I wouldn't dare.'

After he left, Ellie got her laptop, went into the kitchen, put it on the table, poured herself a glass of wine and sat down.

In her last email to Daniel, she'd finally told him about the accident – and the bicycle on her lawn. It had been a difficult one to write: she was confiding in him as she'd confided in Louisa, but the words had looked so clinical on the screen. How would he feel when he'd read what she'd written? Taking a large sip of wine, she presssed the 'On' button.

Dear Ellie,

It's hard to know what to say. I'd like to try to give you some comfort, but I know how you feel and how the accident must have affected you. I see patients come in and some of them are old and some of them are young and I want to save them all – and of course they all want me to save them – but real life doesn't allow for that. In your case, you had an accident. In mine, I can do whatever I can to save a patient, but sometimes that's impossible. It's a different kind of accident. And often it happens to the young ones with the most to lose. It's heartbreaking – as is your story.

206

As for someone putting that bike on your lawn – that's horrible. I wish I knew what I could tell you to do. I guess it can't be a coincidence, but like you said, it's impossible to think who could want to be so cruel. Or why. I feel so powerless over here not being able to help you. If there is anything you can think of I might be able to do to help, just tell me. You know I will, no matter how far away I am.

It's remarkable what a small world it really is, though. All that six degrees of separation business is so right. Last night I ran into an old friend of mine who lives in DC now – he's a journalist, over here on vacation. We saw each other in a pub in Chelsea, if you can believe that. Anyway, he was talking about the Senator Harvey scandal (isn't everyone, I guess – except the English) and I told him I knew someone who knew someone who worked for Harvey. Turns out he's heard of Joe Amory. Apparently his reputation in DC isn't good – he's well known for playing nasty political tricks. I didn't want to indulge in gossip – not my thing – so I didn't press him. In any event, it's none of my business. All politicians probably do those things.

All I really want to say is that I'm so sorry about what's happened and what is happening in your life. It's unfair. No one knows better than I do how unfair life – and death – can be.

As always, I look forward to hearing from you soon.

Love, Daniel.

This was the first time he'd signed off with the word 'love'. Ellie re-read the email, surprised yet again by how much comfort she always got from his words, surprised, too, at the part about Joe and his 'nasty political tricks'. Maybe the journalist was exaggerating. And Daniel was right: all politicians probably had to be tricky and nasty at some point.

Joe Amory – attractive, funny, smart super-hero son of Louisa, or Joe Amory – man who writes lousy fuck-off letters and plays dirty tricks in his working world?

Take your pick, she thought. Except she didn't have to. The woman he was involved with could figure it out.

Daniel had written 'love'. She wanted to figure that out.

Turning off her laptop, grabbing her keys and taking the glass of wine with her, she went out, locked the door, and walked down to the beach.

There was no plan now. She couldn't take Tim away from Lauren. She'd have to stay and keep herself together and hope the bicycle was the end of it. If they wanted to remind her of the accident, they'd done it. If they wanted to scare her, they'd done that too. If they wanted to hurt her, they'd probably find a way to do it wherever she went. And that bicycle was directed at her, not Tim. If they made any kind of threat towards him, she'd send him to Charlie's and go to the police and camp out at the station until they took her seriously.

It was a perfect July night. And Daniel had written 'love'. What would it be like to fall in love again, or was she already doing it? Slowly. Was it possible to fall in love when you were scared shitless?

Kicking off her sandals, she dug her toes into the sand, took a sip of wine, watched the sun setting across the Canal.

No more mistakes, Ellie. Go slow.

She pictured him sitting behind a desk, wearing a white

coat, that lock of blond hair falling across his forhead, his boyish face listening intently to a patient, trying to do everything he could to help.

Did he joke with them sometimes?

What did he do when they cried?

He'd know what to say to them, he'd known what to say to her. Life's unfair – what Louisa had said. So you have to hang on to those moments. Louisa was right.

Daniel's patients dying being a different kind of accident – that had touched her deeply. He'd try his hardest to save them, but sometimes he couldn't. Living with that, *dealing* with that fact all the time, had made him wise as well as compassionate.

No one looked forward to seeing a doctor.

Except she did. Now.

Two years. That was a long time to wait.

Maybe a long time to wait was a good thing.

Or maybe he'd come back to Boston to visit at some point. Doctors got vacations.

When they'd first started emailing, Ellie had been pleased he lived so far away. Now she wished he were closer, that they could spend time together in person. Dinner with him at Acquitaine a second time would be so entirely different. She could imagine them staying up all night talking.

There were never enough words in his emails. She would read them, gobble them up, and be disapppointed when they ran out, wishing he'd written more.

A massive white yacht was going down the Canal. She

turned to follow its progress and caught sight of Joe peripherally. He was standing at the edge of the beach – Louisa's beach – separated from hers by seaweed and a jagged line of rocks. He had his hands in his pockets and a blade of grass in his mouth. Dressed in jeans and a white long-sleeved shirt. When he saw her, he stood still. He didn't wave or call out, she didn't either.

They stood as if they were in a showdown at the OK Corral, neither of them moving for about fifteen seconds during which Ellie considered walking over to him, telling him how unnecessary and hurtful that letter had been. Before she had made a decision either way, he'd turned and walked back towards the house.

Man up, Joe, she said to herself. *You're a coward*.

She finished her wine, picked up her sandals.

Lauren was sitting on top of the kitchen counter, in a blue-jean skirt and white tank top. Tim was on his usual stool.

Her mother was out.

'She has a better social life than I do,' Lauren said. 'And it's not like she drinks or anything. But she and her friends all go out and talk about guys and pretend they're still teenagers. Tragic.'

'Yeah, well, my mother stays in and writes pen-pal emails to some guy in England.'

'Parents.' She turned, opened a cupboard above her, took out a jar of peanut butter. 'Do you ever think about fate?' she asked as she unscrewed the lid.

Curveball. Think fast.

'Fate? Sure. All the time. Fate. Destiny. The meaning of life. It's all I ever think about.'

'I'm serious.'

She was.

'Think about it. OK, bad things happen, right? But maybe there's always a reason. So your parents split up and that's a bad thing for you, and then you blow off school last year and that's not good either . . . but what happens then? You come here. And I didn't want to go to the beach that day with Kerry. Meet some new guy? No, thanks. But I didn't have anything better to do, so I went. I mean, we would have met up in the fall anyway, but then it might have been totally different. What I'm saying is, everything happens for a reason. Sometimes I think maybe if *my* parents hadn't split up we'd all have been driving somewhere together and end up crashing and all be dead now. Do you see what I'm saying?'

She put her finger in the peanut butter jar, scooped out a chunk of it, put it in her mouth.

But then there was this moment . . . he heard Louisa saying.

Getting off the stool, Tim walked up to Lauren, put his hands on either side of her legs, leaned forward and kissed her. He'd kissed a girl before. But not like this.

This was a whole different ballgame.

15

13 August

Louisa couldn't remember a summer so full of changeable weather. Intense rain for a day followed by stunning sunshine and then rain again, like a meteorological see-saw. Today the sun had ceded to a heavy fog and she put on her yellow slicker before walking over to see Ellie, in case it started to pour.

Approaching the cottage, she was surprised to see a white van parked behind Ellie's car. She went and knocked on the door and after a few seconds Ellie opened it.

'Hi.'

'Ellie? What's going on?' There was a sudden banging noise coming from inside.

'I decided I needed new locks on the windows and another on the door, so I called as soon as I woke up. Luckily, I found someone who could do it right away.'

'Good idea.' Louisa was surprised by how upbeat she sounded. 'How are you feeling? You look well. I thought you'd be exhausted after yesterday.'

'I decided not to be.' Ellie stepped out of the house.

'You decided?'

'Yes. Come on, let's take a walk. It's too noisy inside.'

They headed down the driveway towards the end of the Agawam Point Road.

'Do you want to talk about yesterday? We don't have to.'

Ellie was walking quickly; she was wearing jeans and a blue-and-white striped top that really suited her. Louisa had expected her to be in a bad way after that message and their brief talk the night before, but she seemed almost perky.

'It's all right. Like I said, I shouldn't have gone. And I know they weren't responsible for that bike. They're trying so hard to move past it, you know? They have a son now. I don't know how old he is, but the point is, they're trying to look forward. And all I did was bring it back. Anyway, I made some decisions last night.'

'Are you going to call the police? I've been thinking, even if you don't, you really should hire a private investigator.'

'No.' Ellie stopped walking. Louisa could see the determination in her face. 'I'm going to do what the Davises are doing. I'm going to look forward too. The past has been haunting me – I've let it haunt me by not facing it before, and whoever is doing these things is trying to haunt and scare me. But I'm not going to let them.

'I realised that if they wanted to hurt me physically they would have done that by now. They're trying to hurt me emotionally – and they have. But I'm not frightened of them any more. Yes, I've put new locks in, but I should have done that before anyway. You move somewhere, you change the locks, right?'

'Right. But don't you want to find out who it is? Who did these things?'

Ellie began to walk again.

'If I did that, I'd just be playing their game.'

Louisa was struggling to keep pace with her.

Was this another way of repressing an ugly truth? she wondered. Or was it a sensible decision, and a brave one? She didn't know. The real problem, as she saw it, was whether whoever was waging this campaign of fear would continue with it, and, if so, how.

Could she hire a private investigator on Ellie's behalf? It was a possibility. She'd have to think about it.

They continued walking in silence until they reached the end of the road.

'Here's what I realised last night.' Ellie was standing in front of her mailbox. 'I told you my mother watches a lot of cop shows. *Law & Order* is her favourite. Anyway, sometimes when I watch them with her and someone is being threatened but refuses to leave their house because it's their home, I think – "Come on, this is ridiculous. Just get the hell out."' She paused. Just as Louisa was about to say 'That's what I think, too', Ellie continued.

'And yesterday I thought: all right, Tim and I will move to California. But Tim is so happy – and this *is* my home here now. I finally understand that whole concept. It's our *home*, Louisa. I'm not letting anyone push me out.'

214

'That's really admirable, Ellie, but . . .'

'Look, I'm tired of being a wimp. I can handle this. Some clothes thrown around, some garbage dumped, a bicycle? It's pathetic, really.'

Louisa didn't respond. She didn't think it was pathetic, she thought it was sick and evil. But Ellie had clearly thought about it, and she'd made these decisions, and Louisa had to admit she was glad they wouldn't be moving to California. Ellie's newfound resolve was almost catching.

'You look as though you want to go climb Mount Everest.'

'I would . . . if a whole load of sherpas carried me up.' She laughed.

Whoa! Louisa thought. Ellie was in a mood to kick ass. Good for her.

'I'll just check my mail.' Opening the box, Louisa saw it was empty. 'Looks like I'm not very popular,' she said.

Ellie opened hers and pulled out a bunch of envelopes.

'I'm popular with bill collectors. I'd rather be you.'

Retracing their steps, they talked about Tim and Lauren and how pleased Ellie was that Tim had told her how he felt.

'But it does make me feel old.' She smiled. 'He actually said the word "love".' She stopped, the smile still on her face. 'That's big, isn't it?'

'Huge.' Louisa smiled too.

'Huge.'

'Listen, come over for lunch later.' Louisa paused. 'Joe's gone to Boston for an interview. I'll be all alone. We can discuss young love.'

'Great. I'd love to.' They started walking again. When they reached the turn-off to the cottage, Ellie said: 'I'll see you later.'

Rain started to fall as Louisa continued down the road. Putting up the hood of her slicker, she sped up. She'd make a nice salad for lunch and she and Ellie would talk about young love and laugh together and she wouldn't mention Joe.

At some point those two would have to get beyond what had happened, but how they could do that she didn't know.

She did know, though, that when she got to the house she'd find the Yellow Pages and look up private investigators. All right, Ellie didn't want to 'play their game', but Louisa still thought that game was more dangerous than Ellie would let herself admit. If Ellie wouldn't hire one herself, Louisa would do it for her.

Something told her that bicycle wasn't the end of it.

The locksmith had finished; he handed over the new set of keys for the windows and door and Ellie paid him. After he left she wrote an email to Debby, waiting until the end to ask the question she needed to ask. *Daniel signed his last email 'Love' – do I do the same back? I want to, but I'm feeling a little shy.* She still hadn't told Debby about the accident. To go through it all yet again was too much.

Picking up the mail she'd brought back, she opened the first envelope – a credit-card statement. The second was hers and Tim's cell-phone bill, the third an electricity bill. Putting them aside, she looked at the next. Her name was

216

written on the front. No postmark, no stamp, no address, only 'Ellie' in black ink.

Opening it, she pulled out a sheet of paper.

In the middle of it were three typewritten lines:

> *I was dead before I could cry.*
> *I HOPE you're crying now.*
> *You should cry me a river.*

She stared at it until the words began to blur, except for HOPE, which was staring straight back at her.

Ellie stood up, feeling the blood drain out of her, and along with it all the decisions she'd made the night before, every ounce of her strength. She'd made herself believe the bicycle might be the end. But it wasn't. She'd thought she could handle whatever came next, if the bicycle weren't the end. But she couldn't. This was never going to end. It was only going to get worse.

She sat back down.

For minutes she sat with her head in her hands, struggling to rein in thoughts that were flying in every direction. Someone had put this in her mailbox. When? How much did that person know? Did they know she'd gone to the Davises' house the day before?

Had they been at the scene of the accident?

I was dead before I could cry.

I.

HOPE.

Had someone in the psych ward – another patient maybe

– overheard about what had happened and then . . . then what? Decided to do this nineteen years later?

Had Dr Emmanuel gone crazy and was it him, tracking her down somehow?

When he was fifty or sixty years old?

I was dead before I could cry.

Who knew that? Only she and her mother and Louisa. And Daniel. And the Davises. And the ambulance driver. And the police who had questioned her. And people at the hospital when they brought Hope there.

Ellie gripped the table. Or had Hope *not* died? Was she alive somewhere? Had they pronounced her dead but she wasn't and then someone kidnapped her and brainwashed her and she only realised now who she was and . . .

And no and no and no and no.

She picked up the envelope, stared at her own name. Ellie. The bottom of the small 'e' at the end was a longish line.

She'd seen that before. She'd seen an 'e' writtten like that before.

Where? When?

Think. Remember. Calm down and make yourself remember.

I can't calm down.

You've seen that writing before.

It's in longhand.

Who has written something to you in longhand?

It was darting around in the back of her brain. She kept reaching out for it and it kept eluding her.

If she thought about something else, cleared her brain, she might remember it.

On really hot summer nights in her mother's apartment, she used to close her eyes and think of swimming pools.

Ellie closed her eyes. She forced herself to think of the pool at The Country Club. It had two diving boards, it had lanes. It had a little roped-off bit at the shallow end for small kids. It was surrounded by concrete, but the concrete then gave way to grass.

She opened her eyes.

And caught it.

She saw 'Joe' scrawled at the bottom of a page. With the bottom of the 'e' elongated.

16

Louisa was at the kitchen table, the Yellow Pages in front of her. There was a small section of private investigators listed, but she had no idea how to choose one. All she could think of was those old movies with worn-out men sitting behind desks in shabby offices, making wisecracks.

Could she hire someone over the phone or would she have to go visit them? And could she do that without Ellie's permission? The fact that she'd told Joe Ellie's story was still making Louisa feel uneasy. Of course he wouldn't tell anyone else, but if Ellie knew he knew, she'd be upset. She hadn't even told Charlie. Or Tim.

Loose lips sink ships. That old World War II warning was unforgettable. But Joe was safe. And he had removed himself from any dealings with Ellie. He'd have no reason to discuss her past with anyone else.

'Louisa?'

Startled, she looked up, saw Ellie at the threshold.

'I knocked but I guess you didn't hear me.'

'No, I didn't.' She flipped the Yellow Pages shut. 'God, what time is it? I haven't begun to fix lunch. Sorry.'

'I'm not here for lunch.' Ellie took a step forward. 'I need to ask you something.'

'Sounds serious.' She was about to smile, but the expression on Ellie's face stopped her.

Ellie approached, but didn't sit down. 'Is this Joe's handwriting?' She held out an envelope in front of Louisa.

Louisa looked on the table for her reading glasses, then realised she'd put them on when she'd pulled out the Yellow Pages. Peering at the word 'Ellie' on the front of the envelope, she said, 'It looks like Joe's, yes. Why?'

Ellie withdrew the envelope, crossed her arms.

'I need to talk to him.'

'What's going on?'

'Can you give me his cell-phone number?'

'Ellie, sit down. What's this all about? Has he . . . I mean, what's in the envelope? You look so troubled. And you sound so angry.'

'I can't talk about it. I need to talk to him. Now.'

'He's gone to Boston – for interviews. This isn't a good time to call him.'

'I have to talk to him. Please, Louisa. Give me his number.'

Louisa had seen Ellie in fraught situations: she'd seen her hysterical, frightened, numb, resolute; but she'd never seen her look or sound like this. Her face was hard and tight. Her eyes were steely. Something was very wrong.

'I never remember cell-phone numbers. It's on mine. I'll go get it. Sit down. Really. I'll be right back.'

Ellie sat. Louisa went to the living room, got her phone out of her bag.

What had Joe written? What could he possibly have said to make Ellie act the way she was acting?

'*Don't get involved, Lou. This is between Joe and Ellie.*'

'*But I am involved, Jamie. Joe wouldn't do anything to upset her. There's been some misunderstanding. There must have been. Why would he write to her? What could he have said?*'

Back in the kitchen, Louisa was relieved to see that Ellie *had* sat down, and went to sit across from her. But the second she saw her face, still set in its cold, hard expression, Louisa's relief vanished.

'Ellie, I know you and Joe – I know you got close when I was away. He told me, and I'm sorry it didn't turn out . . . I mean, whatever happened, I'm sure he didn't mean to hurt you.'

'I need his number, Louisa.'

'He's still wrapped up in his grief. If you'd seen him after Pam died . . . he would never knowingly hurt you. There's been a misunderstanding, obviously.'

Ellie didn't speak. She was biting her lip, her arms were crossed tightly in front of her, her fists were clenched.

'I would have loved it if you two could be friends. You know that.'

'Where's your cell phone? Didn't you find it?'

'It's here.' Louisa pulled it out of her pocket, was about to hand it over to Ellie, but kept hold of it. 'I don't understand. Why are you acting like this? And why did you ask if that was Joe's handwriting? You must not have known

222

whether whatever is inside that envelope was from him. This doesn't make sense.'

'Don't.' Ellie shook her head. 'Just give me the number. Please.' She reached out for the phone, but Louisa refused to give it to her.

'No. This is ridiculous. Tell me what's going on. Whatever Joe said, you've misunderstood him. I want to stop all this animosity before it goes any further. You've been upset. Of course you have. You may have overreacted to something and I can understand that, but if you call him in this frame of mind, you'll make things worse.'

'Make things worse? That's a fucking joke.'

'Ellie!'

'I shouldn't have come here. I knew it was his hand-writing. I just couldn't believe it.' She stood up.

'Believe what?' Louisa stood too. They were facing ecah other, both shaking. 'You're acting as if he's done something heinous. Joe would never—'

'You don't know him, Louisa.'

'What?'

'You're his mother. You don't see . . .'

'Stop saying these things. All right, he may not have behaved appropriately after what went on between you, and you're hurt by that, I can understand, but I told you before, he's full of grief. Your cottage was theirs, Ellie. Don't forget that. And feeling the way he does, for Joe to show any interest in a woman is remarkable, actually.'

'This has nothing to do with that night. I *am not* hurt.' Ellie was palpably bridling. 'And Joe's not grieving as

223

much as you think he is. He is interested in other women, believe me.'

'You don't know what you're talking about.'

'Louisa, drop it.'

'If it has nothing to do with that night, then show me the letter.'

'No.'

'What's happened to you? Christ, you've gone crazy.'

'*I've* gone crazy?' Ellie threw the envelope down on the table. 'Go ahead then. Read it.'

Louisa picked it up, took out the sheet of paper. And read.

'You can't . . .' She sank on to a chair. 'You can't seriously believe Joe wrote this?'

'That's his handwriting on the envelope. I'm sorry, Louisa, but you wouldn't let it go.'

'This is horrible.' She stared up at Ellie. 'But this is from whoever put the bicycle there. Obviously. This has nothing to do with Joe.'

'You told him about the accident, didn't you? I couldn't figure out how he could know. But you told him.'

'I . . .'

'I knew it.'

'Ellie—'

'Why is he doing this to me?'

'He isn't doing anything. I don't know how this letter got in an envelope with his writing on it but it's not from him.'

'No? He was here every time something happened. I went

over the dates in my mind. He was here when the cottage was trashed, he was here when the garbage was on the beach, he was here that day the bicycle was left. You told him about the accident before then, didn't you?'

'Sit down and listen to me. This letter is terrible. It's grotesque. It must have been awful for you to get it, but Joe didn't write this. You thought before that the Davises might be responsible and you were wrong about that. Joe would never do anything like this.'

'He's done things before. He sent me a patronising, idiotic letter after that night we . . . and, I'm sorry, but people in DC have said . . .'

'People in DC have said what?'

'I don't want to do this. I never wanted to get you involved.'

'You really have lost your mind. Why would Joe want to hurt you like this? I can't believe you could think these things.'

'You can keep calling me crazy, but it's his handwriting, Louisa.'

She looked down at the envelope again. It *looked* like his writing, but the capital E – that looked odd.

'No, I don't think it is. I was wrong. Not that that matters. Joe *did not* do any of these things. Do you understand me?'

'Will you give me his number now?'

'No. I'm not having you making these accusations against him. They're baseless and cruel.'

'I know you want to protect him, I know you love him, but you must see he's the one who's crazy.'

'I'm not having this conversation any longer. I want you to leave now.'

Ellie stood up. She took the envelope off the table.

'I'm sorry, Louisa. I'm sorry he's done this to us both.'

She turned, walked out.

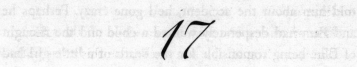

17

Ellie sat on her sofa, holding the letter, feeling sick. Her self-righteous anger had abated with every step she'd taken away from Louisa's.

She shouldn't have shown the letter to Louisa, but what else was she supposed to do? She needed to be certain of the handwriting, and she needed to get Joe's number. Louisa had pushed it and Ellie had reacted. Louisa had defended Joe; she'd defended herself.

I didn't want to hurt her, but there was only so much I could take. I'm not some spurned woman acting out. He's trying to drive me insane.

Now her relationship with Louisa was ruined, probably irreparably. And Joe was waging war against her for no apparent reason, his 'I was dead before I could cry' stabbing at her heart.

What was she supposed to do now? Wait for Joe to come back from Boston, go over there and confront him? With Louisa there watching?

Joe had hated the idea of her moving in, Ellie knew. That might have made him do what he did to the living room and beach, but why escalate matters? Why the bike and this letter? The only possible explanation was that once Louisa told him about the accident, he'd gone crazy. Perhaps he and Pam had desperately wanted a child and the thought of Ellie being responsible for the death of a little girl had driven him over the brink.

But he had a new relationship – why would he react like that now?

It *was* his writing, though. Louisa had tried to take that back at the end, but only after she'd read what he'd written. It had to be Joe. It was his handwriting.

Yet when she heard her cell phone ring, a sliver of hope sprang into Ellie's heart. Maybe it was Louisa saying: Come back over here, let's talk this through. We both said things in the heat of the moment.

She picked it up and saw it was her mother calling.

That's all I need now, she thought, but if she didn't answer it, her mother would only keep calling again until she did, Ellie knew.

'Hi, Mom.'

'Hello, darling. How are you?'

'Not so great at the moment.'

'Oh, dear. What's wrong?'

'It's complicated.' Ellie hesitated. 'But I'm all right, really. You don't have to worry.'

'Is Tim all right?'

'Tim's fine.'

'Good.'

Her mother started in on an anecdote about a downstairs neighbour, some piece of gossip Ellie didn't listen to.

Though maybe this was exactly what she needed now, she thought.

'. . . and apparently she met this man on that computer dating thing some people do. It's shocking, isn't it?'

'I guess so.'

'I heard she's going to wear a white dress. Really! At her age and for her second wedding. That's not right.'

'I guess not.'

'You're not paying attention. What's wrong, Ellie?'

'Mom, can I come visit you for the night tonight? I need a little break.'

'Of course. And bring Tim. I haven't seen him for so long.'

Tim wouldn't want to go, Ellie knew. He hated being stuck in his grandmother's apartment, would hate it even more now because he'd be away from Lauren.

'No, he has school here, remember? I'll arrange for him to stay over with a friend. I'll just come for the night, if that's OK?'

'Of course.'

'I'll get a bus. I should be there in the late afternoon.'

'Good. I'll see what I can find to cook for dinner.'

'Don't worry – I'm not hungry. See you later then,' she said, anxious to end the call and look up the bus schedule.

'*Ciao*.' Her mother had started saying '*ciao*' a few years ago, and it usually struck Ellie as an amusing quirk, but not this time.

'Goodbye, Mom.'

At least she'd be getting out, she thought as she opened

her laptop and searched online for the schedule. Louisa had been furious and Ellie couldn't call and try to make things better between them. It would be pointless. Louisa would keep trying to deny it was Joe's handwriting, and if Joe were there he'd deny it was his handwriting, and then they'd have to hire an expert handwriting analyst and it would be hell being here while it was all going on. Hell.

After she'd found the bus she needed, which left Tedeschi's at 1 p.m, Ellie called Sam's mother, arranged for Tim to stay the night there, then texted Tim to tell him. She went back to her computer, clicked on 'compose message', and typed:

Dear Daniel,

This is going to be a quick note because I have to pack some things and catch a bus to New York. I'm going to visit my mother for a night. I can't explain everything right now, but I know who has been doing these things to me – Joe, if you can believe it. I got a letter from him written as if it were from Hope, the girl who died. It's sick and I don't know why he's doing this, but I recognised his handwriting. And I had a terrible fight with Louisa. I'm sorry, this is all jumbled up, but I was hoping you might be able to call me. It would be so nice to hear your voice. I'll have my cell phone with me and you have the number from before, but just in case you lost it, it's 616-277-0250.

Love, Ellie.

She packed a few clothes in an overnight bag, and walked out the door. Glancing over at Louisa's house, she felt her heart shrink.

Why did Joe Amory have to ruin everything? Was he

jealous of her relationship with his mother? Could that be it? But how could that be possible? How could Louisa's son have turned out to be so sick and twisted?

Joe had called Louisa from a Dunkin Donuts en route, full of hope about the two interviews he'd had that day, one with a female state senator, another with the aide of a congressman. 'I think they went well, Mum,' he'd said. 'Neither of them dwelled on Brad Harvey for long, so that was a relief.' She'd replied, 'Fantastic,' knowing she couldn't tell him about Ellie on the phone, she'd have to wait until he arrived back.

Louisa was still rocked from their encounter. She couldn't remember ever being so angry before, but then she'd never had to defend Joe from anything like those accusations.

How could Ellie? she kept asking herself. How could she possibly believe Joe would have done that?

She'd found herself wandering around the house talking to herself, like some mad old woman, shaking her head and muttering. Finally, she'd ended up back in the kitchen, opened the fridge and saw the ingredients for the lunch she was going to make for Ellie sitting there. Shutting the door again, she went back to the table, sat down.

The letter had been in an envelope with 'Ellie' written on it and, yes, it had looked like Joe's writing at first; it was certainly very similar. Those gruesome sentences were type-written, however. As the note in Ellie's fridge had been.

Which meant whoever had typed it had either found an enevlope of Joe's with Ellie's name on it or had forged his writing. Neither of those scenarios added up. Why would Joe write Ellie's name on an envelope and leave it lying around? Even if he had, how could someone have found it? But how would anyone trying to forge that envelope know what Joe's handwriting looked like?

Equally inexplicably, why would anyone want to set Joe up for this?

The Yellow Pages book was still lying on the table in front of her. For a moment Louisa considered forgetting about this whole mess, and forgetting Ellie too. They could avoid each other from now on. No more coffee together, no more trips in the boat, no more talks. Ellie would have to deal with her persecutor or persecutors by herself.

I've had enough of these dramas, Louisa thought. And I don't believe I can forgive her anyway.

But who the hell *was* doing this to her? Whoever it was had involved Joe, so they'd involved Louisa too.

'Oh, shit,' she said out loud, flipping the Yellow Pages open to the private investigators section. Taking the cell phone she'd refused to give to Ellie out of her pocket, she dialled the number of a name she liked the sound of: George Andrews Agency.

A female voice answered and said, 'Hold on, I'll put you through' when Louisa asked for Mr Andrews.

'George Andrews. How can I help you?' a man asked.

After introducing herself, Louisa said: 'I hope you can help,' following it with: 'I need to explain the situation and it may take a little time. Is that all right?'

'You got me at a good time, my lunch break. Go ahead. Shoot,' he replied.

As she recapitulated Ellie's story, Louisa thought how odd it must sound to him, and was both amazed and relieved when he didn't interrupt – or simply hang up.

'So you see,' she finished, 'I need to find out who is responsible for all this, and that's why I hope you can help me.'

'All right. I've been writing this down as you talked. Give me a second here.'

She liked his no-nonsense voice.

'OK, this woman Ellie . . . an accident like that at an early age – it would mess with your mind.'

'Yes.'

'And she spent – what was it? – six months in a psychiatric ward?'

'That's what she said, yes. Six months.'

There was silence on his end.

'Mr Andrews?'

'I'm here. Listen, I'd be happy to help you. I have time free on Thursday, you can come to the office then. We can discuss my fees, et cetera. But let me ask you something. I'm thinking off the top of my head here, but I've met some disturbed people in my life – it goes with the territory.'

'I'm sure.'

'And people who end up in psychiatric wards, well, those are hard cases.'

'I'm not sure I understand what you mean.'

'What I'm saying here is, sure, we can meet, but I'm not

in the business of ripping people off. So I'm going to ask you this: all these incidents, did you witness any of them?'

'Witness? No. I didn't see anyone break into her house, if that's what you mean.'

'Or . . . hang on . . . put garbage on the beach, or put a bicycle on her lawn, or write that letter?'

'No, obviously I didn't witness that. If I did, I'd know who was responsible.'

Clearly she'd chosen a particularly dumb private detective. Louisa sighed.

'That's not my point,' he said.

'What *is* your point? You've lost me.'

'My point is, you say no one knows about this accident that happened. At least, no one who would do these types of things. So, off the top of my head, like I said, my first question is, could this woman Ellie have done them herself? You wouldn't believe what people do to bring attention to themselves. And she does have a history of mental illness.'

'No. No, that's not possible.'

'If you say so. All right, look, let's make an appointment. For some reason this week is a really busy one, so like I said I can't make it until Thursday. I'd prefer it if you could bring this woman with you. It would make my job a hell of a lot easier.'

'I'm not sure about bringing her,' she said after they'd set up an appointment for Thursday at 2 p.m.

'Well, you're paying. All I'm saying is, it might take a lot longer, cost a lot more.'

'That's all right.' She paused. 'Mr Andrews, I want to ask you something. Do you think I should go to the police?'

'No offence, but the police are busier than I am. I don't think you'd get a great response from them. Firstly, there's no direct threat. Secondly, they're not too good with oddball stuff. And this story, well, it's off the wall, for sure.'

After she'd hung up, Louisa sat pinching the bridge of her nose until it hurt. Then she pinched the top of her lip.

'No. She wouldn't. It's impossible.'

'What's impossible? Mum, you've really got to stop talking to yourself.'

Joe was at the threshold of the kitchen, smiling.

18

Ellie made it to Tedeschi's just in time to catch the bus. There were only a few people at the front, so she went to the back, put her bag on a seat by the aisle, then collapsed in the seat by the window.

That speech to Louisa she'd made this morning about not letting anyone drive her away from Bourne seemed like centuries ago. All she wanted to do was get away.

The bus started up, the doors closed. They took a left-hand turn on to the main road. Looking out of her window, Ellie saw a familiar car driving past on the other side of the street. Joe Amory was at the wheel.

What would happen when he got back home? What would he say to Louisa? 'She's crazy. She has a thing about me. God, Mum, what a nutcase.'

Ellie couldn't stand the thought of going over and over it all again in a brain race, trying to figure out what his motives were.

What did I ever do to you? Is it because I had sex with you? Do you think I'm a whore?

As they left the Welcome to Cape Cod roundabout sign behind and headed on to the Bourne Bridge, Ellie pulled out her cell phone. She'd arranged for Tim to stay at Sam's, but she'd prefer it if he stayed with Charlie, in Boston. When she called Charlie and asked, he was more than willing to pick Tim up.

'I'm sorry I don't have time to talk, El. But I've got a shedload of work, especially if I'm going to be picking up Tim.'

'Thank you for this, Charlie. I really appreciate it. I'll be back from my mother's in time to pick him up tomorrow from school.'

'No problem. And give my best to your mother, will you?'

'Yes, of course.'

Charlie and her mother had always gotten on incredibly well.

'OK, I'll call Tim, let him know I'll pick him up. Have a good trip. Bye, El.'

'Goodbye.'

Maybe we *can* have a civilised relationship, she thought, as she called Sam's mother to cancel, then dialled Tim's number and left a message, telling him plans had changed and Charlie would be picking him up and taking him to Boston for the night.

After she'd said 'Love you' and hung up, she reached over, took her laptop from her bag, opened it up. She'd made a special file of all her and Daniel's emails.

She didn't want to think about Joe and Louisa sitting in that house discussing her. Or the words in that disgusting letter. Or how she'd handle all this when she got back tomorrow. She wanted to read this correspondence, get some sanity back in her life.

Halfway through, as she was reading Daniel's email about a trip he'd taken to Scotland, her phone rang – an unfamiliar number, but then she saw it was a Washington area code.

There was no good place to have this conversation, but a bus was one of the worst ones. She let it ring out. As she had expected, she saw a minute or so later that he'd left a voice message.

Right, she said to herself. I want to hear this one.

'Ellie, it's Joe. My mother told me what happened between you. Jesus Christ. I thought you said you didn't do drugs. I didn't write that hideous note. Why the fuck would I? I can't fucking believe you could think that. My mother said you said I'd written you a letter before – what the fuck is that about? I never wrote you any letter. I have no idea why it looked like my handwriting on the envelope. It wasn't. You told me to leave you alone and I've left you alone. I'm sorry about that note, but I'm pissed as hell you believe I wrote it. I didn't steal the money from the charity box, I didn't put a bicycle on your lawn – shit! Where are you? I want to see that envelope.'

His outrage was so palpable, Ellie was shaking. Of course he'd lash out at her, she thought. The best defence was offence. But what was that part in the middle? She replayed the message, steeling herself against the anger in his voice.

'You told me to leave you alone and I left you alone.'

When? When had she told him to leave her alone? Why would he make that up? Her brain began to hurt.

Joe worked in politics, he was used to lying. Yet that rage sounded so genuine. '*I didn't steal the money from the charity box, I didn't put a bicycle on your lawn –* '

Ellie slumped against the window.

Why the fuck would I?

That was the unanswerable question, the one which had stumped her all along.

But why the fuck would *anybody*?

Why would he want to see the envelope if he knew it was his own handwriting on it?

Why *write* Ellie on the front when he knew she might recognise it from the letter he'd sent? He could have typed 'Ellie'. That thought hadn't occurred to her before.

Because some part of her was relieved in a way, to know who was doing this?

I never wrote you any letter.

He'd already told her he wanted to act as if the night between them hadn't happened. She hadn't contacted him. There'd been no need for that letter. Yet Louisa *had* recognised the handwriting on the envelope – at first. And that same handwriting had been on the fuck-off letter.

Confusion gave way to something else. Exhaustion. She tried to read Daniel's email again but couldn't concentrate.

You should cry me a river.

Wake up, Ellie, she told herself.

Her eyes were so heavy and her body was so heavy and it was too much for her. Her head fell forward, she snapped it back. It happened again and she woke up with a jerk.

Stay awake.

Her eyelids wouldn't obey. They drooped down.

'Sorry, Tim, I can't make it. I'd love to meet your dad, but I have to go to *my* dad's tonight – in Hyannisport. I'll see you tomorrow, though. You're coming back tomorrow, right?'

'Absolutely. I'll meet you after school, OK? I can walk over to your house.'

'That's a haul. I can bike over to school. Whatever. Just give me a call.'

'Right.'

'And don't look up any old girlfriends in Boston tonight.'

'Shit – how did you know?'

'So funny. I can't stop laughing. See you tomorrow.'

'See you.'

Ending the call, Tim walked over to the car park where his dad had said he'd pick him up, sat down on a wall at the side.

So he couldn't have seen Lauren tonight anyway. Going to his dad's wasn't as much of a pain as he'd thought. Tim put his iPod on, stuck the earphones in his ears, put on the Cowboy Junkies, another CD Lauren told him he had to listen to. She didn't like any music less than twenty years old as far as he could tell, but that was another interesting thing about her. She had all these sides to her, was always surprising him, making him think.

Like that fate business the night he'd first kissed her. They'd stopped talking about it as soon as they'd started kissing, but he'd been thinking about it and now he wanted to tell her those thoughts.

Maybe he'd do it tomorrow, ask her how she squared it. Because he sure as shit couldn't. Yeah, OK, *some* bad things turned out good, but how about a little baby who gets sick and dies when he's like two years old? How does that turn out good? Or all the kids in Africa starving to death or dying of AIDS? Tim couldn't see any redeeming part to that: he wanted to know how Lauren could.

Never in a million years had he thought he'd actually want to have a philosophical discussion with a girl, especially a hot girl. Way too many other things he'd want to do with her. Maybe that's what happened when you fell in love, though.

He saw his father's car take the turn into the parking lot and stood up.

So according to Lauren it was a good thing his dad went off with Sandra, Tim thought as he watched his father park. That way she and he got to meet. But how about his mom? Had that played out well for her too?

Tim wasn't so sure about that.

He trudged over to the car. 'Misguided Angel' was playing on the iPod. A kind of haunting, killer song. Lauren was right about these guys. And Tim never would have heard this if he hadn't met her.

Fate. When it worked, it rocked.

Ellie woke up as the bus pulled into the Port Authority station. Is it Joe or not? was her first conscious thought. Sleep had given her a break, but as soon as it ended, she was back where she had been. Nightmares were supposed to end when you woke up – but not hers. It was beginning all over again. Her laptop was still on her lap. Putting it back into its case and taking her overnight bag, she disembarked and started to walk to the subway station.

Almost everyone she knew loved New York City: the buzz, the culture, the excitement of the Big Apple. As far as Ellie was concerned, New York was crowded, dirty, depressing. Whether you lived in a fancy apartment on Park Avenue or a one-room place in Chinatown, you were stuck in a square box, effectively – one with a big park in the middle of it, but still a box. And all these people in the box were waiting.

Pedestrians gathered in throngs at street corners, waiting for a little green man to flash up so they could cross a street. Cabs waited at traffic lights, honking. Customers formed lines at delicatessens, waiting to be served. Waitresses waited tables, waiting to be discovered. Dog walkers waited for their dogs to poop so they could scoop it up and go home.

Her mother sat in her apartment, waiting for her life to get better. And doing absolutely nothing to make that happen.

Right now, though, Ellie was relieved to be among this throng, riding a subway, safely anonymous. No one knew who she was, or cared. All these people were in worlds of their own, just as she was. They all had their own stories and they didn't want to know hers.

She wanted to tell her mother what was going on, confide in her, but if she did, she'd only succeed in worrying her, and Ellie had been the cause of anxiety to her for too long.

First the accident, which had traumatised her mother as well, she was sure, then her nervous breakdown, and then, just as her mother thought Ellie was on an even course – a happily married mother – the divorce.

Her mother wasn't like Louisa. She wasn't free-spirited, she hadn't had a happy marriage. And she'd had no idea how to deal with her daughter when she'd shut herself away in her room and refused to leave. She'd been anxious and frightened, and at times, Ellie thought, she'd not only been afraid for her, but afraid of her, too – this unreachable daughter who had turned in on herself.

When she'd come back from the hospital, she could see her mother was tiptoeing around her, desperate not to say something that might send her spiralling down again. And she'd been so fragile, she'd tiptoed too.

Occasionally they'd manage moments of mother-daughter connection, especially when Charlie had been around, but most of the time they stuck rigidly to banal conversations on banal topics.

Ellie knew what she'd find as soon as she got off the subway and walked into the apartment on the Upper West Side: her mother would be stretched across the sofa watching *Law & Order*, a cup of coffee on the floor beside her.

How could *Law & Order* manage to be on screen practically 24/7? she wondered as she got out at the subway stop and made her way across Broadway and down 110th Street towards West Side Drive. There was always a *Law & Order* episode playing: if not that, then *Law & Order Special Victims Unit*, or *Law & Order: Criminal Intent*. Detectives Briscoe and Green and all the others had become, over the years, Ellie's semi-siblings. She knew all their little habits and facial gestures, their astounding ability to solve cases. At times, she imagined running into one of the actors on the street and sympathising with their plight; all those horrendous dead bodies they dealt with on a daily basis.

She was right: *Law & Order* was on when she let herself in to the apartment. She could hear the familiar voices.

'Hi, Mom,' she said, as her mother got up off the sofa. 'How are you?'

Her mother gave her a quick hug, stepped back.

'I'm fine. How are you? How was the trip?'

'Good. I slept through most of it. I'll get myself some coffee, if that's all right?'

'Of course. It's right there, ready and waiting for you. Get yourself some and come sit down.'

Putting her bag and laptop on the hall floor, Ellie did just that, then went to the living room and sat down on the chair beside the sofa, at right angles to the television. Her mother was dressed in her usual sweatpants and top, with no shoes on but with immaculately coiffed hair. After retiring from her work in an accounting firm three years before, she could have done something creative or fun with her free time. Instead she'd discovered the wonders of crime TV.

'Do you mind if we wait to talk until this episode's over?' she asked.

'That's fine,' Ellie replied. What she longed to do was go into her old bedroom, curl up and fall asleep again. But falling alseep like that on the bus had been bad enough.

Because it had been *that* kind of sleep, the escape kind of sleep she'd fled into after the accident.

Someone had once told her that when they found the black boxes after an airplane crash, nine times out of ten, the pilot's last words would be: 'I love you, Mom.' Looking at her mother staring at the screen, Ellie wished she could pour everything out, say, 'What do I do now, Mom? Help me.' But there was an invisible barrier between them, one that had locked itself in place nineteen years ago, one neither of them knew how to break down.

Looking away from her mother, Ellie zeroed in on the television. In this episode of *Law & Order*, an army officer's wayward wife was smuggling cocaine in from Colombia and had gotten herself involved with a murder. Ellie had seen it at least twice. Which meant her mother must have seen it scores of times.

'You know how this turns out, Mom,' she stated.

'I know. But Sam Waterston's about to come on. I love him.'

'Doesn't everybody?' Ellie sighed, settled in for the long haul.

Yet in its own odd way watching TV in the two-bedroomed, bleak, sunless apartment was comforting. It was a hell of a lot better to watch this show than feel as if you were on it yourself when you opened an envelope, read what was inside and felt so sick you almost threw up.

When it ended, and Sam Waterston had the final words with his black-haired assistant whose name Ellie could never remember, her mother paused the TV.

'So,' she said, 'how's Tim?'

'Tim's fine.'

'That's good.' Her mother snuck a quick glance at the TV, then reached for the remote control and turned it off. 'I told you about the widow downstairs, didn't I?'

'Yes.'

'And whatever was bothering you – that's all fine now?'

Ellie nodded.

Her mother picked up her mug from the floor, took a sip.

'How's that new place you're living in?'

'Bourne. It's fine.'

'That's good. And how is Charlie?'

'I talked to him today. He said to send you his best. He's marrying Sandra Cabot in December.'

'Oh, no. No, I don't think so.' Her face looked pained.

'I know so, Mom.'

'I think you're mistaken.'

'I'm not, OK? Can we drop this subject?'

'You should give him another chance, Ellie. He's a good man. He made a mistake, that's all.'

'Like Dad did?' She hadn't been able to stop herself.

'This is nothing to do with your father.'

'You're right.' Ellie sighed. Her mother adored Charlie. Whenever he'd see her, he'd sit down, ask her all the right questions, say all the right things. Because he'd paid attention to her stories from the beginning, remembered the details and who was who, he made her believe he was as interested in her world as she was. There was no point in trying to point out the similarities between Charlie and her father – her mother didn't want to know.

'So how's Aunt Sarah?' she asked, lobbing what she knew was an easy ball for her mother to catch and run with. While her mother indulged in family gossip for ten minutes, Ellie tried to keep up, but her thoughts kept reverting to Joe's message. Should she go into her room and call him back? Or would that be tantamount to saying she believed him? Did she believe him? Circles. Endless fucking circles.

'Ellie? Did you hear what I just said?'

'Yes, Joel's going to medical school. That's great. I think I'll go unpack my things.'

Collecting her bag and laptop, she went into her bedroom. Looking around, she wished she'd asked her mother to redecorate it a long time ago. It was the same as it had been since they'd moved in, after her father had left, when Ellie was six years old. The same *Wizard of Oz* books on the shelves, the same glass horse she'd won at a school fair when she was eight. The only thing that had changed were the walls. The day after the accident, she'd ripped off the poster of Brad Pitt she'd put up when she was eleven. Her mother, for some unaccountable reason, had replaced it with one of George Clooney when Ellie had been in the hospital. He was still there, looking suave.

She took her cell phone out of her bag, sat down on the bed. She could call Joe now, she *should* call Joe now. If he wasn't the person who had written those words . . .

I'm so tired.

If I could just lie down for a second . . .

'Ellie.'

Her eyes flashed open.

Her mother was standing over her.

'Ellie – you've been in here for forty-five minutes. It's only six thirty and you said you slept on the bus.'

'I'm . . . I'm sorry, Mom.' Sitting up, she rubbed her forehead. 'I haven't been sleeping well lately. I'll get up now, I'll be right there.'

'Are you sure you're all right?'

You *could* rewind the tape. She just had. Her mother was looking at her the way she'd looked at her all those years ago, the same tone of anxiety and helplessness in her voice.

'I'm fine, honestly. I'll be right in.'

19

Part of bringing up a child was creating rituals. There was a sense of safety in repetition which appealed to kids – and especially, Louisa thought, to Joe, who otherwise led a hectic spontaneous life when he was growing up. Coming to Bourne for summer vacation was one of these rituals for Louisa, Jamie and Joe: they always packed the night before they left, took the same flight to Boston on the same airline, arrived on the same day in June, left on the same day in September. And the three of them always went to the Clam Shack when they wanted to celebrate something, or if the weather was bad and they wanted to cheer themselves up.

Luckily, the Clam Shack didn't change either. It had existed when Louisa was a child, and it was still there, living up to its name, a little shack with a few tables, on the road to Buzzards Bay, wedged in between an amusement centre and a gift shop selling saltwater taffy and Cape Cod mementoes.

The day had been beyond disturbing. Her scene with Ellie, Joe's furious reaction when she'd told him about Ellie's accusations, a whole cloud of nastiness polluting the atmosphere.

Meanwhile Ellie had vanished. Joe had called and left a message – God knows what he'd said in the frame of mind he was in. Ellie hadn't returned his call, probably not wanting another blast from him. Despite her own anger, Louisa couldn't help but worry. She phoned Tim, who told her his mother had gone to his grandmother's in New York.

It was just as well she had, Louisa decided. Maybe Ellie would come to her senses in New York.

Joe had gone for a long run and afterwards a swim. When he returned from that, he'd sat down with her on the porch and she'd told him about the private investigator.

'You were right about hiring one,' she said. 'We have to find out who is responsible for this. The PI, Mr Andrews, said something strange, though. He thought Ellie might be doing all this to herself – to get attention.'

'That's nuts.'

'I know. But then, you do hear about those kind of people. What's it called? Munchausen Syndrome by proxy? The people who pretend they're sick and have needless oper-ations . . . no – they're the people who pretend other people are sick. Just plain Munchausen's Syndrome? I don't know. It's all nuts.'

'All I know is, I didn't do anything. Ellie's the one who wrote *me*, telling me to keep away from her.'

'She never told me that.'

'Yeah, well, she wouldn't. It was a crappy letter.'

They sat in silence for a minute, both wrapped up in their own thoughts.

'Hey.' Joe put his hands in the air. 'Maybe you can throw

me another party, with a ton of people who have been falsely accused.'

'Joe.'

'Come on, that was funny. Kind of. Shit – I still can't believe she could think it was me.'

'Neither can I. I was so livid when she said those things. God, it was awful.'

They'd finally decided to get out and come to the Clam Shack, but they hadn't exactly cheered up. Uneaten fried clams lay on paper plates in front of them. Louisa speared one with her fork, looked at its fat belly.

Can You Forgive Her? the title of a Trollope novel she'd read years ago popped into her brain.

Ellie was going through hell. That message had been disgusting and frightening. The handwriting *had* looked like Joe's.

Could she forgive her?

Putting the clam back down on the plate, she took a sip of her Diet Coke.

It keeps getting messier. There are no answers. It's a good thing she's gone away. We need some peace. And she needs some space where she can sit down and think rationally.

'Louisa, Joe, hi!'

Tim Walters had suddenly appeared at their table in his ominpresent jeans and T-shirt, smiling happily.

'Tim, hello.' Louisa struggled to sound pleased to see him and hoped she'd managed to. 'What are you doing here? Sorry. Stupid question. Getting some clams, obviously.'

'Yeah. I came here with my dad. We're on our way to

251

Boston for the night, but I wanted him to have some of these clams. Dad . . .' he called out to a man who was about to sit down at a table a few feet away. 'Come over here. I want you to meet some friends of mine.'

Glancing at Joe, Louisa saw him roll his eyes. This was all they needed now. But she rose to her feet politely as Charlie Walters approached their table, and Joe did as well.

'Dad, this is Louisa Amory. And her son Joe.'

'It's very nice to meet you both.' Charlie shook hands with Louisa, then Joe. He was short, with a head of thick brown hair, close-set eyes and a narrow face. Dressed in a dark blue suit with a perfectly pressed white shirt and a tie that most probably had 'Brooks Brothers' embossed on the back, he stood out among the shorts and T-shirts of the Clam Shack clientele. But he didn't look uncomfortable at all.

'We don't want to interrupt your dinner, but I've heard such nice things about you from Tim. It's wonderful to meet you in person.'

He spoke quietly and slowly, as if each sentence counted.

'It's nice to meet you too,' Louisa replied, trying to picture Charlie and Ellie together. He'd be taller than she, but not by much.

'Tim told me you took him to the batting cages here,' Charlie addressed Joe. 'I wish I could help him with that, but I'm uncoordinated when it comes to baseball. The only sport I was any good at was wrestling.'

'Wrestling Brewster,' Joe murmured.

'Sorry?'

252

'Wrestling Brewster. That was the name of one of the Pilgrim kids on the *Mayflower*, Dad.'

'Really? What a great name. Tim also tells me constantly about how fantastic your house is, Mrs Amory.'

'It's Louisa, and thank you,' she said. 'And thank you too, Tim. Why don't you two join us?'

She avoided looking at Joe, knowing he wouldn't be pleased. But something about Charlie Walters's politeness required matching politeness from her.

'That's very kind of you.'

'Dad, is it OK if I go play a quick game of pinball before we eat? The pinball place is just over there. I won't be long.'

Charlie looked at Louisa. She nodded.

'All right, Tim. Go ahead. But not for long. When you come back, we'll get a table for ourselves.' Then Charlie looked over at Joe, who was staring at his plate. 'There's a time limit to entertaining unexpected guests.'

Joe glanced up then, but Louisa couldn't read what he was thinking. She watched as Charlie got a chair from an empty table beside them, placed it at theirs and sat down.

His eyes went from Louisa to Joe and back again.

'You two have the same eyebrows.'

Louisa found herself staring at Joe's eyebrows.

'You're right. I never noticed that before.'

'Do you have the same sense of humour?'

'Why?' Joe spoke up. 'Do people with the same eyebrows always have the same sense of humour?'

'I doubt it.' Charlie paused. 'But it would be interesting if they did.'

Ellie was right, Louisa thought. If I were at a party and he were standing in a corner, I'd want to go talk to him. And I'd be intrigued by whatever he had to say.

'You know, Tim has an artistic streak,' she said.

'Well, he doesn't get it from me.' Charlie smiled. 'I'm a lawyer. Lawyers destroy, they don't create.'

'I don't think pro bono lawyers destroy,' Joe stated.

Thinking of her brother's descriptions of his huskies, Louisa decided Joe was behaving just like a dog, sniffing around Charlie, challenging him.

'You're absolutely right, Joe.' Charlie nodded.

There was nowhere for Joe to go with that response. Louisa, seeing him struggling, wanted to tell him to stop trying. Charlie Walters was way ahead of him.

'I've interrupted your meal long enough.' Charlie stood up. 'It was very nice to have met you both. And thank you again for all you've done for Tim.'

'We haven't done anything we didn't want to do. He's a terrific boy.'

'Thank you.' He seemed about to walk away, but stayed, resting his hands on the back of his chair. 'I know it's not my place to say this, but I do worry about Ellie. When I last saw her, she looked upset and worried. She has a delicate nature. Sometimes she . . .' His eyes swivelled away, swivelled back. 'I hope you'll look after her. No, I'm sure you will.'

'We'll do our best. It was nice to meet you too and I hope you enjoy the clams here.'

'What's not to like about clams? Unless you get a bad

one. Which couldn't possibly happen in a place called the Clam Shack, could it? I'll go get Tim away from those infernal pinball machines.' He gave a little nod, walked off towards the amusement arcade.

'Whoa!' Joe said as soon as Charlie was out of earshot. 'He's something else. I can't believe she married him.'

Louisa didn't respond. She could believe Ellie had married Charlie. His soft voice, the way he carried himself, how his eyes focused on the person to whom he spoke. There was a stillness to him, and a natural authority. It would have been easy to fall for that; especially easy after what Ellie had been through. She had said he was a corporate lawyer, yet Louisa could picture Charlie Walters trying criminal cases, with the jury all leaning forward to hear what he was saying, rapt.

'He's a jerk.' Joe took a French fry from his plate, gobbled it. 'Let's get out of here.'

'All right. I'm not hungry anyway.'

He took a handful of French fries with him as they went to the car. On the trip back they were both silent.

Yes, Louisa thought. Charlie Walters would take care of everything. And he would care about being polite. Ellie said he was thirty-eight, but he seemed older. In her experience, most people who were driven were nervous types. They couldn't sit still for long, were always up and doing things. Charlie looked as though, in other circumstances, he could happily have sat at their table for a long time, asking slightly offbeat questions, listening, all the while taking in every detail. Ellie was right, Louisa thought. She had liked him.

Or perhaps she'd simply been fascinated by him. Whichever the case, he was defintely interesting.

'I'm going to take a shower,' Joe said when they got back to the house. 'I feel grubby.'

'Are you all right, Joe?'

'I'm OK. I'm sorry you had to get dragged into all this, though. I know how much you like Ellie and now it's all mixed up with me and that can't be easy for you.'

'I don't think anything is easy for anyone right now. But that's not your fault.'

He walked over to her, gave her a big bear hug.

'I'm coming to see that detective with you. No way are you going alone.'

'That would be nice. Thanks.' She hugged him as hard as she could. 'I wish your father were here.'

'Dad?' Joe stepped back. 'I didn't think about that. Dad would be right in the thick of it, wouldn't he? He'd be seeing conspiracies everywhere. Shit – he'd think the FBI were behind it all.'

Louisa laughed – truly laughed.

Joe had Jamie's sense of humour. And his lean and hungry look. And that light he carried with him which dazzled her heart. She watched him as he went upstairs, full of pride and love. He'd be gone again soon. Maybe living closer – in Boston – but in a place of his own. He was home with her now, though, and even with all the drama and sadness and pain of today, she adored having him here.

As she went and sat on the living-room sofa, Louisa heard Ellie saying: 'I wish I could talk to my mother the way I talk to you, but I can't. I don't know exactly what it is, but we have these meaningless conversations and then watch television. As if watching TV were our default mode.'

Guilty pleasure had snuck into Louisa's heart when Ellie had told her that over coffee at Atwoods. She didn't want Ellie to have a bad relationship with her mother, but she couldn't help but feel complimented.

I would have loved to have had a daughter, too, she'd said to herself then. *I would have loved to have had a daughter like Ellie.*

Can I forgive her? she asked herself.

What had Charlie been about to say before that 'Never mind'?

'*I do worry about Ellie. Sometimes she . . .*'

Sometimes she what?

Louisa thought she knew Ellie; that over these weeks they'd spent together she had become closer to her than she'd been to anyone in a long time. Yet that's exactly what it had been − weeks. And she'd conveniently swept aside the characteristic of Ellie she hadn't wanted to think about: her unnatural ability to hide things. After nineteen years of repressing an essential truth in her life, how much else had she managed to keep in the dark?

Just as Louisa had been pleased when Ellie said she'd wished she could talk to her mother in the way she talked to her, she had to admit she had also taken satisfaction from being the person who had helped Ellie start to deal with the pain and grief of the accident. It was egocentric of her, she knew, yet she had felt useful − and needed.

Because of this, had she fooled herself into believing Ellie really was coming to terms with her past? Or was Ellie in even worse shape than she could have imagined?

If I tried to find out who was doing this, I'd only be playing their game.

But who wouldn't want to know who was doing this? Unless . . .

She does have a history of mental illness.

No – it was impossible.

It had to be.

20

14 August

Ellie came out of her sleep into a daze, not knowing where she was or whether it was night or day; only conscious enough to be aware that there was a phone ringing somewhere. Just as she remembered she was in her mother's apartment, she realised too that her cell phone was on the bedside table and quickly lunged for it before the ringing stopped.

'Hello,' she said as she reached over and switched on the lamp, terrified by the thought it was Charlie and something had happened to Tim.

'Ellie?'

'Yes.'

'I'm sorry if I woke you up.'

A man's voice and there was music in the background.

'It's Daniel. Oops! Wait a second. I need to get out of this noisy room.'

Daniel? She checked the radio clock and saw it was five minutes past midnight. Which meant it was 5.05 a.m. his time.

'There . . . that's better.' The music had disappeared. 'I'm really sorry. I was out in the country today. No bloody reception. And these drug company people took a group of us out and it's turned into an all-nighter. On a Sunday. How crazy is that? But I just checked my iPhone and saw your email. Are you all right?'

'Daniel. God, I can't believe it's you.'

'Well, it is. A little the worse for wear, but that email sounded so distraught. I needed to know if you're OK.'

'I'm OK. Wait a second.' She put a pillow behind her, sat back against the bedhead. 'I'm sorry. I didn't mean you had to call when you're out like that. Oh, God, I don't know what to say. I feel foolish. I shouldn't have written that email.'

'Don't be ridiculous. I'm glad you did.' He coughed. 'Sorry about that. I have a bug. Doctors aren't allowed to be sick but it does happen. But listen, it's time we talked. All this crap you're going through there . . . I can't believe it. I wish there was something I could do to help.'

'Calling me like this is a big help. It's been so long, I'd forgotten what you sound like.'

'Well, you're welcome to give me shit if I've picked up an English accent. It's hard not to but it sounds so fake, you know?'

'How is everything there?'

'Hectic. But listen, I don't want to talk about me. We're not at dinner.' His laugh turned into another cough. 'No, seriously. Tell me what's going on. Joe wrote you something? You think he's the one who put the bicycle there?'

'I did, but I'm not sure now. I can't be certain about anything any more, Daniel. Except that I hate all this. I

260

thought it was Joe, but it's all so complicated and so much of it doesn't add up. I keep falling asleep too, which isn't good. But all I want to do is to sleep.'

'Ellie, listen. There's an oncology conference in Boston this week and one of the other oncologists dropped out so I get to go. I'm flying in tomorrow night – no, wait, tonight – I forgot it's five in the morning already. Anyway, I'm getting a plane this afternoon. I could rent a car and come see you at the cottage as soon as I land.'

'You're coming tomorrow? Oh my God, I can't believe it. I'm going back to Bourne tomorrow. I'll get my car there, and then I can drive to Boston and pick you up at the airport . . .'

'Hang on a second.' He had a short coughing fit. 'I don't think you should pick me up. You're exhausted and the plane might be late – it's easier if I just hop into a rental car and come to the cottage. Will you be all right being there? In the cottage, I mean?'

'Yes. I need to . . .' She sat forward, clutching the phone tightly. 'I need to pull myself together. And you're coming. It makes a big difference, knowing that. God, that sounds so needy, sorry. I don't want to put any pressure on you. It's just that it will be so nice to see you again.'

'Ditto. We've come a long way since that night in Acquitaine, haven't we?'

'Yes.' She pulled her knees up to her chest.

'We've shared so much. And it feels to me like we're on the same page, in all senses of that phrase, you know?'

'Yes, I do know.'

'Ellie, I've had a fair amount to drink. I don't want to put any pressure on you either, but, hell, *in vino veritas* or whatever, I have to say something. It may sound crazy, I know. We've only met once. But it feels as if I've known you for a long time. You're a huge part of my life now. I wait for your emails. Oh, Christ, I'll just say it. I love you. There. I've said it. I love you.'

'I love you too, Daniel.'

'Wow.'

Every cell in her body smiled.

When she was a kid Ellie used to play the rocks/scissors/paper game with her friends. Scissors beat paper, rock beat scissors, paper beat rock. She'd always be careful not to hurt anyone when she won – she'd give just a light tap on the wrist. And she always wondered why paper beat rock.

Now, as the bus made its way on to Route 195, she wondered whether falling in love beat fear. Because she was still afraid, but not in the same way she had been. After she and Daniel had hung up, she'd gone back to sleep but hadn't felt that overwhelming lassitude. It was normal sleep. When she'd woken up, she'd gotten out of bed quickly, taken a shower, had a cup of coffee with her mother, even willingly participated in another round of gossip. Yes, her thoughts were still being diverted by that note, by Joe's message, but she kept flashing back to Daniel's 'Wow' and she kept feeling herself smile when she did.

Her 'I love you too' had come out unbidden – an immediate response. As as soon as she'd said it, she knew it was the truth.

They were on the same page, in all senses of that phrase. They'd come to know each other in an unusual way, but because of the distance between them, they'd been able to share things it might have taken years to share otherwise. She'd fallen in love with Daniel because of his words, which came from his soul, not because her stomach churned every time she saw him.

He knew all her history, he knew *her*. This wasn't some madcap romance or yet another mistake. It was real. They had approached love from a different angle, getting to know each other before hurling themselves into each other's arms.

Looking out the window, she saw the sign for Plymouth and her thoughts returned to Louisa and Joe. When she got home, she'd have to face them both. If Joe hadn't written that note – and the more she thought about it, the more uncertain she was that he had – Louisa would probably never forgive her. Even if Joe were responsible, how could Louisa continue to be her friend?

She knew she'd have to try to deal with that loss. She'd have to deal with whoever was doing this to her too. Perhaps that note was close enough to a threat for her to go to the police without them thinking she was some crazy woman ranting about bicycles on her lawn and trash on her beach.

Daniel was coming. She could talk about it all rationally with him. They were in love, but they were friends, too – that was the beauty of taking time to get to know someone. She and Charlie had been passionate, but when that passion

263

had dwindled, as it almost inevitably did in a marriage, they hadn't had a real friendship to fall back on. Charlie had had all the power in their relationship – she'd given it to him willingly. They weren't equals.

Maybe he and Sandra were friends as well as lovers. That thought didn't hurt Ellie as it might have before.

She'd get off the bus, go pick Tim up from school, call Joe, hear what he had to say.

You should cry me a river.

Ellie stared out the bus window. Love might not beat fear, but it sure as hell helped fight it.

21

When his mother picked him up, Tim had asked her if she could drop him off at Lauren's. She'd seemed a little anxious to get back to the cottage, but he'd come out with 'Pretty please?' and she'd laughed and said: 'OK.'

On the drive there, she'd started talking about her pen pal, and how he was coming over from England and was going to visit the cottage that night.

'You must be pretty excited about that,' he'd said. 'So what's the deal, Mom? How serious is this?'

'You sound like a parent, Tim.' She'd laughed again. 'It's pretty serious. I want us all to have dinner together so you can get to know him. What you think is important to me, you know that.'

'Hey, Dad set the bar low. He can't be worse than Sandra.'

'How was Dad? Did you have a good time last night?'

'It was OK. How was Granny?'

'Fine.'

'Cool – you take a left here, and it's the third house on the left.'

After they'd swung in to the driveway, he said: 'Why don't you come inside for a few minutes, say hi to Lauren?'

'I don't know.'

'Come on, you keep saying you'd like to meet her again.'

'OK. I'll come in for a few minutes, but then I have to go.'

They got out of the car, climbed the three stairs to Lauren's porch. Tim rang the bell. When Lauren came to the door, she said, 'Hello, Mrs Walters. It's nice to see you again. Come inside. Can I get you anything to drink?'

His dad would love that whole polite thing Lauren did. He could see his mom appreciated it too.

'That's nice of you, Lauren. A glass of water would be great.'

Lauren went to the fridge while Tim sat on his usual stool and his mother sat on the one beside him.

'Ice?'

'Yes, please. This is such a nice house, Lauren. I like how it's open-plan – you can cook and talk to people at the same time.'

'It's functional.' Lauren handed the glass of water to his mother. 'But I like your place too. It's got that whole homey thing going for it.'

'Thank you. And I love that Bonnie Raitt CD you gave Tim.'

'I'm trying to educate him.' Lauren raised her eyebrows at him.

'Yeah, well, I'm trying to help her draw a straight line. It takes patience, believe me.'

'Sorry,' his mom said then because her cell phone was ringing. She fished it out of her bag, looked at it.

'There's no number but I better take this. It might be Daniel. Maybe he missed the plane. Excuse me for a second.'

'Who's Daniel?' Lauren asked when his mother took the phone out on to the porch.

'Mr Pen Pal. He's flying in from England and coming tonight. She's psyched.'

'Maybe she'll get some action tonight.'

'Don't go there.' Tim put his hands up.

'My bad, yeah, but it's not as if—'

'Stop it! Stop it! Leave me alone! Stop it!'

It was his mother screaming. Tim bolted out of the house, saw her standing at the bottom of the steps, the phone clutched in her hand.

'Mom?'

She didn't say anything; she was turning around, looking all over the place.

'Mrs Walters?' Lauren was behind him.

'I can't do this,' she said. She was still looking around everywhere.

'You can't do what?' Tim went up to her. 'What happened, Mom?'

'Why? Why?' She looked at him then, but it was as if she didn't know who he was.

'Why what? Mom?'

Lauren had come up too. He looked at her, she looked at him.

'Has something terrible happened, Mrs Walters? Did you get bad news?'

'I'm sorry, I have to go.' She walked to the car, opened the door, got in the driver's seat.

'You better go with her.' Lauren nudged Tim with her elbow. 'Call me.'

'Right.' He sprinted over to the car, got in the passenger seat just as his mom was starting to reverse out.

'Mom – hold on. Tell me what happened. What was that call about?'

They were on the road; his mother kept looking into the rear-view mirror.

'Can you look behind you? Is anyone following us?'

He swivelled, looked over his shoulder.

'No. Mom, you're really scaring me. What's going on?'

'No one's behind us?' She looked in the rear-view mirror again, so did he.

'No one's there, Mom.'

'I can't . . . I have to . . .' She pulled over abruptly to the side of the road, into a random driveway. Her hands were gripping the steering wheel.

'Wait a second, Tim, all right? Just wait a second . . .'

He sat, not knowing what to say or do or think. She'd gone mad. Had she taken some drug accidentally or something?

She finally spoke. 'I'm sorry. I'm not feeling well.'

'Not feeling well? Mom – you were screaming back there.'

'I got a crank call. A really horrible one. It frightened me.'

'What did they say? And why do you think someone might be following us?'

'I can't talk about it now. I have to . . . I have to pull myself together. You should go back to Lauren's, Tim. I'll turn around now, drive you back there.'

'I don't want to go back to Lauren's. We should go home.'

Another bout of silence and then she mumbled something.

'What?'

'Nothing. It's OK. Everything will be OK. I was frightened by the call, that's all. I have a headache, too. Right.' She put her hands back on the wheel. 'We'll go back home now.'

But on the way back she kept looking into the rear-view mirror.

When they got to the cottage, she fished in her bag and it took her forever to find the keys.

'Can you open the door, please, Tim?'

He could see she was shaking too much to do it herself, so he did, then went and grabbed his backpack while she opened the back of the car and got her laptop and overnight bag out.

'Why won't you tell me what they said in the call?' he asked as they stood in the living room. 'I've heard a lot of bad stuff, Mom. It wouldn't scare me. Maybe I can help you feel better. And give me your phone – I can call that number back, give them shit.'

'Tim, sweetheart, there was no number. You can't call back. I need you to do me a favour, though. Can you go over to Louisa's? Ask her to forgive me, tell her I know I was wrong? And ask her to please, please come over here? And if Joe's there, stay there with him in the house until I call you, OK?'

'Mom . . .'

'That would be helping me. A lot.'

He hated the way she wasn't telling him anything, but he couldn't force her.

All that looking in the rear-view mirror – that had been seriously weird. But the way she was asking him, the panic in her voice – he couldn't say no.

'OK, I'll go. But you're going to have to tell me what that call was at some point, Mom. That whole screaming thing – it was bad.'

'I'm sorry. Go to Louisa's now, please, Tim. Tell her I was wrong, ask her to forgive me and come here. Please?'

'What were you wrong . . . ?' He stopped because he could see how desperate she was for him to get out of there, like when he was a kid and had hurt himself and she was desperate to make the hurt go away. 'OK. I'm going.'

When he got outside, he started walking over to Louisa's. Then he broke into a sprint, and then a run. He was running faster than he'd ever thought he could.

'Mom got some crank phone call. She was screaming "stop it" and then . . . and then . . .' He was out of breath, standing in the centre of Louisa's living room, saying this to Joe and Louisa who were sitting down. Both of them had been reading books when he'd burst in without knocking. 'And then, on the way back, she kept asking if there was a car behind us. Like she thought we were being followed . . .'

Louisa stood up, came over to him. 'A crank phone call? What kind of crank call?'

'*I* don't know. We were at Lauren's. Mom got a call, went outside to take it. And went apeshit, started screaming. She asked me to ask you please to go and see her, Louisa. She says to tell you she was wrong and to please forgive her and go over. She won't talk to me. It was freaky. I've never seen her like that. Something's really wrong.'

He saw Louisa glance at Joe quickly before she said: 'I'll go over there now.'

'I'll come too.' Joe got up.

'No, stay here with Tim. It's better if I go by myself.' Louisa reached out, put her hand on his arm. 'I'll handle it, Tim. She'll be fine. Don't worry.'

'Why?' he asked, unable to keep the childlike note from his voice. 'Why can't everything just be normal?'

22

Ellie had obviously been waiting for her. She opened the door while Louisa was walking up to it.

'Louisa. Thank you so much for coming.'

'Tim said you got a crank call,' she said as she walked into the living room. 'He's frightened.'

'I'm sorry. I'm so sorry I accused Joe.'

They were standing a few feet apart. Lousia was struggling, her anger vying with her concern for this woman who looked both scared out of her wits and full of remorse. Yet she'd come here. Which meant she'd already made a decision; only she couldn't bring herself to go hug Ellie. Or keep the stern tone out of her voice.

'What was the call?'

'Louisa, please forgive me. I know what I said was wrong and horrible. Please.'

'We can talk about all that later. Tell me about the call.'

'It . . . can we sit down?'

Louisa walked over and sat in the chair beside the sofa, knowing she was signalling that the distance between them hadn't been entirely breached. Ellie sat in the middle of the sofa, her hands crossed over her chest as if she were shielding herself.

'It was this woman and she was singing – at first. That Police song, "Every Step You Take". And then . . . and then she said, "It's Hope." And then . . . she started laughing. This terrible fake laugh. After that she said: "You're mine." I think she said that twice. I don't know, I'm not sure. And it ended – the last thing she said was: "If you call the police, I'll know. And there'll be another accident. You don't want another accident, do you?" And then that horrible fake laugh again.

'I can't take this any more. I just can't. I can't keep it together, and Tim . . . I didn't want to scare him, but I couldn't tell him, and . . . she knows *everything*. Where I live, my cell number, my past – *everything*. And she's watching me. She could be outside right now, watching.'

'Oh, Ellie.' Louisa felt herself melting, rose, went and sat beside her. 'That must have been hell. Did you recognise her voice?'

'No.'

'How old was she. Could you tell?'

'No. It was a strange voice.'

'We have to call the police.'

'She said not to. She said she'd know if I did. She'd know if you did too. She knows everything. How? Who is she? How can she know everything?'

'I don't know.' Louisa found herself looking around the

273

place, as if she'd be able to see a bug or a hidden tape recorder.

'I'm going crazy, Louisa. When I went back to my mother's I started sleeping again. The same kind of sleeping I did before. And I'm afraid I'll do it again. I'll end up back in that hospital. It's all going to happen again. Only this time there won't be a Dr Emmanuel. I'll never get out.'

'No, you will not go back to a hospital. We'll find out who is doing this and stop them.'

She took Ellie's hand in hers, squeezed it.

A woman had phoned? It was a woman who was orchestrating this madness? Louisa had always assumed it was a man. Ellie was positive it wasn't Hope's mother; it couldn't be Ellie's own mother. What woman would do this to another woman? Use the death of a child like that?

'And Daniel's coming soon. Do you think she knows he's coming too? But how could she?'

'Daniel? That doctor you email? He's coming here?'

'Yes. He called me last night. He's coming to a medical conference in Boston and he's driving down here tonight. I love him, Louisa. But what will it be like for him, walking into all this? I should call him, tell him not to come. But I want to see him. Oh, God.' Ellie put her head in her hands. 'I don't know what to do or think any more.'

As far as Louisa had been told, Ellie had a nice email correspondence with a man she'd met once who had moved to England. Suddenly it had blossomed into love?

She'd fallen in love with a man she'd met on an internet site?

'I'm worried about Ellie. Sometimes she . . .'

I'm worried about her too, Charlie.

'I don't understand. I thought you two were writing emails to each other, that it was a friendship.'

'We are friends. But we've fallen in love with each other too.'

'I see,' Louisa said. What was this? Some sort of variation on that *You've Got Mail* movie, during a period of Ellie's life which had been especially fraught? After that encounter with Joe, she'd rushed headlong into the metaphorical arms of another man?

'What am I going to do? What if this woman . . . ? What did she mean by an accident? Is she talking about Tim? She can't be, can she? But I didn't want him to be here in the cottage. She could be outside right now.'

Ellie stood up, went over to the front windows, peered out.

'Where would she hide? How did she get my number? If you'd heard that laugh . . . Wait – that's Joe's car driving out. And he's got Tim with him. Where are they going?'

'I don't know, but I'm sure it's a good idea to get Tim out. He really was scared, Ellie.'

Again, Louisa could hear her own tone of voice shifting as doubts began to assail her. This was all so – Louisa searched for the word – improbable. A woman singing a pop song then laughing maniacally? Lurking in the bushes? It sounded like something a Hollywood scriptwriter on speed would dream up.

'I know, I know. I tried not to scare Tim, but I couldn't stop trying to see if someone was following us.' Ellie was still beside the window, looking out. 'Whoever she is . . . she couldn't have called Joe, could she? Gotten him to bring Tim to her?'

'Joe would never put Tim in any kind of danger.'

'But I have, haven't I?' Ellie turned away from the window, faced Louisa. 'It all started when we moved here. We've got to get away from this place. If we leave, maybe it will stop. Oh, God.' She looked at her watch. 'Daniel's plane might have landed. I need to find out when he's coming. Maybe I can call him and tell him not to. I'll just check the flight details on my laptop. I'll go do that – it won't take a second.'

Ellie went into the kitchen.

Louisa sat, trying to put all the facts together in a straight line.

The break-in, when nothing had actually been stolen.

The typewritten note on the milk carton. Scary, but not a direct threat.

The trash on the beach: again, no direct threat.

The bicycle on the lawn: horrible, but not something the police would get wrought up about. 'They'd think I was crazy,' she remembered Ellie saying.

The note in that envelope – disgusting, but that 'Cry Me A River' business wasn't 'I'm coming to kill you'.

And finally the phone call with a woman saying not to go to the police. Or else.

A campaign of terror which skirted bringing in the police. Deliberately?

But the envelope – she'd forgotten about the envelope with handwriting that closely resembled Joe's on it. He said he'd never written Ellie a letter. Had he left things around the house . . . notes or anything? No. He always used his BlackBerry. So there was no example of his handwriting Ellie could have seen.

'Joe's handwriting is neat and tidy,' Louisa remembered a teacher's comment on a report card when he was in third grade. 'Although I'm working on that habit he has of lengthening his small "e" at the end of a word.' She'd laughed as she read it, thinking how absurdly petty some teachers could be. If Joe wanted to do that with his 'e', what was the harm? He'd always done it.

Oh, shit. Louisa saw herself and Tim and Ellie standing in that room where the heights were written on the wall. Joe's name, in his handwriting – as soon as he had been able to write – was all over it.

But why, in God's name, why, would Ellie do this to herself?

'He made me feel safe,' she'd said about Charlie. 'He took care of me.'

Now this oncologist was flying over from England and he was going to walk in and find a distraught woman who needed him to look after her.

Looking after women appealed to some men – probably doctors especially.

Joe had stayed out of the whole drama, hadn't gotten involved. Was that why Ellie had written him, telling him to leave her alone? Because he wasn't taking care of her the way she would have liked him to?

Louisa had taken care of her too, those weeks after Ellie had told her about the accident. They'd spent hour upon hour together.

Was this a pattern of behaviour brought on by the accident? Did she desperately need that kind of attention?

'Louisa? You look like you're a million miles away.' Ellie was beside her on the sofa, had taken her hand. 'His plane landed on time. I have to decide whether to tell him not to come. I want to see him so badly but I'm not sure it's fair on him. What do you think?'

'I really don't know.'

'You sound angry. Oh, God, I haven't apologised the way I should have, have I? I'm so sorry about thinking it might be Joe. I'm so sorry to drag you into this again, too, but I needed to see you. I missed being able to talk to you. I missed you. I can't bear it if we can't be close again.'

'Can I ask you something, Ellie? When you were in the hospital, did your doctors put you on any medication?'

'I was on antidepressants for a while. Why? Why are you asking me that?'

'You never told me – did they actually make a diagnosis? Post-Traumatic Stress Disorder or something like that?'

'I don't know. I guess so. Maybe my mother would know. But why are you asking these questions?'

'You've been under a lot of stress. I'm really worried about you.'

'I'm worried about me too. Some psychotic woman is following my every move. What does she want? Maybe she wants this cottage? Could that be it? She terrorises me so I'll move out and then she'll buy it?'

'I doubt that.'

'I know, it sounds ridiculous, but I can't think straight.'

'As you said, whoever is doing this knows everything about you, even your cell-phone number. Tim said . . .'

'Tim said what?'

'Nothing.'

'You and Joe are the same. You both start sentences and don't finish them.'

'I don't think you should say anything negative about Joe, Ellie.'

'Louisa, what's going on? Why are you looking at me like that? I didn't mean to be negative about Joe, I promise. I just hate it when people start sentences and don't finish them. What were you going to say? Tim said what?'

'He said that you left Lauren's house when you got that crank call. You went outside to take it.'

'So?'

'Nothing.'

'What are you trying to say, Louisa? What difference does it make if I went outside to take it?'

'None.'

'Then why . . . ?' Ellie tilted her head, narrowed her eyes. 'Wait a minute. I think I get it. You think I'm crazy. You think I'm so crazy, I'm doing all this to myself?'

'Ellie—'

'You do, don't you?'

'Ellie, I never said that.'

'But you think it. I can see it in your eyes. You *think* it. That's why you were asking me about drugs and my diagnosis. You think I've done all this to myself!'

'Ellie, we need to talk about this. I—'

'Leave me alone. I mean it. Get the fuck out of my house!'

23

Tim was shifting from foot to foot, looking so distressed and pissed off, Joe couldn't think what to do with him. The poor kid was shit-scared and confused, partly because Ellie had kept him in the dark about her accident – not a wise decision when all this was going down. Tim should have been in the loop. But it wasn't Joe's place to tell him the whole story, one that was obviously continuing if Ellie had started screaming outside Lauren's house.

Whoever was doing this just kept ratcheting it up. But what was their goal? That's what he'd like to figure out. One thing he'd learned in DC was that no one did anything without a purpose. So what was it? Terrify some poor woman, play on her sense of guilt . . . and then what?

'Hey,' he said, suggesting the only thing that might keep Tim from bouncing off the walls. 'Why don't we go to the batting cages, hit a few balls?'

'Yeah.' He stopped shifting. 'Sounds good.'

'OK, come on.'

They went to the car, Joe thinking as he got in the driver's seat that OK, now Ellie knew he wasn't responsible for this shit, why hadn't she called him back? And why had she written that crappy 'Dear John' letter to him in the first place? It wasn't as if he had gotten in touch with her or tried to resurrect that night in any way. He'd been the one who had walked out, and the one who had told her they should treat it as if it had never happened. He'd behaved badly, he knew. But not in a way that would lead her to write a letter like that.

'Do me a favour and don't keep checking the rear-view mirror, OK?' Tim said, doing up his seatbelt.

Joe glanced at him, said: 'OK.'

Ellie had maintained he'd written her a letter. So what the fuck was going on? Maybe there was some kind of conspiracy. Hell, maybe the FBI *was* involved.

His mother wished his father were here. So did he. His father would have dealt with all this differently, Joe knew: he would have stepped in the second that bike was put on the lawn and taken control. He would have done the private investigating himself, hunting down every lead or clue. Thrown himself at it all with abandon, as he had done with everything. Whether he would have figured it out, Joe didn't know. But he sure as hell would have tried.

Whereas his son had stepped back and removed himself. Because Ellie had told him in that letter that she didn't want him to get the wrong idea, she had no interest in him at all, he should keep out of her life. A total overkill letter, given that last scene between them, but it had effectively quashed the thoughts he'd been having. Those thoughts that he'd overreacted wildly after sleeping with her, that he'd like to get to know her better, that he shouldn't have taken his own guilt and pain out on her.

'Is it all right if I turn on the radio?' Tim asked as they passed the driveway to the cottage.

'Sure. Just no heavy metal.'

'I'm not into heavy metal.'

He should have asked Tim what music he was into, but that same scene was replaying in his head. The one that had branded his heart.

Pam was lying in bed, wearing a Red Sox baseball cap, worn out and feeling lousy from the chemo. He'd brought her in a cup of peppermint herbal tea she said made her stomach feel better. After he'd handed it to her, she put it down on the bedside table, patted the bed beside her, asked him to sit down and hold her hand. When he did that, she'd delivered a speech. She'd started by saying she knew she shouldn't say this, but she had to, and she'd gone on to tell him she couldn't bear the thought of him with another woman.

'Good people, when they're dying, tell their partners to carry on their lives and find happiness with someone else,' she'd said. 'If I were a good person, I'd say that to you now. But I'm not good, I'm bad. I can't stand the thought of you with someone else. It kills me just thinking about it – which is absurd, right? I mean, I'm already almost dead. So it shouldn't matter. I wish it didn't matter. But it does. It's terrible. I hate myself for feeling this way.'

Joe had done what he always did when she said she was

going to die: told her she was wrong, she'd be all right, everything would be fine. But she'd interrupted.

'That's crap, Joe, and you know it is. It's funny – there's retrospective jealousy, isn't there? But there's no word for future jealousy. Especially a future dead person's jealousy. It's pathetic, I know, but I want to be the love of your life.'

'You are.'

'OK. Good.' She'd smiled then. 'But keep it that way, will you? And if you don't, baby, I'm going to haunt you.' She laughed. 'Or haunt *her*, whoever that bitch turns out to be. All right, I feel better now that I've expelled every evil thought from my heart. Let's see if I can manage a walk. I want to breathe in the sea air.'

It was impossible to banish that conversation from his head because that's exactly what he would have felt if he'd been in the same position. There was no way he would have been able to bear the thought of Pam with another man. And that visceral jealousy would have been exacerbated a billionfold if he'd pictured her with another man in *their* cottage, in *their* bedroom. So swept up by desire, she hadn't thought of him – not until it was over, when the weight of the betrayal descended like piles of heavy, crushing stones.

He had hated himself then. And he'd resented Ellie for being the person who'd made him forget Pam. So he'd treated her like shit by walking out like that and hadn't done much better the next morning.

He should have realised that letter he got a week later didn't sound at all like her. Someone was playing a seriously devious game . . .

As he reached the end of the road, he found his thoughts veering into the surreal: all this happening to Ellie and no one had any idea who was doing it. Instinctively he looked up at the sky. 'OK, Pam – enough.'

'What?'

'Nothing, Tim. I was talking to myself.'

'Yeah, right. You're going nuts on me too. When is someone going to tell me what that phone call was about? And why Mom wanted me to apologise to your mother.'

'She'll tell you, I'm sure. Once my mother has talked to her.'

'I wish I'd had your parents.'

There was no useful response Joe could make to that comment.

'Yeah, well, it seems to me we're both feeling pretty lousy at the moment. But at least you didn't spend two years of your life working for a paedophile, right?'

'True,' Tim nodded. 'That does really suck.'

'Big time. So – it's looking like Bourne might win the league.'

They were both relieved, Joe knew, to move on to baseball as the topic of discussion. When they reached the batting cages, just down the road from the Clam Shack, Tim leaped out of the car and headed straight for them. Trailing behind, Joe paid for their time, and joined Tim in finding hard hats to protect their heads.

Joe watched as Tim swung and missed when the first ball fired out of the machine.

'You're swinging behind it,' he said. 'Lower your bat a

little. It's too high up.' After a few more whiffs, Tim began to get his eye in, whacking the balls into the far nets, one after the other. He was hitting them venomously, taking his frustrations out in the best possible way.

'My turn,' Joe said. 'I need a little of that.'

When he took Tim's bat and stepped up to the plate, he blasted the first one so hard Tim clapped.

What do women do? he wondered at one point when he'd made contact so perfectly, he grinned. How do they take out their frustrations?

By talking to each other.

It couldn't be half as satisfying as this.

Handing the bat back to Tim, Joe stepped aside, lost in the sound of bat meeting ball, forgetting everything except the thought of actually being on a real baseball diamond, doing this. Hitting the ball over the Green Monster wall at Fenway Park, rounding the bases. Getting high fives from his teammates.

They'd batted for about twenty minutes when he turned and saw there were people waiting to use the cage.

'We better go,' he told Tim.

'I want to stay here forever.'

'So do I.'

They took off their helmets, put the bat back into the box, walked slowly to the car.

'My mom's got this guy coming tonight.'

'Oh?' Joe made himself keep walking. 'What guy is that?'

'Some guy she emails in England. His name is Daniel.'

'Right.' They reached the car and Joe opened his door.

'He's a doctor. My mom said he's an oncologist.'

'Uh-huh.' He got in.

An oncologist. One of those people who couldn't save Pam.

'She says she's pretty serious about him.'

Great, just great. There goes any chance I had of making up for how I acted, getting involved in trying to help her. Talking to her about how we were both conned by those letters. The doctor won't appreciate me hanging around.

'Hold on. That's my phone.' Joe got it out of his pocket. 'Mum, what's happening?'

'I need you to come back. I wouldn't advise you to try to see Ellie. Come straight here. I need to talk to you.'

'OK. We're just leaving the batting cages now. See you in a little while.'

He hung up, started the car.

'Is Mom all right?'

'I think so.'

'Joe?'

'Yes?'

'Can we just keep driving? I mean, can we go pick up Lauren and go to Mexico or something?'

'I wish.'

24

Ellie sat at her kitchen table, staring at a blank piece of paper. She wanted to make a list, write down exactly what had happened and when, and prove she wasn't crazy. But she didn't pick up the pen beside her because she knew, whatever she wrote, it wouldn't prove anything.

Louisa had only done what she'd done to Louisa, she realised a few minutes after ordering her out of the cottage: she'd put things together and come up with the wrong answer.

Of course Louisa thought she was crazy. Ellie had showed up at this cottage in June, proceeded to have a hysterical fit when she saw Joe's old bike a few weeks later, presented Louisa with all these lunatic goings on and then blamed Joe for them.

I'd probably think exactly what she's thinking now.

In the past forty-eight hours, she'd managed to terrify Tim, alienate Louisa, falsely accuse Joe. Whoever was responsible for this was about to get what they wanted. Ellie could feel tears starting up. And if she let them escape, she'd cry a goddamn ocean.

She had a choice. Either she could get up, walk to her

bedroom, fall on to her bed and stay there, or she could get up, make a cup of coffee and deal with this whole nightmare by herself. She couldn't run to Louisa, not again. Or her mother.

For so many months, she'd wanted to be independent and strong, move away from the girl who got married at twenty, the one who had felt not only joy but also relief as she walked down the aisle – relief because now she wouldn't be alone. Or the thirty-six-year-old woman who'd half-wanted Louisa to come with her to see the Davises and face her past – she'd wanted to move past that and she had. She'd insisted on going alone.

But she'd called Louisa immediately afterwards.

Now she really was alone. Tim would stay with Louisa and Joe until she called him, but she wasn't going to call him yet; she didn't want him near her in case he'd be in danger.

She was on her own with a blank piece of paper and lurking tears.

'The mind is more powerful than a speeding bullet,' Dr Emmanuel had said at their first meeting. 'It can leap tall buildings with a single bound.'

'So the mind is Superman,' she'd said, surprising herself, because she'd hated talking to the other doctors so much.

'The mind is every super-hero rolled into one, Ellie,' he'd answered. 'It can do anything.'

Could she will herself to get up and make that coffee? She'd been pretty expert at willing herself to deny the accident – she should be good at that.

'But first of all . . . this is very important . . . the mind has to be fed, Ellie. The body has to feed the mind, and you have to feed the body. You have to eat.'

All she'd had to eat so far was coffee at her mother's. Which didn't count as food.

I should eat something too.

Food.

Dinner.

Daniel.

Ellie looked at her watch. He must have gone through Customs and Immigration by now, gotten his bag, hired a car. She'd emailed him the directions from her mother's that morning. If she wanted to stop him from coming, she should try to call him now.

Daniel didn't think she was crazy. He loved her. He said he wanted to help, but she hadn't asked for that help, he'd volunteered it.

The Ellie he knew was the Ellie she wanted to be now. If she got up, made that cup of coffee, ate something, pulled herself together, she could find herself again. He wouldn't walk in on a demented woman spying out of the window and yabbering like a coke fiend.

She wouldn't be using her mind to hypnotise and trick herself, she'd be using it to find the willpower she needed to fight off this exhaustion and despair. She had to. Whatever else happened, she and Tim would have to leave Bourne and she'd have to find the energy to arrange that. Being here this one night after that phone call was horrible enough – her first instinct watching all those shows had

290

been right. Forget about the concept of home. Get the hell out.

OK, Ellie, get up. If some psycho woman is outside spying on you, let her spy.

Tim's with Joe — he's safe.

After tonight you'll get out of here. Daniel will show up soon.

You can do this.

The mind can leap tall buildings in a single bound.

He went into the kitchen, saw her getting some coffee out of the cupboard.

'Mom?'

'Tim? I didn't hear you come in. What are you doing here? I told you to stay with Joe until I called.'

'I made Joe drop me off. I'm fifteen years old.' He sat down purposefully at the table, folded his arms over his chest. 'You have to tell me what's going on, Mom.' He felt as if he were the adult now and she was the kid. 'Why was the front door locked? I thought you'd gone out. I want to know – now. You can't keep hiding things from me.'

'You're right,' she sighed, and sat down across from him.

She started talking. He knew as soon as he'd heard a few sentences that this wasn't going to play out well. This was bad. As soon as she said 'She died', Tim's eyes widened in disbelief.

'You killed someone?'

'Tim.' She reached across the table, took hold of his

forearm. 'Look at me. It was an *accident*. Please look at me, sweetheart. It was an *accident*.'

He shifted in his chair; his eyes went to the fridge and stayed fixed on it.

'Tim, I swear I didn't mean to hurt her. She lost control of the bike. It was an accident. I'd just gotten my licence. I was driving really slowly, I promise. She came out of nowhere. I couldn't have stopped in time. I felt so guilty I ended up in a hospital. It's taken me a long time to forgive myself.'

'What do you mean, hospital – were you hurt too?'

'Not physically hurt, no. I told you, I felt so guilty, I couldn't cope with it.'

His mother had run over a little girl. The little girl had died. His mother had been in a hospital. A mental hospital.

Fate sucked and life sucked. Everything sucked.

'Please look at me, Tim.'

He did, but only for a second before his eyes went back to the fridge.

'What do you want me to say? I can't change what happened. If you only knew how much I wish I could.'

'I don't want to talk about this any more.'

'But—'

'Mom. I mean it.' Now he was looking at her.

He didn't know the little girl, it wasn't his mom's fault she was dead, but he couldn't get past it. This was his mom. His mom had been in a loony bin.

'We have to talk about it, Tim. Because that crank call I got – it had to do with the accident. And there were other things. Like that garbage on the beach. Someone is trying

292

to get revenge, or drive me crazy – I don't know which, I have no idea why they're doing these things – but the point is, we can't live here any more. So I've been thinking. Maybe we could go to California and visit Debby.'

'Because someone threw garbage on the beach and made a crank call? No way.'

'There's more to it. I don't want to frighten you, but it's scary and it all started when we moved here. If you don't want to go to California, maybe we could go to Europe. I have enough money to take us on a trip there, like a summer vacation. We could go to Paris. Or London. Or—'

'London? With this Daniel guy?'

'We might visit him there, yes. But—'

'What about summer school?'

'A trip to Europe is an education in itself. And you could bring books along and we could go to museums and—'

'Forget it.'

'I know you think you're in love with Lauren and you don't want to leave here, but maybe she could come with us. I could talk to her mother.'

I know you think *you're in love with Lauren. Gee, thanks, Mom. You understand me so well.*

'You don't get it, do you?'

'I don't get what?'

Tim could feel it building up inside of him. Two and a half fucking years of it. There was no way he could stop it from coming out, not now.

'You and Dad. Both of you. You do all this crap and expect me to suck it all up. Which makes sense, I guess, because I have. I've sucked it up. You tell me you've grown apart and that's why you're splitting up – as if I didn't know he'd been having an affair. What am I, an idiot? But, OK, I'll go along with that bullshit. And *of course* – I mean, of course – I have to be polite to Sandra who's a total dickhead because, hey, being polite, that's crucial. I'm not about to break one of the Walters rules, am I?

'Then, it's like – I flunk out of school and no one asks me why. Instead of asking me why I flunked out, Dad just gets pissed off at me and you decide to move – that will fix everything, right?'

'Tim, I did ask you. You wouldn't talk to me.'

'Yeah, right, as if you wanted to hear. All either of you want to hear is that I'm fine, everything's fine, you don't have to worry about me.'

'That's not true.'

'Do you have any idea? I mean, really? Do you know what it felt like when you started screaming outside Lauren's house?'

'Oh, Tim, I'm sorry.'

The way she was looking, the way she said it – he knew she meant it. But so what? The way this was going, he'd end up in London with some guy he'd never met, and shit – it would probably turn out his father had met his mom when they were in the loony bin together. And his dad would have some good reason for moving to Brazil.

His mom looked like she was about to start crying; he knew he should stop, but he couldn't.

He stood up. He was in the batting cage now and he was going to slam that ball as hard as he could.

'You can't do this to me, Mom. You can't drop all this shit on me and expect me to suck it up. You wanted me to stay with Louisa and Joe? Well, that's what I'm going to do. Your pen pal's coming, right? You can ask *him* how he feels.'

'Tim!' he heard her call out.

But he was out of there.

Ellie sat, reeling, her heart feeling as if it had been shot with a thousand arrows, each more deadly than the next.

Should she run after him?

And say what?

She'd tried to get him to open up to her about the divorce before, but he'd always said he was fine and then changed the subject. Obviously she should have probed more and *made* him talk.

How did he know about Charlie's affair? She'd been so careful to try to keep him away from that. Obviously she'd failed there too.

And he was right, she'd come out with all this in one fell swoop: her accident, her stay in the hospital, the threats – although she hadn't told him everything, to try to protect him – and her wanting to move away.

How must that have felt for him? Ellie cringed, remembering how she'd screamed outside of Lauren's house. What teenager wouldn't be inwardly dying when his mother acted like that in front of his girlfriend?

No wonder he'd gone to where he felt safest – Louisa's. Where he *was* safe. Despite what had happened between them, Ellie knew Louisa would never tell Tim she thought his mother was crazy. She'd do everything she could to make him feel better, and so would Joe.

She had to talk to Tim, but she had to give him some time. If she could call Daniel, tell him not to come, then wait a while and call Tim and get him to come back? But then Tim would be in this cottage and that wasn't safe if that woman was watching . . . and she didn't have Daniel's number – it hadn't registered on her cell when he'd called the night before – and . . .

Slow down. One thing at a time.

Ellie went to her bag to get her keys and lock the door again. Her cell phone was lying beside them. She took the keys and phone out, went and locked the door. When she'd gotten that call outside Lauren's, she'd turned her cell off. Now she switched it back on.

Maybe Daniel had left her a message.

She waited as it powered up. There were three messages.

Were they all 'I'll be watching you' ones? She never wanted to hear that laugh again.

Walking over to the sofa and sitting down, Ellie held the phone in her hand. After a minute, she dialled the message retrieving service.

The first was from Debby.

'Hey, babes. Sorry to be so delinquent and out of touch. Love can make you crazy. In fact, so crazy I might even marry the guy. Can't decide whether to take the plunge or hold out for Rob Lowe. Weirdly enough, Rob hasn't called me yet. Anyway, how are you doing? It's been way too long.

Give me a call and let me know what's happening. So did you bite the bullet and sign off with "love" to Daniel? Oh, God, all I can talk about is romance now. I've got it bad. Give me a call.'

The next message kicked in.

'Ellie, I'm on my way. I've put the address in my Sat Nav and I think I should be fine. If I get lost I'll call you, so can you keep your phone on, please? My ETA is now 8.35. And my cell-phone number is . . . I'll wait 'til you get a piece of paper . . .'

Ellie scrambled over to the table beside the sofa, found a pen, tore a page out of a magazine lying in front of the lamp.

'OK, got it? It's 617-277-0350 if you need to call me.'

Writing it down, she checked her watch. It was almost 8.30.

Message number three.

Had something happened? Was there traffic? Was he going to be delayed?

She could barely hear the voice, but it was definitely a man's so she pushed the button to make it play again. It was muffled, that male voice, but this time she heard the words properly.

'Time's up, Ellie.'

25

'I fucked up, Louisa. I made everything worse,' Ellie had said in her message after going to see Mrs Davis. And that was exactly how Louisa was feeling now.

When Joe came back from the batting cages, he'd listened as she told him what had happened at the cottage, and his face fell. 'I told you before that was nuts, Mum,' he said. 'It doesn't fly. It's way too convoluted. There are a hell of a lot more easy ways to get attention. Besides, as soon as Ellie told you she thought it might be me, she screwed up her relationship with you. You'd be one of the people she most wanted attention from, you know. So it doesn't add up.'

Joe was right, but Louisa had already realised that herself as she trudged back to her house after Ellie had told her to fuck off. She'd allowed herself to suspect Ellie because of what that detective had said, and probably because she'd been so wounded by her before. When she saw the hurt and in-comprehension on Ellie's face as it dawned on her what Louisa was thinking, she'd wanted to take it all back immediately. But it was too late. It was out there. After that talk with Joe she'd tried to think of how to rectify the situation, but then Tim had arrived at the door, full of anger and angst.

He'd spilled it all out to her and Joe, standing in the middle of the living room, ranting about his parents, the gist of it being that no one ever consulted him or cared enough to ask him how he felt. 'So now she wants to move to England. And she says I can bring Lauren with me. Yeah, right. That's a real possibility. And that pen pal guy is about to show up. Great. I *really* want to meet him.' He flopped down on a chair then, rolled his eyes. 'This so sucks.' Springing up, he said, 'I have to go call Lauren. I'll call her in the kitchen if that's OK?'

'It's fine,' Louisa had said, and turned to Joe after Tim left the room. 'What do we do now?' she asked.

'We let him blow off steam. He's fifteen years old, Mum. He's confused and pissed off and he needs to talk to his girlfriend. Do you remember me at that age? When I was so in love with Leslie?'

'I'm not about to forget that.' Louisa smiled.

'Neither am I.'

I love him, Louisa.

If that doctor hadn't been about to arrive, Louisa could have gone to see Ellie again and done her best to make things right. In these circumstances, though, the only way she could think of to help Ellie now was to take care of Tim.

'Who could be doing all this, Joe?'

'Fucked if I know.' He turned his gaze to the window. 'The big question is, what do they want?'

Time's up, Ellie.

A man's voice. But it had been a woman before. How

many of them were there? How many people were involved in this?

Time's up.

She looked at her watch. 8.35. Daniel's ETA. Would he get here before they did?

Getting up from the sofa, she went and checked all the locks. They were secure, but someone could throw a rock through the window. Or try to bash down the door. She was trapped in here. If she went outside, she was trapped too. They were watching her.

She went to the front window, hid behind the curtain at the side.

It wasn't too late to call the police. If her time was up, it didn't matter if she called the police. Tim was safe with Louisa and Joe. They couldn't hurt him. But the woman had said she'd know if the police were called. If she knew, the man would know too. And they might do whatever they were going to do more quickly, before the police could arrive. Daniel would be here any second. If they were watching the cottage, they'd see his car. They'd know she wasn't alone.

Should she go get a knife from the kitchen while she waited for Daniel?

As she was about to do that, she saw a car appear, coming down the road to the cottage. It had to be Daniel. Or it could be them. She stood, paralysed, watching it as it swung into the driveway.

It was a classic old blue Mercedes convertible.

What?

What's he doing here?

26

'Hello, El.'

'Charlie. What are you doing here?'

'I had a meeting with someone who lives in Hyannis. I thought I'd drop by on my way back.'

It wasn't Daniel, but it was someone. Whoever was watching would have seen Charlie arrive. They'd know she wasn't alone.

'You look terrified, El. What's going on?'

'Someone's stalking me. I can't explain, it's too complicated. And a friend of mine is about to arrive.'

'If someone is stalking you, you shouldn't be here on your own. I can wait until your friend comes.'

'Would you?'

'Of course.'

She stepped aside and he came in.

'You should tell me what's happening. Maybe I can help. Have you called the police?' He sat down on the sofa, leaned forward.

'I can't call them. And I can't tell you, Charlie. It's all too complicated.'

'So you said. What have you gotten yourself into, El?'

'I didn't get myself into anything. It's not my fault. She sat down in a chair, looked at her watch.

'This friend you're expecting. Is it a man or a woman?'

'Charlie, Jesus. What does it matter?'

'Don't get spiky, El. There's no need. I was wondering if you'd met someone special. I shouldn't be surprised if you have, I guess. You're not the type to be on your own for long.'

'What does that mean?'

He was dragging her into this ridiculous conversation and she was letting him.

'Only that you need someone to take care of you. You always have.'

'I'm different now, Charlie. I've changed.'

'Really?' He sat back. 'I'm not sure anyone ever changes. They only think they have.'

'I changed when you left. I had to. And now I'm glad. Because I wasn't myself with you.'

'Uh oh. That's a dramatic statement. It sounds as if you've been reading self-help books.'

'Don't patronise me.'

If only she could kick him out. But Daniel must have broken down or got lost. Right now having Charlie here was better than having no one. And he clearly knew that.

'I'm sorry,' he said. 'I didn't mean to patronise you. All I meant was that you should have someone. I only wish that someone could be me.'

'What?'

'I'm being honest with you, El. I made a mistake.' He sat

forward again, his eyes drilling into hers. 'I should never have left.'

Unknown people were hounding her, Tim was furious with her, Louisa thought she was a madwoman. And now Charlie was telling her he'd made a mistake, he shouldn't have left.

'El? Did you hear what I said?'

'Yes.'

'And?'

'And there's nothing I can say. It's over. You're with Sandra now.'

'But I'm not.'

'I don't understand.'

'It's simple. Sandra and I are finished. I never should have left you. I love you and you love me. We belong together.'

The same words he'd used when he'd proposed. 'I love you and you love me. We belong together.' Followed by, 'Will you marry me?' The exact same words and the same tone of voice. The tape had rewound again, as it had when her mother had woken her yesterday. Sixteen years ago, she'd said 'yes' immediately.

His eyes were still fixed on hers. He was drawing her to him, the way he had that first night they'd met.

'No. It would be like falling asleep.'

'What?'

'If we got back together, Charlie. It would be like falling asleep.'

'Now *I* don't understand.'

303

'I don't love you any more.'

'Yes, you do.'

'No, Charlie, I don't.'

'Is that because you're in love with someone else?'

'No. Yes, I mean, I am in love with someone else, but that's not the point. The point is, I don't love you.'

'I think it *is* the point, El. You love *him*, whoever he is.'

'I . . . listen, he should be here by now. He must be lost or have broken down. I have to call him. But I'm not going to change my mind about us. You have to understand that. It's too late, Charlie. Too much has happened.'

He crossed one leg over the other, raked his hand through his hair.

'All right. I can see you mean what you say and I won't push you. I'll stay here until this man arrives and then I'll make myself scarce. I won't bother you any more, El. I wanted to tell you how I feel. I'm sorry you don't feel the same.'

He didn't say it with any bitterness or anger. He had accepted what she'd said with real grace.

'Thank you, Charlie.'

He wasn't a creep. Or a social-climbing egotist. Debby was wrong: no one who hadn't met him could judge him. He was Tim's father. He was a fundamentally decent man.

'Go ahead, call him. Find out where he is. You look so worried.'

She pulled her cell phone out of her pocket, along with the piece of paper with Daniel's number on it. Phoning him with Charlie sitting so near felt odd, but she wasn't going to have a romatic talk with Daniel, she was just going to find out why he was late. Ellie dialled.

The sound of a phone ringing in the cottage confused her and she looked towards the door, her cell phone at her ear. Daniel must have arrived. But no one was there. She saw Charlie shift position on the sofa. He reached into his pocket and brought his phone out.

He was getting a call at the same time she was making one?

'Hi there,' he said.

The same two words coming to her over the phone and over the space between them.

After he'd hung up from his call with Lauren, Tim stayed in the kitchen. He needed a little time on his own to think. Just before he'd made that call to Lauren his father had phoned, asking him where he was. Tim had told him he was with Louisa and Joe, and then admitted he'd had a fight with his mom. He was beginning to feel shitty about that, but he didn't know how he was going to fix it.

'Don't worry,' his dad had said. 'I'm in the area as it happens and I'm going to drop by and see her. You should give us some time together. We have things to talk about. You and your mother can work things out between you later. It's probably best if you stay with a friend tonight.'

'I guess I could ask Lauren if I could stay at her house. On the sofa or whatever.'

'Good idea.'

He hadn't asked what things his dad had to talk to his

mother about because he was relieved his dad was taking charge. He was also busy thinking how much he'd like to stay over at Lauren's, if her mother would let him. He'd sleep on the sofa, no problem. But if he could stay, he'd be able to chill with her for a long time. As much as he liked Louisa and Joe, it had been a lousy day. The only person who could really make it better was Lauren.

So he'd called her and asked and she'd said 'Wait' and then she'd gone and asked her mother, come back and said, 'The sofa it is. But turn on the charm, OK? Dial it up.' And he'd said, 'Done deal.'

Now he was sitting by himself for a second, wondering what things his parents had to talk over. Maybe his mother had called his father and said she wanted to move to England. Who knew? He did know his dad, though, and no way would his dad agree to that. So everything would be OK.

Tim looked over at the two mammoth sinks. You could take a bath in either of those, he thought. It would be seriously cool to throw a party in this house. Louisa would have to let him, and his mother would have to say it was OK too, but as soon as she dealt with this stuff going down with the crank calls and whatever, she'd get back to normal and then a party would be possible.

Seeing her go nuts like that – it had really scared him. So had hearing about that little girl and then the loony bin. So, yeah, he'd gone too far, he knew. But his dad would fix everything. When he wasn't pissed off, his dad was ace at fixing things. People always listened when he talked.

Tim got up, went back into the living room. Joe and

Louisa were in the middle of a conversation but they both stopped talking and looked up at him.

'Would it be possible to get a lift to Lauren's?' he asked. 'I'd really like to see her and she invited me over. I'm going to stay there.'

'Sure, I'll drive you,' Joe said.

'I'll come too. I need a little air.' Louisa stood up.

Joe got his keys, Louisa threw on a white sweater, they all left the house.

'You're not going to lock the door?' Tim asked.

'No. Hippies don't lock their houses, Tim. I know I don't live in a commune, but I can pretend.'

They got into Joe's car, started down the road. When they passed the turn-off to the cottage, Tim saw his father's car.

'Dad's here already,' he said.

'Your father?' Joe asked, sounding kind of shocked.

'Yeah, he told me he was going to drop by and see my mom. There's no other car so that doctor hasn't come yet. I guess Dad might meet him.'

'That could be interesting,' Louisa said, then: 'I'm glad your father's there. I'm glad your mother's not alone.'

How could she have called Charlie's phone? Ellie couldn't fathom it. She'd been looking at the piece of paper with Daniel's number on it, hadn't she? Clearly not. She wasn't thinking straight, she must have dialled Charlie's number out of habit, because he was there.

Charlie looked puzzled, held his hands up in the air, put his cell phone down on the coffee table in front of him.

This time Ellie concentrated on the numbers, taking it slowly, pushing one after the other then putting the phone back up to her ear.

When it rang, so did the phone on the table.

Charlie leaned forward, picked it up. 'Here we go again.' He pressed a button. 'Hi there, El.'

'What?' She stared at him.

'I said "hi". Now it's your turn to say it. At least, that's what normally happens in phone calls.'

'How? I mean . . . how do you have Daniel's phone? I don't understand.'

'It's a mystery to me too.'

'I don't understand,' she said again. 'Wait. I must have copied the number down wrong.' She'd deleted Debby's message and the 'Time's up' message, but saved Daniel's. All she had to do was replay it. When she did, she checked each number he said with the numbers she'd written down.

They were exactly the same.

'It's his number. It must be his phone. How did you get his phone, Charlie? Did you run into him on the way here? But how could you . . . I don't understand. Where is he?'

'I'm not sure where he is, El. In Cornwall, maybe? In a little fishing village?'

'What?'

'On the other hand, I don't think he's the type to go to a fishing village. But, oops, I may be wrong about that. Maybe he is.'

Her brain began to reel. Why did he say Cornwall? Why

had he said a fishing village? He'd said 'oops'. Charlie would never say 'oops'.

'El? Are you all right?'

'You know about Cornwall? How? You must have met him. And you have his phone . . . Did you do something to him, Charlie? You couldn't have. Please tell me you haven't hurt him?'

'Hurt Daniel? Never. I wouldn't harm a hair on his head. Which reminds me – you know the way he pushes that little lock of blond hair back off his forehead? It's quite beguiling, isn't it?'

None of this could be happening. None of it made sense. Ellie couldn't take her eyes off Charlie, who was acting as if they were having a normal conversation, completely relaxed.

'Still – he isn't really your type, is he? A little too Hugh Grantish, I'd say.'

'*What?*'

'And honestly – do you care about universal healthcare? I mean, we might think it's a good idea in principle, but who needs all those details? Leave that to the politicians. That's what I'd suggest.'

'I don't . . . what . . . how do you know? How can you know all this? I don't understand.' Ellie's heart started to pound.

'It's simple.' He shrugged, uncrossed his legs, leaned forward. 'You didn't fall in love with Daniel, El. You fell in love with me.'

27

Joe needed a drink. Or ten. They'd dropped Tim off at Lauren's. Her mother had asked them to come inside for a few minutes, they'd sat and made polite small talk with her, then left. Tim was going to spend the night there.

Joe didn't think there'd be any creeping down the corridors, though. Lauren's mother looked pretty fierce.

Now they were heading back to the house, but Joe didn't want to go back there, spend hours discussing who could be doing this to Ellie. Charlie Walters was with her now, her new boyfriend was about to show up, she'd have two men in that cottage. And it wasn't as if he and his mother could figure out who had made that call or written those letters.

Joe had to admit it: he'd behaved like an asshole when they'd met Charlie, he'd flinched when Tim had told him about the doctor. Which had to mean he was a little jealous.

He needed a drink.

'I have an idea,' he said, as they were about to turn down the road that led to Mashnee. 'Let's go to that Chinese place past Buzzards Bay.'

'Where they have the karaoke nights?'

'Yeah. Why not? We can listen to all those aspiring stars and eat some lousy food.'

His mother pulled over to the side of the road.

'You're serious?'

'Absolutely. Let's take some time out of all this.'

'I was just wondering if we should go back and call the police.'

'Charlie's with Ellie, the doctor's about to arrive. And then the police show up? I don't think she'd appreciate that. We can go over there tomorrow. We can call the police then. She has her ex-husband *and* the man she has a serious thing with. She's safe. Let's take a break. Besides, I'm craving some pork lo mein and whisky.'

Louisa nodded, turned the car around.

'What do you mean, I fell in love with you? I fell in love with *Daniel*. We wrote all those emails to each other. You have nothing to do with it. You're insane.'

But Charlie didn't look insane. He looked pleased with himself and in control.

'I suppose all lawyers are insane in their own way. At least, the successful ones. All those long hours of work – it's enough to drive anyone crazy. So point taken, but I'm afraid it's not applicable to this situation. What *is* applicable is due diligence.'

'What?'

'Due diligence. Prior to signing any contract, we are obliged to act with a certain standard of care. Which means we have to investigate, do our homework, as it were.'

All Ellie could do was stare at him.

'In this case, the due diligence was remarkably straightforward. I wanted to keep tabs on you, so I did. Really, you should be more careful, El. You should know cyberspace is a whole new world, and there's no such thing as privacy in it. Especially when you never change your password. And you don't delete your emails immediately. It's sloppy to let them pile up like that.'

'You read my emails?'

'Of course.' He said it as if he were saying 'Of course I paid the phone bill'.

'I think coffee would be a good idea now. Would you like some too? You seem to have lost the power of speech. I'll take your silence as a no, then. Don't move, El. I'll be right back.'

She couldn't move.

He'd been reading all her emails. Since when? He'd read all her and Daniel's emails. He had Daniel's phone. Had he intercepted Daniel at the airport? Somehow stolen his phone?

'You know I don't like instant coffee, but I had to make an exception. So – where were we?'

Sitting back down, Charlie put his cup of coffee on the table by his phone – by Daniel's phone.

'Right, I know where we were. As I said, I read all your emails. Your new friend Debby has a good sense of humour when she's not being crass. In any event, there was nothing to worry about there, it was all pretty anodyne, but then, well – the real shock came. Online dating. That's not only beneath you, El, it's dangerous. And utterly disrespectful to me.'

'Charlie, what are you talking about? I don't understand. You were with Sandra. We were divorced. I . . .'

Why was she defending herself? She had every right to go out with other people. He kept putting her on the back foot. He'd been the one who had invaded her privacy, yet still she felt the need to justify her actions to him. She didn't want to hand over any more power to Charlie, but he'd manoeuvred her into doing just that.

'Please don't keep saying you don't understand. I never thought you were stupid, El. But you're beginning to make me doubt myself on that.

'Obviously I wasn't going to let you go on that date alone. One piece of good fortune, I must admit, was that our friend Daniel chose a restaurant with a crowded bar for your meeting. I was at the back of it but I had a good view. You know, when I saw the way he looked at himself in the mirror, I was surprised you didn't walk out right away. I know how much you hate that.'

'You were there? In the restaurant?'

Ellie's mind was whirling, trying to remember the layout of Acquitaine, attempting to picture the bar as she'd walked by it. But she hadn't been paying attention; she was too nervous, too intent on finding Daniel.

'I watched you both. Remember when you and I first met? It wasn't like that, was it? He really can't stop talking. Forget about cancer – I'm sure he bores his patients to death.'

Panic seized her. This was even worse than that phone call, but she couldn't scream.

'You've hurt him, haven't you? Oh my God, Charlie. You really have hurt him.'

'Please.' His expression was one of pure exasperation. 'Daniel Litman is in London.' He leaned forward, put his elbows on his knees, his chin on his fists. 'As far as he's concerned, you ended what really can't be dignified by the word "relationship" when you emailed him and told him you were both starting new lives and you hoped he had a good one, or whatever you said exactly to brush him off. It was polite, obviously. You're like me, El. You care about manners. And I'm sure he took it well.

'I took over from Daniel after you got rid of him. I created a new account under his name – not difficult if you know how to do it. Do you *understand* now? Every email from London was from me. All the ones you enjoyed so much? I wrote them.'

All her cherished beliefs were like little ducks lined up in an amusement arcade. With each sentence Charlie spoke – bam! – another one was blasted out of the water.

No, no, no. It wasn't possible. It couldn't be.

'So, you see, you fell in love with me. You've fallen in love with me twice.'

'No. I didn't . . .' Ellie put her head in her hands. She was shaking, trying to take in what he was saying, trying to remember what Daniel had written in those emails – except Daniel hadn't written anything. That was what Charlie was saying. Her mind searched for some way out of this, something in his story that didn't fit.

'Wait – it couldn't be you. In that first message he sent

314

from London, he talked about the "Happy Birthday" song – you couldn't have known that.'

'You're losing it, El. What did I just say? I was there at Acquitaine. I even joined in on the song.' Charlie picked up his cup, took a sip of coffee. 'Is it sinking in now? It looks that way.' He took another sip. 'It's a lot to take in. I understand that. Take your time. Go through it all.'

Think. Think. All those emails . . . Charlie had written them. Daniel hadn't. Daniel had stopped writing after she'd sent that one saying they were better off not keeping in touch. Daniel had gone to England and not writtten again.

But if that were the case, if Charlie were doing it all, Daniel wouldn't have been on that plane.

Which meant . . .

'You're lying.' She stood up. 'You're lying through your teeth. You're making all this up. Daniel called me . . . You didn't call me. *He* called me when I was at my mother's. You didn't know that, did you? You didn't know and you're sitting there looking so smug and I *know* it wasn't you who called. He did.'

'Sit down, El.'

'No. You're lying. He called me. You're lying!'

Charlie stood up, came to her and took hold of her wrist.

'Come sit down with me. I'll explain that call. You'll want to hear this.'

Tightening his grip on her wrist, he pulled her with him, forced her to sit on the sofa beside him.

'Let go of my wrist! You're hurting me.'

'I'll let you go when you've heard what I have to say next.

315

You really will understand then. I know I hurt you deeply when I left. It's natural for you to resent me for that. Your pride would stop you from admitting to yourself that you still love and need me. That's human nature, isn't it? "Hell hath no fury", et cetera. You were still in love with me but you wouldn't allow yourself to express that. You buried your feelings the same way you buried the accident.

'And that, El, was a problem for me. But I'm a problem-solver, as you know. And I remembered that first night we met. Do you? Do you remember that you told me you'd just read *Cyrano de Bergerac* for an English course you were taking? Do you remember saying how much you loved it? I remembered. So I became Cyrano de Bergerac. Problem solved. You could fall in love with me without your pride getting in the way. It really is one of the great love stories of all time.'

'Shut up and let go of me!' She pulled her wrist away, but he yanked it back. 'I can't stand this. It's bullshit, Charlie. You *didn't* call me. I know your voice. It wasn't you. It was Daniel.'

'Really?' He coughed. 'Oops, I think I have a bug. Doctors aren't supposed to get sick, are they?'

'You bugged my phone? You read all my emails and you bugged my phone?' She closed her eyes, felt herself sinking. The weight of his words was pushing her down into a hole, a terrible black hole of nothingness.

'I don't like coughing, as you know. Another exception. I make exceptions for you. But, no, I didn't bug your phone. Am I boring you?' He patted her cheek. 'Are you falling asleep? Well, this should wake you up. I didn't bug your phone. *I* made that call. As it transpires, the marvels of modern technology are boundless. See – you are interested. Which you should be because it's fascinating. Listen to this and don't interrupt.

'There are machines that can transform the human voice. Not those old digital fake-sounding ones you hear on television. State-of-the-art ones. The amazing thing is, they're not that expensive either. And there are spy shops, did you know that? Spy shops that sell this equipment to ordinary people like me.

'I knew you'd want to talk to Daniel at some point and I had to be prepared for that. It was a risk, I know, but I tested the machine out on other people and I knew it worked. When you asked me to call you in that email, how could I not respond?

'I decided you wouldn't remember his voice very well. It *was* noisy in that restaurant, and I saw the way you were leaning forward, cupping your ears, trying to hear him. Also, it had been a while since that night. And I called late so I'd wake you up. That would help too. You'd be a little fuzzy. I threw in the cough for good measure.

'The hard part was trying to talk the way he talked. I could give myself licence when I wrote. Strangely enough, people can converse like idiots and yet write like angels. So I had to think of the way Daniel Litman would phrase things. What words he'd use in speech. The way I see it, anyone who would use the word "oops" would say "ditto", and, of course, "wow".

'El, snap out of it! Don't close those beautiful eyes again. This is really good news, you know. It proves you love me and you need me. Look who you turned to when things started to go wrong. Not that no-hoper Joe Amory. No. You needed Daniel. You needed me.'

When things started to go wrong.

Ellie's eyes flew open.

Of course. Charlie.

A man and two women were standing on the makeshift stage, finishing the last verse of 'Bad Moon Rising'. The three of them looked embarrassed, unlike the woman who had been on before, who'd belted out 'Black Velvet' with complete confidence.

Joe and Louisa applauded loudly after each song, especially 'Bad Moon Rising' because those three had hung their heads as they walked off, obviously wishing they'd never gone up there in the first place. Although the man had a good voice.

Louisa wished she could join Joe and have a drink, but she was driving. When they got back home, she'd pour herself a glass of wine – a large one.

Coming here had been a good idea, though. They'd eaten, they'd relaxed, they'd listened to a few surprisingly good singers.

They'd taken a break.

With about twenty other people who were taking their own breaks. In a dark generic Chinese restaurant where you could gather up your courage and go stand in the spotlight.

Louisa wished she could carry a tune. Or have enough to drink not to care that she couldn't. Get up on that stage and follow the bouncing ball and screech out a Rolling Stones song – that would be perfect. Although 'Bad Moon Rising' would have been even better if it hadn't already been taken.

The bad moon had already risen; it had been hanging around for a long time now.

She wasn't going to wait until Thursday to see Mr Andrews. She was going to go over to Ellie's tomorrow and convince her to go with her to the police, whether Daniel was still there or not.

Louisa picked up her chopsticks, took a mouthful of noodles.

Charlie and Daniel might have met by now. Whatever Daniel was like, he'd be hard-pressed to come out of any encounter with Charlie looking like a star.

Charlie Walters judged situations instantly, knew exactly how to handle himself. Always the lead dog in the pack.

Would Daniel, like Joe, attempt to challenge him?

When they got back home, she'd pour herself a big glass of wine, go to her computer and Google Daniel . . . What was his last name?

Litman – that was it.

It would be interesting to find out a little more about the man Ellie had fallen for.

Looking up from her food, she saw two forty-something women dressed in short shorts and tank tops getting ready to sing.

'Ten bucks it's an Abba song,' Joe said.

Louisa was just about to say 'You're on' when she heard the music to 'Take a Chance on Me' start up.

28

Charlie.

She'd thought it might be Hope's parents.

She'd been sure, for a while, that it was Joe. She'd actually accused him.

Charlie.

It had never come close to entering her head that he could be the one.

Wrong.

So unbearably, unbelievably wrong.

He was sitting beside her, dressed in a blue suit with a crisp white shirt and a red and blue striped tie. She could smell his 4711, the aftershave he always used.

Charlie. The man she'd been married to for almost seventeen years. Her husband. Sitting there calmly. Watching her. She could tell he knew exactly what she was thinking. He knew she had realised. Yet he didn't blink.

'You did it all. The beach, this room, the bicycle, the note, the phone calls. Why do you hate me so much? You left me. I never hurt you. Why do you hate me?'

'Say it again, El. Tell me you love me.'

Her wrist was aching from his grip. Her brain was on

fire. She'd fallen in love with him. She'd married him. They'd had Tim together. He was a corporate lawyer. He worked hard. He was successful. He was powerful. People listened to him.

'Why did you do those things to me?'

'You needed to know you needed me.'

He had his rules. He was a perfectionist. But he wasn't crazy. Too tough on Tim sometimes, but not deliberately cruel.

The Charlie she knew would never throw clothes around a living room. He'd never do any of these things. What hadn't she seen?

Ellie shrank back, but he pulled her forward.

'You were going off the rails.' His voice was so quiet it was a whisper. 'You thought you could be independent. Have your own life in a new house with a new man. You can't do that. Look what you did, El. You kept vodka and wine in here – where Tim could easily get them. So negligent. And that little beach. You were so proud of it, weren't you? A measly little patch of sand. As for those tacky little seagulls – what *were* you thinking?'

'Why did that matter to you? Why would you care? You were with Sandra. What happened with her, Charlie?'

'There's an excellent Herman Melville short story – you might know it from that English course. *Bartleby, the Scrivener*. Throughout the story, Bartleby repeats one phrase: "I would prefer not to." I'd prefer not to discuss Sandra Cabot.'

He'd pretended to be Daniel – to make her fall in love with him again. He'd messed up the living room and the beach because he didn't want Ellie to have a life of her own. Something had gone wrong with Sandra. Something had gone wrong with her, and Charlie had lost his mind.

Ellie had never felt afraid of him before. He'd made her feel safe.

'Charlie, please let go of my wrist. You're hurting me. This isn't you. You know it isn't.'

He tightened his grip so hard she let out a cry of pain.

'Why didn't you tell me about the accident?'

'Charlie, you're scaring me. You're really scaring me.'

'You can't answer, can you? You know how wrong you were not to tell me. How many times have people said to me, "I've never told anyone this before, but . . ."? People I don't even know. *They* tell me their secrets. But my wife? She keeps an enormous secret. From the man she vowed to love for eternity. She doesn't even tell me she's been in a mental ward. I could probably sue you, you know. Withholding information like that.'

'Don't say that. You don't understand. I had convinced myself it hadn't happened. I did all these things to stop myself remembering. Self-hypnosis and—' She could see he wasn't listening. He was looking around the room, as if every word she said bored him intensely.

'Charlie, how did you find out?'

His eyes came back to her. He smiled.

'Your mother loves me. In a very well-intentioned effort to bring us back together, she told me. She said I didn't understand what you'd been through, she had no idea why you hadn't told me before. I'm like a son to her, you know.'

Her mother. Of course. 'I think you're mistaken,' she'd said when Ellie had told her Charlie and Sandra were getting married. She'd been talking to Charlie. She must have known he wasn't with Sandra any more.

But why had he emailed her that he was getting married?

To make it easier for her to fall in love with Daniel? To make absolutely sure she'd never suspect him of being involved in anything to do with her life?

It was so well planned. So well executed. He'd covered all the bases.

But that could mean only one thing. He expected her to fall at his feet, tell him she still loved him, agree to go back.

Yet Charlie was psychologically astute. He had to know that after all this she could never go back.

As soon as that thought was processed, her fear escalated so much she couldn't swallow.

Fast forward the tape. There's no acceptable end to this, not for Charlie. Or me.

'So your mother gave me all the details and I used them. I suppose you would say I was punishing you. Perhaps I was. But that's nothing compared to your not telling me. And it's less than nothing compared to that sordid little escapade with Joe Amory.'

He knew about Joe?

Of course he did.

He was Daniel.

He knew everything.

'You had sex with him the first night you met. Oh, I know, you didn't actually say that in your email to me, but really it was so obvious. How disgusting. Did you paint your nails that day? The way you painted them when you went to meet Daniel? You were turning into a real slut. You have no idea how difficult it was for me – sorry, for Daniel – not to email you back and tell you what a slut you were becoming.'

She had to make him let go of her. Then she could try to escape.

In so many scenes in those crime shows her mother watched, the victim attempts to talk to the criminal down, get through to him. But Charlie would see that tactic coming a mile off.

'As it happened, Joe Amory played right into my hands, behaving as he did. However, it was incumbent upon me to protect you from him in case he tried to rehabilitate himself. I bet you want to know how I discovered what his handwriting looked like.'

He was speaking as if this were all a fun practical joke and he was bragging about how he'd pulled it off. He was speaking as if she were in on it with him, as if it would amuse her. He'd said 'Of course' when she'd asked him if he read all her emails. 'Of course.'

As if he had every right to.

Something had slipped inside him, tilted his whole psyche.

This was real insanity. She'd seen it before, in the ward. In patients who had completely lost touch with the world. Some of them screamed their heads off constantly, some of them ranted about aliens pursuing them, but some of them were quiet. The quiet ones were the scariest. When they spoke, they spoke logically. They created a fabric of seeming logic to sustain what was entirely illogical and entirely crazed.

She'd been in there with them. But she hadn't been insane, she'd been sick.

'Yes, I want to know about the handwriting,' she said.

Keep him talking.

While he's talking, think.

'Joe doesn't lock his car. On one of my trips here, I waited until 2 a.m., walked over there, opened the car door, took out my flashlight and studied the rental agreement he'd signed. With that distinctive "e" at the end. Sometimes I wonder about fate, El. You know me, you know I don't believe in that nonsense, but at times like that, well, you can't help but speculate. I'd like to think the gods were on my side.'

The only sport Charlie had excelled at was wrestling. He wasn't a fast runner . . . he'd always refused to race in any of the father/son games at school sports days . . .

But he had to let go of her before she could run.

'Could I change my mind about the coffee, Charlie? I need some.'

'I don't think so, El. Not now. You should be listening to me. This is important. I sent a letter to Joe, from you, and I sent a letter to you from Joe. One of my clients was going to DC. I asked him to mail the one to you from there. See what I mean about fate?

'I knew exactly what to say to you to get you to avoid him like the plague. Just as I knew exactly what to say to you when I was Daniel. I shouldn't have to make this point again, but I will. I *know* you. I know you better than you know yourself. Everything that has happened only goes to prove that. Excuse me. Goes only to prove that. I keep telling Tim he constantly misuses "only" in that way.'

Tim.

'Tim will be back soon. You don't want him to see us like this. With you holding me like this.'

'Tim's not coming back tonight. He's staying at Lauren's. I took care of that too.'

Relief and despair coursed through Ellie simultaneously. Charlie wouldn't let her go because Tim wouldn't be back, but Tim had no chance of being involved in this. Tim was safely at Lauren's.

'I've almost finished my little discourse, El. I'll try to wrap it up quickly. As you know, I don't normally talk so much. I'm not Daniel. Thank God.' He snorted. 'I wrote that "Cry Me A River" note and put it in an envelope and used Joe's handwriting for your name. Looking back on that, it was a mistake. Because it was unneccesary. I didn't need to cast suspicion on Joe. But never mind, I did it. For my own amusement. That call today was for my own amusement too. Again, unnecessary. But my new machine is so seductive. It can turn me into a woman and I don't even have to pay for the operation.

'That was a joke, El.'

He didn't jog or run, but he lifted weights at the gym. Not regularly, but enough to maintain his upper body strength. She'd seen him lift heavy furniture with no problems.

'Before I came here, I left that message from Daniel. Then, when I was driving here, I left that "Time's up" message. Obviously I couldn't use my machine in the car – it's like the mixing desks DJs use, it's not portable. So I put a handkerchief over the receiver, the old-fashioned way.

'There are other little details, of course. Getting another cell phone, that kind of thing. Working this all out so the police wouldn't take it seriously if you tried to get them involved – until this afternoon when my female alter ego warned you off. But you don't need to know about those.

'There,' he sighed. 'I'm done.'

'Then you can let me go.'

'Tell me you love me.'

What would he do to her if she didn't?

'I love you.'

'Oh, El. That was tragic. Let's do it the way we did it on the phone. "I love you." There, I said it. I love you.'

'I love you too.'

It was a huge deal. So he had to think about it, not just blurt it out like a kid. He and Lauren were sitting on the sofa together, watching TV. Her mother had gone out, but she'd given Tim a pointed look when she'd said, 'I'll be back by ten. No fooling around, you two.'

Lauren wasn't making her usual funny comments about the show, so maybe she was in a bad mood.

Maybe this wasn't the right time. She'd been amazing before, listening to him talking about his mom and even saying, 'Look, I would have screamed too if some nutcase

327

had made a crank call to me. Don't worry about it. And so what if she went to a loony bin for a while when she was, like, seventeen? There are tons of times I think *I* should go to one. Think about it: no homework.'

He'd so wanted to say it right then. She knew exactly what to say to make him feel better. Everything she did was right.

But it might freak her out. He thought she felt the same way about him as he did about her, but how could he be sure? The last thing he wanted was for her to look at him, say: 'That was a joke, right? It better be.'

Maybe he should wait.

Uncertainty sucked. When was the right time to do anything? No one ever told you that stuff.

His arm was around her; she was snuggled against him. All of a sudden, she broke away, turned around to the side, sitting cross-legged so she was facing him, picked up the remote control, switched the television off.

'I've been thinking,' she said.

She was using her serious voice.

This could be the run-up to 'I've been thinking. I need space' – or whatever girls said when they were ditching you. He waited, trying to work out how he could deal with that if it happened, how to be cool, how not to react like an idiot.

'Your mother running over that little kid . . . That must have been so bad for her. If I were her, all I'd want is to take that day back. Something like that must change your life forever. And I've been thinking that everyone at some point has something that changes their life forever. Someone they love dies or they get really sick. You know what I mean, right?'

'Right. I think so.'

'I know I said before Fate works things out for the best, but I'm not sure about that any more. I mean, maybe it does, but you can still have that "I want to take this back" moment, that "please say this isn't happening" time. And we haven't hit that yet. OK, our parents got divorced and that changes things, but not in that kind of way. I mean, I know some kids never get over the whole divorce thing, but not us, right? We're still the same people. We're not spending all our time wishing something hadn't happened. And . . .'

'And what?'

'And I hope it doesn't happen to us until we're really, really old, when there's less time to wish you could take whatever it is back. Sorry.' Lauren raised her eyebrows, rolled her eyes. 'I think about shit like this too much. You must think I'm really weird.'

He reached out, put his hands around the back of her neck, pulled her towards him. 'I love you.'

29

'Charlie, what are you doing?'

'Isn't it obvious?'

He was pulling her towards him, trying to kiss her. Ellie pulled back, but he caught her other hand in his, pulled her in again.

'Let go of me.'

'You love me, El. Come on.'

'No.' She squirmed so her face was turned away from his.

'What the hell is your problem?'

'Let me go!' She started to struggle, jerking back, trying to get out of his grip.

'Don't be coy.'

'Charlie, stop it.' She was pulling away from him as hard as she could, but he wouldn't let go of her wrists.

He pushed her down so her head was on the sofa, got on top of her, his legs on either side of her body, his face looming over hers. Her wrists were pinned to the sides of her shoulders.

She jerked her leg up, kicking his back with her knee. The impact was feeble, though. She tried to do it again, but he'd moved back slightly, his weight on her thighs.

'You lied to me. You don't love me. You lied.'

'Charlie—'

'Is this where you did it with Joe? On the sofa here? Is this where you fucked him? Or did you do it on the floor?'

Her wrists were numb, she could feel the blood circulation in her thighs cutting off.

'Don't do this,' she begged.

'Don't do what? If you love me, what's the problem?'

'I do love you, but—'

'But? There are no buts, El. You know, I think you've turned into such a slut you need it this way.'

He was too strong. She couldn't win a physical battle. She had to make him get off her, let go of her.

'We should go into the bedroom, Charlie.'

'Really? I don't think Joe did it in the bedroom. I think he did it right here.'

'We were in the bedroom. I promise.'

'I don't believe you. You've turned into a lying little slut.' He let go of her left wrist, slapped her across the face. It burned. Her face burned from the pain. And she hadn't been quick enough to punch him when he'd let go of her. He had her wrist again.

'You like it this way, don't you?'

'No.'

This time when he slapped her, she drove her free hand as hard as she could into his ribs.

'Ouch,' he said. But he didn't budge. He didn't grab her wrist again, so she kept punching at his ribs, her fist flailing.

'Ouch ouch ouch. That really hurts.' He didn't get off her, he didn't move.

'I know I'm short, but I'm strong. And you're tiny, El. You can't hurt me. Go ahead, keep punching.'

A feeling of utter powerlessness swamped her. Her punches turned into small thumps, as if she were drumming on his ribcage.

There was no way out.

But there had to be.

'I wasn't lying. We did it on the bed, Charlie. I swear to you, we did it on the bed.'

She could see his eyes searching hers, looking for the truth.

'Maybe.' His face scrunched up. 'Maybe.' He relaxed it, his eyes bored into hers again. She forced herself to stare back at him without blinking

'It's the truth.'

Keeping hold of her wrist, he got off her, yanked her up, twisted her arm so it was behind her back.

'Half nelson,' he muttered. 'Come on.'

Her legs were so dead she stumbled as he frog-marched her into the bedroom. She'd thought he might have let go of her momentarily when they went to the bedroom. She was wrong.

'We always had great sex, didn't we?'

They were beside the bed.

'Didn't we, El?'

He jerked her arm up and she cried out, 'Yes.'

The only way she could get away from him was if he

were distracted. He was so focused, though. Screaming wouldn't distract him. And no one would hear her scream. If she screamed, he'd hit her again.

Charlie didn't get distracted. When he concentrated, he concentrated entirely. Once he'd bought a jigsaw puzzle for Tim. It was such a difficult one Tim didn't have a hope of putting it together. Charlie sat down and concentrated. He didn't look up until he'd finished it. She remembered thinking then he'd obviously bought it for himself.

All this was running wildly through her head as he let go of her arm, pushed her down on to the bed, stood in front of her.

'Don't be stupid now, El. You know if you try anything I'll hit you again. But I'll hit you harder. Of course, if you'd like that . . .'

'No.'

'So tell me, how did Joe do it? Did he rip off your clothes or did you take them off yourself?'

Charlie was so driven he never lost concentration.

'I took them off myself.'

'Go ahead then. But, remember, don't be stupid.'

He hovered above her as she unzipped her jeans.

But . . . but there was always that one moment when he relaxed. Always. That one moment.

'I have to stand up to take these off.'

He stepped back, but only a pace. If she tried to run now, it would be simple for him to stop her.

She wriggled out of her jeans.

'Take off your shirt.'

She did.

'Your pants and bra.'

She unhooked her bra, dropped it, took off her pants.

'Sit back down.'

She sat.

And closed her eyes as he took off his clothes.

'He was on top, wasn't he?'

'Yes.' She opened her eyes. She couldn't stop herself from shrinking back at the sight of him. His hand flashed out, he slapped her again. Tears leaped into her eyes.

'Make yourself comfortable.'

Thank God. Thank God.

She backed towards the middle of the bed, stretched out.

He launched himself on to her, grabbed her forearms.

'If I were you, I wouldn't fight me, El,' he whispered in her right ear. 'You won't win.'

She screamed in pain when he entered her. She could taste the tears that were rolling from her closed eyes. He kept saying 'You're mine' with every thrust he made. 'You're mine, you're mine, you're mine.'

He wasn't stopping. He kept going and going and going.

You're mine, you're mine, you're mine

She didn't know this man. But she did. This was Charlie. And because it was Charlie she knew when he was reaching a climax and she knew he was finally getting close.

'You're mine . . .'

He was yelling now. The only time he ever really raised his voice.

Get ready. Be ready.

His whole body shuddered.

And then he did what Charlie always did. He rolled off her, turned his body to the side, away from her.

Ellie sprang up. She ran. She ran out of the bedroom and through the living room and out the door. She ran the way she ran in nightmares, her legs pumping with fear. She ran to Louisa's.

'Have you had enough?' Louisa asked Joe. 'I'm getting tired.

'I'd like another whisky but I shouldn't, so I won't. Yeah, let's get going.'

They'd already paid the bill.

Louisa and Joe stood up.

A large woman in a bright blue flowing dress launched into a song.

And Louisa was back in California, at an outdoor concert, sitting on the grass with Jamie, listening to Janis Joplin sing 'Take Another Little Piece of My Heart'.

She sat back down.

30

Ellie couldn't stop or look behind her; she didn't dare. The sandy gravel of the driveway was cutting into her bare feet, but she didn't slow down. Racing up the steps, she grabbed the handle of the front door, flung it open.

'Louisa?' she yelled. 'Louisa?'

There was no answer. The light was on in the living room, but Louisa wasn't there. Joe wasn't there. No one was there.

The phone.

The landline phone was on top of the bookshelf, underneath the photographs. Ellie ran to it, picked it up, dialled 911.

'I was raped,' she said as soon as a woman answered. 'He's coming after me. I'm in the Amory house at the end of Agawam Point Road. Help! Please help. Send the police.' The woman started to say something but Ellie hung up. Charlie would be seconds away.

He'll know I've come here. I have to hide.

Where?

She ran up the stairs, tripped on the next to last one, picked herself up, got to the top, turned to the right, then left.

The attic.

No, he'd think of that. It had to be a place he wouldn't think of.

Wait . . . when Joe told her about Burt and the medicine cabinet, she'd said if she were playing Sardines, she'd hide in that cupboard in the sewing room.

There were no lights on in the hall. Charlie didn't know this house the way she did. He'd have to find the switch or else feel his way down the hallway. And he'd have to find the light switch in each room.

That would give the police more time. He'd search each bedroom. The sewing room was at the end. But would he be smart enough to start at the end?

Move.

She ran to the left, passed the bedrooms, raced into the sewing room. Moonlight was streaming through the windows in it.

Shit. Shit. He can see in here without a light.

But I don't have time to change my mind.

The cupboard was like a small hidey-hole set into the wall to the right of the piano. It could be full of junk.

What if it were full of junk?

Crouching down and opening it, Ellie saw board games stacked up. She could push them to the back, still climb in. She was small enough . . . she had to be. She got down on her knees, picked up a few of the games, pushed them back against the far wall.

She crawled inside and pulled the door shut.

She just fitted – just. She was curled up, holding her knees, her head down.

How long before he found her in here?

How long before the police came?

They'd come – they had to. They always responded to 911 calls, didn't they? But what if they thought she was making it up? What happened in those *Law & Order* shows? Had anyone ever said the police always responded to 911 calls or not? She couldn't remember.

Where was Louisa? Where was Joe?

Wherever they were, they'd have to come back at some point.

What point?

What would Charlie do to her if he did find her?

He'd rape her again. Or he'd kill her. Or he'd do both.

It was airless in here. Stuffy and boiling. How long had she been here? The sweat off her legs was making her hands clammy; drops of hot sweat were dropping off her forehead on to her knees. She couldn't start to sob; if she did he might hear her.

He wouldn't shout out for her. He'd search the house quietly. And thoroughly. He might start on the other side, though. Or even downstairs.

If she could have fitted into the medicine cabinet, he'd never find her. Or she could have hidden under one of the eaves in the attic. Or in the bushes outside, Joe's special place. But it was too late now.

She lifted her arm slightly, trying to see the time, but her watch didn't have an illuminated dial. She had no idea what time she'd escaped from him anyway. She had no idea how long she'd been in this closet. It could have been

338

five minutes since she'd made the call. Or more. Or less. Probably less.

Her face still hurt. She touched one side then the other with her wet hands. He'd slapped her so easily, as if he always slapped people.

But Charlie didn't slap people. He charmed them.

He wasn't Charlie.

He wasn't Daniel.

He was insane.

She held her breath, listened for the sound of movement. There was none.

He might not be here. He might have gotten dressed, gotten into his car and left after she ran off. He might have realised what he'd done, understood and been so ashamed and . . .

No. He'd been plotting all this for a long time. This wasn't a momentary spell of madness. He'd cultivated it all, carefully, with intent.

There was a sound. Or was she imagining it? She held her breath.

Nothing.

She must have imagined it.

'That's nice. A piano. A very old piano,' Charlie said.

'Let's take the longer way,' Joe said.

'Why?'

'I want to see Buttermilk Bay in the moonlight. Don't you love that name? Buttermilk Bay.'

'Are you drunk?'

'No. What's wrong with seeing Buttermilk Bay? Remember

when you and I and Dad went there in the boat? That day it was so choppy? Remember how rough it was?'

'Yes. I was actually frightened.'

'I was shit scared. But I didn't want Dad to see how scared I was.'

'He wouldn't have minded.'

'I know. But I did.' Joe yawned. 'Come on, Mum. A little trip down Memory Lane? Who's that going to hurt?'

When the sound blasted out, Ellie's head jerked up, hitting the top of the cupboard.

Had he heard it? Or had the notes he struck masked it?

'Out of tune. Careless, Louisa.'

He was moving. Where? Back towards the door. He was leaving. He was going.

Another sound and then light seeped in at the bottom of the cupboard. He'd found the switch.

He was moving again. Towards the window.

'This is so stupid.'

Did he know she was there? Was he talking to her?

'Due diligence.'

He was moving again, to the far end of the room. There was a clothes closet there. She heard him open the door. And then close it.

If only she'd hidden in the attic. He must be leaving the attic for last. Why hadn't she hidden there?

Footsteps. They were heading straight for her.

The door swung out and open. Charlie crouched down. His face was level with hers.

'Please. Charlie. Please!'

He reached in, grabbed her ankle, began to tug her out. Her hands flailed to get a grip on something but there was nothing she could hold on to. He was dragging her out.

'I called the police,' she cried out. 'The police are coming.'

'I don't think so, El. I called 911 too. I told them my wife was having an hysterical fit, not to pay attention to any call they might have received.'

He let go of her ankle.

'No offence, El, but you look like a mess.' He crouched down, took hold of her arm above the elbow. 'An unsightly naked mess.'

The police weren't coming. Louisa and Joe weren't coming.

It's over.

She closed her eyes.

This isn't happening.

It's not happening.

About ten seconds after they passed Buttermilk Bay, Joe fell asleep. Louisa began to hum that Janis Joplin song to herself as she kept on the Buzzards Bay Road, passing the now-defunct movie theatre, thinking as she always did when they passed it about the other old movie theatre – the one in Onset, a town five minutes away. That one had closed too, a long time ago. Someone had rented it one summer, turned it into a club with live bands playing and called it Sergeant Pepper's.

She and Jamie used to go there and listen to a band called Rigor Mortis and the Standstills. Sergeant Pepper's closed after that one summer. Which was also a shame. She would have liked to imagine Tim and Lauren going there, dancing the night away.

She sped up a little because she was tired too. It had been a good idea of Joe's to go to the Chinese/karaoke place, but she was feeling worn out. Too much music. Which definitely meant she was getting old. There never used to be such a thing as too much music.

There was barely any traffic. She crossed the Bourne Bridge easily. When Ellie began to tell her the actor playing Superman who thought he could fly story, she'd stopped her, saying, 'That's one of the bridge myths. The other is that one of the men working on it fell asleep on the job and another worker poured concrete over him by mistake. So his body is still in there, doomed to be trapped forever in the bridge. That one always scared the wits out of me until I heard the exact same story – only this time the worker was buried in the Golden Gate Bridge.'

Louisa was trying to decide whether she should inform Joe that he snored when she saw Tedeschi's and realised she needed to pick up a bottle of wine. She was tired, but she wanted that glass before she went to sleep. And there was no wine in the house.

'Wake up, Joe. You're snoring.'

31

It's not happening.

It's not happening.

I can shut out the sound of the siren, I can shut out every-thing.

The brain is every super-hero rolled into . . .

The siren?

Ellie opened her eyes.

'Shit,' Charlie said. He was kneeling over her again. Her wrists were pinned to the floor.

'It's the police . . . The police are coming.'

'They can't be. I made that call.'

'It's a siren, Charlie. It's getting louder. They're coming.'

'Shit.'

He looked wildly around the room.

'I can . . .' He stopped. Shook his head. 'Come with me, El. Now.'

'No.'

'You have to.'

'No.'

He stared down at her.

343

'What the hell happened to you, El? You've gone crazy again.'

Letting go of her wrists, he stood up. And ran out.

Ellie sat up, put her head in her hands, stared at the floor. *He's gone. He's really gone. He's gone.*

Within seconds her relief disappeared with the next thought.

The police would catch him now. They'd put him in jail. She might have to testify against him.

Tim.

How could she possibly tell Tim about this?

But she couldn't let Charlie go free.

He'd raped her. He'd hit her. He'd threatened her. If the police hadn't come, he would have . . .

Tim.

I'm her mother, it was my job to protect her.

How could she protect Tim?

Could she lie to the police? Say it had all been a misunderstanding and hope Charlie somehow magically became himself again?

Someone was yelling 'Hello?' from downstairs.

Ellie stood up. She picked up the blanket that was draped over the piano bench, wrapped it around herself. She took one look at the closet with the board games, then walked out of the sewing room.

When they passed the sign for the Aptucxet Trading Post, Louisa remembered the first time she'd met Ellie and Tim. Ellie had been so sweet, and so welcoming. Making a move

344

like that must have been a huge step – especially huge after having lived with a man like Charlie. She could imagine him 'taking care' of Ellie; she could imagine the power he had in any relationship.

'You know, when I went to the men's room back at the Chinese place, one of the guys there said that the first guy we saw . . . the one who was singing "Bad Moon Rising" with the two women? . . . he's the CEO of Home Depot, apparently.'

'Really?' Louisa smiled, remembering how shy and embarrassed he'd looked. 'That's a nice spin on a typical CEO. And he can sing. Any hardware we need from now, we're going there.'

'Christ – look at that lunatic . . .'

A car sped by them on the other side of the road, going so fast Louisa wondered how the driver could keep control.

'That's a crash waiting to happen.'

She turned on to Agawam Point Road, thinking: Almost home. A glass of wine. Bed. I'll Google Daniel Litman when I get up tomorrow.

'No other car in Ellie's driveway.' Louisa slowed down, looked over at Joe. 'Where's the doctor? She must be alone. That's not good. Do you think we should stop and go in? The lights are on.'

He sat up straight.

'There's a police car outside our house, Mum.'

She turned her head, saw it.

'Oh, no. Oh, God. What the hell has happened?'

They pulled up behind the police car. Before she'd

turned off the engine, Joe was out of the car, running up the steps.

Louisa turned the key, left it in the ignition, got out and went after him.

Ellie was sitting on the sofa wrapped up in one of Louisa's blankets. A policeman was sitting on the chair next to her. Joe was standing in the middle of the room, saying: 'Ellie, are you all right?'

'Ellie?' Louisa rushed up to her. 'Sweetheart. What—'

'Mrs Amory?' The policeman stood up. He was thin and tall, like Joe, but older, with greying hair.

'Yes, yes. I'm Mrs Amory. Louisa. Are you all right, Ellie?' She rushed to the sofa, sat down beside her.

'I'm OK.' Ellie nodded. 'Sergeant Powell has been very nice to me. I've been telling him. I've been telling him . . .' Her voice died away.

'She's been through a bad experience, Mrs Amory. Maybe it would be a good idea if you got her a cup of tea or something.'

'Coffee,' Ellie mumbled. 'Please?'

Did she have any clothes on under the blanket? Louisa couldn't see any. He'd said a bad experience. A bad experience and she didn't have clothes on. Louisa felt her heart lurch.

'I'll get it,' Joe spoke up. 'You stay here with Ellie, Mum.'

'Joe is Louisa's son,' Ellie said to Sergeant Powell.

'You told me that before. But thank you. Maybe we could all use some coffee, Joe? If that's all right by you? And my name is David, OK? Forget the sergeant business.'

'OK. I'll get it now.'

Joe disappeared to the kitchen and Louisa grabbed Ellie's hand.

'Sweetheart, I'm so sorry. I should never have left you. I should never have—'

'It was Charlie, Louisa.'

'What?'

'It was Charlie.'

'Mrs Walters's ex-husband attacked her in her home.' The policeman, David, said. 'She ran here to escape him, but he followed her. He was in this house but he managed to elude my partner and me somehow. He must have gone out the back way, through the kitchen door. My partner is trying to find him now. We're a little short-staffed tonight. As usual.'

Louisa turned back to Ellie.

'Charlie? He . . . ? God Almighty. Are you sure you're all right? Shouldn't you go to the hospital?' She swivelled around to face David again. 'Shouldn't she see a doctor? Now?'

'One second.' He pulled a phone out of his pocket. 'I need to get this.' Standing up, he walked over to the stairway.

'Ellie, you need to see a doctor.'

'What am I going to tell Tim, Louisa? I couldn't lie. I couldn't pretend it hadn't happened. But Tim . . . He'll never understand. This will ruin his life.'

Joe came in with a trayful of cups, put it down on the floor, picked up one and handed it to Ellie.

'I put a shot of rum in yours, is that OK?'

'Yes.' She nodded. 'Thank you.' Pulling the blanket tighter around her with one hand, she took the mug with the other.

Her hand was shaking, but she managed to get it to her mouth and take a sip. 'Thank you.'

'Mrs Walters?' David Powell approached Ellie. 'My partner found your husband's car.'

'Where is he? Where's Charlie?'

Louisa saw the rank fear on Ellie's face.

'He was in the car. It crashed. He died, apparently on impact. It would appear he wasn't wearing a seatbelt. And it's an old model car. It doesn't have a safety bag.'

Ellie turned her face away and looked out the window.

'He died before he could cry.'

'What? Mrs Walters . . . I'm afraid you'll have to come with me to identify him.'

The speeding car, the crash waiting to happen. Charlie Walters. Jesus.

'Was anyone else hurt?' Ellie turned back to David Powell. 'In the crash?'

'No. It would appear he drove straight into a tree.'

'Straight into one?'

'That's what my partner told me.'

Ellie hung her head.

'Louisa, can I borrow some clothes?' She put her cup of coffee down on the floor. 'I need to see Tim.'

15 August

Someone was shaking his shoulder. He sat up, rubbed his eyes, saw it was Lauren's mother.

'Tim, your mother's here. She needs to talk to you.'

The lights were on; he looked at his watch. It was one

o'clock. He'd slept until one o'clock? But it was dark outside. His mother was walking towards him. At one o'clock in the morning.

He hadn't done anything bad. What had he done? He was on the sofa, not in Lauren's room.

'We'll leave you alone,' Lauren's mother was saying.

He searched the room for Lauren. She was standing by the island unit, and she was looking straight at him, and she looked scared. He'd never seen her look scared.

His mother sat down beside him. She took hold of his hand. She was crying. Lauren and her mother were leaving the room.

'Don't go,' he called out to Lauren, his eyes fixed on her. She stopped, and he knew. From the way Lauren was looking at him, he knew. This was it. This was the thing that had happened that would change his life forever.

'Tim—'

'Don't say it, Mom.'

'Come on, Lauren, we should go.'

'No. Stay, Lauren. Please.'

'She'll come back in a few minutes, Tim,' Lauren's mother said, taking her hand and leading her away, up the stairs.

'Tim, your father—'

'Don't say it.'

'Look at me, Tim. Please.'

He looked down at the floor. It was a tan-coloured carpet. Sandra didn't like the word 'carpet', she said people should say 'rug' instead. Tim had said 'carpet' every time he possibly could say it, to annoy her.

'Dad had an accident.'

He'd been going to fix things. He was going to make it all OK with his mom. He wouldn't have let them move away.

'He had an accident and he—'

'Don't say it.'

He hadn't said 'I love you, Dad' before he'd hung up. He'd never talked to him the way he had to his mother in the car after that time at The Country Club.

'Tim.' His mother had her arm around his shoulders. She was hugging him. His dad never hugged him. But that was OK. He wasn't a hug type of person. He should have told his dad that was OK. He should have said 'I love you' before he'd hung up.

'He wasn't in any kind of pain, Tim. I want you to know that. He didn't suffer.'

Wrong – his dad *had* suffered. He'd suffered because his son had fucked up at school, and now he'd never know that his son *wanted* to do well, that his son would have worked really hard, that his son would do anything to make him proud, only his son hadn't done it yet.

And now he never would know.

'I got an A. In my History test. I didn't tell him.'

'Tim, listen to me.' His mother took his face in her hands, made him look at her. She was crying. 'When he came to see me, he told me how proud he was of you. He told me how much he loves you and how you're the best son in the world. He said that, Tim.'

'You're making that up.'

350

'No, I'm not. Your father adores you, Tim. He always has and he always will. You should have seen him the day you were born. I've never seen anyone so happy and proud.'

'Really?'

'Really. I promise you.'

'Can we go home?'

He didn't want Lauren to come back and see him crying.

How could he be thinking like that when his dad had just died?

His father was dead.

'Of course we can. Lousia and Joe are in the car outside. Is that all right?'

He nodded.

That thing that changed everything had happened to Louisa. Her husband had died. It had happened to Joe. His wife had died. It had happened to his mom, too. They were all OK. They'd figured it out somehow. Maybe it could happen and life would still be OK.

But life wasn't OK. Not without his dad.

32

Louisa was sitting on the balcony off her bedroom, trying to make some sense of the world. Sleep was impossible: she wondered whether Ellie and Joe and Tim were actually sleeping or had been roiling around in their beds as she had before she finally decided to get up.

She could hear the Mamas and the Papas singing that line about the darkest hour being just before dawn. What had she read about them a while ago? John Phillips had slept with his daughter. For years. Even on the night before her wedding. Some Papa.

Maybe I don't mind getting old. I used to listen to 'California Dreamin'' over and over again – I loved it so much, it probably influenced my decision to move to California. And the man singing it does that *to his daughter.*

I'm beginning to want out of a life where people do these monstrous things on what's starting to feel like a regular basis.

She breathed in the sea air, remembering the times her brother and she used to sneak out of their rooms late at night and sit on this balcony, wolfing down candy bars and Cokes they'd hoarded. This house was her history. She'd been a little girl once, in short-sleeved shirts and shorts,

352

running up and down the stairs, racing around the garden, going out in the boat, not caring about anything except the sun shining. And the delight of black and white frappés.

Her father used to take the train from Boston to Buzzards Bay on Friday afternoons in the summer. When he arrived, he always brought special little presents for John and Louisa. There was one magical one, a blank sheet of paper, which, if you scribbled on it with a special pencil, came to life as a pretty picture.

Maybe she should go see a shrink, and tell him or her that's why she had expected things to be beautiful. 'That special present represented the *tabula rasa* of life we all fill in with our scribbles,' she'd say. 'I never thought I'd fill it in and see ugliness, sadness, monsters.' And then she'd say: 'All I want to do is be five years old again and throw myself into my mother's and father's arms. How do I do that?'

Pulling her sweater tighter, she considered going down to the kitchen and making herself a coffee. It wasn't as if she were going to get any sleep. But she could see the sun beginning to make its appearance on the horizon. She wanted to watch every second of its ascent.

It had to make a difference, that sun. It had to mean the beginning of something better.

The sun should *care*, she thought. Why doesn't every animate and inanimate being *care*?

Ellie hadn't stayed in the hospital long, but when she'd come out, she and David Powell had gone to the police station. Joe and Louisa had followed, waiting outside while Ellie was interviewed. Then they'd all gone together to Lauren's house. When Ellie and Tim emerged, Louisa had driven them straight back here, not stopping at the cottage, and Ellie hadn't demurred. She was in the back seat with Tim, her arm around him, holding him close.

Tim hadn't spoken, but Louisa could hear him quietly crying. When they arrived, all four of them had immediately gravitated to the kitchen. Louisa poured out four glasses of water, threw some ice in them all and handed them out.

When she was thirteen, Louisa's grandmother on her father's side had died. She remembered her family sitting around the living room in their house in Boston a few hours after they'd heard the news, talking about her grandmother. She'd kept looking at her father, thinking how insensitive everyone was being. Talking about her would make him so unhappy, she'd thought. They should talk about something else, anything else.

She hadn't understood then that when you lost someone you loved, you wanted to keep hold of them. Make them alive and present. You *needed* to talk about them.

'I only met your father once,' she said to Tim. 'But I could see how intelligent he was. And perceptive, too. You know, he noticed that Joe and I have the same eyebrows. I'd never seen that. Tell me more about him.'

'Dad would have . . .' Tim swallowed, looked down, looked back up at Louisa. 'He would have said, "I met your father only once. Everyone misuses that word 'only'."' He smiled. 'He cares about stuff like that.'

'He's right to care.'

Louisa knew, too, that you kept shifting tenses after someone had died. Present, past, present – always wishing you could stay in the present.

'What else did he care about?'

She had to put aside what she knew, what Charlie had done to Ellie. This was a boy grieving for his father. This was separate.

Tim began to talk, and when he did, Louisa saw how he was building the myth, as everyone always did. His father was the smartest, best man in the world. Everything his father touched, he turned into gold. Whether Tim would ever let go of that, Louisa didn't know. Right now that wasn't important.

Jamie and she had gone to a funeral decades ago. The dead man had been a singer/songwriter and a Lothario *par excellence*. One of the speakers at the service, a good friend of his, stood up and said: 'Right, we all knew Luke and we all loved Luke, but boy, Luke was something else when it came to women. He couldn't stop himself. And women couldn't stop themselves from responding. I mean, take a look around you now, guys. Have you ever seen a church so packed out with women? And if you're a woman out there, I'm sorry, but don't even begin to think Luke had two hundred sisters.'

Everyone had cracked up.

But Luke hadn't had children. No fifteen-year-old son was listening to that.

They were all listening to Tim talk about Charlie. And Ellie talked too, telling little anecdotes about Tim and his father, all of them touching.

After about forty-five minutes, Tim said: 'I think I want to go to sleep now, Mom. We can stay here, can't we?'

Ellie looked over at Louisa and she nodded.

'Why don't you two share the bedroom across the hall from mine? The beds are made,' she suggested.

'That would be perfect, thank you.'

When Tim stood up, Joe rose, went to him and put a hand on his shoulder.

'It gets better, Tim,' he said. 'I'm not saying it gets better right away, because it doesn't. All I'm saying is that it gets better.'

Tim nodded. Joe gave him a quick hug and stepped back.

Ellie took Tim's hand and they left the kitchen together.

'What happened, Mum?' Joe sat down heavily. 'She didn't talk on the way back from the police station. What the hell happened?'

'I'm not sure. She'll talk when she wants to.'

'He attacked her. She had that blanket, she didn't have on any . . . He must have . . . That bastard. I know we have to think about Tim, but shit. How could he do that to her?'

'I don't know. I don't know how anyone could to that to anyone.'

'Where was that doctor guy?'

'I don't know, Joe.'

'Shit. Poor Ellie. This is awful.'

'Yes. It is.'

A few minutes later, Louisa went up to check on them. The door to their bedroom was open and she poked her head in. Tim was stretched out on one of the beds, face down. Ellie was sitting on the other, watching over him.

She looked up, saw Louisa.

'He's asleep,' she whispered. Standing, she came to the doorway. 'I need to talk to you,' she whispered again.

'Come into my room,' Louisa whispered back. They walked across the hall. Ellie sat down in the rocking chair, Louisa sat at the bottom of the bed, facing her. She was wearing some tracksuit bottoms Louisa had found which were too long for her, and a dark blue T-shirt – the first one she'd found when she'd opened her drawer. She looked like a teenager, Louisa thought. An innocent, bewildered teenager.

'I don't know how to start.'

'Start at the beginning. What was he doing at the cottage? Why did Charlie come to see you?'

'Charlie was Daniel.'

'What?'

'All right, I'll start at the beginning.' Ellie paused. She wiped the bottom of her eyes with her palms.

And then she began to talk.

What she said should have been unspeakable. It should never have happened. No one should have had to go through what she had. Within seconds of the story unfolding, Louisa wanted to jump up and say 'That fucking devious little bastard', but she made herself stay quiet. She couldn't interrupt. Ellie had to get it all out.

When she'd finished, Louisa said: 'You poor baby. You poor, poor baby. How he could do all that to you – the mother of his child . . . It's monstrous.'

357

'I didn't suspect him. If I had . . . but I thought he didn't know about the accident. I didn't know my mother had told him. I can't believe she did that.'

'I want to kill—' Louisa stopped herself.

'He drove into that tree on purpose, Louisa. He'd realised what he'd done. He did it for Tim.'

Louisa felt herself frown. She could let Ellie think that; maybe it would help her if she did think that. Charlie Walters had come to his senses, enough anyway to take the honourable way out and spare Tim. She could enable Ellie's myth-making.

No. Ellie was a thirty-six-year-old woman.

'He didn't. We saw him driving when we were on the way back here. He was speeding like a bat out of hell. Did you see the wreck and the police car when you passed it on the way to the hospital? I know that spot. If you're driving that fast, there's a corner there, a big bend in the road, and if you don't take that corner carefully, you go straight into that tree. People have crashed there before. Not fatally, but they've crashed.'

Ellie was silent. She began to rock back and forth. After a minute, she stopped.

'I need to take a shower. Can you check on Tim while I do? Make sure he's still sleeping.'

'Of course. Use the bathroom at the end of the hall. That way you won't wake him.'

'Thank you.' Rising, she came over to Louisa, sat down beside her. 'I felt so weak . . . when it was happening. I tried to be strong, but nothing I did . . . I punched him and punched him but it didn't make any difference. I was so weak.'

'Listen to me, you're not weak. You've gone through absolute hell, the worst kind of hell, and you've not only survived it, you've protected Tim. You sat there in the kitchen with us and listened to him talk about his father, and *you* talked about Charlie too – for him. That's strong, Ellie, that's unbelievably strong.'

'It hurt. When Charlie . . . it hurt so much.'

'Oh, Ellie.' Louisa was crying. 'I'm so sorry. And I can't tell you how sorry I am about what happened between us before. I let you down so badly. I can't believe I even consid-ered—'

'I would have considered it if I were you, Louisa. Charlie's whole purpose was to wreck the life I was trying to make. And when Charlie has a purpose – when Charlie *had* a purpose – he'd make sure he succeeded. But . . .' She took Louisa's hand. 'Tim can't know about this. Only you and I and Joe and the police know. He *can't* know. This is a secret we have to keep. It's not like before, me not admitting the accident. It's different. Tim needs a father he can be proud of. You can understand that? You must.'

'Yes.'

'I need to take a shower.'

Louisa stood at the threshold of Ellie and Tim's room until she came back from her shower.

'I got you a pair of PJs' she said, handing them to her. 'Tim's still asleep.'

'Thanks. I think I should try to sleep too.'

'Ellie, you're an amazing woman. And an amazing mother. You need to know that.'

'All I care about now is being a good mother.' She looked at Tim's bed. 'All I care about is Tim.'

The sun was rising, sliver by sliver. A lone tanker chugged down the Canal towards New York. Louisa remembered how excited she and John used to be when they saw a submarine going through. She hadn't seen one of those in ages. Shifting her gaze, she looked over to Mashnee Island – where Ellie used to sit and look over to this house. Dreaming of a different life.

Charlie Walters had raped Ellie physically and emotionally. He'd brutalised her in unimaginable ways. There had been no end to his stealth and deceit.

Louisa hadn't seen it, not in those few minutes at the Clam Shack. Would Jamie have seen it? she asked herself. Possibly. Joe hadn't liked him, but she'd put that down to testosterone.

It was impossible for her to imagine what could make a man do that to someone he'd once loved, much less the mother of his child.

No, I don't mind getting old. None of this is palatable.

He'd been in this house, stalking Ellie. Going from room to room, trying to find her. He must have been in this bedroom, too. If Ellie hadn't remembered that little cupboard in the sewing room . . . if the police hadn't decided they had to respond to her call, despite Charlie's subsequent call to them.

Louisa had never, in all her life, wished anyone dead. Yet she was glad Charlie had driven into that tree.

'Your death solved a lot of problems, you bastard,' she said out loud. 'And I will not let your presence in this house touch anything.'

Getting up, she went into the bedroom, over to her dressing table. She picked up a beautiful, tiny porcelain box she'd bought years ago, went back outside to the balcony with it and threw it against the wall at the corner. When it shattered, she said, 'Go. Get the hell out of here.' She waited for a minute then bent down to gather up the pieces.

'Louisa?' Ellie was at the balcony door. 'What are you doing?'

'Evil spirits hide in beautiful places,' she said, piling the pieces into a small heap. 'I learned that from a Turkish man. When something beautiful breaks, you don't get upset. You get rid of the evil spirits.'

'So you're exorcising Charlie?'

'Yes.'

Louisa went over to the other side of the balcony, sat down and patted the ground beside her.

'You couldn't sleep either?'

'No,' Ellie said, joining her. 'But Tim's still sleeping. I think that's good. Unless he starts sleeping too much.'

'Tim will be all right, Ellie. He has a lot of people who love him.'

Ellie pulled her knees up to her chest, hugged them.

'I had that shower but I still feel so unclean. I feel filthy.'

John, when he was in his twenties, had brought a girl

down here. He'd taken her out on the boat for the day, then driven her back to Boston. Her name was Sophie. She'd looked so anxious and pale that Louisa asked him the next day if she were sick. He told her that Sophie had tried to kill herself, but had cut her wrists the wrong way, and not severely. She'd refused to go to the hospital, but had called him.

'I brought her down here because she needed to get out on to the water. The ocean can heal, Lou. Nature can do things people can't. I know Soph will have to get professional help, but I wanted her to start off with a different kind of help. She told me she felt much better after coming here.'

Louisa rose, put her hand out to Ellie.

'Come with me.'

She went to her cupboard, found a bathing suit for herself and one for Ellie.

'We're going swimming? Now?'

'Dawn is the best time. You'll see.'

She changed in her room as Ellie changed in the bathroom; Louisa found some towels and they met up in the hall and walked down the stairs.

'We won't go into the garden. We'll go out to the wall, climb down on to the big stone there. I can't explain it, but when it's high tide like this, swimming there is better than swimming from the beach. There's something different about the water there. I bet Tim would be able to describe it.'

'I don't want to leave him for long in case he wakes up.'

'We'll take a short swim. He's only been asleep for a few

hours.' She almost corrected herself on the 'only', but thought: fuck that.

Ellie and she walked out, went to the wall. Louisa hoisted herself down, waited as Ellie followed her.

'Joe used to sit on this slab by himself for hours, daydreaming.'

'I know.'

'It's a little rocky here, but we'll be fine.'

Wading out together, they both stopped when the water reached their waists. It was perfectly calm, there were no boats on the Canal, the sun was waking up, spreading its light over the sky.

Diving in, Louisa swam a few strokes then surfaced. Ellie was swimming further, doing the crawl, her arm reaching above her head, coming down, rising again as she breathed.

Halfway to the Rock Pile, she stopped, turned and faced Louisa, treading water.

'It's beautiful,' she said.

33

The funeral had been surreal. Charlie didn't have any other immediate family, but he had friends and three of them spoke, extolling his intelligence, his wit, his virtues. Ellie had sat listening, trying to disassociate the man they were speaking about from the man who'd done what he'd done to her. But she couldn't. When one of his friends mentioned Boston University, she could hear Charlie saying: *You fell in love with me twice, El.*

His voice was back in her brain. The clinking chains of Jacob Marley.

She'd fallen in love with him once, when she was nineteen and still reeling from the accident. Maybe she would have fallen in love with him even if she hadn't had the accident. She didn't know. But she hadn't fallen in love with him again. Whatever he wrote in those emails, he was writing with the intention to deceive. He knew her well enough to know what she'd respond to. He'd played her, and he'd played her well. But that didn't count as love.

Her mother was in love with Sam Waterston because of the way he played his part. If she met him in real life, she'd say, 'Jack! Jack McCoy! I adore you.' And as polite and charming as Sam Waterston might be, it would all be downhill from there. He wasn't Jack McCoy.

At the end of the service, when Tim got up and read a poem, Ellie cried. Not for Charlie, but for her son.

The funeral had been in Boston. Joe, Louisa and Lauren had all come as well, for support. When it was over, they'd driven back to Bourne, to Louisa's house: Ellie couldn't face going back to the cottage, and Louisa had insisted they stay with her. Tim had started at summer school again and Ellie found herself gravitating to Joe's slab after breakfast in the mornings, sitting there and thinking.

This morning she watched as a sailboat loughed in the Canal, not making any headway. Louisa had explained to her what the word 'loughing' meant and now she was seeing it in action. The people in the boat were trying out different sails to catch the wind, attempting to get some forward momentum and failing. Slipping backwards instead. She could see the boat had an engine at the back.

Just start the fucking engine, for Christ's sakes. She wanted to stand up and shout at them. The longer they kept trying, the more angry she became. After ten minutes, they gave up, started up the motor and headed towards the Railroad Bridge.

About fucking time, you jerks.

Loughing was like being stuck in traffic, only worse. Loughing was sitting on this slab thinking of Charlie.

She'd deleted the Daniel file from her laptop. She'd found someone who would collect all the furniture from Charlie's apartment and hopefully give it away to people who needed it. She'd taken so many swims and showers, she had to have shed the skin of that night.

But she was still sitting here thinking of Charlie. And still hearing his voice, especially in her dreams. In some of them he was the old, charming Charlie. In some a terrifying, monstrous man. But at some point, in every dream she had, however innocently it started, Charlie would gate-crash. And she'd wake up thinking about him. She didn't love him or hate him or feel anything towards him, but she was so angry. So full of fury.

'Hey, that's my slab you're sitting on.'

Looking up, she saw Joe sitting above her on the wall.

'I'll vacate it,' she said, but he was already jumping down.

'No, I'll join you.' He sat down on one side of the slab. She was on the other.

'You must be tired of us being here in the house. Tim and I will move back to the cottage soon, I promise.'

'I'm not tired of it. But you look tired, Ellie.'

'Thanks.'

'Sorry. All I meant to say was, you look like you need a break.'

'It feels like such a long time ago – that night we sat up there on the wall.'

'It was. Maybe not calendar-wise, but otherwise.'

'Yes.'

'I need to apologise to you. I acted badly that night. I felt I had betrayed Pam.'

They hadn't spent any time alone together since it had

happened. They weren't avoiding each other: no opportunity to be alone had arisen and neither of them had engineered one.

'I understand. I understood then. It was the letter I didn't understand.'

'You know, that day I saw you on your beach – if I'd gone over to talk to you, we would have figured it out. We would have realised neither of us wrote to the other.'

'But we wouldn't have known who did write them.'

'True.' He paused. 'It really was a shitty letter.'

'Was I disgustingly patronising?'

'Absolutely.'

'So were you. It's a miracle we're still speaking to each other.'

He laughed, then got off the slab, began to search through the stones at his feet until he found a smooth one. He crouched down, skipped it across the still water.

'I've always wanted to do that.' Ellie rose too, found a stone, tried to imitate his action, but it sank without skipping.

'You have to try to be on a level with the water. Bring your arm back horizontally.'

'OK.'

They took turns skipping stones. Ellie improved but she couldn't get near Joe's record of ten skips. The most she could manage was three, and the more she tried, the angrier she became.

'Ellie? You look upset. We're skipping stones here, not harnessing nuclear energy.'

'I should be able to do it.'

'You can do it. I've been doing this all my life. You need to practise, that's all.'

'I'm sorry, Joe. I'm sorry for ever thinking it was you. I'm sorry for bringing Charlie into your life and Louisa's. I'm sorry about everything. I have to go. I hope we can talk again soon, but I have to go now.'

She walked off, not getting back up on the wall but continuing around the point, past Louisa's beach, to her beach and up the path to the cottage.

She'd been back twice, once to get her laptop, once to get some clothes. She hadn't locked the door when she'd left either time. Walking straight through the living room, she went to her bedroom and sat on the bed.

He'd been stronger than she was. He had physical power. And she'd let him do what he'd done at the end without fighting him because she'd decided it was her only chance to escape. When he'd said 'Get comfortable', she'd been relieved because she'd known it would be easier if they were in the middle of the bed: he'd have more space to roll to the side, away from her, as he always did.

But he'd been physically stronger. When she'd hit him, it hadn't made any difference. When he'd hit her, it had.

Almost any man could overpower almost any woman. Brains didn't enter into the equation. Nothing but brute force did.

You're mine.

He'd possessed her body. She'd escaped him finally, but only because the police had come. He'd been tricking her every step of the way and she'd fallen for it. Maybe anyone would have, but that thought didn't help her.

She was acting as if she were all right, but she wasn't. Back there with Joe, she'd been so consumed with rage, she'd wanted to pick up every stone beneath her feet and hurl them all into the water. There'd been times lately when she'd almost snapped Tim's head off – for no reason. And Louisa's too.

If she kept on like this, something was going to give.

And if something gave, Tim would suffer.

She didn't want to keep imposing on Louisa, but she couldn't bear the thought of coming back to this cottage, sleeping in this bed.

Maybe if she smashed every beautiful thing she possessed here, she could exorcise Charlie and her fury too.

Maybe she should try and find Dr Emmanuel.

No.

Don't go backwards, Ellie.

Start the fucking engine.

34

'You look terrific,' Louisa said as soon as Ellie stepped off the bus at Tedeschi's. She gave her a hug. 'How was the flight?'

'Fine.'

The driver had descended the bus stairs, was standing beside the luggage compartment.

'Thanks. Those two in the front are mine,' Ellie said to him. He stopped down, retrieved the bags, then turned to help the woman behind her.

Louisa picked up one, Ellie the other, and they walked to her car.

'Does it feel as if you've been away forever?' she asked as she opened a door.

'In some ways. I can't wait to see Tim.'

'He told me he's been Skyping you.' They put the bags in the back and Louisa opened the driver's door.

'I know, it's great, but it's not the same as being with him.'

They got into the Saab, both put on their seatbelts.

'You know, Debby said: "God, El, if Tim or I had told

370

you about Skype, none of this would have happened.' But she said she was a latecomer to Skype herself, and I guess Tim didn't have any reason to use it.'

'She's right. Charlie would have been hoist on his own petard of modern technology. Unless he found some machine that made him *look* like Daniel.'

This conversation was worrying Louisa. Ellie had spent three weeks in California with Debby. Before she'd been back for two minutes, she was talking about Charlie.

'Joe got a job. Did I tell you? He's working for a state senator in Boston. A woman.'

'You did tell me. Remember? Last time you called me. That's fantastic.'

'Uh-oh. Repetition. Senility alert.'

'As if.'

Ellie *was* looking terrific – a lot less tired. A lot healthier. When they passed Atwoods, Louisa asked her if she wanted to stop there for a coffee.

'No, thanks, I want to get back.'

'I have a surprise for you. I hope you'll like it. I think you will.'

'The last time you said you had a surprise for me, you wheeled out Joe's old bike.'

'Oh, Ellie. I'm sorry, I—'

'Louisa, that was a joke. Spending three weeks with Debby, well, you can't help but get caught up in black humour.' She laughed. 'Don't worry. Whatever it is, I won't drop my coffee cup and turn into a wreck.'

She laughed again. Louisa glanced over at her. Ellie looked

relaxed. Apparently Debby was a maths genius. She was also clearly a tonic.

'You know, Lauren's been around a lot and now *I've* fallen in love with her,' Louisa stated. 'I have a fantasy that she and Tim will get married and we'll have a huge party for them at the house. And then I remember they're only fifteen years old. The odds are stacked against them lasting.'

'You never know, Louisa, Tim still believes what I told him, that a crazy person from my college days made that call, that we found out who it was and it's all taken care of – right.'

'Yes.'

'That's good.' Ellie nodded.

They were passing the tree Charlie had smashed into. Louisa felt herself tense up, but Ellie didn't apppear to have noticed.

'It's too bad you didn't have time to go to San Francisco.'

'I know. Debby went there a few months ago. She got this tattoo – in Haight-Ashbury. You'd love her, you know. She said she'd come visit soon. Her last romance didn't pan out. She's still hoping for Rob Lowe, though. She wished Charlie were alive so she could get some good pointers on stalking.'

'Whoa. She really does go in for black humour, doesn't she?'

'You'd be surprised how much it helps. She left me alone a lot, too. That helped as well.'

Face it – head-on. That's what Debby must have done.

She hadn't tiptoed around Ellie, she'd brought it all out in the open.

'Just enough solitude, black humour, beaches, cocktails and talk. They all helped.'

'A different version of therapy?'

'Yes.' Ellie nodded. 'But, believe me, I'm not pretending it didn't happen. Not this time.'

'I believe you.'

When they turned into Ellie's drive and parked, Louisa saw her hesitate about getting out.

'It will be all right, sweetheart.'

'I know,' she said, but still didn't move. 'You know, I had a dream when I was in Long Beach. I'm allowed to tell my dreams now, even if they are boring. Anyway, I dreamed that Charlie was back here, sitting on my sofa, telling me it was all an accident. He hadn't meant to do what he'd done to me. It was all an accident. And I said, very calmly: "No, Charlie. I know about accidents. What you did wasn't accidental." And then I woke up.'

'Have you dreamed about him since?'

'No.' Ellie reached out, opened the car door.

'Before we get the bags, I want you to go in,' Louisa said when she'd got out. 'Come on.' She went to the front door, took the key from her pocket, opened it. 'This is my surprise. What do you think?'

Ellie stood at the threshold, gazing around the room. Louisa had had the walls repainted in a turquoise shade. She'd bought a variety of new little seagulls, scattered them around the place. She'd moved the sofa and chairs to different positions, re-covered them in a rough white cotton material. And she'd had Venetian blinds fitted on the windows.

'I love it.' Ellie took a step inside, then another. 'I love it. Thank you so much. You're brilliant.' She turned back, came to Louisa and hugged her hard. 'The perfect surprise.'

'You said you dreaded the idea of walking back in here and sinking into bad memories, so I repainted your room and moved your bed too. I hope you don't mind?'

'I can't tell you how relieved I am.'

'Good. Then I'm relieved too. Should I get us some coffee?'

'Absolutely, but I'll get it. Come into the kicthen.'

Louisa followed her and sat down at the table as Ellie found a jar of instant and took it out of the cupboard, then filled the kettle with water.

'It's funny, you know.' She leaned against the counter facing Louisa. 'Debby made a joke about me emailing Daniel Litman again. And, for one second, I was tempted. Just to find out what the real Daniel Litman was doing. But then I thought about typing that name again and knew I couldn't do it. It's so strange. What if we had hit it off? I mean, really hit it off? Then Charlie wouldn't have been able to do what he did.'

'He was at the restaurant watching you. He would have seen you two hitting it off. You know, you may have saved Daniel Litman, Ellie. I doubt Charlie would have stood by and watched you ride off into the sunset with him. He would have taken him on. And that wouldn't have ended well for the doctor.'

'I never thought of that. You're right. Daniel will never

know, though. How strange.' The kettle boiled. Ellie turned around and picked it up.

'I was worried you'd want to move out to California, you know. Sell this place and never look back.'

'I couldn't do that to Tim,' she said, pouring water into the mugs. 'Besides, I belong here. I like living with the Indians.'

EPILOGUE

27 September

It was boiling hot outside, which was more than unusual for late September. But the restaurant was air-conditioned, thank God. It was a nice restaurant too. And he was a really nice-looking man, and a nice-acting one. This was all going far better than she'd expected.

'You know, I never would have done this myself. What I'm saying is, a friend convinced me to do this. I guess everyone always says that, but it's true.'

'Same here,' he said. 'A friend conviced me to, too. She said it was criminal to be forty-two years old and single. She said everyone does this now.'

'I guess so. It's really hard to meet people. Everyone is so paranoid at work. You know, I was thinking, on the Tube ride here, your work must be so difficult. Dealing with sick people the whole time.'

'It's not fun.' He nodded. 'But it's rewarding.'

'I'm sure.'

'You have a wonderful smile, you know. Really captivating.'

'Really?' She was going to blush, she knew. 'Is it all right if I have another cocktail? I was so nervous about this whole business, I'm afraid I drank that first one quickly.'

'Of course.' He signalled for a waiter and got one straight away. Other men she knew would wave their hand around forever without anyone paying attention.

He had chosen a fairly expensive restaurant. He was a doctor. He was a fit, single doctor. More attractive even than his online picture. She'd done well to choose him. But she shouldn't drink too much or she might end up pissed out of her brain and destroy any chance she had.

'Another mojito, please,' he said.

'No, actually, a glass of wine would be fine. A glass of house white. That would be perfect.'

'Are you sure?' he asked.

'Yes.'

She liked his American accent. She liked the idea of an American, anyway. It was different. And he wasn't obsessed with football.

She did well through the meal, careful to sip her wine, not chug it down. He was asking her lots of questions and she was trying to be funny. He laughed so she figured she was being funny enough, anyway. If she had to take a bet, she'd put money on him asking her out again. She was looking hot, she knew. And he was appreciating that, she could tell.

So she wasn't exactly surprised when he said at the end, when the bill came: 'You know, I'd really like to keep talking. My car's outside. I've only had one glass so I'm fine to drive. Let's go somewhere. I don't mean back to my place, don't worry. I won't pounce on you, I promise.'

'I didn't think you would. Where would we go?'

'I don't know – out on the M4 a little way? We could try to find a nice pub. We have enough time. I promise I won't drink there either. But it would be good to get out of London.'

She hesitated. But he was a doctor and she'd Googled him and it was so hot. A hot, sunny night in September? It didn't happen in London. She should take advantage of it.

He smiled. He had a really nice smile. Good teeth. Of course. He was a Yank.

'So what do you say?' he asked.

'I say absolutely, why not?'

It fascinated him. What made one woman spark your interest and another woman not? It wasn't always about looks. Or intelligence. Or humour. It was that certain something you could never define.

He'd spent so long looking and now that he'd found her, he had to ask himself if it could be something as simple as an accent. She hadn't dazzled him with her wit; and though she was attractive, she wasn't a complete knock-out. But her accent. He couldn't resist it. He'd heard plenty of English accents since he'd been here, but hers was different. She said she'd been born in Wales – maybe that was it.

It didn't matter, though. He'd finally found her. He'd felt that click. He'd *almost* felt it a few times before, but almost never caught the train.

Some of the ones he'd been hesitant about he'd contact afterwards, seeing whether he might change his mind. Or they might change theirs. Because of course there were the ones who didn't take to him straight away. He could accept that. He'd never been vain enough to think he was God's gift to women.

He was always really careful not to hurt a woman's feelings, of course. He'd always email and say, 'let's keep in touch' and if they said 'great' he'd have fun for a while, trade a few harmless emails and then disappear from cyberspace. No harm done, no hurt feelings. He hated hurting people.

She had kicked off her shoes and put her feet up on his dashboard. Mildly annoying, but it wasn't worth saying anything.

'I know a nice pub outside Windsor,' she stated.

'That sounds perfect. We could take a walk in Windsor Great Park afterwards. If it's not too late.'

They'd eaten early. They'd have plenty of time.

He was getting excited. He'd waited so long and this was it. He'd finally found her. You *could* fall in love at first sight – or at first sound. He'd been beginning to doubt it, but now he knew it was possible.

He felt sorry for the ones he hadn't fallen for, though. If they knew, they'd have to ask themselves: why didn't he choose me? But they'd never know he'd finally found the perfect woman. No harm done. It wasn't as if they'd read about it in the papers.

He pushed his hair off his forehead, put his foot down on the accelorator.

No one could explain these things. Not rationally. It was all about that click.

He wouldn't have to try to explain anyway. Because he was smart and he'd planned it all out. *His* name wouldn't be in the papers. He wasn't going to get caught.

Tainted

Brooke Morgan

How far would you go to protect the ones you love?

When Holly Barrett meets Jack Dane, she falls rapidly and passionately in love for the first time in her life. Within six weeks they are married and Jack opens up a whole new world for Holly and her young daughter Katy, offering them a way out of the small-town Massachusetts existence in which they have become trapped.

But Holly knows very little about the enigmatic Englishman who has come into their lives so unexpectedly. Parts of his life story seem destined to remain forever shrouded in shadow yet, happier than she has ever been, Holly sees only inter-ference and jealousy when her beloved grandfather, Henry, and best friend, Anna, tentatively start to raise questions about Jack's past.

However, as the truth starts to emerge, it soon becomes frighteningly possible that everything that Holly has ever believed in could be a terrible lie. And that rather than marrying the man who will save her and Katy from their safe but small world, Holly may have brought a monster into all their lives . . .

Read on for an extract . . .

1

Holly liked to sit at the front of the bus. The wide windshield gave her a feeling of space and a view forward which quashed any potential travel sickness. And she liked watching the bus driver swing the heavy front door open and closed. There seemed always to be big men driving the route between Boston and Cape Cod; heavyweights with gruff voices and a palpable command over their vehicles. Sometimes they'd crack jokes and talk to her. 'This is my ship of the road,' one had once commented. 'I'm the captain, sailing her over the highways.' He must have been in his fifties and over three hundred pounds, but there was such a wistful romance in his voice as he said it, she gave him a nickname: the Poet. Every subsequent time she boarded a bus, she hoped she'd see the Poet again, but he'd disappeared. To another highway, another ship.

She was early enough for the eight-thirty a.m. bus to be the first on and snag the front seat, the one beside the window. If she was lucky, no one would come and sit beside her and she could stretch out, have the front all to herself. People trickled on behind her: an elderly couple who went straight to the back, a lone middle-aged woman who took a seat a few rows behind her to the left, two teenage girls who

1

wandered down the aisle toward the middle. *Keep going*, she thought. *Keep going past and down the aisle. Maybe I'll get lucky.* But then she looked out the window and saw a line beginning to form. It was going to be pretty crowded, she gauged. She probably wouldn't get away with two seats to herself.

She almost didn't see him. He had been stooping over, pushing his bag into the cavernous luggage holder and she had almost turned her gaze away from the queue of people when she caught sight of him as he straightened up. *Faintworthy.* That was the expression Anna had come up with to replace 'drop dead handsome'. 'Look –' Anna had pointed at a guy in the bar the night before. 'Look, Holly – there's a faintworthy over there. At least, he's close to being faintworthy. Let's go talk to him.' Holly had laughed and told her to be quiet. She wasn't going to go talk to some stranger in a bar. Anna could, and Anna usually did. But last night Holly had managed to rein Anna in and they'd stayed where they were, finishing their drinks and then leaving to get some supper.

He was tallish, dark, thin and tanned. He'd rolled the sleeves of his white shirt up over his elbows. Clean-shaven, straight-nosed, strong-chinned. Wearing khaki trousers and loafers. No sunglasses. An old watch with a leather strap. Looking serious and nonchalant at the same time. So, so handsome she felt his looks hit her in a punch of pleasure. Like the first sight of a beautiful painting. He was staring ahead, not up. He couldn't see her looking at him, so she allowed herself to and was reminded of the time she'd been

2

sixteen, in Friendly's, waiting to get an ice-cream cone and seeing, suddenly, at the front of the line, a man she thought she recognised as Noah Wyle, one of the actors in *ER*. She'd stared and stared, taken aback by his looks. He was more attractive in person than on TV and for a second, when he'd bought his cone and turned, he'd caught her eye and she'd blushed. He'd smiled and walked out. Later, she'd learned he was filming a movie around Buzzards Bay, so it was definitely him. When she'd told Anna, all Anna could say was, 'Why didn't you get his autograph, Holly? God, how could you let that opportunity slip?' and she'd thought she was much happier with that one fleeting smile than a tangible piece of paper.

Faintworthy had handed the driver his ticket and was climbing the stairs. Quickly, Holly turned her stare to the floor of the bus, feeling that same blush she'd had at Friendly's begin to rise. *A blush is like being sick to your stomach*, she found herself thinking. *You can't stop it. You have no control. It just happens. But he'll walk by and not notice me and as long as I keep my eyes down, I'll be all right.*

'Do you mind if I sit here?'

'Sure.' She had to look at him. 'I mean, I don't mind, no. You can sit here. I don't mind.' She knew she was sounding supremely inarticulate. Her whole body was blushing.

'Thanks.' He sat down.

Her eyes dived back to the floor.

'I know there are other seats, but I like to sit at the front,' he explained. 'I like to see out.'

'Right.'

He had an English accent. So his voice was as attractive as his looks. It wasn't fair. She'd have to spend an hour and fifteen minutes with him beside her and she'd doubtless be hot and sweaty and monosyllabic the whole time. She hadn't brought a book, she had nothing she could do to pretend to be engrossed. He was empty-handed as well, sitting there quietly, his arms crossed.

Holly had yet to meet one person who didn't say he or she was shy as a child; even the most outgoing, rambunctious personalities, even someone like Anna, would say, 'Oh, but I was such a shy kid. You wouldn't believe it.' And Holly always felt like saying, 'No, I don't believe it. Because I was a shy child and I'm still shy and I don't see how you grow out of being shy, ever.'

The last passengers were boarding the bus. A woman came on holding a toddler in her arms and sat down in the seats behind them. She looked tired and stressed and so grateful for a chance to sit down she hadn't even noticed this impossibly handsome man she'd just passed in the aisle. *Children do that*, Holly thought. *They make you concentrate on the really important things – like collapsing into a seat and taking a break from the constant demands for an hour or so.*

She could feel her blush finally subsiding as the bus driver climbed into his seat and swung the door closed. *Pretend you're Anna*, she told herself. *Say something feisty and funny. Make him think you're completely comfortable in this situation. As if it happens every day. A gorgeous man sits beside you and you start a scintillating conversation.*

As if.

She remained mute.

'It's interesting. The word "mind". In England, in London, at tube stations, they say, "Mind the gap," meaning, "Watch out for the gap." Between the train and the platform. And then there's "mind" in the sense of, "Do you mind me sitting here" like I just asked. And then there's "mind" as in "brain". Not that . . .' he paused. 'Not that you're interested in me banging on about a word. Sorry. I'm going for a job interview. I'm a little nervous.'

'No. It *is* interesting. I promise.' His anxiety immediately wiped out hers. She allowed herself to look up, into his eyes. They were a dark shade of blue, the same colour as the sweater Billy had worn when she'd danced with him. *Bad memory. Cancel it out and move on.* She smiled and he smiled back, offering his hand.

'Jack Dane.'

'Holly Barrett.'

A brief, strong squeeze.

'My grandfather always shakes hands with his left hand. He says it's closer to the heart.'

'Makes sense.' Jack Dane nodded. 'But it might be difficult to retrain the entire Western world.'

'I don't think he's trying to convert anyone. In fact, I think he likes it being his private idiosyncrasy. Anyway, what job are you interviewing for? Or is it bad luck to talk about it?'

'Bad luck? No. I hope not. It's not a big job. Just a waiter at a new restaurant in a small town. But it's by the sea and I've always wanted to be by the sea.'

'Where by the sea?'

'A place called Shoreham.'

'You're kidding. Figs? Is that where you're interviewing? That's where I live. In Shoreham.'

'That's the place.'

'Figs is the first fancy restaurant we've ever had. It's big news in town. We're used to diners and clam shacks and Dunkin' Donuts and pizza places. I looked at the menu in the window just a couple of days ago. It's seriously grown up.'

'Seriously?' Jack Dane laughed.

'Very, very seriously. They have exotic sauces. They have pomegranate cocktails. I think I even remember some herb-encrusted salmon dish.'

'The restaurant I used to work at in Boston has salmon cocktails with herb-encrusted ice cubes.'

'That's ridiculous. What are they think—' Holly saw his sly smile and another blush started. 'Oh, God. I can't believe how stupid that was.'

'No – it wasn't stupid at all. Yes, I was teasing, but I wouldn't put salmon cocktails past that place. Or herb-encrusted ice cubes either.'

'You're just being nice.'

'No way. I worked there, remember?'

'You're from England, aren't you?'

'Yes. But I've never met the Queen, Prince William, Prince Harry or David Beckham. I'm such a disappointment to Americans. I'm beginning to think either I should pretend that I *have* met them or I should lose my accent. Not raise false expectations.'

'Oh, no, you shouldn't lose your accent, it's—'

A child's wail came from behind them and then a woman's voice saying wearily, 'Stop it, Tom.' But Tom wasn't stopping. His cry moved up a pitch and Holly could hear him pummelling the seat – Jack Dane's seat – with his little legs. Jack turned and rose, putting his face over the seatbacks.

'Could you control your child, please?' he asked.

'He's tired and irritable,' the mother replied. Holly could hear her exasperation. 'I'm sorry. Tom – stop that now.'

Jack Dane turned back and sat, frowning.

'What were you saying?' he asked.

'Only that you shouldn't lose your accent.'

He flinched as another bout of flailing legs hit the back of his seat.

'Tom, Tom, stop. I mean it.'

Holly peered through the crack between the seats and saw the mother struggling to keep hold of the squirming little boy, but he was determined to keep kicking. 'You're bothering that man, Tom. Stop it or I'll put you to bed as soon as we get home. Do you hear me?'

'Bloody useless,' Jack Dane muttered.

'She's trying.'

'Not hard enough.'

Whack, whack, whack – unrelenting tiny feet pounded the seat.

He stood up.

'This is really annoying and it's not going to stop. I'm off.'

Don't go. Please don't go. Can I say I'll move with you? No.

7

I can't. I'll sit here like an idiot and you'll be sitting beside someone else, teasing someone else as this bus hits Route 128.

'Come on.' He leaned over, took hold of her hand and pulled her up. 'There are two seats in the middle back there. Let's go.'

She followed him as he led her down the aisle, not looking at the mother and child, knowing how embarrassed that mother would be. He motioned for her to go in first and take the window seat, a row behind the two teenage girls she'd noticed before.

'That's better.' Settling in beside her, he immediately relaxed. 'I hope you don't mind me dragging you with me.'

'I don't mind,' she smiled. 'And we're right back where we started – with that interesting word "mind".'

'The secret of a good dinner party is a running theme – or two. Some story or joke the table shares and then can refer back to, embroider on. Food and drink count, but it's the conversation that really matters.'

When had her father told her that? She had to have been young, maybe eleven or so. He'd been sitting with the *Boston Globe* on his lap; it was in the morning and her mother was in the kitchen. Preparing for a dinner party? Holly didn't know. She remembered thinking she'd have to try to create running themes when she gave dinner parties. Whatever running themes were. Now that she did know what they were, the other part of the equation was missing. She'd never given a dinner party. She couldn't imagine ever giving one.

'So tell me. What's Shoreham like?'

'Wonderful. At least I think it is. It's basically a one-street town. You know, like you see in old movies. A bank, a fire station, a hairdresser's, a grocer's, a liquor store, a diner and that's it – we used to have a movie theatre but that was ages ago. And now of course we have Figs.'

Shut up, she told herself. *You're babbling. You're so used to being the one who listens, you get nervous when someone asks you a question.*

'So he's like asking me out on a date, but I don't know if it's a date date or just a going-out thing. It's so not clear. And I'm like trying to figure him out.'

The obnoxiously loud voice came from one of the teenage girls in front of them. Holly waited for the other one to reply but the first one kept talking.

'You think so? I mean, I'm with Teresa on the bus here and she's been saying it's a date date but I'm not so sure and what does that mean anyway? I mean, what do I wear?'

'Oh, no.' Jack Dane shook his head. 'We know how to pick them, don't we?'

'No way. The pink top sucks.'

'They have cellphone-free places in the trains, but not in the buses,' Holly said apologetically, thinking, *And I'm just as bad as she is. I'm acting like a teenager too. When you asked me to move seats with you, when you just said 'we', my heart did a little dance.*

'OK, OK, I hear you. Look, I gotta go. Teresa is handing me a sandwich and my stomach's like empty. Talk later. Yeah.'

Jack Dane scrunched down in his seat so his head was level to hers; he leaned over and whispered, 'She's going to eat. We're saved.'

His breath was warm, clean, so intensely male, she held it inside her as if it were a drug.

'Which is worse?' she whispered back. 'The little boy kicking the back of your seat or the cellphone screamer?'

'It's a tie. Although I should be used to cellphone screamers. They inhabit restaurants too. Someone like me who hates noise shouldn't work in restaurants – but I do, so I should be used to it. Anyway, tell me, Holly Barrett. How old are you?'

'Twenty-three.'

The tones of their voices, the softness of the whispers and the proximity of their heads made Holly feel as if they were side by side in bed, plotting something. Except she'd never been side by side with a man in a bed. But this was how she'd imagined it would feel.

'I'm twenty-six, so those days are even longer ago for me – but what were you like when you were a teenager?' he asked. 'Did you have a group of friends who all talked too loudly and too fast?'

'No. I didn't have a group. Aside from one friend, I was pretty much a lone wolf.'

'I doubt it.' Jack Dane was studying her face so intently, from so close up, it took all the courage she had not to turn away from him. 'No, you weren't a lone wolf. Lone wolves are the ones who get kicked out of the wolf pack. They straggle along behind, at a distance, hoping to gain re-entry into the pack. Whereas you, Holly Barrett, were the quiet, shy one who was serious at school, who studied hard and who didn't go in for silly teenage stuff. Which may have set you apart from the pack, but it wasn't a pack you wanted to join. You had a different world, a world of your own, a much more adult one. You're an old-fashioned girl.'

'Yeah, it's me again. Yeah, it was a fucking tiny sandwich. So what do you think? If I wear that black top with the pink pants – you think that will send the right signals?'

He threw up his hands in a gesture of surrender and drew back from her.

'It's useless. No one knows how to put a sock in it. Wankers. Listen, I think I'm going to take a kip for a while – a nap, I mean.' He put his hand in his pocket, pulled out a small iPod. 'We can't talk properly with the cellphone screamer in full flow, so I'm going to tune out. I don't mean to be rude. But I had a late night last night. I need to recharge. Sorry.'

'You don't have to apologise,' she said quickly. 'No problem.'

'You don't mind?' he smiled.

'I don't mind.'

Putting his earphones in, Jack Dane leaned back in his seat, fiddled with the iPod controls and closed his eyes.

Holly was still feeling his physical presence, the closeness of him. She'd felt something almost like it once before, the time she danced with Billy. Billy's sweater had smelled of autumn leaves; he'd held her close to his chest, she'd breathed in the scent, she'd felt herself melt into him. When they'd had sex a few weeks later, there'd been no melting, only his rank desire and her desperation.

Looking out the window, she saw that they were passing

the Foxboro racetrack, so they'd reach the junction with Route 495 soon. Which meant they didn't have that much further until they arrived in Shoreham.

There were certain types of people who took pleasure in telling you about yourself, Holly knew. Anna being a prime example. 'I saw this great ad for white-water rafting. I might go. You'd hate it though, Holly, I know. You never take risks,' or, 'Hey, Holl – I was going to buy you a skimpy top for your birthday but I knew you'd never wear it.'

Exactly how, Holly wanted to ask, did Anna know? Maybe Holly would have liked white-water rafting, or the skimpy top. *I took a risk,* she'd wanted to yell. *I took a huge risk with Katy*. But Anna had her typecast as a mouse from the age of thirteen and nothing Holly could ever do would change that.

Jack Dane was different. Out of nowhere, he'd looked straight into her and pulled out the truth of her early teenage years. Aside from her unlikely friendship with Anna, Holly had been apart from the pack. She had had her own world – with her parents, her books, her imagination. And yes, it had been largely an adult world, although she'd never thought of it in that way before.

The only part Jack Dane was wrong about was her not wanting to join the pack. She'd wanted to, all right. But she hadn't known how to. She was so self-conscious, she felt paralysed. Other girls could be wild and fun and funny, but she felt as though she was outside herself, watching, and would appear foolish if she tried to join in. Every time she had worked up the courage to make an effort, she'd been ignored. Not rebuffed exactly – no one bullied her or was mean. They just didn't notice her, except as Anna's friend.

'I can't figure out why Anna hangs out with Holly Barrett,' she'd overheard a girl named Debby say in the gym one afternoon. 'I mean, what's the deal? Holly Barrett isn't exactly a winner. What's Anna doing with her?'

'She probably does Anna's homework for her,' another girl, Wendy, had replied.

And Wendy had been right.

'Hey.' Jack Dane nudged her, offering her one of his earphones. 'Listen to this.'

Holly took it, placed it in her left ear. It took her only a second to identify the song: Coldplay's 'Fix You'.

'Brilliant, isn't it?' he said when the song ended, holding his palm out. 'It's possible, you know.'

'What's possible?'

'To get fixed. Hang on, don't look so frightened. I didn't mean drugs. I meant, it's possible to feel better. You looked sad staring out the window, that's all.'

She put the earphone into his outstretched hand, smiled. 'Thanks.'

He rearranged the earphones in his ears, closed his eyes again. Was he going to sleep for real this time? Holly wondered. Or would he be watching her as she stared out the window?

She wasn't wearing nice clothes; instead she had on her usual worn jeans and black T-shirt. No make-up. No jewellery. No perfume. Dirty white sneakers. Who dressed up for a bus trip? Holly wished fervently she had. She

13

wished even more fervently that she had figured out some-where along the way how to flirt, but most of all, she wished she knew what was supposed to happen next. Would he ask for her phone number? If he didn't, could she ask for his? No. Definitely not. It would be way too embarrassing. The odds were he was already going out with someone anyway. 'Spoken for' as Henry, her grandfather, would say. He'd been making conversation, he'd been having a little fun. He'd probably call his girlfriend in Boston straight after the interview and she'd meet him at the bus station when he got back.

Closing her eyes too, Holly tried to recapture the smell and texture of his breath when he'd whispered to her. She wanted to put herself back into that moment of intimacy and stay there for a while, savouring it. Instead, images of him walking hand in hand with a tall willowy blonde appeared. Her eyes flew open and she turned to look out the window again.

Way too quickly, the Mill Pond Diner was in sight. The bus driver signalled, braked and pulled into the car park.

Holly touched him on the arm; his eyes opened, he dis-engaged the iPod.

'We're here?'

'Yes.'

'Excellent.'

The pneumatic door swung open with a swishing sound of air and Holly and Jack both stood. They appeared to be the only two on the bus getting out at this first stop. Jack Dane stepped into the aisle, motioned for Holly to precede him. She did, conscious of her sloppy clothes. Neither spoke as they climbed down the bus stairs then grabbed their bags from its underbelly.

'Nice meeting you, Holly Barrett.' He extended his right hand. No 'Can you give me your cell number?', no other words followed. Once again, they exchanged a brief, strong shake.

I can take a risk, Anna. I have to take a risk.

'If you need a lift into town, my car's here. I can drive you to Figs.'

'Thanks, but the manager said he'd meet me.' He put his hand over his eyes to shield them from the summer sun. 'There's a man over there, by that blue car. Looks like he could be waiting for me.'

'Charlie Thurlow. Yes, I heard he's the manager.' Wanting to say more, but knowing he was anxious to leave her, Holly said, 'Good luck, Jack Dane. I hope you get the job. It was nice meeting you too.'

By the time she had reached the 'It was nice' part of the farewell, Charlie Thurlow had waved to Jack, Jack had started off towards him and her final words ended up directed to his back.

I don't mind, she said to herself, hoisting her bag on her shoulder and walking to the other side of the car park where her car sat baking in the heat of the sun. *I was crazy and deluded to hope for anything more. I don't mind at all.*